Photo: Chuck Bradley

Susan Duncan enjoyed a 25-year career spanning radio, newspaper and magazine journalism, including editing two of Australia's top selling women's magazines, *The Australian Women's Weekly* and *New Idea*. She now lives in her own patch of offshore paradise, Pittwater, with her second husband, Bob, in the beautiful home built for poet Dorothea Mackellar in 1925.

Susan's bestselling memoir, *Salvation Creek*, won the 2007 Nielsen BookData Booksellers Choice Award and was shortlisted for the prestigious Dobbie Award, part of the Nita B Kibble awards for women writers. Its sequel, *The House at Salvation Creek*, was also a huge bestseller.

She has now turned her hand to fiction and is the author of two novels: *The Briny Café* and *Gone Fishing*.

Also by Susan Duncan

Fiction
The Briny Café

Non-fiction
Salvation Creek
The House at Salvation Creek
A Life on Pittwater

SUSAN DUNCAN

Gone Fishing

BANTAM

SYDNEY AUCKLAND TORONTO NEW YORK LONDON

A Bantam book
Published by Random House Australia Pty Ltd
Level 3, 100 Pacific Highway, North Sydney NSW 2060
www.randomhouse.com.au

First published by Bantam in 2013. This edition published in 2014.

Addresses for companies within the Random House Group can be found at www.randomhouse.com.au/offices

National Library of Australia
Cataloguing-in-Publication Entry

Duncan, Susan (Susan Elizabeth), author.
Gone fishing/Susan Duncan.

ISBN 978 0 85798 076 2 (paperback)

A823.4

Cover and line illustrations by Nettie Lodge
Cover design by Christabella Designs
Typeset by Midland Typesetters, Australia
Printed in Australia by Griffin Press, an accredited ISO AS/NZS 14001:2004 Environmental Management System printer

Random House Australia uses papers that are natural, renewable and recyclable products and made from wood grown in sustainable forests. The logging and manufacturing processes are expected to conform to the environmental regulations of the country of origin.

For
Shane Withington,
Friends of Currawong,
and
the anonymous benefactor who followed his heart and
every eco-warrior who never loses sight of what matters

CHAPTER ONE

With the early-morning sun beating through the cabin window and a dawn breeze pleasantly cool on the back of his neck, Sam Scully steers the *Mary Kay* off her mooring, checking behind to make sure the stern is well clear before pushing forward the throttle. Through the cabin windows, he looks rock solid. Square. Shoulders as wide as his hips, powerful legs, all muscle. His hair is a helmet of tight squiggles — as though it's been singed all over by a sudden burst of flame. His clothes, faded by the sun, look dusty: he could have stepped out of a drought-stricken paddock instead of onto a working timber barge. He spins the helm with a single finger, his ear tuned to catch the slightest off-note from the diesel engine thrumming under his feet. At one with the sea and his vessel.

The light, more orange than pink now, fires up the escarpment, treetops; it drills into the water before bouncing back, poker sharp. He is struck, as he often is, by his good fortune. How many men can claim they live and work in paradise? He quickly reaches to touch a small overhead trim made from golden Huon pine. Like all good seamen, who understand the deep blue waters are dark, mysterious and endlessly unpredictable, he's as superstitious as hell.

In the distance, he sees Kate Jackson's half-cabin, snub-nosed fibreglass runabout explode out of the shadows of Oyster Bay, going so fast it skims the satin-smooth water like a bird. A dead ugly commuter boat but stable as a cement slab, it barely rolls in even a heart-stopping sea. Perfect for over-confident novices who often fail to grasp the force and fury of the physical world until they are threatened by it.

He watches her through narrowed eyes. Nearly a month, he thinks. Certainly not long enough to accurately call it a relationship but long enough to pin down what makes her tick and truthfully, he doesn't have a clue. Some days, he feels like a yo-yo. Wound in tightly one moment and unspooled the next.

Up ahead on the mainland shore, The Briny Café tilts haphazardly eastwards, blasted every August by winds straight from the South Pole. It's haloed by a shimmery heat haze or sea mist: he's not sure which. He points the bow towards it, noting for the umpteenth time that the warped and rusty corrugated-iron roof badly needs replacing. If the café's new owners can continue their promising start through the short dark days of winter, when locals rush past to avoid bumping blindly home over a black sea, he'll gently suggest it.

He swings the barge alongside the creaky rear deck, throws a rope around an oyster-crusted pile worn needle-thin by more than a century of tides. Ties up. Picks his way through a motley collection of tables and chairs, cast-offs donated by Cutter Islanders: the financial status of the café is still precarious. Arrives at the café's private pontoon in perfect time to help Kate, who's drifted dockside with a centimetre to spare, secure her boat. Not such a novice any more, then.

'You look a million dollars,' he blurts, happy to see her. She looks at him blankly. 'The clobber,' he continues, steadier now. 'Nice jacket, trousers well cut. Silk shirt that's seen the flat side of a hot iron, for chrissake. First-rate professional gear. And those heels will knock the bluff out of any lawyer.'

Kate glances at her clothes as if she's seeing them for the first time. 'The heels are tame, Sam. Trust me. And city people will take one look at my shaggy hair and see *country hick* at a hundred paces.'

'You'll knock 'em dead, love. You're a dead-set star turn. Sure you don't want me to come with you?' A tinny roars past. The wake strikes out and whacks the pontoon with a thump. He thrusts out a hand, huge, scarred, sunburned to a crisp, and grabs her arm to keep her steady. 'Freaking moron,' he mutters. 'One born every day.'

'Gotta run, Sam. I'll call you.' Her slight figure disappears up the gangplank, the sun casting blue highlights on sleek black hair. He sighs. She might have let him get away with the *moron* bit but the *one born every day* was a lay down misère loser line. Made him sound like a die-hard whinger looking back on years of disappointments when all he really cares about is her wellbeing. He glares as the renegade tinny is noisily rammed into a row of equally decrepit boats further along the sandstone seawall at commuter boat dock. Feels an uncharacteristically violent urge to garrotte the driver. Love does your head in, there's no doubt about it.

Had they met in her former life as a globe-trotting journalist interviewing the men and women who make the top-end decisions, he is painfully aware Kate would never have given him anything more committed than a nod. Blame the sea.

The sun. Summer madness brought on by the warm and sexy north wind, he thinks, not sure whether to curse or bless it. Essentially, they are an improbable coupling: a journalist and a bargeman. One end of the cultural stratosphere and the other.

He'd read the signs last night. Never mind the frigidly cold beer that was shoved hospitably in his mitt the second he walked through her front door. Never mind the cosy dinner with candles that smelled like a French tart – the kind you scooped onto a spoon with plenty of thick cream – and never mind the fact that, after less than a month, you'd expect to skip the foreplay and head straight for the main course. Which was the giveaway, when he thought about it. A barrage of social rituals aimed at softening the news that she'd prefer him to cross the enclosed waters between Oyster Bay and Cutter Island to sleep in his own empty bed. Feinting and demurring when all she had to do was say she felt like a night alone, thanks very much. At least he hopes she meant a night alone and nothing with more of a nasty streak of longevity attached to it.

'Just spit it out straight and to the point, Kate,' he'd told her, trying to lighten the load by smiling over the words. She'd given him a look that was part relief and part ice because he'd seen through the rigmarole and seized the upper hand. 'Old habits,' she said. 'Journos spend their entire careers coming in from oblique angles to arrive at the main point.' (Jeez, he thinks now, the media is a roaring cacophony of white noise that no one trusts for that very reason.)

Later, crossing plate-glass water under stars that snatched away the importance of any human-sized moments, he'd wondered if she believed sneaking towards the main goal had its own nobility. If she did he was in for some rough crossings.

He shakes himself like a half-drowned dog. He isn't himself this morning. A lonely night in a bed where the sheets needed changing and the dust was thick on the floorboards – he slaps the palm of his hand against his forehead, eyes squeezed tight with relief. No coffee yet. No wonder he's ratty. The caffeine fix is long overdue. A large mug with a double shot is all that's required to set him back on track. If it's combined with one of Ettie's fragrant raspberry muffins, he'll be a happy man. Sex or no sex last night.

'Ettie,' he shouts through the patched flyscreen door of The Briny, 'I'm a man who's teetering dangerously on the edge of complete physical collapse from lack of proper nourishment. A coffee and one of those delicious raspberry muffins that turns a dull morning into pure ecstasy. If you please.'

But he can't shake the niggling feeling that a forty-year-old man who turns himself inside out for the love of a woman is headed for the kind of beating that leaves him crippled for life.

Ettie Brookbank, the aging hippy co-owner of The Briny Café, is dealing with a long queue of tradies. With Kate en route to the big smoke to sort out her mother's last will and testament, god help the girl, she's knee deep in orders without any back-up and everyone in a tearing hurry because it's Monday and they're late for work and ferociously hung over.

One-handed, she cracks eggs on the smoking hot flat-plate, checking the whites are firm, the glossy yolks perky – which means the supplier isn't trying to slip her dud stock while she's not looking. She lines up ten bread rolls like roundly plump soldiers, loads them with bacon strips and scrambled eggs. Her homemade tomato chutney is spooned on top. She gets a whiff of the spices. Mustard seeds. Cumin. Cinnamon. Fennel seeds. Mixed in with a cayenne pepper kick that would wake the dead. As good a cure-all as her famous chicken soup. For hangovers anyway. Ten bleary-eyed blokes, barely out of their teens, with hair sticking out from their sunburned scalps like corn stalks and wearing groin-skimming Stubbies that only serve to emphasise their knobbly knees, pounce on the food like starving dogs. 'Thanks, Ettie. Ya saved the day.' She shakes her head, tempted to warn them about the evils of alcohol but bites her tongue. Not so long ago, the number of mornings that found her with a blinding headache had been turning into more of a problem than a social ritual.

The young fellas exit the café, a ragged platoon, grease running down their sharp young chins. A lone straggler, avoiding Ettie's eyes, mumbles a request for the price of a buttered roll. He's broke, she thinks, and he's ashamed to admit it in front of the others. 'Yesterday's are free,' she says. With her back to him, she reaches for fresh bread, fills it with ham, cheese and tomato. Whacks the sandwich in a white paper bag and twists the corners. 'There you go. Would've had to toss it to the fish so you've done me a favour.' He hesitates. Unsure. 'Quick, off you go,' she adds, 'or you'll be left behind.'

He nods his thanks. Taking a quick break, she follows him out of the café and watches as he races off towards a small armada of barely seaworthy tinnies, outboards raspy as an old man's last gasp. The tradies jump lightly on board and ship themselves off to various building sites. Spilling not a single drop of Ettie's famously frothy cappuccinos.

She makes a mental note to keep an eye out for the straggler tomorrow morning. He has the look of a half-starved dog. Not long off one of the boats, she reckons. And she's not talking about cruising pleasure yachts.

While he waits for his order, Sam pulls a small book out of the back pocket of the shorts he wears year-round no matter how far the mercury dips, thinking it's a bloody slim volume to claim it contains *The Concise History of the World*. Still, Kate told him once that she had a sub-editor who reckoned the bible could be cut back to twelve hundred words if you put your mind to it, so who was he, a bargeman who took his daily cues from the sky and sea, to judge? He silently chastises himself for referring to his beloved lighter as a barge. Habit. Tell people you have a lighter and they think you're talking about a Bic. He'd always been a matches man back when he indulged in sweet-tasting rollie tobacco. The stuff that gave off a scent – now that he thinks of it – not unlike the candles Kate'd whipped out last night to soften him before giving him his marching orders. He feels his emotions spiralling downwards again. Opens *The Concise History of the World* to page one to take his mind off the precariousness of romance.

Global cooling around six million years ago wiped out tropical forests in sub-Sahara Africa and triggered the rise of savannahs. The change in environment saw the development of new carnivores and omnivores, including hominines, the ancestors of modern man.

He wonders what global *warming* will give rise to and quickly decides that on an evolutionary scale of six million years – or six hundred years, which seems to be the equivalent time-frame in the current high-speed world – it's not going to be his problem. And, looking on the bright side, who knows what amazing creatures will evolve out of the heat and dust? His eyes track the glitter of a plastic bottle floating under the deck. He's tempted to hazard a guess that wet footprints will be the next significant evolutionary step if the current epidemic of two-legged water guzzlers continues. The bottle emerges into daylight. Sam swoops on it like a hawk and heads inside the café to locate a bin.

Finding the café deserted, he leans on the polished counter and raises an eyebrow in hope.

'Give me five,' Ettie says, still looking frazzled, even though the pressure is off. 'I'm having trouble getting my head sorted this morning. Monday, eh? Bugger, where did I put the oven mitt?' She spins full circle. Wipes her brow. Goes bright pink.

'No rush, love. Take your time. Er, the mitt's in front of you. There.' He points. Ettie snatches it up. 'Bloody hell. Must be going blind,' she says, crossly, her face beetroot now.

Sam grins, joking: 'Senior moments compressing, eh?'

Ettie gives him a look that shrivels his kidneys.

In Bertie's day, Sam recalls, the counter was a dusty mess of tins of antique baked beans, melted globs of sweets and green-fringed bread. Cantankerous old bastard that he was, he'd done the right thing by selling The Briny to Ettie for a knockdown price. Understood money wasn't much use to a dying man and he might as well do something useful before the rock-hard knobs that had latched onto his lungs cut off his oxygen supply forever.

The community had rocked in shock when Ettie announced she was taking on Kate as a partner. The woman was newly arrived and more inclined towards loner than joiner, so everyone – him included – thought Ettie was nuts and that once again her instinct to nurture was over-riding her common sense. Kate couldn't cook and even wearing jeans (ironed, razor creases) and a T-shirt (ironed, blinding white) she looked more corporate than café. For Ettie's sake, they'd all given Kate the benefit of the doubt and she's done a good job, he admits. Slipped into dishes, mops and waitressing without a quibble. Even learned a couple of failsafe recipes (her spaghetti Bolognese with finely diced celery and carrots was right up there with Ettie's). But skills are really just window dressing. Personalities – their hard core – might broaden but do they ever switch gears completely? Truthfully, if he had to put money either way, he still wouldn't know how to place his bet.

'You heard the news?' Ettie asks, lining up two white china mugs, punching the espresso machine and plating up a raspberry muffin in one fluid movement that's as much about instinct as practice.

'What news?' he asks, his neck twisted sideways so he can read the newspaper headlines without bothering to pick up a copy from the stack under the counter.

Ettie turns off the steam, wipes the spout: 'They're going to build a bridge to Cutter Island then plonk a flash resort in the middle of Garrawi Park.'

'Eh?' Sam jerks up from the headlines so quickly pain shoots up his neck to his head. 'You're joking, right? Setting me up for some shocker community job like carting Portaloos to the next big fundraiser so it looks good in comparison.'

'Serious as,' Ettie says. 'Check out the development notice in the Square. Found it there first thing this morning. Thought someone was having me on but Fast Freddy says he ferried two dark-suited blokes with a fistful of posters and pamphlets around the public wharves in the dead of night. Looks like it's a fact all right.'

'Where's Freddy now?'

Ettie slides Sam's mug across the counter and picks up her own. Takes a long sip, shoulders rounded, hands circling the hot creamy brew like it's winter instead of midsummer outside. In a dry voice, she says: 'Think about it, Sam. He's a water-taxi driver who comes off a twelve-hour night shift at first light. He's where he is every morning by nine o'clock. Racking up the zzz's.'

Kate finds the address she's searching for located between a fast-food joint and a (borderline) porno lingerie shop. Limp hamburgers and even limper sugar-coated fries (to turn them golden instead of brown, according to a story she once wrote about the hidden ingredients in fast food) alongside fire-engine red frilly knickers, shiny black boots with metal stiletto heels, rubber aprons (not the kitchen clean-up variety), and lacy corsets. She checks the scribbled note in her hand to make sure she's not mistaken and pushes open a dirty glass door. She wonders how on earth Emily, who revered glitz and glamour and judged everyone and everything by appearances, managed to put aside her prejudices to engage the services of Mr Sly. This is low-rent territory at best, slum territory at worst. Without the shadowy existence of a brother she's hoping to either confirm or deny, she probably would have done a runner. She tells herself to expect nothing, a lesson she learned early to avoid the disappointment of forgotten birthdays, worthless promises and – at best – an abstract acknowledgement of her existence. Out of the blue, she has a sudden and completely uncharacteristic compulsion to whitewash the facts – or did she mean acts? – of the dead. Dead. Not *passed*, which seems to be the new, dreadfully twee and slightly ambiguous euphemism for an essentially unambiguous state. What is, after all, uncertain about lying six feet under a marble slab? Emily hasn't *passed* by, she hasn't *passed* the salt and pepper, she will never again sail *past* in a froth of floral chiffon and a cloud of complicated millinery and heavy perfume. Kate angrily wipes a tear off her cheek. Surely she doesn't feel *guilty* for outliving her volatile mother. It is, after all, part of the natural order. Emily is dead. Move on. Survival of the fittest. It was ever thus. Law, according to Emily. So why the empty hole in the centre of her chest? The dull ache that constricts her throat? Why the awful, tippy feeling that nothing is quite in alignment any more?

Kate finds the office of Sly & Son easily. So absurdly Dickensian, she thinks, wondering whether names go hand in hand with careers or vice versa. She wonders if Emily was attracted by the irony of hiring a firm with a title that accurately summed up the dodging and weaving that made up the fabric of her existence. Probably not. Emily was never a deep thinker. Devious, yes, but not deep. Kate swallows, clenches her fists and angrily wipes away another tear, appalled by the see-sawing going on between her head and heart, reminding herself of the pointlessness of regret. Death changes everything, she thinks, and nothing.

She knocks lightly. Opens the door swiftly and decisively without waiting for an invitation. 'Hello,' she says brightly to the aged receptionist who points her index finger at a seat without a word of acknowledgement.

After a while a tall man, probably in his early forties, wearing a well-cut charcoal suit – Armani or a good copy that's lounge-lizard sleek – emerges from an office. Kate assumes he's a client on the way out. More well-heeled than she would've expected given the location. An observation, she reassures herself, not one of Emily's snap judgments.

'Ms Jackson? Neville Sly. My father looked after your mother's affairs until he retired a few months ago. On the face of it, it all seems pretty simple. Would you like tea? Coffee? No? OK, let's proceed then.'

'Great.'

'It's not a complicated will,' Mr Sly adds. 'She's left everything to you.'

'No mention of anyone else?'

He looks surprised. 'No. It's quite clear. Just you. As soon as outstanding debts are paid and probate is cleared, the estate will be settled.'

'Thanks.' Kate gets up, holds out her hand politely.

'Aren't you going to ask about the value of the estate?'

Mr Sly sounds less smooth, more shocked, which makes Kate wonder how most of his clients respond to the news they're sole beneficiaries. 'There can't be much. Enough to pay your fees, I hope, but if not, don't worry, I'll settle the account.'

Mr Sly is thoughtful. 'I see. Odd then. After everything is taken care of, our fees included, there should be a balance remaining of about $70,000.'

'I beg your pardon?' It's got to be a cock-up, she thinks. He's muddled her up with some other client. 'Are you sure? We're talking about Emily Jackson, right?'

'We don't make mistakes, Ms Jackson,' he says tersely.

'Sorry, I'm in shock.'

The idea of Emily hoarding cash when she had a lifetime history of scatterbrain financial profligacy that consistently involved running up debts and then stepping back until first Kate's father and then Kate bailed her out is baffling. Emily was a born squanderer. Unable to resist the sparkle of pretty trinkets, the lure of a silken fabric. Kate, who thought through the long-term ramifications of even the smallest purchase – an instinctive mechanism to counter her mother's extremes, in all probability – frantically scrabbles back through Emily's history, trying to find a possible source for this kind of windfall. As far as she is aware, the family fortune, such as it was (her father's small country grocery shop wasn't worth much in the days before they morphed into trendy bakeries serving exotic teas and a mind-boggling range of flavoured coffees), was frittered away in one failed Emily-inspired business venture after another. To put it mildly, money turned to dust in her hands. At least that's what she'd thought until now.

'As far as I knew, Emily never had two coins to rub together.'

Mr Sly remains silent, uninvolved in family drama. He closes the file. Folds his hands on top of it, signalling there's no more business to be done. Kate glances at her watch. The wrapping up of the final details of Emily's life has barely taken ten minutes. Her mother would have been outraged by the lack of flourishes and rigmarole, the rigorous attention to details unembellished by colourful asides. She would have said yes to the coffee, refused a biscuit and requested cake. Chocolate was her preference. It made her feel happy, she said. She would have taken two small bites. Left the rest. Then she would have embarked on a long account of the deceased's life, or more accurately, her role in the deceased's life. The reading of Gerald's will had turned into a circus, Emily giving an award-winning performance of a grieving widow, switching on tears as easily as a light. By the end of it, Kate, who never uttered a word throughout the whole shabby show, saw that the solicitor couldn't work out whether to applaud or commiserate.

'By the way, you don't happen to know how Emily came to use this firm, do you?' she asks.

'We're one of three recommended by the retirement village. Does it matter?'

'Not at all,' she replies quickly. 'It's just . . . I was wondering . . . Well, if there'd been a long association. Whether she kept old documents here, you know, such as birth and wedding certificates. For safekeeping, I mean.' She is tempted to tell him about Emily's deathbed (as it turned out) confession.

How somewhere deep in a past that Kate, and presumably Gerald, knew nothing about, Emily had given birth to a son and then – for all she knew – abandoned him. Her mother's periodic disappearances, which she'd put down to illicit affairs, could have been about the boy. Maybe he'd been institutionalised for some reason. Perhaps if Mr Sly searched Emily's file one more time, he might find a clue so Kate could nail the ghost and move on. Her thoughts remain unuttered.

'This probably sounds odd, but there are huge gaps in my knowledge of my mother's life. I'm trying to unravel a few, er, complications she left behind. You're sure there's not another file lurking out there in one of those huge stacks . . .'

'We have the current will and a copy of her earlier will. Nothing else. Is it possible your mother used the services of two solicitors at some time?'

'I doubt it.' Emily would resent paying one bill, forget two. *How rude*, she'd explode whenever one popped up in the mail. Queen Emily. Bestowing favours. Her fingers holding the request for money like a bag of dog poo before flicking it towards her husband.

'Yeah, well, it was a long shot.' Kate reaches for her handbag. 'So it's all a mystery then.'

'Lawyers tend to be incurious. It's often a mistake to know too much about your clients.' He smiles to show it's a joke. 'Probate usually takes from one to three months, if anyone wants to challenge the will . . .'

'Challenge?' Kate asks, too quickly.

'As a general rule, only children and grandchildren have grounds, although theoretically anyone can challenge. In your case, there shouldn't be any problems. Expect a cheque around late April. Sorry I can't be of more help.'

Kate turns back at the door, her hand already on the knob. Now is the time to mention a half-brother, she thinks. 'I'm curious. When does time run out on challenging a will?'

'Once probate is settled, it's very difficult to revoke the terms.'

On a street thick with exhaust fumes and rushing lunchtime crowds, the noonday heat hits Kate like a blow. She leans against the gaudy underwear shop window, her eyes adjusting to sharp sunlight. Feeling frazzled and confused, she ducks into a dimly lit and smelly basement pub next door, compelled by a force she can't define. She orders a cognac for the first time in her life. A tired barmaid, either drug or alcohol affected, pours what Kate recognises as a cheap brandy into a shot glass and slams it on the counter.

'Fifteen bucks, love, on the nose.' The woman sways slightly. Kate fishes in her bag, looking around the room. Furtive men in raincoats – or the equivalent.

'Oh hell.' She pushes a twenty over the counter, sculls the drink and flees. Outside on the street, she puts together the lingerie shop and the bar. If it's not a front for a brothel, her name's not Kate Jackson. Her stomach feels like it's on fire. Her mouth is raw. Too late, she realises she's just done exactly what her mother would have done in the same circumstances. Feel good? Order a brandy? Feel bad? Order a brandy. Feel hot, cold, happy, sad – order a brandy. Does anyone ever travel a long way from their original DNA?

She thinks: Seventy thousand dollars? There's got to be a catch. Nothing to do with Emily is ever clear-cut. There'll be a debt somewhere. An Emily-created catastrophe that will emerge one day – probably quite soon – and take every penny, and probably more, to put right. She grabs hold of anger like a lifeline, burying what she doesn't even realise is grief and loss under a blanket of rage and confusion.

CHAPTER TWO

Outside in the Square, where even the spindly leaves of the casuarinas seem plumper after a week of heavy summer rain, it's still too early for the January holiday crowd and the chaotic early-morning offshore commuter dash is well and truly over. A couple of elderly tourists are installed at one of the picnic tables, sipping café coffee out of cardboard cups. On the foreshore, a lone dog walker struggles with a sleek and self-satisfied mutt the colour of toffee, tugging on a lead. A cyclist zooms in and out of sight. Two joggers flash by. Otherwise there's no one. It's almost nine o'clock and Sam is virtually on his own.

He fronts up to the community announcement blackboard. Skips past a few wind-chewed, mostly out-of-date notices (*House to Rent. Moving Sale. Reliable tinny – Reasonable price. Babysitter available. House cleaners wanted.*). Hones in on screaming red letters plastered on a poster-size sheet of paper: *BRIDGE. RESORT. SPA.* And shouting loudest: *EXCLUSIVE DEVELOPMENT!*

Sam swears. Moves closer to read it carefully, paying particular attention to the small print where, he's learned through painful experience, the real information is found. The notice has the stink of authenticity. This isn't some die-hard Island prankster gristing the local rumour mill to see how far it runs before someone susses it's a joke. Some anonymous bastard is serious about trashing Cutter Island.

A bridge from the mainland to the west-facing foreshore of Cutter Island, Sam thinks darkly, feeling a twist in his gut. All this bloody beauty of place and people with fine instincts and some philistine plans to blitz the golden sand, turquoise waters and a fresh-water creek that rushes over mossy boulders from the knobbly peak of the Island for . . . what? A bridge and a freaking resort. As far as he's concerned, the world is already brimming with resorts. Lined up next to each other so even if you scratch around you can never find the paradise that titillated the developers in the first place. Not that he's ever been a paying guest in one, of course. But he's seen pictures of tropical destinations where blank-faced high-rise shockers – with a couple of token palms at the front – are lined up closer than a Briny Café knife and fork wrapped in a paper napkin. The palms replaced, no doubt, after the originals were ripped out. They don't need a resort 'cause no right-thinking Islander wants an influx of visitors pushing Island resources to breaking point. And who needs a bridge when ninety per cent of the pleasure of going home comes from crossing the water in a boat with the wind in your face and your lungs full of sharp, salty air?

'Sam! Where ya bin? Bin waitin' on the barge. Me and Longfella. We got a job on, remember? The steel beams, Sam. They're due in Blue Swimmer Bay. Doc's house. Remember?' Jimmy, the *Mary Kay*'s sartorially colourful deckhand (lime-green shorts and a purple T-shirt today), heads towards him at a cracking pace, his fluffy black-and-white Border Collie pup close on his heels.

'They're going to build a bridge, mate. A bridge and a bloody resort on Cutter Island. It's enough to make a grown man weep.'

Jimmy skates to a stop, dances and prances with anxiety. 'Ya sure?' His sunburned face (clashing puce against the purple) is earnest.

'The bulldozers first,' Sam says, his emotions running hot. 'Then landfill. The contours of the site will be moulded to some wanky architect's vision of nirvana.'

'Ya sure?'

On a roll, Sam continues: 'The beach will be lined with glass and steel. Then the racket of jet skis and high-powered boats dragging screaming water skiers . . .'

'What about the turtles, Sam? And the stingrays?'

'And the jellyfish? The constellations of starfish?' The kid nods violently, in full agreement. Sam, angry now: 'This whole magic world, mate, is going to be ripped and gutted by tourists here for a week or two before roaring off, never to be seen again. Everything the Cook's Basin community holds sacred wrecked forever. And that's aside from the trashing of the park.'

'Ya sure?' the kid asks again, teary now.

On the verge of another tirade, Sam notes Jimmy's growing distress and bites his tongue. Jimmy's already fragile hold on the basic routines of daily life, all that keeps him balanced, is threatening to snap altogether. Sam fixes an easy smile on his face, places a comforting hand the size of a dinner plate on the kid's bony shoulder, lowers the tone of his voice: 'Relax, Jimmy. It's early days yet. Nothing to worry about.

You had breakfast?' he asks, trying to switch the kid's head from mayhem to manna before he has a complete meltdown.

''Course. Mum put out twenty-four Weet-Bix when I told her about the steel beams. Reckoned I'd need me strength.'

'Right. So let's get going, eh? Before we miss the peak tide.'

'What are they gunna rip up the Island for, Sam? When's it gunna happen?'

Not quite back on track yet, Sam decides, scrabbling to come up with a new distraction. He pulls out the book from his back pocket. 'On your mark, get set, and it's time for history lesson number one.'

'Aw gee, Sam.' The kid slumps, scrapes a toe along the ground like he's about to sign his name. 'I thought ya were kiddin'.'

'Education, Jimmy. It's the key to self-improvement. Now. Did you know that it's taken nearly six million years for you and me to end up with shorter arms, longer legs and a bigger brain than our primate relatives?'

Jimmy shrugs: 'What about me dog, Sam? How long's it taken for him to grow four legs insteada two?'

Sam sighs. Snookered at the opening gambit. But the kid's head is back in neutral territory, which has to count for something. As the two of them march across the Square to board the *Mary Kay*, Sam wonders if educating Jimmy is his ham-fisted way of disguising an attempt to better himself so that when he and Kate sit down politely to a candlelit dinner (presuming he wasn't being turfed off the premises for good last night) complete with meticulously ironed and folded cotton napkins (not serviettes), he'll be able to impress her with little-known but exciting facts. There is, he admits wryly, more than a pathetic grain of truth there. Yep, love does your head in. True as night follows day.

Beams craned aboard and on a swollen tide, the *Mary Kay* sedately cruises to one of a hand-spread of blue bays hemmed by golden beaches and crowned by towering eucalypts, their leopard-spotted trunks washed clean by the recent rain. The sea drifts from navy blue to turquoise. The barge comes to rest deep in a corner where mangroves are a corps de ballet on a stage of shifting sand and sea. Sam kills the engine. Listens to the whispery song of cabbage palms while tree ferns, delicate as lace, spread like giant umbrellas in a damp green gully. The high humidity hangs like a bridal veil. Mysterious. Magical. Wondrous. 'Over my dead body,' he whispers, so the kid doesn't hear and get knocked off his hinges again. In his ears, though, it rings like a war cry.

On the way back to Cook's Basin, Kate veers off the road home and heads towards the retirement village where Emily lived, presumably loved and took her final breath. Was she deep in a pleasant dream when the Grim Reaper came to claim her? Or did she wake, a pain so sharp in her chest she was unable to find the strength to press the emergency button strategically placed by the bed of every resident in a place where each night – she'd once told Kate – she could hear the discreet roll of mortuary vans creeping in to spirit away their once-in-a-lifetime clients. *Hardly inspiring, being forced to consider death on a nightly basis*. Survival of the fittest – law, according to Emily.

By the time Emily moved into her neat little unit, though, she'd run out of options. Kate had questioned the rationale of the red button. Better to roar off into the great void of death than hover at the edge in pain and anguish, she'd said. *Wait until you're old, then you'll understand the will to live gets stronger and stronger.* And yet, seventy wasn't a great age any more, not by 'forty-is-the-new-thirty' standards. So Emily must have slept peacefully through the point where she quit one world for another, depending on your school of spiritual thought. The bottom line was always the same, though. Everything that is born must die – one of the rare absolute truths.

The village looms. She swings into the pretty driveway with the pretty herbaceous borders before she can change her mind. She unlocks the door and steps inside. Emily's heavy perfume, trapped in her pink frills – chairs, clothes, curtains, lampshades – hits her like an assault.

Here to empty the unit so village management can erase any lingering traces of Emily with new carpet, a fresh paint job and a new stove top before offering it *as new* to the next cab off the mortal rank, she stumbles for a second. She'd planned to ask Vinnies, the provider of luxuries small and large in Sam's impoverished childhood, to blitz the place but kept putting off the call. Now, with the lawyer unable to shed any light on her mystery brother, she's glad. Somewhere in the detritus of seventy years there must be a clue.

Kate takes a deep breath and enters the bedroom to open the wardrobe. Suddenly finding it hard to breathe, she leans against a wall, slowly sliding to the floor. Eyes closed, she scrolls through the past like a black-and-white movie show, searching for hints, clues, answers. Or even a flimsy link she might be able to follow up.

She remembers conversations between her parents that suddenly went silent when she, still a little girl, entered the room. She remembers her father's quiet acceptance of Emily's frequent absences. Once, when she plucked up the courage to ask where Emily had gone, he simply said, 'Out.' She knew the question was off limits forever after. Sometimes Emily'd be gone only a day and night. Sometimes a week. Once, she heard her father ask, 'The money ran out, did it?' Her mother's response a murmur too low to catch.

Out of the blue, Kate remembers being dragged along on a flight to the city to tour one of the few Australian navy battleships in operation. It seemed so weird at the time. Emily, a battleship nerd? Even weirder in hindsight, unless one of the sailors – no, never a sailor, Emily was a snob – one of the officers, then, was the father of her child. Or maybe her son had joined the navy? But why drag her daughter along? For appearances? As an equaliser? To prevent a nasty scene?

Kate's head is beginning to throb. *It's not called rotgut for nothing, Kate, so don't bother buying me the cheap stuff, I'll only throw it out*. Birthday and Christmas gift law, according to Emily. Kate goes into the kitchen where a used coffee mug sits on a bench that needs wiping. She scours it, fills it with tap water, drinks thirstily.

Revived and back at the wardrobe, she gingerly fingers clothing arranged fastidiously in strict colour order: red, green, blue, turquoise, yellow and pink, pink, pink. Underneath, a rack of shoes reflects the same colour code. She counts twenty cardboard hatboxes stacked on the top shelf.

All of them almost certainly crammed with over-decorated hats representing the most outlandish fashion fads for the past fifty years. Kate had never considered her mother capable of such forensic order.

'The Secret Life of Emily Jackson,' she murmurs.

How her mother adored hats. It didn't matter what style she placed on her head, it always looked fabulous. *I've got the right bones, Kate, very few women do.*

She opens a hatbox and, against her will, finds herself impossibly seduced by a gauzy emerald-green fascinator with a jaunty little feather (no doubt from an endangered species – survival of the fittest, Emily would poo-poo) propped on top in a swirl of silk. It must have cost a bomb, she thinks. And suddenly she can't bear the thought that her mother's great passion for outrageously glorious hats will end up on Vinnie's crowded and shabby shelves. She puts them aside to take home in what she hopes isn't a bout of grotesque sentimentality. The Island Players, she tells herself, might be able to use them for their next theatrical production.

After a while, Kate stumbles on a plastic supermarket bag stuffed with old photos of the blurry, bleached-colour kind, and her heart leaps. Unable to bring herself to sit in one of Emily's frilly floral armchairs, she sinks to the floor again and sifts through the shots. Her journalist's eye is tuned to pick up odd emotional nuances among groups of wedgie-wearing, frizzy-haired 1960s diehards in washed-out psychedelic shirts and skirts who smile mechanically into the lens. Were they all saying *cheese* back then? Or had that free-love generation invoked *sex* to loosen lips? She has no idea. Nothing leaps out at her. There's not a baby in sight. She finds two pictures of her father and puts them aside with the hatboxes.

Late afternoon. Hot. Sunlight corkscrews off the water but not for much longer. Soon shadows will lengthen, casting a gentling haze over sea, sky and landscape. Back onshore in the Square, Sam and the rest of the Cook's Basin community is gathering in groups of growling dissent. News of a luxury resort planned for Garrawi Park has rocketed around the Island. Even isolated bay residents, usually the last to hear the gossip, have been alerted to a travesty that everyone agrees will scar an already ecologically vulnerable coast beyond redemption. *No bridge. No resort.* Agreement is universal.

Sam licks his lips, tasting the last of the beer on them, sticky and yeasty, leaving a gluey film on his tongue. He vows never to leave an emergency stash of the amber ale on board again. His head feels woozy. Thick and slow. He wanders over to the tap, turns it on full bore and shoves his head under the water, hoping the cold will shake off the booze. What kind of a warrior gets pissed before the battle even begins? The cold feels like a sharp blade cutting through his scalp. It's all he can do not to yelp.

'You OK, Sam? You forget to wash your hair after work?'

'I'm good, Jimmy,' he fibs. 'Just clearing my head for business, mate. How'd you go this afternoon? Did you do a good job for Frankie?'

'Yeah, Sam. I was the best.' Before Sam can inform him that self-praise is no recommendation, the kid goes on. Bouncing up and down in his mucky sandshoes, his iridescent clothes subdued by grime, spiky red hair gluey with the gel he applies in an almost religious ritual every morning, he points across the sun-struck water. 'See her, Sam. She's a beauty now. Better than a facelift, me mum says.'

Sam squints into the distance. The *Seagull* is riding higher than usual after a three-day overhaul that knocked about a tonne of hitchhiking crustaceans off her underbelly.

Sam turns back to the kid. 'She looks good for another century, mate. Does Frankie need you again tomorrow or are you back on board the *Mary Kay* full-time as first mate?'

Jimmy's beams. 'I'm with ya, Sam. Me and Longfellow. Reportin' for duty. What time, Sam? What's on?'

Sam looks at the pup tucked in the crook of the kid's arm. 'Give your mum a hand in the morning and then report on the afternoon high tide. And give that mutt a bath when you have your own tonight. There's enough marine life stuck on him to make a meal.'

Jimmy studies the pup. 'You reckon?'

Sam sighs. Turns towards the crowd. 'Three o'clock sharp,' he says, giving the kid's hair a rough-up before he walks into the thick of a ropeable community with violence and bloodshed up front in its mind. Metaphorically speaking, of course. He wipes his sticky hand on his shorts, checks his watch. No sign of Kate. No word from her either. Even putting a good spin on it, the signs aren't too auspicious. He'd at least expected an *I'm OK* call after she finished her tricky legal appointment in town. Serious couples communicate. Real couples support each other. Committed couples share even the most boring minutiae of their lives and find it fascinating. Or pretend to. He's getting the distinct sense of being an accessory good for occasional use but inessential in the greater scheme. She's going it alone on the big stuff. He shakes drips of water from his hair. Get busy, mate, he tells himself, or you'll fry what's left of your thumping head. If only he hadn't off-loaded Jimmy for the afternoon. He'd never dream of getting pissed in front of the kid. Lead by example. Not as easy as it sounds. His kingdom for a couple of painkillers.

Fast Freddy, kitted out for his night-time taxi shift in fluoro orange, appears out of the throng as if by magic. 'You look awful, Sam. Migraine?'

'Nice of you to put it so politely, mate. Tied one on. Fell asleep. Now I feel like someone's ramming a boot into my skull.'

Fast Freddy reaches into his pocket and comes out with a couple of small white pills. 'Good old-fashioned aspirin. You'll be right as rain in a tick.'

Sam grabs the pills like a lifeline, swallows them dry.

'Er, they're meant to be dissolved in water,' says Fast Freddy, who's a stickler for following instructions. 'You might experience a bit of fizz making a rocket-fast return trip from your gullet.'

'Feel better already,' Sam insists, punching Freddy's shoulder in thanks and honing in on Lindy Jones, the shapely real-estate agent who seems to be able to discover the secrets of the universe by clicking on one in a row of bewildering graphics on the bottom of her computer screen. He wonders nervously whether it's time he embraced the new technology. 'It's been around for thirty years,' Kate had lectured him the other night when he made some disparaging remark about the invasion of electronics and the abandonment of nature for what seemed to him to be a load of time-wasting trivia. 'The web,' she replied – almost impatiently, now that he looks back on the conversation – 'means no one needs to suffer in silence and ignorance ever again. Used correctly, it's the tool – the weapon if you like – of the masses. All you have to do is hit one key and you can galvanise an army to march for the common good.' He was unconvinced. Now he wonders if her words were prophetic. If ever there was a time to galvanise an army, it's right now.

But army? He checks out the beads, sarongs, shorts, T-shirts, thongs and bare feet; kids splashing about naked in the shallows; the same old Island die-hards glued to their seats in their regular corner, fists curled around stubbies dripping condensation like a dodgy hose. He marches up to Lindy, pushing aside Jason, her good-looking, always-amenable husband, with a business-like shove. Squashing down a ping of envy for this bloke who has it all, Sam kisses Lindy on both cheeks to show he's up with at least one of the current social fads. 'We need to do a bit of research, love. Find out where this shower of . . .' He pauses; Lindy's two excellent teenage kids are in earshot. '. . . shinola emanates from. You got any ideas?'

'For god's sake, Sam. Keep up,' she replies impatiently. 'Why do you think everyone's here? The developers stuck up a sign at lunchtime to say they'll answer any questions at six o'clock. Or, in their words, *bring the community up-to-date and on board*. They're distributing plans and prospectuses so we'll all be absolutely clear about what's happening. Considerate, eh?'

Sam fights down the queasy sensation of being caught wrong-footed. He looks around at the crowd. To an outsider, it might appear to consist of aging hippies, yobbos and beach bums, but they're people he's laughed with, drunk with, eaten with, grieved with, worked alongside and even battled. They'd never let you down. You could get arrested for knocking off your mother-in-law and they'd risk smuggling a frigidly cold beer behind bars before giving you a quiet nod of understanding: *Must've been having a crap day, eh?* Right now, they've gathered to protect everything they passionately believe in and damn the consequences. 'The law on our side or theirs, Lindy?' he asks.

'Too early to say but it's not looking good. Just so you know, that shiny-headed stirrer with the filthy temper who lives on the eastern side of Garrawi has bought all the bordering properties over the last couple of years. My guess? He's in this up to his eyeballs and not the temporary blow-in we thought he was.'

Sam scans the crowd, searching for light bouncing off a baby-pink skull. 'How'd he manage to get under your radar?' he asks.

'Company names. If there was a connection I failed to see it and I look hard when people buy stuff over the internet because there's no knowing who might pitch up as your next-door neighbour. There were eleven separate organisations. I thought they were one-offs triggered by the current volatility of the stock market. The grey brigade funnelling retirement funds into property. Big mistake.'

Sam thinks back. 'Nah. Don't blame yourself. The signs were there for all of us to see. We just didn't take them seriously.'

Two years ago, Eric Lowdon had turned up in his deeply eccentric golf-course clothes to take up residence in the waterfront house left vacant when Joycie Bancroft broke her ankle rushing for the ferry and decided that at the relatively *young* age of ninety-three, it was probably time to give up offshore living. Eric descended on Cutter Island like a puffed-up parrot, accompanied by six flashy barge loads of glass-and-chrome furniture that outshone the bay on a blaster of a day. Making enemies from the start. 'One chip in my glass table top,' he told Glenn the removalist, 'and I'll personally hold you responsible for a replacement. Seats thirty. Twenty grands' worth.' The thick plate glass, beaded with coloured sparkles that skewered the eyeballs of anyone brave enough to look at the thing, hung over the front and back of the barge by two metres. Eight men moved it into the house. Sam included. All of them tempted to chuck the glittering monstrosity overboard and let the bastard sue. Glenn didn't have a cracker anyway. But a bloke had his pride. Glenn couldn't let a runty little arsehole with no taste win a single round.

Not long afterwards, Eric Lowdon began appearing at the fireshed fundraiser dinners. Scraped his plate clean of top nosh cooked by noble, sweaty volunteers before he whinged about the lack of value for money. 'It's a fundraiser, mate, not a loss leader,' Sam told him. 'And tell me where else would you get a three-course dinner for fifteen bucks?' Lowdon ignored him and banged on about how it was time to bring Cutter Island into the twenty-first century. A bridge, he preached, cafés, restaurants, sparkling new marinas, a helipad. *Glamour*: the word presented like a gift on a silver platter. And they'd all laughed smugly in his face. Explained patiently that the whole point about Cook's Basin was the fact that it was managing to hold back the over-regulated, over-crowded, over-stressed, *glamorous* current world. They'd thought he'd up and go one day without a peep, like the deluded weekender who'd bolted when he found out what the community thought of his idea to upgrade the fire tracks into major access roads. Jeez. How did you fight an enemy when you couldn't see it coming?

'Here they are,' says Lindy, tipping her chin towards three very clean, sleek black sedans purring up to the Square and coming to a standstill on the sandy track. All eyes turn and fix on the six hard men who emerge from the soft leather innards of the vehicles. They're wearing suits and ties, dark glasses that hide half their faces but not their smirks. The murmuring crowd goes deathly quiet, like the curtain's just been raised on a Greek tragedy. One hundred pairs of accusing eyes track the movement of the men but not a soul moves to ease their way to the seawall, where they eventually line up to sit like well-fed crows on a country fence. Oozing power and arrogance, protected from any possible rear-guard action by a tide that sloshes lazily behind their backs, they (bizarrely) fold their hands primly in their laps like schoolgirls at a class photo-shoot.

'They think it's in the bag,' Sam says through clenched teeth. He grabs Lindy's hand and pulls her forward with him, turning sideways to squeeze through narrow gaps in the crowd. 'They think we'll just roll over with idiot grins on our faces while they tickle our tummies, not notice when they bully us into submission and destroy everything we believe in. Are they dead-set morons?'

'No sign of Eric,' Lindy says, on tiptoes, searching the heads. 'But I know he's the lynchpin. Every instinct in my body tells me I'm right.'

'He doesn't strike me as a man who likes to get his hands dirty. But I'm with you. He's got to be up to his eyeballs in this.'

Two of the dark suits are handing out pamphlets and flyers, smarmy, touching shoulders, arms, like they're trusted friends spreading comfort and hope at – given their weird black outfits – a funeral. A few people flinch. Some look at a hand laid on their body like it's a violation. Others grab the written material and retire to the far end of the seawall to get the facts in black and white. The suits forge on, immune. Sam has to fight the urge to roar. 'They have no idea what they've just stepped into. No freaking idea at all,' he mutters to Lindy. 'I'll fight this to the death. Trust me on this, Lin. The only way I'll give up is if I'm dropped over the side of the *Mary Kay* wearing concrete boots.'

Before she can reply, he snatches a copy and stomps off towards The Briny. He doesn't trust himself not to hurl empty bottles at those unblemished black cars, or slam his fist into the even rows of sparkling white teeth. At the last minute, unable to contain his anger, he spins on his heel and marches back into the crowd. He picks the closest suit, and twists the bloke's designer silk tie as tight as he can without totally cutting off his oxygen. His face so close he's almost knocked flat by a shocker dose of halitosis, Sam hisses: 'You can't do this.'

With the sixth sense of professional thugs, the other five blokes dump their pamphlets and converge on Sam. Close around him like a cloak. 'Are you taking us on?' They make hee-haw sounds. Grin. 'Are you taking us on?' they say again. Fingers pointing, prodding the open air, then making circular motions at their temples like Sam's a full-blown loony.

The locals step forward, edgy, spoiling for action. 'Bring it on,' says Glenn, puny fists raised to his face like a boxer.

'Kids and dogs splashing about, Glenn,' says Bill Firth,

the mild-mannered, art-loving president of the Cook's Basin Community Residents' Association, who materialises behind Sam. 'This is not the time nor the place.' Fast Freddy, a newly practising Buddhist, spirits Glenn away before the goons turn him into fish food. Bill says soothingly, 'Let it go, Sam. Save the fight for when it matters. Punch-ups never settle anything.'

Sam hesitates, eyeballs the buffoons one by one, his reflection bouncing back from the blank screens of their mirror sunglasses. Under his work shirt he's shaking with rage. 'Yeah,' he says, dredging up a careless grin from god knows where. 'Sure.'

The suits shake their heads like Sam's a tragically lost cause and break away. One holds his hand in an L-shape against his nose. 'Loser,' he whispers, like a kid in a schoolyard brawl, making it sound like a deadly disease. Sam watches their backs. Pinheads. No necks. Wide shoulders. Narrow hips, legs descending into steel-capped Cuban heels. Satiny carapaces. A plague of freaking cockroaches. He stares. Remembering details. Still as the air before a terrifying storm breaks loose. It's on, he thinks. It's bloody on.

The sun is low in the sky. Kate feels drained and defeated. She scoops Emily's leaky cosmetics from the bedside table into a bin and strips the bed, shoving the linen into a garbage bag and knotting it tightly. Twenty bags in all and a few of Emily's picnic baskets filled with crockery and glassware. Picnic baskets? She racks her brains trying to remember going on even one family picnic. Draws a blank. The Secret Life of Emily Jackson.

She's decided to keep her father's old writing desk, where he sat and instructed her on important financial matters: *Red means debt, Kate, black means credit – aim for the black and you'll always have choices.* The law according to Gerald Jackson. Emily never caught on. Aside from the designer hats that she supposed were couture back in the day, and one crocodile skin handbag circa 1970, judging from a race book she'd found inside (was Emily a punter? Is that where her windfalls came from?), she can't help thinking it's a lacklustre tally after a lifetime of avid consumption. Did it make her mother happy? Not as far as Kate could tell. For a moment she seriously considers simply taking the money and forgetting the possible existence of a half-brother. But the truth, no matter how awful, can never be as bad as your imagination. Law according to Kate Jackson.

On a hunch and feeling vaguely absurd, she goes back into the bedroom she's stripped bare and runs her hand under the mattress. Why not? After all, Emily was a woman who thrived on melodrama. Spun it out until long after her audience lost interest or, in the case of Gerald and Kate, admitted defeat. And there it is. Cold metal. A box, perhaps. Certainly not part of the inner workings of the bed. She pushes aside the mattress. A dented old container sits dead centre on the bony metal springs. A cash box of the kind country shopkeepers once kept hidden under the counter with the key hung on a string around their necks for safekeeping. It might have belonged to her father. Kate stares at it for a long, long time, as though she's waiting for it to either speak or explode. Eventually, she pulls Emily's house keys out of her pocket and checks each one. Nothing is small enough to fit the tiny lock.

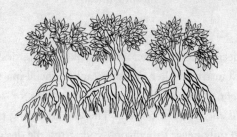

CHAPTER THREE

Inside The Briny Café after a shockingly frantic day of fielding orders, cooking, serving and washing dishes, Ettie Brookbank is too tired to move from the swivel chair. Too tired to check the day's takings. Too bloody exhausted to make it up the stairs to her all-white *penthouse* apartment for a glass of restorative white wine. Under normal circumstances, with the Square chockers with potential customers, she and Kate would've stayed open and boosted the day's takings, ears tuned to the breaking news about a bridge and a resort. But she'd hung out the *CLOSED* sign on the dot of six-thirty pm and then hidden herself at Kate's desk under the stairs so no hopeful with an empty stomach would think his pleas might find favour. With the lights off and the café in darkness except for the ghostly glow from the fridges, she hoped everyone would think she'd shut up shop to attend the briefing.

Truthfully, she is not just tired. She's furious. Kate was due back around lunchtime. She should've called or at least responded to her text message. They are partners. They are meant to care about each other's wellbeing. In Ettie's world, you communicate and you never let anyone down. By nature a giver, nevertheless she doesn't like to feel used. And right now, she's feeling used and bruised. And, let's face it, worried sick. It's out of character for Kate to vanish without explanation, but with her mobile phone going straight to message bank, short of calling the police she's stymied. She gives a start when a fist bangs on the locked door. 'What?' she yells angrily from her dark hole. 'Are you bloody blind? Read the sign. We're closed.'

'Ettie, you OK?' Sam rattles the door. Dashes around the side of the café and vaults the railing to charge in the back entrance. 'Ettie, love, what's up? You sick?'

She laughs for the first time all day. 'God, how ironic,' she says, hauling herself to her feet so wearily Sam reaches to give her a hand. 'A little fit of exhausted pique and people think I must be sick.'

'No offence, love, but you're not looking crash hot, if you don't mind me saying so.'

'Just tired, Sam. It's been a long day on my own.' It's on the tip of her tongue to point out that a solo fourteen-hour shift without a break is too much to ask of a fifty-five-year-old woman, but she swallows the words, unwilling to concede a single round to age. You're as old as you feel, she reminds herself firmly, which, right now is about a hundred and ten.

'Yeah,' he says, relieved. 'It's the drama of the bloody bridge and resort. Wearing us all out already.'

She shuffles painfully towards the stairs. Her feet feel broken. Her legs are two dead weights. Her knee joints hurt like a bad toothache. 'You want to come upstairs to my lavish penthouse for a beer? Tell me what happened out there?'

'You're the answer to every man's dreams,' he says, worrying again when Ettie fails to pull him up for a corny line he's worn to death over more than twenty years. With the force of a fist landing hard on his solar plexus, he realises she isn't getting any younger and neither is he. He's overwhelmed by a sudden sense of undirected urgency and leaps the last three steps to get it out of his system.

Upstairs, the old storeroom – converted to a live-in apartment by ever-practical Kate to save Ettie paying rent on a tiny cottage at the peak of two hundred steps on Cutter Island – is hung with her whimsical paintings of seagulls and ferries, cormorants and tinnies; the floor is awash with the jewel colours of a Turkish carpet.

'Marcus on his own tonight?' Sam asks.

'It's a new moon and a high tide. Perfect for prawning. He's out with a torch and a net. God, what was I about to do? Oh yeah.' Stoic and normally unflappable, Ettie wrings her hands. Fusses with her hair, her apron. Fusses in the fridge. Fusses in cupboards searching for a wine glass. Fusses with a cheese board. Fusses for the first time in Sam's living memory. Her behaviour does nothing to ease his concern. He feels an unspecified alarm building once more.

'You hear from Kate today?' Ettie asks, when they're sitting out on the deck nursing their drinks. The open waterway is a stretch of black glass. A few stars begin to twinkle. The Square is nearly deserted; everyone's gone home to mull the contents of the developers' screed.

Sam picks up a knife and cuts himself a large piece of crumbling cheddar, his face deliberately blank. 'Nah.' He shrugs, throws the cheese into his mouth, reaches into his back pocket. Spreads the future plans for Garrawi on the table. Not quite believing the gist, but unable to disbelieve it, he sees plans for eighty holiday units in a building twelve metres tall, as well as a design for a massive swimming pool, gymnasium and tennis court. A reception area measures twenty-five by fifteen metres. Bigger than the local kindergarten with the playground thrown in. 'They're calling it a *health and beauty spa for the body and spirit*,' he tells Ettie, spitting out the words. He looks up, his face twisted. 'They've aced the great cheese tree, love. The cheese tree is bloody gone.'

Ettie reaches across and pats his wrist. 'God. It's a desecration of a holy site.'

'They're going to build it four storeys high, Ettie. That's enough to knock out the views of every house behind. It's more than bloody desecration, love. It's rape. Rape of the bush, the wild life, the sea and the whole Island itself. Why would you want a pool when you're surrounded by a rising and falling sea that lives and breathes? It's – '

'You know what? I just can't handle this tonight. Do you mind? I'm totally knackered. Can we just sit here like the two old friends we are and finish our drinks in silence?'

'You're worried about Kate, aren't you?' Sam says, unable to avoid the matter of her disappearance any longer but driven to defend her even though he's fully aware he may be on shaky ground. 'She's different from us, Ettie, that's all. Never put down real roots in a community before. She also spent years in the media world where values seem to shift faster than chocolate at Easter. She needs time. Six months isn't long in a place like Cook's Basin. Not long enough anyway, for new ways to set rock solid once and for all . . . And it must've been a shocker day. Even if they didn't get along, a mum's a mum. She'd feel a whole . . .'

Ettie puts a finger to her lips. 'Shhh. Do you hear the water? A fresh wind? The casuarinas singing? I swear I can hear oysters breathing. Fish playing. Simple things, Sam. They keep us grounded. If Kate needs time off, I'll ask one of the Three Js to help out. Pushing a person where she doesn't want to go is pointless.' She smiles, the weariness wiped from her face. 'I just heard that wisdom on the wind.'

'You're not gunna go all poetic on me, are you, Ettie? Not when right now we need fighters . . .'

'Listen to the wind, Sam. And bend with it.' She takes his empty beer bottle from his hand. 'Now I'm going to bed. See yourself out.'

Ettie takes a long hot shower, slips into one of her faded cotton nighties and lies back in the narrow converted cupboard that's her bedroom, on a single bed, feeling stifled by the confined space, the lack of a window. Her aches and pains are duller now but her head is a mess. Kate's disappearance, Marcus off fishing alone, café business, tomorrow's work list, the dodgy roof, the rickety tables and chairs on the deck, the whole damn drama of surviving each and every day. It's all too bloody much. She holds back tears. Her toes begin to tingle. Breathless, fighting off panic, she throws aside the sheet and heads for fresh air. On the deck, she scans the night sea for the beam of a single torch. Sees the red, green and white lights of Fast Freddy's water taxi, the flashing green shallow-water marker at Stony Point. No torch.

Riddled with mounting anxiety, she pours another glass of wine even though she knows it's a very bad idea. Takes a sip.

Her face flushes, her head spins. The old black dog of despair begins plodding lugubriously over to take up residence at her feet. She makes a serious effort to pull herself together: it's still early days but the business is going well. Marcus is a consummate fisherman and would never take unnecessary risks. Barring a shocker storm, the roof will hold. The tables and chairs may not be new but they're loaded with what she likes to think of as character. And Kate? She sighs, pours the wine down the sink and goes back to bed. Only time will tell.

As she does every night, she mentally calls up a list of her chores for the following day. Finds she can't remember a single one. Wonders if she's going mad or showing signs of early dementia. Teary again, feeling childish and abandoned, she wants Marcus – the feel of skin on skin, her head resting on his broad, comforting chest, the sound of his breathing like a meditation. And god forgive her, she yearns for a spacious, luxurious bedroom with windows that let in the golden light of the moon. Next time, she'll go fishing with him. Far better than lying, sleepless, worrying the sky is about to fall on her head.

Alone in the wheelhouse of the *Mary Kay*, Sam spins the helm, turning the barge towards Oyster Bay. If he sees a light he promises himself he'll turn around. He wants to know she's safe, that's all. That the boat that's missing from the café pontoon is tied fast at the bottom of her garden and not floating out to sea after coming adrift. He tells himself it's time he checked on Artie anyway. He's been a bit slack since Kate started delivering café leftovers to the old fella at the end of every day; since

Jimmy and his mum decided to take responsibility for cleaning the yacht, washing the bed linen and making sure Artie changed his underwear at least every second morning.

The bosomy *Mary Kay*, her golden timbers curving from bow to stern, surfs the rising chop, barely acknowledging it, steady under his feet. The reliability of a good vessel, he thinks. Ah, get over it, he tells himself out loud, seeing Kate's house ablaze with lights. He swings the barge around all at once, too fast and tight so he bounces over his own wake with a ball in his gut that feels like lead.

He tries not to think of the number of times he's followed her home, his eyes on the slim dark shape of her, unable to believe she's chosen him to share her bed. The first time, when he looked at the grease embedded in the cracks of his hands, even though it was Christmas Day and he'd scrubbed until his skin started to flake, he thought she could so easily change her mind once the festive spirit from a long lunch on Ettie's deck wore off. He'd hung back, waiting for a signal, not sure he could laugh off disappointment if that's how it ended up.

He'd been overwhelmed by the cleanness of her clothes, her skin, her hair, her spotlessness. The sweet soapy scent of her. Then the two of them tangled in white cotton sheets that crackled and snapped. He wonders now if she changes the linen every morning because the house nestles into the folds of a rainforest gully backed by a sky-high red rock escarpment that blocks the sun for most of the day. Damp creeps in with the stealth of rumour and takes hold like a vice. But then they were still in drought four weeks ago, the land dusty and raw with the singed, spicy smell of parched eucalypts. The air so dry it caught in your throat. He stares into the darkness, amazed at how little it takes to rattle something he thought was new and beautiful. Time to get real. He's forty years old. Love is a two-way deal or a one-way ticket to misery.

There's a park to save. A bridge to oppose. If this relationship is meant to be, it will find its own way. Did his mum say that? Or someone famous? Buggered if he can remember. Maybe he'll find a reference in *The Concise History of the World*. Not as silly as it sounds, he thinks. Didn't he read somewhere that love'd changed history over and over? Cleopatra and Anthony, Napoleon and Josephine, Edward and Mrs Simpson, Lola Montez and some king whose name he can't remember. He fingers the solid form of the book in his pocket. Might get his money's worth out of it yet. King of Bulgaria. No Belgium. That was it. Lola and the king of Belgium, who was mad as a hatter, apparently. Even putting a sympathetic spin on it, Emily was a piece of work, and she'd read Kate like a first-grade primer. Ruling from the grave. No, much more than that. Setting the seeds in motion for her daughter's destruction. What kind of a mother desired failure for her child? He gives himself a mental shake. Starts to feel a little manic. He suddenly needs company. Real bad.

He slides alongside Artie's yacht, which even in the dark of a new moon he can see needs a good bum scrape. Knocks lightly, not wanting to disturb the old bugger – he's famous for waking up crankier than a bear with a sore head. Not that Sam's ever seen a grizzly, but, like he said to Kate the other day when she pulled him up during a cliché-ridden (he's happy to admit it) conversation, sayings turn into clichés because they're true. And that's the truth.

A voice like gravel floats up from the pit of the yacht. 'You have permission to come on board, Sam. And don't forget to hang your bloomin' fenders out so me paintwork doesn't get scratched.'

'Give me a break, Artie. When have I ever failed? And there's more scratches than solid paint on your hull anyway.' He lightly slaps his forehead with the palm of his hand. Bad move opening the door on that subject.

'Doesn't hurt to keep you on your toes, son. We all need reminding now and then. As for the paint-job, I'm still looking for a volunteer. Got any ideas?' Sam grabs hold of the lifelines and pulls himself on board, pretending not to hear.

Inside a tidy cabin with portholes open to admit a quickening wind, Artie waits on the portside banquette. In front of him, there's a bottle of rum and two glasses lined up on a spotless table. 'Medicinal?' Sam queries, eyebrows raised, figuring the lingering smell of detergent and the shine on the glassware means Artie's had the company of Jimmy's hardworking mum, Amelia, for most of the day.

'Not tonight, mate. Never felt better in me life.'

'Well, if you're just being sociable,' Sam says, pointing at a glass, thinking a rum might ease the terrible cramp gripping his gut.

'Amelia sparkles me up till I almost feel these useless old legs of mine could come good in a minute or two.' Artie slaps his withered thighs, grinning. They both know the part of his brain that passed on instructions to stand, walk and run died when a tiny blood vessel decided to explode as he was reaching into the fridge. He was found lying on the floor, his head swimming in spilt milk and nobody home when they checked his muddy brown eyes for signs of life. A miracle he lived, the doctors said. Artie returned from hospital, moved on board his pretty timber pleasure yacht and immediately tossed his wheelchair overboard in a gesture he confessed was irresponsible and driven by anger and frustration. But he couldn't stop himself and he figured the minute or two of pure power he felt was well worth virtually ripping up the hard-earned dollars he'd spent to buy the bloody thing. For months, he roared at any nosy social worker who managed to get close enough in a water taxi to suggest he'd be better off in a nursing home. 'Locking him up would kill him,' Ettie told the nurse one day when she nobbled her at The Point. 'The community will take care of him.'

'So,' says Artie, slumping on plumped orange floral cushions, his yellow T-shirt riding up his back to reveal a roll of pasty white skin, 'no hot date with Kate tonight?'

Sam takes a slow sip, feels the burn in his throat, the spreading warmth in his stomach. 'None of your business, Artie,' he says quietly.

'Ya'r right, of course. Forgive me if I lose me sense of perspective occasionally. Not much entertainment around for an old bloke whose arse is nailed to a boat.' Artie sighs heavily.

'Spare me the self-pity and try the heartstring tango on some other sucker. You've been flat-out shooting the breeze with Amelia all day if the condition of your usually, er, homey boat is anything to go by. You're a nosy old bastard. That's the truth.'

Unoffended, Artie grins and taps the side of his nose with a finger that's nowhere near as clean as his clothes. 'Just tryin' to keep abreast of daily events,' he says. 'You're drinkin' my prize rum like orange juice, mate.' He lifts the bottle in a question.

Sam holds his empty glass up at eye level then slams it on the table upside down in the negative. 'A bunch of blue-collar thugs in shiny suits reckon they can steal Garrawi Park from the community,' he says. 'And correct me if I'm wrong, Artie, but that bottle looks suspiciously like the one I gave you for Christmas so I reckon I'm entitled to drink it any bloody way I please.'

'Simmer down. Just complying with me duty of care. You in charge of a barge and all. Garrawi, eh? Heard the scuttlebutt but couldn't credit it.'

'I'm going to fight them, Artie. I'm going to fight them even if I bleed to death in the process. Not sure how to go about it. That's the biggest problem facing me right now. Feel like a tiger looking around a big empty cage for somewhere to sink his fangs.'

The old man uses the strength in his saggy-skinned arms to shift further back on the banquette until he rests against the bulkhead. He nods at Sam, points at his glass, out of reach now. Sam slides it across the table to him. 'In me own day . . . Now, now, Sam, relax. I'm not about to give you me entire life story, even though a drop of this amber rocket fuel is enough to set an old man down the sometimes melancholy path of memory. But I've fought me share of battles. Ran a union once, one of the tough ones, back in the days when Jack Mundey was king. 'Course, forty years ago, there wasn't any other kind.'

'How old are you, Artie?'

'What's that got to do with the price of rum?'

'Just curious.'

'Bullshit. You think times were different then, don't ya? Well nothing changes, mate, and I've been around long enough to know that for a definite fact. And me age is none of your business. If you don't mind me quotin' someone sittin' right here in this cabin.'

Sam holds up his hands. Surrendering.

Artie hitches his trakkie daks with the underside of his forearms, like he's scratching an itch. 'Them silvertails didn't have much time for union members. Thought we were riff-raff and they could bully us into workin' our guts out for the privilege of livin' on the breadline.'

'Hard days, eh?' Sam says, fiddling with his empty glass, almost tempted to go for one more slug to see him through what he senses will be a drawn-out soliloquy.

'That was the point, mate. One of the most prosperous times in history.'

'So what did you do?'

'We lit spot fires. One after the other. Just as one trouble spot got doused, we'd light another. On and on until the factory was shut more than it was open and it was costin' 'em more than givin' us a decent wage.'

'There's no factory floor. No identifiable bosses. No bloody union.'

'Oh, there'll be a boss somewhere. Find him then put the pressure on. It's all about money, Sam. Keep hittin' them in the pocket till it hurts so bad they go away.'

'Not sure how you do that.'

'Talk to your girlie. Kate.'

'You ever call her girlie to her face?' He is curious. If he tried it, she'd probably knock him to the ground. Half his size or not.

'Do I look like a nincompoop? Me legs might be buggered but me brain still functions. Once worked as a financial journo at the big end of town, didn't she? She'll know where to start.'

Sam leaves Artie and goes back to his own home for the second night in a row. Forgetting to eat, he sits on the deck. All night he reads the development proposal over and over under the weak yellow outside light, wearing out the print with the force of his thumb and forefinger, hoping he'll be hit with a genius idea.

When he was nine years old his mum and dad took him on his first holiday ever. He was shivery with the excitement of sleeping somewhere other than the bunk bed in the primitive rented boatshed the three of them called home. God, the excitement of crossing the water from Oyster Bay to Garrawi Park on Cutter Island – what would it have been, five hundred metres? But it felt like an ocean voyage even though he'd done it a million times because this was a *holiday*, not just a visit to play with friends.

He helped his dad put up a tent his mum had bought second-hand from Vinnies, a rare and exotic find that had sparked the whole holiday madness to begin with. The park, already noisy with kids running wild on the first day of the school break, was alight with dancing campfires. Families sorting billies, frying pans, plates, searching before it turned dark for somewhere flat to spread a sleeping bag so the blood didn't run to your head and give you a headache in the morning. A rite of passage it was, now that he looks back on it. And all of it free, which was the only kind of holiday his family could have afforded. 'This is how you light a campfire safely, son, so you don't burn yourself or endanger the bush. See up there? Stars. Look hard. Learn their names. That's how ancient mariners travelled uncharted waters and found their way back home. You can always get your bearings from the stars, son. Remember that when you're out in a boat with nothing but the sea all around and you feel like you've lost your way.'

He'd stolen his first kiss from Carly Atkinson under the spreading arms of the old cheese tree that weekend and fallen head over heels in what he'd thought was everlasting love. 'I've got a girlfriend,' he'd raced to tell his dad, who saw the glitter of infatuation in Sam's young eyes and took him aside for a chat. 'Man to man,' he'd said in a serious tone. Sam nodded, his chest bursting with a whole host of sensations he could hardly define let alone control. They sat together, cocooned in that same tangle of massive roots at the base of the cheese tree. His father placed a protective arm around Sam's young shoulders. 'There's love and there's sex, son,' he said. 'It's wise to be able to pick the difference.' Sam's understanding of life changed forever in the next half hour.

On the second day, a threatening sky turned on a solid downpour that didn't look like shifting for a week. Water filled the tent like a swimming pool until his dad couldn't pretend it was *only condensation* any more. Sam feels a tear run down a groove in his face to the corner of his mouth. He licks it away, tasting the sting of salt.

Near dawn, with the wind dropped to a breathy murmur and the sea flat calm, his anger compressed into a tight little kernel and stored away for the time being, he knows he has to make a start somewhere. He feels pressure build again, time running out. Maybe a visit to the address in tiny print secreted away in the bottom corner of the last page. Find the head honcho where the buck always stops and force the bastard to see sense. How hard can it be? He hits the sack to grab a couple of hours' sleep.

Cook's Basin News (CBN)

Newsletter for Offshore Residents of Cook's Basin, Australia

JANUARY 14

This is a special edition due to extraordinary reports that Garrawi Park is under threat by developers. We must FIGHT this proposal with every means at our disposal.

NO BRIDGE
NO RESORT

An open discussion will be held on a drastic issue facing all Cutter Island Residents. Bring your ideas on how to fight this travesty so Garrawi Park remains untouched for future generations to enjoy.

Where? Cutter Island Community Hall

When? This Saturday

(Afternoon tea will be served).

RED ALERT

On another note: Red algae has shut all ocean shoreline beaches. While it is not toxic, it is certainly unpleasant and can cause skin irritations. The eradication of the bloom depends on wind and surf conditions.

N.B. At least two and possibly more, massive great white sharks (approximately six metres, according to water police called to investigate the cause of the frenzied waters) are currently feeding on the remains of a whale carcass near Cat Island. If you're out cruising on a pleasure jaunt and thinking of a quick, refreshing dip over the side of the boat . . . DON'T!

Dear Parents

If you would like to enrol your child (age 2–6) in our beautiful kindy, with qualified staff, please call in to collect an enrolment form. This needs to be competed and returned by February 27. Places are limited so get in early!

Open Tuesday to Friday from 7.30 am to 5.30 pm. Mondays are a possibility, depending on interest.

Trudy Wentwhistle, Director

CHAPTER FOUR

Sam wakes to the screaming harangue of cockatoos, the loony racket of kookaburras and a low-grade clench in his gut that he knows from long experience is born of dread. Hot and sweaty for all the wrong reasons, he throws back the sheet. The sea breeze is long gone; the mercury is rising. He pulls together the pieces from yesterday until they fall into place. Garrawi, he remembers. They're trying to steal Garrawi. He glances at the clock his mum bought for his eighth birthday and that he's kept ever since even though the tick tock is loud enough to shatter the peace of the kitchen four doors away. Swings his legs to the floor. There's work to be done. He reaches into the wardrobe for a clean pair of jeans, a halfway decent shirt. He's going calling.

Ten minutes later, showered, shaved and out on the flat, shimmery water on the magnificent *Mary Kay*, he passes the usual early-morning commuters, all of them barefoot to avoid ruining their good shoes in the petrol scum that pools in every hull. He waves a hand out of his cabin door. Gets a nod, a flick of the wrist in return. Bob the Rower raises a leg in acknowledgement, not missing a stroke of the oars. The morning light is fuzzy with heat. It's going to be a scorcher.

A civilised chat with the people at the top. That's the go. He'll mention storms that wash fragile beaches out to sea. How it can take years for nature to repair the damage. He'll tell them about towering eucalypts and their frail grip on the land. How they suddenly let go and keel over, destroying anything in the way as they crash to the ground. Then there are death adders. Spiders big as a man's hand – although it's the smaller ones that carry enough poison to kill. Goannas that rip your guts out if you get in their way. He'll point out that the Island survives mainly on tank water. How many tanks would they need for a resort catering for . . . He hauls the development pamphlet out of his back pocket, slowing the *Mary Kay* to a crawl to avoid rear-ending a yacht on a mooring. Eighty. No change since he last looked. With more staff quarters at the rear. Insanity. It won't work. It's a bad investment. Sam likes the leaden certainty of the phrase *bad investment*. Surely they'll see the risks, the downside of a still-raw paradise that is not necessarily everybody's cup of tea. Feeling like he's on stronger ground, he pushes the throttle forward.

He's on the road in his battered white ute twenty minutes later, the already burning hot bitumen shimmering wetly, pollution thick in his nostrils, his vision blurred by salt scale glued to his windscreen like dry skin. Suburbs unfold on either side of the road in different shades of baked brick. Red. Cream. Brown. Speckled. Grey. Liver. Solid and serious houses, crafted to last for generations. He's a timber man himself but in Cook's Basin, where white ants are voracious, just about the only houses still standing after a hundred years are built from brick or sandstone or both. One day, he thinks, when he and Kate have a brood of kids . . . Ah jeez. He's fairdinkum off with the pixies. Everyone steps off on the wrong foot once or twice in the early days of a new romance but the core issue – the fact that he is besotted and she is engaged in a disengaged sort of way – is hardly the stuff of firm foundations. Boil their personalities down to the base ingredients, and they're a different species. She analyses. He feels. She likes crisp linen and cutlery laid on the table in the right order. He prefers to sit on the end of a pontoon with his feet in the water and his hands slippery from the shells of fresh prawns. She's a woman who enjoys a good glass of wine. He wouldn't cross the road for a glass of fermented grape juice but he'd scrabble over ten tradies on a murdering hot day to get to a frigidly cold.

It's never going to work, he admits, feeling what's becoming that familiar clench in his gut. He's on a hiding to nothing. To hang on and hang in is just a weakling's way of putting off the hurt that he remembers vividly from when ruby-lipped Carly dumped him for suave Billy Morris and he thought his eight-year-old heart might die of the pain. 'C'mon, Sammy. Let's get busy.' His mother had grabbed his hand and a couple of hessian sacks and dragged him along the wallaby track leading from the boatshed into the bush on a search for firewood. By the time they staggered home bent almost double under the weight, the moon above white in a fading summer sky, he was almost too buggered to eat his dinner. 'Keep busy, love, and you won't feel as bad.' She'd cooked the Sunday roast on a Thursday for him. Maybe because in her heart she knew it wasn't quite that simple but it was as good a place to start as any.

He skids to a stop at a red traffic light, burning rubber. Scaring himself rigid. Longing for the open waterway where there is room to move. He's way out of his comfort zone and the pressure is like a vice squeezing his chest so he can hardly breathe. He urges himself to take it easy. Drives on when the light goes green, accelerating a fraction of a second too slowly. The car behind him honks. Sam gives him the finger. A P-plater passes him at double the speed limit. Dead meat in a month, he thinks, more sad than angry. He recites his bad-investment spiel out loud to take his mind off the numbing stop-start drive. His voice bounces back, failing to convince even him. He hasn't a hope. He hasn't a choice. No wonder commuters go nuts, he thinks, hitting the brakes for the tenth time in as many minutes and yearning again for the snap of clean air in his lungs, the freedom of open water.

The café is humming. Clattering, banging, hissing. Sweet scents of sugar, cinnamon, vanilla, lemon, baking, knock back the smell of the sea and wet sand. A low murmur of voices comes from inside. Ettie, who didn't fancy another brutal day if Kate decided not to appear, has called in help. Marcus, a former top city chef and *two hats* restaurant owner, is working the customers, the food, the cooking, like a virtuoso performer. He tosses pancakes, swirls maple syrup, spins delightedly from grill to counter. Every so often, his eyes land on Ettie, who has returned to her usual joyous self, and his faces softens. He is a man in love with a woman he believes to be a treasure above all others. He is contemplating a quick little behind-the-counter waltz of happiness when he catches the change in Ettie's demeanour. He looks behind. Kate stands in the doorway. Ettie takes a deep breath. Marcus steps aside. Kate has shame or chagrin hanging off her like a cloak. Ettie moves forward. Marcus watches. Kate appears to be fighting an urge to flee. Ettie holds out her arms. Kate heaves in a bucket of air, swallows and walks straight into them.

'I will make coffee, yes?' says the chef, pleased with the outcome of what could have been a tricky moment. 'You girls, you wait outside in the sunshine. I will come with everything in a few moments.' He flits around the café, shooing them away with the flick of a tea towel when they fail to move fast enough.

Ettie slips an arm around Kate's waist and guides her onto the deck. 'He's happier on his own. He's a chef and I'm a cook, both noble in their way, but with little in common beyond ingredients. God,' she adds, referring to Marcus and smiling brightly, 'how did I ever get so lucky? Fifty-five years old and he calls me a girl. Love, thank the lord, is blind.'

'I'm so sorry, Ettie . . .' Kate says.

Ettie reaches across the table for Kate's hands, holds them tightly in hers. 'Next time, call me. I was worried something had happened to you,' she says softly. 'There's always a fall-back position but I need to know what's going on.' She lets go and leans against the back of her chair, eyes closed, letting the sun wash over her, enjoying an unaccustomed break. 'So how did it go with the lawyer yesterday? Any nasty shocks? '

'Nothing unexpected.'

Ettie stirs from her languor. That's it? she thinks. Kate disappears for a whole day on the basis of *nothing unexpected*? Ettie frowns. Checks out Kate's body language: back ramrod straight, eyes focused on the table. She's lying, Ettie thinks, tilting her head sideways, considering whether to push for more information or to leave it alone. Before she can make up her mind, the chef swoops on them, plates balanced on his arm as if they're glued in place. With a theatrical flourish, he delivers five-star service. 'Two coffees. Two of my exquisite almond croissants. Two each, of course. One is never enough.'

'The ego of the man,' Ettie says, when he's gone. She's laughing. Happy. Rips off a corner of her croissant, chewing with her eyes closed. Ecstatic again. She mentally gives the subject of Kate and her mother's will the flick. If Kate wants to tell her, she will when the time is right.

'Now . . . Let's move on. We've got a business to run. OK? Eat your pastry or Marcus will be offended. If you can't eat both, I'll help you out.'

'Ettie!' Marcus Allender roars from the kitchen, his normally velvety tone so distraught that Ettie leaps to her feet, almost knocking over the table. Kate follows at a run.

Inside, the chef's tope is askew; he twists the corner of his apron, points to a corner near the soft-drinks fridge. 'You have a rat in this kitchen. Look. There. Shit. A rat has made this shape of a poo. I know these things.' The chef's voice has climbed an octave, he's reverted to a strong German accent, he looks about to collapse.

'God, is that all?' Ettie says, relieved, the colour coming back into her face. 'I thought you'd had a heart attack. I'll find a trap. He'll be gone by tomorrow, Marcus. I promise you.'

The chef dabs his neck, flushed lobster red, with his trademark black-checked kerchief – a remnant from his glory days – then stuffs it back into his breast pocket and frowns at Ettie. 'This is serious, my pet. This rat can close you down. He must be gone quickly.'

Feeling like he's travelled into territory so foreign he should have brought his passport (if he owned one), Sam feeds a small fortune into a parking meter that allows him exactly half an hour to do his business. As he's a fair way from his destination, he almost jogs to the address on the flyer. He'd read the penalty notice. The fine was worth four hours of Jimmy's labour on the *Mary Kay*. He picks up his speed.

At the end of a long corridor in an aging building dwarfed by downtown's plate-glass skyscrapers, built before the money stream dried up in a global fiscal meltdown, he finds black lettering peeling off a smoky window. *New Planet Fountain of Youth*. Fountain of Youth? Bollocks. Varnish from the bottom half of the door flakes at his feet. Shysters, he thinks. The whole development plan is a scam. Someone testing the water. Nothing to worry about. He tries the knob, expecting to find it locked. It turns under his touch. He steps inside.

A dark-suited goon – Sam can't tell whether or not he's from the amorphous group that turned up at the Square – perches on a corner of a naked 1970s standard veneer desk with two drawers on either side and not even a telephone to dignify it. Looks more and more like the place has been hurriedly rented to provide a temporary but legal address to print on the posters. The goon's ankles are casually crossed; dark glasses cover most of his face despite the gloom. He's drinking a can of imported beer. The whole set-up is like a bad joke. Black suits. Sunglasses. Cartoon character stuff. Too weird to take seriously.

'Gidday,' Sam says, prepared to be civil.

The goon grins. 'Got some advice for you, *mate*. Real good advice. You don't want to take us on. Believe me, you take us on, and I'm warning you, you'll get kicked to death.'

'Now hang on, *mate* . . .'

The goon rises. He flicks at an imaginary piece of dust on his sleeve, removes the dark glasses. His eyes are shiny bright – half crazy or just plain stupid: it's too hard to know. He drains his beer and flattens the can in his hand. Crosses to open the door and chucks it into the deserted hallway. He sneers at Sam, then turns on his heel and disappears into the bowels of whatever lurks darkly and silently behind the reception area. Sam feels like he's stepped into a totally surreal parallel universe.

So stunned by the crazy eyes and the casual act of vandalism he fails to react before he hears a key turn, a bolt slam home. Finally finds his voice.

'If there's one thing I can't cop, you bastard, it's bullies,' he yells, blood rushing to his head, his face reddening fast. He strides to the door, yanks hard. It holds firm. 'You picked on the wrong bloke, mate. Believe *me*.' He pounds on the timber. Kicks the door in frustration. What kind of a pea brain brushes the fluff off his clothes but doesn't hesitate to chuck an empty can into a clean corridor? They're all bloody nutters without a single grey cell between them, he thinks. It's a full-on, blue ribbon tin-pot organisation. Are they serious about Garrawi? What the hell is really going on here?

Fuelled by anger, he yanks open the desk drawers one by one. Hits gold in the last one in the form of a glossy pamphlet with a long-haired bloke dressed in white robes – a ringer for the Jesus in his Sunday School book – holding his hands out for . . . what? Alms? That'd be right, he thinks. It's always about cold hard cash. He shoves the pamphlet in his pocket. In the hallway, he picks up the can, chucks it back onto the reception desk. 'Shit in your own nest, mate,' he shouts into an empty space.

Back on the street, he stops short, looking up and down with a frown on his face. Where the bloody hell did he park the ute? North or south? How do people spend all day in these soulless concrete canyons, where the only breeze comes from the dirty exhausts of crawling traffic? South, he decides, setting off in a hurry, anxious to put the city behind him and aware he's achieved absolutely nothing. Lighting spot fires isn't as easy as it sounds.

He arrives back at the Square by late lunchtime and marches into The Briny in search of sustenance. Ettie can't keep the shock out of her eyes. 'Someone die?' she asks, not joking.

'On a mission, love. Had an appointment in the city,' Sam says casually, although they both know it's almost historic for him to quit Cook's Basin for any place more distant than the local supermarket. 'And I'll have the beef pie, easy on the grassy stuff. Don't hold back on the spuds. A napkin in case I spill a drop on my pristine clothes that I'm very pleased to see that you've noticed.'

'You're up to something, Sam Scully. Duplicity is hanging off you like a bad smell.' Ettie leans forward on the counter, ignoring his order.

'Kate around?' he asks, avoiding the subject.

'Upstairs with Marcus. They're setting a few rat traps,' she says. She goes pink, looks around for a chair. Heat builds from her toes like a tidal surge. She has the weird sensation the ceiling is about to crash down on her head. Her heart thumps loudly in her ears. She could be drowning.

'Rats?' Sam's voice is an underwater echo. His worried face swims in front of her. 'Settle, Ettie. It's no big deal. Couple of traps and you're as sweet as a nut.'

'Want me to tell Kate you're here?' she says, feeling steadier by the second, wiping a sudden eruption of perspiration from her brow, her upper lip. The impulse to rip off her clothes is abating.

Sam visibly swallows. He makes a point of looking at his watch. Feigns surprise. 'It's getting late. Make it a take-away. I've got a job on. What's the damage?'

'Fixing two chairs on the deck,' Ettie says, realising Kate still hasn't called Sam and he hasn't called her.

'Done!'

Sam grabs his tucker and skedaddles like a man who's mislaid his backbone. He makes it into the Square where the luscious scent of pastry and tender beef wins out. He rips open the package and takes a bite, leaning forward to spare his going-to-town clothes a gravy hammering. Sauce. Not gravy. Gravy, Ettie tells him, is old-fashioned even though it's basically one and the same. He checks out the blackboard. Sees the Cook's Basin Community Residents' Association has called an extraordinary general meeting at the community hall to discuss the plans to develop Garrawi Park. *Volunteers needed: tea and scone duty*. Sam toys briefly with the idea of offering to make his world-famous sausage rolls and then comes to his senses. It will be a full house. Two hundred irate locals equal four hundred sausage rolls. His knees go weak and he feels a light sweat break out on his forehead as though he's had a narrow escape. He scoffs the last of his pie, wipes his chin with his forearm and heads for the communal tap, where he rinses and refills a dog water bowl wired tightly to the pipe so neither a king tide nor a thieving bastard can whip it away. Washes his hands. He catches sight of the two Misses Skettle, octogenarian twins resplendent in starched pink cotton shirts and skirts, deep in conversation with the Three Js – Jenny, Jane and Judy. All of them born and bred Cook's Basin women. Tough as nails. Soft as mush. Depends on the day and the circumstances. They look cool in loose cotton dresses and sandals, despite the heat and the meagre shade from the casuarina. He joins them in the far corner of the Square, where they're seated around one of several scabby picnic tables carved with the initials of four generations.

'Ladies,' he says, mock bowing. 'Sorting scone duty, are you? What do you reckon about cheese scones for a change? My mum used to make the lightest cheese scones in the world in her kero stove. Fairdinkum magic, they were, with enough hoist to see you through to dinner time.' He breaks off. The five women are giving him hard looks. Too late he remembers the unwritten Cook's Basin rule: Never question a volunteer. You risk scaring them off. And landing the job.

Jenny slides closer to Sam, a sweet smile on her face that instantly makes the hairs on the back of his neck shoot up. He waits for the crunch moment. 'You need a job too, Sam. How about whipping the cream?' She cracks that killer smile again. Sam scrabbles to suss the catch that he knows is hurtling towards him like a locomotive. She adds: 'The cream has to be good and stiff or it makes the scones go soggy. We'll need ten litres. Might take a while with that old egg beater of yours.'

The women laugh. Pleased with themselves. Three (mostly) kind-hearted and good-natured women, he thinks, automatically excluding the eternally sweet and compassionate Misses Skettle. You'd never guess at the killer instinct lurking just under their skin.

He finds Jimmy waiting for him on the barge at Cargo Wharf. 'Ya gunna tell me who died?' asks the kid, grinning widely, pleased with his witticism. Sam sighs. Wonders if everyone's reading from the same script. Lets the comment ride. 'You give that mutt a bath last night, mate?'

'Yeah, Sam. Used me own shampoo so he smells real good.' The kid bends to scoop the pup into his arms. He shoves the warm, wriggling mass of fur under Sam's nose. 'Go on. Have a sniff.'

Sam grimaces, reels back. 'Smells like a bloody fruit salad, mate. You might want to change your shampoo . . .' The smile is wiped off the kid's face. He dances up and down. Anxious. Sam wants to cut out his tongue. He back-pedals.

'Er, deliciously enticing as it is, mate, maybe you should find one that's more suitable for a dog. Something that works on fleas and ticks. Know what I mean?'

'Sure, Sam.'

But the spark has gone out. Sam searches for a way to redeem himself. Guide Jimmy, who gives the smallest, most inconsequential task everything he's got, back on track. He seizes the pup, holds him high against the empty blue sky, feels his emotions go slightly haywire at the sight of an exposed pink tummy, trusting brown eyes: 'He's a lucky dog to have you, Jimmy. And Christ, he smells good enough to eat.' He holds the dog against his neck, suddenly embarrassed because he doesn't want to let go.

Jimmy senses the shift. Grows a little taller. 'Watch the tide, Sam. You gotta concentrate, cap'n. Where's this stuff goin' anyway? You got a sling ready? C'mon on, Sam, get it together: we got work to do.'

'How much you saved, Jimmy?' Sam asks, as he does at the start of every job.

'Not enough yet, Sam.'

'Well, mate, Rome wasn't built in a day and cars don't come cheap.'

'How long did it take to build Rome, Sam?'

'Grab the sling. Thread it under the cargo pallet like I've shown you. Hurry up, mate. Then I'm leaving you in charge of the *Mary Kay* for a while, which means I expect her to shine brighter than the stars by the time I get back. You getting my drift?'

'Aye, aye, sir. You want me to work my scrawny backside off. Is that it?'

Sam smiles, gives the kid the thumbs up, strips to his jocks in the wheelhouse and pulls on his work clothes. They load without another word and set off. Jimmy sits on the pitted deck by the pup's basket, his skinny knees pulled up against his cheekbones. Every so often, the pup twitches in his sleep. Jimmy rubs a furry ear until he settles once more.

Just on dark. A low, brooding sky. The smell of rain on the way. Out on the deck of Ettie's penthouse, the two tired owners of The Briny Café sip frosty glasses of white wine. Ettie bunches her voluminous blue-and-red tie-dyed skirt around her knees, kicks off her sparkly sandals, and hoists her throbbing feet up to the top rail. Her toenails are painted to match her clothes. I'm not entirely losing the plot then, she thinks. She briefly considers investing in orthotic footwear. Then her vanity kicks in and she quickly ditches the idea. Kate rolls up her jeans. Ettie drops her feet, covers her legs to avoid comparing Kate's smooth young skin with her own battle-hardened extremities.

It's been a gruelling afternoon; busloads of dithering white-haired tourists, clumsy on Zimmer frames in small spaces; dripping wet kids on school holidays, impatient to eat and then plunge back into a warm and tender sea; a constant stream of anxious offshorers dropping in to chat about the plans for Garrawi even though they could see the two women were flat out.

'Felt like hanging out a sign announcing it was *all quiet on the eastern seaboard* except no one would bother to read it,' Ettie says.

A few lights switch on over at the southern end of the Island. The faint sound of laughter carries across water that's battleship grey and matches the sky. The *Seagull* hoots three times. The last commuters make a dash, beers in hand. It's the final run for the day and a long swim to Cutter Island.

'I've heard the timber ferry is borderline. A big swell or a killer storm and she's liable to give one last moan before sinking,' Kate says.

'Chris says he's stacked toddler-sized lifejackets at the entrance. Reckons adults can fend for themselves.'

Kate says: 'Yeah, well, I guess it's a doable swim to shore in any direction, barring sharks.'

The *Seagull* eases away. Ettie wipes a pool of sweat from under each eye. She tries to recall the last time she saw a shark part the clean blue sea with a fin like a small black sail. Three years ago? Five? She measures time by ingredients, now. If she's run out of eggs, it's Wednesday. Ready for a fresh delivery on Thursday. If the milk has reached its use-by date, it's Sunday. The butcher delivers on Monday. The greengrocer on Tuesday. She has to work out the ingredients for the Saturday special on Sunday. A whole week accounted for in routine chores.

'Maybe a bridge isn't such a bad idea . . .' Kate says.

Ettie's feet drop to the deck; she rounds on Kate, furious. 'That better be a joke and if it is, it's not funny.'

'I'm not supporting the development. I'm just saying. Times change. You can't hold back progress.'

'Depends what you call progress.' Ettie suddenly stands and waves. Marcus Allender is coming towards them in his swish commuter boat with its highly polished timber bow and white padded seats. A Riviera runabout, straight out of a gossip magazine. Ettie turns back to Kate, suddenly almost teary. 'Mention one word about how you feel and you'll kill our business overnight. Not a single offshorer will ever walk through this door again for even a box of matches. No one will forgive you – or me, because I had faith in you. Think about where you stand, Kate. Let me know what you decide. Oh, and by the way, I – by that I mean we – volunteered to cook dinner to serve after the community meeting on Saturday. We've all got to do our bit, eh?'

Marcus stands and waves madly with both hands, his silver hair flying. The boat skews sideways. He loses his balance for a second. A huge laugh booms across to Ettie. She rips off her bandana and brandishes it like a flag of victory. 'Lock up, will you? I'm out of here.'

CHAPTER FIVE

Night falls. The Island becomes a carnival of lights. Voices drift across the water. A lone tinny struggles past, the outboard coughing. The driver curses when the motor dies. Kate hears the snap of the starter cord. The engine catches limply. The boat coughs on.

She lingers, sifting through the realities of her current existence and how they fit with what she knows of herself. She casts her mind back over the fewer than one handful of lovers in her life – so different from Ettie, whose past included a philandering ex-husband and a string of good-looking bedmates who came and went with the sailing season. Kate remembers the claustrophobia, the struggle for ascendancy that inevitably culminated in endless compromises until they leached the marrow from each other's bones and she felt hunched over from the weight of another's expectations. None had lasted as long as a year. Each excision felt like a release from prison. Not for the first time, she wonders what curious force drives humans to think that they'll find salvation through love. In her heart, she is aware that Sam is that rare thing, a good and decent man, but she can't shake the feeling that if you let it, love exacts too high a price. Too high for her, anyway.

*

A hand on her shoulder wakes her. Kate jumps to her feet, groggy with sleep.

'Café door was wide open. Didn't know whether to leave you in peace or not,' Sam says. 'Then I figured you wouldn't want to wake in the morning with a sore back and a stiff neck.'

'Ettie said you went to town?'

'Yeah.'

'Garrawi business?'

He nods.

'Want to talk about it?' she asks.

'I'll put the kettle on. Unless you'd prefer a beer or a glass of wine.'

'Tea's fine.'

'Think I'll opt for a beer, myself. As days go, this one hasn't exactly been gold star.'

'How so?'

'You got an electric beater hidden anywhere in your house?'

'Eh?'

'Nah. I'm kidding. I called into the not-so-swank offices of the New Planet Fountain of Youth this morning. You could say the meeting didn't quite go according to plan.'

Back on the deck where the air is cooler, they sit with the table between them, both staring into a sky the colour of tar. 'I thought I could make them see sense, you see, get them to understand that the success of a community is far more important than dollars in the bank,' Sam says, earnestly.

Kate shakes her head in disbelief. 'No offence, Sam, but if you think the sudden appearance of a well-meaning but – in their view – misguided bargeman in a downtown office might influence their multi-million dollar decisions, you're a five-star idiot.'

'Jeez, Kate –'

'Look at it from their perspective. You turn up alone in blue jeans and – sorry – ratty boat shoes without any facts and bearing a banner for peace, justice and the Cutter Island way. Don't you understand that your idea of nirvana is their idea of hell? They like nightclubs. They enjoy resorts. They think they're improving the quality of living and the community should be on its knees with gratitude. Quite frankly, they have a case.'

'What are you saying?' Said in a whisper. His face as shocked as if she'd just slapped him.

'A resort would bring local employment. A bridge would reduce the risk of fatal boat accidents . . .'

Sam cuts in: 'Guess it depends on what you value, eh?'

Kate slumps back in her chair. 'Those goons, they're probably just front men. Not smart enough to tie their own shoelaces. You'll need to wade through three thousand pages of listed companies to find the source . . .'

'There are certain basic principles that are sacrosanct,' Sam continues quietly, as though he hasn't heard her. 'The first is that you protect your environment. The second is that it only takes a minute to destroy the landscape. The third is that you never get it back.'

Kate opens her mouth. Before she can say a word, Sam continues. 'Hear me out. OK? Maybe I'm delusional or naïve, but I've always believed the best things in life come without a price tag. And yet every time I turn around, there's some new project that destroys something free and precious for short-term gains and long-term losses.'

'You're exaggerating –'

'Take farmers. Decent, hard-working people who suddenly find they haven't the right to stop miners from drilling into land they've nurtured for five generations in the mistaken belief that when they were handed the title deed it meant they called the shots.

'Then there's quiet little coastal towns – not unlike the off-shore clusters all over Cook's Basin – and one morning, locals wake up to find there's a swank hotel blocking their view and access to the beach. Or one day, the pristine wetlands rich with birdlife in your country-town backyard have suddenly been re-zoned for housing. Surely "wetlands" is a pretty strong hint that the location might not be ideal for a string of villas aimed at retirees. Not unless they've got webbed feet, anyway.'

'Pressure of population, Sam. Too many people. Not enough land. And even the strongest dissenters can lose track of their scruples when a hefty cheque is waved under their noses.'

'Maybe. But if we all stand back and let some shonky idiot rip into the heart of Island life for the sake of a few dollars, we'll never forgive ourselves. Something's got to give sometime. Or we're all buggered in the end. But where do we bloody start when we don't even have a name to call the enemy?'

'Quis licit, Sam,' Kate says, sounding resigned.

'Not following you . . .'

'Who profits? Track the money, Sam. You'll find the culprits when you uncover the source of the money.'

It's on the tip of his tongue to ask for her help. But suddenly he's not sure where she stands. If he has to guess, he reckons she'll sit quietly on the fence. A bull-at-a-gate man, he'd once asked her about her tendency to observe instead of act, hoping some of it might rub off on him. Turned out it was another of those journo habits she couldn't shake. 'Journos look at every angle, never take sides. It's all about objectivity.' In Cook's Basin, he almost said at the time, the fence-sitters were regarded as a waste of space. 'So all we have to do is find the source, eh, and twist his arm until he gives in and buggers off?'

'There's one other thing you need to check,' she says. 'There are often little-known and frequently changing state regulations that allow large projects to by-pass local councils and head straight to the State Housing and Development minister who can tick them off without even notifying parliament. Sadly, it doesn't take much to buy a politician.'

'Jeez, Kate, they're bloody strong words.'

'Trust me, if this is already a done deal – and in my view it probably is – you'll be able to smell the rot all the way to the premier.'

Sam pulls from his pocket the brochure he nicked. 'Found this in a drawer. What do you reckon? A bunch of unrelated bible-bashing happy clappers or the real deal?'

Kate gets up to turn on a light that casts a soft yellow glow across the water. It's still hot as hell. The sea smells swampy. A swarm of insects hones in on the glow. *Bang. Bang. Bzzt.* Ducking the barrage every so often, she studies the front page for a long time. Breaks off to fish out a Christmas beetle that's fallen down her shirt and latched on to her left breast. Sam sits waiting. He watches her face intently, like it's a book he might be able to read. She catches him. Gives a quick smile. Opens to the inside blurb and reads every line. When she looks up, she's frowning. 'Could be dealing with a cult, Sam. I'll check into it, if you like.'

He feels a swell of euphoria. She's moved off the fence and onto the sidelines. It's a start.

With a half-smile, she asks: 'Your place or mine?'

In the dark, the cloud cover thick again, Sam follows Kate's boat across a flat sea all the way to Oyster Bay, guiding the *Mary Kay* around the winking green shallow-water marker at Stony Point. Lamplight shines through the windows of the Misses Skettles' home. Sleep, they tell him, eludes the aged. He politely refrains from revealing that he's often arrived in the early afternoon and found the two of them dozing peacefully in their rosy armchairs, wearing their rosy pink outfits, rosy pink lips hanging slack. Out behind him, phosphorescence plumes and skitters like sparkling green goblins in the black wall of a merging sea and sky. The night feels syrupy.

Inside Kate's sandstone house it's much cooler but the air is still thick with moisture. Here and there, he notices condensation trickling down a wall. First it's drought, he thinks. Six long anxious years of tapping tanks to check water levels and holding back from flushing the dunny until it verged on a health hazard. Now if a dry spell doesn't kick in soon, everyone in Cook's Basin will be wiping mould from nooks and crevasses and dragging their one good suit out of the cupboard before it shuffles off unassisted. He follows her into the whitewashed kitchen where the timber benches are scrubbed to paleness. The room holds the promise of warmth and succour but seems trapped in rigid, clinical order. Like Kate, he thinks, wondering – not for the first and he's sure as hell it won't be the last time – what strange, untrustworthy chemistry keeps sucking him back into her orbit; why a romantic confluence of two consenting adults can sometimes feel more like punishment than pleasure.

She opens the fridge door, her eyebrows raised. 'A beer?'

He nods. Senses her mood has slipped a little. Can't think what to do about it. He goes back to square one. 'Track the money, you say?' He takes the frosty bottle, feels the cold on his hand like a blast of air-conditioning, twists off the top. Watches as she grabs a bottle of white wine from the fridge, a glass from a high shelf so she has to balance on tiptoes, stretch her arms. Dark hair falls across her face for a second and it's all he can do not to reach out and tuck it behind her ears. 'You need to start by forming a committee,' she says. She opens a drawer near the sink, rummages for a pencil. She rips a sheet of paper from a notepad near the phone. Returns to her chair. Sam leans in: is she moving in from the sidelines now? He watches her chest rise and fall. Wonders at the pulsing softness of women.

'You'll need a spokesperson. Passionate but cluey, who understands libel laws. A media liaison person who can write press releases. Of course a few celebrities on board is essential. It guarantees media attention.'

'You're kidding, right? What am I supposed to do? Call Nicole Kidman? Hey, Nicole, got a little problem you might be able to help out with. God, Kate . . .'

'Celebrities make good copy. Soon as they open their mouths, ratings soar, newspapers sell. Doesn't matter whether they're smart or dumb as long as they can learn a few lines. And you'll need a strategist to organise rallies and demonstrations. Also a website and a web master to keep it updated . . .'

Sam feels his optimism drizzle away in the cacophony of foreign jargon. What the hell is a web master? How do you find a spokesperson? Where in god's name do strategists appear from? Why does she keep using the word *you* when he was hoping desperately to hear *we*? Christ, she has all this knowledge at her fingertips. If she put her mind to it, she could orchestrate a campaign single-handed. 'This is starting to sound like Swahili, Kate,' he says. 'We're a small community . . .'

'A long time ago, I interviewed a man who saved a national treasure. He wasn't a genius, he didn't have much money and he didn't have contacts in high places. He had nothing going for him except an unshakeable belief that his motives were pure and his fight was for the greater good. Every time he was pummelled to the ground, he laughed in their faces and bounced back. That's the weird thing about the rich and powerful. They're so used to stomping on the well-meaning poor until they cave in, they have no idea how to handle idealists.'

'Jeez, Kate . . .'

'You might as well know, I don't think you have a chance of winning. Men like the one I just described come along once in every four lifetimes. Mostly, people just plain get worn out and walk away. Or someone breaks from the ranks and lets the enemy in.'

'Never! Not in Cook's Basin . . .'

'Don't be too sure. Here's how it happens: you're getting old. It's becoming harder and harder to look after your house and pay the bills. One day, someone turns up on your doorstep, offers you a magic price for your property and guarantees ownership of a brand spanking new unit in a tasteful little development right where your house is. Bottom line: easy-care home, money in the bank, and you don't have to make new friends. Happens all the time. And you know what? It's a good deal. Even the neighbours see that. They'll all line up for their share and – *snap!* – the foreshore has a new identity. Times change, Sam. And there's sweet Fanny Adams you can do about it.'

'So you wouldn't bother fighting this if some old bloke was getting a golden handshake and a change of lifestyle opportunity?'

'We all have to adapt. Cook's Basin can't hold out forever.'

Sam slumps, the foot he's been tapping so hard that the table rattled, goes still. The enormity of the job overwhelms him. He's a bargeman, for chrissake. He cruises the waters of Cook's Basin with the sun on his face, the tide coming and going under his feet. He does a job, he gets paid – well, ninety-nine times out of a hundred. He loves his life. He may not be a genius but the people he cares about understand the skill and concentration it takes to judge times, tides, loads and weather so no one's life or property is ever at risk. They trust him. What if she's right? What if this is a mad, pointless and potentially painful folly? What if the community bursts its collective gut and comes out with nothing to show for it but cracked heads and busted noses? Then he remembers reading a newspaper story about a cattle farmer from Burrell Creek who took on the state energy giants to stop construction of a huge new power grid in a pristine valley. Against all odds, he won. Sam leans over the table, his face close to the list, straining to read the words in the dim light. 'Give me one job at a time.'

'Get yourself a committee, Sam. Then take it from there.'

All through the night, the temperature stays stubbornly in the low thirties and the humidity is as thick as pea soup. Prime conditions for a cracker storm to rise out of nowhere. Sam and Kate lie side-by-side but not touching, too hot, too wired, for sleep. In the end, with eyes wide open but shielded by the dark, they talk to each other in soft tones. She asks him about his mother, his father, his boatshed life. Who built the barge? What timbers were used? The Misses Skettle – what were they like when they were much younger women? Tough eh? But oh so girlish with it. Ettie and the chef? Has he noticed Ettie seems more anxious lately? The roof of The Briny needs replacing or does he think it will see out the winter? Isn't Jimmy's pup well behaved? So roly-poly sweet. Once or twice, he questions her on subjects he considers safe but, like a good journo, she flicks them back. He retreats with grace, holding back from gushing on about love, marriage, kids, an ordinary life together. He's forty years old and in a rush to pin down the future. His problem, not hers. Her responses drop to a slurred murmur and her breathing grows deep and rhythmic. Using a corner of the sheet, he dabs gently at the sweat gathered in the hollow of her neck. Careful not to wake her.

*

Not long after dawn, the heat wears him down and he gets up to brew a cup of tea. Pours another when he hears Kate stirring. He takes it in to her. An ancient, dinted cash box of the kind his father once kept hidden up the chimney in the boatshed where they lived, takes up most of the space on her bedside table. He's never seen it before. She reaches for the tea with a smile that tears his heart. Just in time, he swallows what he was about to say, knowing she's not ready to hear that he'd be happy to bring her a morning cuppa for eternity. A cool breeze sneaks in from nowhere and skates across the floorboards. In the distance, thunder rumbles. The air is thin and feverish now. The first few drops of rain hit the roof like the tap of a hammer. 'Want to fill in time till the rain stops?' he asks, grinning.

'I might get fired if I'm late for work.'

'That's the beauty of being a boss. You call your own shots.'

She slides easily into his arms where she stays until long after the tea goes cold.

After she's gone, he takes his time showering, washing their mugs and making the bed, pulling the sheets tight as a drum, tucking the corners neatly. He finds he enjoys the process of completing these small domestic chores to the best of his ability when, mostly, he used to race through them.

Outside, the morning sky is dull and low. The rain-swollen tail-end of a cyclone that's already hammered northern Queensland is on the way. In the wheelhouse, he finds a note weighted with a small shackle. *Have a favour to ask. Could you bring a writing desk from Emily's unit? It belonged to my father.* The pick-up address is written in block letters. Below, there's a PS. *Deliver it to Frankie at the boatshed.* No signature. Short, sharp and to the point. For a former journo, he thinks wryly, she's bloody frugal with words. Sam carefully folds the paper and places it in his back pocket. He points the duckbill bow of the *Mary Kay* towards Cutter Island, which climbs out of the deep blue sea like an upended cone, wondering why he suddenly feels like his engine's blown and he's adrift on a rising sea without even a piece of canvas to rig to bring him home.

CHAPTER SIX

The rain sets in steadily and heavily right up to Saturday morning, when it eases off until it's light enough to be mistaken for a sea mist drifting in from the tropics. The bush, flattened for so long by the drought, rises in the heat and damp and runs rampant. Cissus vine curls upwards looking for light, bringing down weak young trees that collapse untidily across paths. Lantana reaches new infestation levels despite last year's backbreaking weeding weekends (even the most dedicated bush regenners are feeling defeated). The land is awash with ticks, sand fleas and every other kind of garden pest that stings, bites or just plain aggravates. In backyards all over Cutter Island and the Cook's Basin area, washing hangs limply on Hills Hoists, wetter than when it was first put out to dry. Soon, it will stink of damp and need washing again. One or two mothers with large, dirty broods of tear-away kids begin to hanker for a few weeks of drought – though they keep their thoughts to themselves, knowing to voice them would be sacrilege.

Miraculously, the rain eases at lunchtime and in the clammy afternoon, the residents of Cutter Island shuffle along steaming pathways and tracks mined with puddles towards the community hall, to plan a strategy to fight the development of Garrawi Park. There's a record attendance that has nothing to do with the fact that Ettie and Kate have volunteered to provide a light early supper of roasted potato, zucchini, capsicum and pumpkin frittata – considering the enormity of the problem, the meeting is certain to flow into dinner time.

To combat what they all agree is a bad dose of heat fatigue, the crowd – covered by only enough clothing to remain decent in public – pounces on the crusty scones provided by the Three Js and anointed with the Misses Skettles' homemade strawberry jam. Most of them skip the cuppas and move in soldier-crab formation towards the bar. Gasping for a frigidly cold, they insist it will only take a couple of quick swigs until they are sufficiently resuscitated to be of some practical and intellectual (heh, heh) use to the proceedings, which have been delayed anyway by the late arrival of Bill Firth, who finally appears full of apologies. He'd lost track of time, apparently. Paradise, eh? Who could blame him? As it turned out, paradise had nothing to do with it. His septic tank was overflowing and he couldn't leave before he'd organised and overseen an emergency pump-out. Given the inclement weather, he suggests it might be advisable for the community to get together to make a group booking with the pump-out barge to keep the cost down should the rising water table plunge more of them into a similar deeply odourous and undesirable situation.

By the time the scones have been demolished and the crowd is well into the third beer, feelings are running as hot as the oven-like temperature in the hall. The president calls for order, aware that a move towards a fourth stubby might end all hope of rational discussion.

'Right now, we're all angry and upset. We feel like our park is being stolen . . .'

'That's because it is, mate,' shouts Davo, one of the old Island hippies, whose two kids – according to rumour – were conceived like many others on a hot summer night under the spreading arms of the ancient cheese tree. Wearing nothing but a yellow sarong accessorised with a beer, he rises purposefully from his seat.

Bill Firth smoothly cuts him off. 'A good point, Davo, but before we go any further, we need a few facts. Let me give you a quick outline of the history of Garrawi Park before we get started.' He clears his throat, shuffles around a few pieces of paper until they form some sort of order.

'The park was left in trust to the people of Cutter Island in 1946 by Teddy Mulray.' The crowd begins to murmur. Bill Firth holds his hand up for silence. 'Yes, yes, I know we're all aware of this fact.'

'There's a bloody engraved plaque with all the details under the cheese tree, for chrissake, Bill. Tell us something we don't know!' Davo reties his sarong grumpily. Anyone within eye-line turns his or her head sharply in the opposite direction, acutely aware of what lies under the fabric. Davo is renowned for attacking his wild and woolly garden buck-naked except for a hat and a chainsaw. How he's remained un-castrated is one of the great local mysteries.

'The point I'm trying to make – if you'll let me, Davo – is that the park is actually controlled and cared for by a private trust –'

'Oy, oy oy, back up, Bill,' shouts Davo angrily. 'Islanders have always looked after the park . . .'

Bill wipes a fresh outbreak of sweat from his brow. 'Yes, yes. But the point is, technically and legally, a private trust has the last word on what happens to the park.'

'Get the names, mate. We'll deal with them in our own way and it won't cost a penny,' Davo shouts, shaking a fist.

'Hear, hear!'

'The real enemy, Davo, is the developer, not the trustees. Although I suppose neither could function without the other.' He breaks off, aware that going down the long and convoluted path of explaining the rights of trustees and developers, combined with the heat and booze, would send the crowd straight to sleep. 'Anyone ever fought a development proposal before?' A hand shoots up at the back. 'Not your neighbour's plans for an extension that's going to block a corner of your view, Ernie, I mean a full-on campaign against bona fide, large-scale developers.' The hand sinks. 'Right, well anyone got any sensible ideas about where to start with all this? Do we want to hit the legal trail and wear the costs – and frankly it could run into hundreds of thousands of dollars? Or do we want to come up with a program of what I can only refer to as our unique and traditional Island way of handling a problem? By that I mean we find a way to handle it ourselves.'

The crowd roars. 'Let's do it the Island way, Bill. Let's show the bastards!'

Bill Firth, his face now puce, his shirt sodden at the neckline and under his armpits, scans the equally heated faces in the airless hall. 'So where do you want to start?'

The silence – broken only by the lazy buzzing of an early March fly – is deafening.

'Right,' Bill says, sighing heavily. 'We can all agree, at least, that no one wants Garrawi Park to be desecrated by developers.'

'Hear, hear.' Enthusiastic shouts.

'Well, we've made a start. Not much of one, but nevertheless, it's a beginning.'

Davo again: 'Pretty bloody good, if you ask me. Can't remember the last time we all agreed . . .'

'Thanks, Davo.' Bill Firth actually bangs the table with his fist, bringing to swift closure what everyone is fully aware could have turned into a long Davo-paranoia-rant.

Sam places his empty stubby on the floor at his feet and rises from his chair. 'Artie reckons . . .' There's a collective groan. 'No, wait a minute and hear me out. He was a big-time union boss in his day and what he said made a bit of sense.'

'Before or after the first glass of rum?' shouts someone from the back.

The rotund president raises his hand for silence. 'Give the man a hearing,' he orders, nodding at Sam to continue. Outside, the breaking clouds take on the golden hues of sunset. A dog barks. White cockatoos go ape-shit. A goanna must be raiding a nest. 'Everyone's a critic,' someone yells, getting a laugh.

Sam begins: 'Artie said the best way to tackle the problem was to light spot fires. Keep the bastards jumping so they never know what's going to happen next. Any delays cost money. Artie reckons if you start costing them enough, they give up and go away.' This time the crowd stays quiet.

Heartened, Sam continues. 'Kate – you all know Kate from The Briny Café . . .'

'Not as well as you, mate.' There's a ripple of uncomfortable laughter. Sam chucks the culprit a dirty look and continues with his case.

'I know there are a lot of smart people here tonight. But Kate, well, she used to be a top journo and she's reported on environmental and property development issues in the past. We had an impromptu meeting . . .' Sam breaks off and eyeballs a sniggerer, who sinks lower in his chair and raises his beer in apology. 'Any of you blokes speak Latin?'

'Aw jeez, Sam, get to the point. We're melting in here.'

'Two words, my friend: *quis licit.* Who profits, in other words. Follow the money and nail the shady deal-makers behind this travesty of a development.' He ends with what he believes is the core point of the crusade: 'How can we feel proud if we don't save Garrawi? How do we tell our grandchildren we failed because we didn't try hard enough?'

People are sitting higher in their sweaty, sticky, scratched white plastic chairs now, their faces aglow with what Sam hopes is enthusiasm and not just the booze. 'With enough passion and plain old bullheadedness, I believe we can pull off a coup and roll a plan that looks like a certainty right now,' Sam says. 'Let's face it. Most of us are born anarchists and rule benders. We're used to fighting for what we believe in and if our methods can be a little, er, unorthodox at times, at least we end up with the right result. Well, nine times out of ten.'

'So when are we going to light the first fire?' calls Marty Robinson, a ruddy-faced Islander with a huge thirst and a legendary wild streak.

'Hear, hear,' echoes the crowd, clapping cheerfully. Aren't most of them volunteer fireys who are experts at lighting spot fires for hazard reduction burns?

'Well, we need to start with a few volunteers to form a committee . . .'

There's rustling and shifting as people begin to stand and make their way to the kitchen to grab a plate. Beer in hand, the Islander with a big thirst comes over and wraps his arm around Sam's shoulder. He leans in to Sam's ear to whisper in a beery breath: 'Details bog us down, mate. Think of the total picture and go for it. We'll back you all the way.' He whacks Sam hard and moves off, his long skinny legs not quite steady as he makes a beeline for the bar.

One by one, Cutter Island residents shuffle up to Sam and stand alongside him, rocking on their heels, nursing their beers. 'We'll support you all the way. And that means with cudgels or swords, mate. Whatever you think is best. Every war needs a general and you've been unanimously elected. Good on ya. We won't let the bastards win.'

The offshore artists approach him in a group. Their spokesperson, John Scott, a short bloke with a Roman nose and deep brown eyes, who is a skilful and diplomatic organiser, outlines a plan in a rush to cover his shyness. 'We're going to need money to fight. Count on one painting from each of us. We'll hold an auction and a BYO knees-up party to follow. Or maybe the other way around. Nothing like a few stiff drinks to loosen wallets and run up the bids. Phoebe's already come up with a fabulous idea for a logo. She's a genius, that dame. Did you know Garrawi means cockatoo in the local Aboriginal language? Trudy thinks a giant papier-mâché bird would look good in the Square. Draw attention to the cause. She's going to get the kindergarten kids to help. We'll need a couple of weeks. OK? Lord, it's a sweat-bath in here, isn't it?'

The two Misses Skettle, looking fresh as two pink daisies despite a long stint in the kitchen alongside Kate and Ettie, coyly sidle up to Sam and offer to distribute material as soon as it comes off the presses, to combat the developer's evil propaganda. 'Thank you, ladies, from the bottom of my heart,' he says, gallantly kissing their powdered and rouged cheeks. Evil propaganda? What bloody presses?

Halfway through the evening, discussions about the proposed development peter out from lack of fresh fodder. Talk inevitably shifts to the problems caused by the recent rain; the rise in giardia cases and the multiplying swimming-pool-size potholes. The track needs bulldozing so the community ute doesn't crack an axle. Long after dark, when these topics too have been hammered to death, the weary but well-fed and -watered people of Cutter Island and the bays head home under swollen black clouds that block out the silver sparkle of the night sky. Even during war, life goes on.

CHAPTER SEVEN

Over the next twenty-four hours, Sam hits the phone. He decides to do away with Kate's ritzy committee job descriptions, which, when he broke them down into everyday language, lost their terror. All they needed was a leader, a thinker, a doer and a heap of support staff. Anyway, nothing beats all hands on deck, he figures. And human nature being what it is, the right people will put up their hands for the right jobs. No mug wants to volunteer and make an idiot of himself. Which, he tells himself swiftly, is not the same as fearing failure. Different kettle of fish completely.

First, he dials Marcus on his mobile. 'Mate!' he says enthusiastically. 'You have just been unanimously voted onto the Save Garrawi committee. Congratulations. Yes, mate, completely aboveboard and legit.' He ends the call after accepting an invitation to dinner on Monday night so the chef can fully discuss his role and thereafter fulfil it to the best of his ability. Sam tells himself that only a full-blown pea brain would turn down the chance to sup at the chef's bountiful table and, by tomorrow night, he'll have thought of an appropriate way to use the chef's many and wide-ranging skills.

Next, he phones Siobhan O'Shaughnessy, an Irish firebrand who lives on the Island and once produced a top-rating talkback radio show with the power to make or break governments, careers and causes. Touchy, volatile, explicit to the point of rudeness, she was famous far and wide for battling for the underdog no matter what the cost. Once, she had two black eyes to prove it (a difference of opinion, Siobhan explained wryly at the time, regarding the rights and roles of women). According to local gossip, she carries the home phone numbers of every celebrity from Hugh Jackman to Ricky Ponting in her head. Sam makes a mental wish list of big-name converts to saving Garrawi, throws in a few top athletes to broaden the spectrum. Comes back to earth with a thump when his call goes to voice mail. He leaves a message.

Next, with the mobile burning hot against his ear, he wheedles, entices, cajoles, seduces and, once, bribes with the promise of a same-day delivery of his (arguably) world-famous sausage rolls still warm from the oven. Glenn the Removalist, who'd been humming and haa-ing on the basis that he didn't have much to offer in the way of brains or even – despite his chosen profession – brawn, couldn't resist.

With the *Mary Kay* swept clean and safely bedded down on her mooring for the night, Sam makes a dash to the supermarket, where he scrabbles together the ingredients he needs to keep his promise. A man's only as good as his word, as his father used to say.

Not long after sunset, he's pulling four dozen sizzling concoctions of his newest creation – minced lamb tickled with mint, parsley and chilli – from the oven. He uses tongs to pluck a dozen from the tray, wraps them in a tea towel to keep them warm and almost jogs to Glenn's back door. 'Good to have you on board, mate,' he says, slapping his friend on the back. In an almost simultaneous motion, he whips away the tea towel, grabs a roll, and bites into it with gusto. 'Just making sure they're up to standard. Wouldn't want to think I left anything out in my rush to keep a promise.'

Glenn gives him a hard look. 'I'd be more impressed with your attention to detail if I didn't know for a fact that you've got a heap more at home waiting to be stashed in your freezer.'

'You wouldn't have a beer anywhere, would you?' Sam asks, heading for the fridge. 'A sauso roll and a frigidly cold. Marriage made in heaven.'

'Next you'll tell me kings used to live like this.'

'But they did, Glenn. Trust me, they did.'

By Monday, the rain is back again and the air so still and heavy the clouds don't look like shifting – ever. Some bright spark posts a notice in the Square on how to recognise early symptoms of trench foot and cure it. It triggers a sudden rush of toe and feet inspections, followed by thorough washings and dryings, among the Island kids. Adept at dealing with ticks, leeches, spiders and sand flies, they had been unaware of the threat of trench foot until now. Parents are stoked: 'Don't want to wash your feet before bed, eh? Well, don't blame me if you get trench foot.' Grumpy holiday sailors are forced to anchor in sandy coves where rain tapping on cabbage-palm fronds is a steady wall of noise. Disappointed day-trippers stash their bait in the freezer, replace their fishing rods and cancel their dinghy hire. Working boatsheds postpone anti-fouls, paint and varnish jobs and concentrate on below-deck tasks such as servicing engines and electrics, plugging leaks, cleaning the bilge. Only the day-to-day routine that keeps the infrastructure of offshore living intact continues without a nod to the wet weather. Trucks are loaded onto massive barges to make their stately circuit of public jetties to collect garbage from large dump bins. A smaller barge makes the rounds of the bays and private jetties to swap empty wheelie bins for those loaded to the max with stuff that even the canniest recyclers can find no further use for. Septic pump-outs continue to do a roaring trade.

Inside The Briny Café, business has slowed to a trickle but Ettie, who hasn't quite recovered from Kate's blasé announcement that times change and Cook's Basin residents better get used to the idea, is heartened to see her partner using the down time to research the New Planet Fountain of Youth on the internet. After their disagreement about the development of Garrawi – which she knows would have escalated to a full-on row if the arrival of Marcus hadn't interrupted – she'd worried Kate still didn't quite understand the underlying forces that drove Island life. Or far worse – unthinkable, in fact – that she *did* understand but wasn't convinced they were worth fighting for. Once, she glances at the screen over Kate's shoulder. Shocked, she flees back to her oven to remove a tray of golden shortbread. The comforting scent instantly steadies her nerves. She gives a silent thank you to unknown forces for the small blessings of her daily life.

Then, without permission, her mind cunningly slips into what she blithely referred to as *cranky old lady* back in the days when she thought she'd somehow (miraculously) avoid the nasty trap of aging. She finds herself launched on an internal rant against the idiocy of war, the pointlessness of cruelty, the horror of modern waste, the necessity of hoarding every empty glass jar along with last year's leftover Christmas gift ribbons until there's no room on the shelf for full jars and the moths have devoured the ribbons. She bemoans the absolute tragedy of seeing smooth-skinned, angelic boys grow ugly facial hair at the same time as their sweet voices drop and they develop shifty-eye syndrome when asked a simple question such as *What are you up to tonight?* Before she knows it, she's on the verge of tears. She's broken-hearted by the threat to Garrawi Park, Island life, innocence; she's worn down by the worry that doing two loads of washing a day is going to cause a worldwide water shortage and lead to failed crops and ceaseless, catastrophic famine; she's tormented by the thought that if she uses one more supermarket shopping bag – ever – she will seal the fate of humankind and tip it irrevocably towards extinction.

Flushed, sweaty and on the verge of a panic attack, she finds she's unable to think of a single strategy to get through the next two minutes, let alone the next few years. She swallows a sob and reaches for a piece of shortbread. It's all too, too much, she thinks, at the same time as she registers that the shortbread is perfect. She sighs; the heat leaves her face. When she considers the baffling alchemy of combining a correct balance of butter, sugar and flour to achieve this crisp, dry but infinitely rich result she is suddenly more hopeful about the condition of humanity. She tells herself it's the sticky wet weather that's making her morose, that she will be back to her old self when the sun comes out again. Or I'll die of a brain tumour or dementia, she thinks, finding a skerrick of her old hubris at last, and all my worries will be buried with me. She covers the shortbread with a clean cloth while it cools and hopes the humidity doesn't turn it soggy before she's sold every piece. 'What do you think Marcus will cook us for dinner?' she asks, as much to switch her focus as to satisfy her curiosity.

Kate shrugs without looking up from the computer.

'Whatever it is, it will be superb,' Ettie says, almost dreamily.

Two drenched cyclists step inside the café. Long skinny black bodies with aerodynamic helmets at one end and luminously shod feet at the other, they remind Ettie of a couple of praying mantises. 'How can I help you?' she asks. They order coffees and drink them thirstily at the counter. She mentally swings completely back on track, pegged firmly by routine. Grind the coffee beans, mugs under the spouts, hit the button for hot water. Heat the milk. Outside, the rain keeps falling.

Near closing time, Kate says: 'I'll finish cleaning and lock up. You go ahead.'

'You sure?' Ettie dithers. Without a word, Kate takes Ettie's arm and steers her through the fly-wire slammer, across the back deck, down the jetty and onto the pontoon. 'Go! While there's a break in the weather. I'll see you soon with my research. Hope you've all got strong stomachs.'

Ettie steps into her ancient tinny, resurrected so many times by Frankie that the locals have dubbed it Life Everlasting. She hoists her skirts out of the greasy bilge water with a wrinkled nose. 'God, Marcus and his spiffy boat have spoiled me. It's amazing how quickly a girl gets seduced by luxury.' Despite the odds, the engine catches first go. Kate shoves off the boat with her foot.

Ettie chugs to the mustard-yellow eight-knot marker, where she hits the revs. At high speed, she swerves around the newly spiffy *Seagull* to a cheer from commuters perched on the back deck like pigeons. She waves, grinning. For a moment she feels immortal. Why would anyone want to destroy a paradise like this? Her heart blips erratically with the awful resonance of the word *destroy*. Despite the wind in her face, the cool sea spray misting over the bow, her dazzling display of daring, Ettie starts to burn. Strong stomachs? She swallows a surge of bile. Looks towards the horizon where the rolling blue hills are like a frozen sea. Fights the urge to leap overboard and end the worry once and for all. Suddenly, the gloom lifts. The grey overcast sky breaks into a mass of tiny clouds like fat curls and picks up the last light, changing from pink to red to apricot while she watches. She focuses on the magic. It's all good, she thinks, crossing her fingers. All good.

'Kate's late,' Sam says, scanning an empty void of suddenly glowing water, a hand shielding his eyes. A table is set on the deck. White linen, tall wine glasses, bone china plates. Like something out of a travel brochure. Marcus hands Sam a beer from an icebox at his feet. Frigidly cold. 'Took a risk with the weather, mate, if you don't mind me saying so,' Sam says.

'No, of course not. I am a careful man. I checked the radar,' Marcus explains. 'The rain, it was due to shift. And Kate? She will have a good reason to come after the designated time. She is not a thoughtless person.' He pours himself a glass of sparkling wine. 'This is a very decent drop that will take on the French winemakers at their own game and in my opinion as a chef who knows these things, will either beat or at least come close to surpassing them.'

'Yeah,' Sam says, barely listening, his eyes on the water. He takes a long swig. 'Your dinner going to spoil, chef?'

'I have cooked chicken tonight. Slowly braised in red wine and my homemade stock – stock is the key, of course, to a fine cassoulet – with bacon and mushrooms and flamed with brandy. A classic coq au vin. You know it, of course.'

'Ah, chicken, yeah, I'm familiar with chicken,' Sam replies, floundering.

'Perhaps we will eat it warm instead of hot, which suits the weather. Yes? This way, the chicken will not dry out.'

'Ah! Reckon that's her now.' Sam takes off, beer in hand. He can't wipe the grin off his face. He waits on the pontoon until she's close enough to swing in. She tosses him a rope, cuts the engine. Passes a manila folder thick with papers.

'Don't drop it,' she says. 'I'd hate to waste a day's work.' She climbs out of the boat. Bare legs and arms. Shoeless. Her tanned skin giving off a low sheen. 'It's mind boggling, Sam. Deeply crazy stuff. They're all mad as cut snakes.'

'Could have told you that from day one and saved you a lot of effort,' he says cheerily.

Kate freezes. 'Really?'

Sam swallows, loses the grin, curses himself for an insensitive blockhead. She's worked hard. All he needed to say was 'thank you'. He suddenly feels worn out, unsure if she was genuinely offended by an essentially harmless, throwaway line or whether she's using irritation as a way of seizing the moral high ground. But, jeez, if you can't laugh in the face of disaster . . . He backpedals. 'A joke, love. The whole community is grateful for everything you're doing.' He bows, mock serious, looking for lightness. But he can't help feeling that his foot comes down on a freaking twig that lies in wait far too often for comfort.

'I don't mean to be unkind,' she says, 'but I wonder, sometimes, if this great and wondrous community you're always rattling on about is nothing more than a sheltered workshop. Out in the real world, I doubt too many of this lot would survive beyond the first day.'

He feels his hackles rising, a rare surge of anger. This time, he doesn't back off. 'Depends where you're coming from, I guess. I prefer to think we understand our responsibilities to each other which, in turn, makes us feel strong and safe in our environment. Which, in another turn, means we feel free to be individuals instead of blindly following the pack mentality. You're part of it too, Kate. Where do you reckon you fit in?'

Without a word, Kate takes her file from him as though he can't be trusted with it. He follows her along the jetty in silence. He suddenly feels flat. Wonders why the two of them so often seem to be failing to thrive, as Fast Freddy would say. Up ahead, he sees Ettie emerge from the house. The chef rushes to her side. He takes her hand, leads her to a chaise. Cups one hand around her cheek. Sam can feel the tenderness in the gesture even from a distance. He catches up with Kate. Rome wasn't built in a day, he reminds himself. Give it time. Give her time. And while he's about it, he could take a few cues from Marcus and make more of an effort to understand the great divide between the casual requirements of summer romance and the concessions and compromise he'd watched his mum and dad make to richly sustain their long-term commitment. Jeez, he thinks, if he's worried he might not be up to it, how must Kate feel? He catches up to her and slips his arm around her waist. He scrabbles for a line to sum up love, respect, appreciation, and even his fears that he'll be unable to live up to her expectations. 'You're a deadset cracker,' he manages, almost shouting with relief when she laughs out loud.

'The night is suddenly so beautiful so we eat outside to appreciate this glory around us every day,' the chef announces.

Ettie smiles agreement but silently yearns for a fan or even a zephyr to stir the air.

Kate says: 'It is all quite exquisite, Marcus. You spoil us. But tonight, if you don't mind, I'd also like to tell you what I've found out about the company that wants to destroy Garrawi.'

'Ah, so this is the reason for coming just now. So! We share this information over dinner. Yes? Although I think, perhaps from the worried look in your eyes, that it may interrupt our enjoyment of this fine food that is waiting for us.'

'Do you need help?' Ettie asks, as the chef heads towards his kitchen.

'Thank you, Ettie, no. The arm of a strong man only will do. Sam?'

Sam returns with a heavy cast-iron pot that's as black as shoe polish. The chef, who follows carrying a salad and a dish of creamy mashed potatoes with melting butter in the centre, points towards a small table. Sam puts down the pot with suitable reverence.

The chef lifts the lid. Steam rises in a rush. The aroma is rich. Mouth-watering. Marcus takes a moment to close his eyes and inhale. 'It is perfect,' he says with pleasure and not a hint of conceit. Ettie can't help smiling. *He* is perfect. 'So first, you take your potatoes according to your desire and hunger, yes? Then I will arrange the chicken on top. The salad we will have after.'

When everyone is served and seated, wine glasses topped up, Kate begins.

'The New Planet Fountain of Youth is in reality a cult. As far as I can tell, one of the worst kinds. It pretends to be about spiritual wellbeing but, in essence, it's a massive money-making machine that lines the pockets of just a few people. The leader is a man called John James, who first appeared in a few isolated newspaper stories in the 1980s.

'Back then, he was written off as a nutter who'd probably disappear after a year or two. One thing the reports agree on is that even though he is mad, he is also quite charismatic.'

The chef nods without saying a word.

Kate continues: 'The basis of his faith – if that's the right word – is fear. He preaches that the world is going to explode one day and fires will rampage across the earth's surface, burning everything and everyone. The only survivors – no surprises here – will be his followers.'

Sam breaks in. 'How's he going to save all these people if the world's blowing to pieces?'

Kate smiles, like it's a no-brainer. 'Easy, Sam. He's going to teach them to fly.'

'Eh?' Sam almost drops his beer. Ettie's eyes open wide in disbelief. The chef merely nods once more.

'Yep. They'll be told the secret of personal flight. No carpets, no gliders, no ultra-lights. It's all a matter of mind control. You've got to love it. When the time for Armageddon is close, he says he will call his believers and they will rise up and hover high in unassisted flight above the holocaust until it passes. When the furore ends, they will descend from the heavens to earth to become the new leaders in a fresh and perfect world.'

'You're having me on, right? I mean, you're talking about a bunch of weirdos that no one could take seriously in a fit! How the hell can they possibly snatch our park from under our noses? What do they want with Garrawi?'

'Money, Sam. Quis licit. Remember? It's always all about money.'

Ettie cuts in, more curious than outraged. 'Do people really believe they'll learn to fly? Surely no one's that gullible in this day and age.'

'People believe what they want to believe, my pet,' Marcus says, reaching across the table for her hand. 'The realities of life, for some, are boring. They are looking always for more. This is why scammers have success, no? Drugs too. They promise excitement at the beginning. Deliver disappointment at the end when the damage is all done. In this case I think, when the money runs out, so does membership. Is this right, Kate?'

She nods. 'There are plenty of sites on the web where former members spell out what was offered to them, how their money was gradually siphoned away and what they were left with by the time their bank accounts were empty and they had nowhere to run. The stories are pitiable – lost and vulnerable people are pathetically easy targets.'

'So what's this bloke worth when everything's tallied?' Sam asks. 'What kind of hard-core cash are we up against?'

Kate reaches for her file. Shuffles through a few papers until she finds what she's looking for. 'There are more than three thousand learn-to-fly centres established around the world. He has thousands of followers who operate profitable businesses – everything from manufacturing and selling health and beauty products to massive property development projects such as Garrawi. They also own vast tracts of valuable real estate.' Kate flicks through a few pages of notes. 'Ah. Here it is.' She reads: '*John James rules from a shiny black marble palace on a rugged bluff overlooking the Pacific Ocean in Qualupe, a small and very poor town on the east coast of South America. He lives in splendid comfort with state-of-the-art technology and a band of assistants, none of them women. His faithful acolytes are housed within the compound in less glamorous accommodation: corrugated iron huts with only basic facilities, including shared kitchens and communal bathrooms. Each day, John James emerges to sit on a carved, throne-like chair on an elevated platform. He calls for prayer and then for alms, which are collected by his assistants, who are recognisable by their clothes – black suits and mirrored sunglasses. They are known within the sect as John James's enforcers.*'

She looks up from the page and continues. 'And to complete the picture, John James has an international reputation for fraud and mismanagement but he's avoided prosecution so far. No extradition treaties exist between our countries and, as far as I can tell, any others. Lengthy investigations by the US government into his net worth estimate his global empire at about three billion dollars.' Kate closes her file. 'There's plenty more but you get the picture.'

'Three billion? You sure that's right?' Sam asks, stunned by figures so far beyond his hourly barge rate of two hundred and fifty dollars that he feels his brain cells fizzing. 'Am I missing something here? I mean how can a shonky cult leader who lives on the other side of the world end up stealing public property at Cook's Basin?'

'Good question. Let me explain.'

Marcus holds up a hand. 'A few minutes, please. I will clear the table and bring dessert. It is best to have sugar in the brain at this time of the night. It is for alertness, no?'

Ettie, closest to the icebox, offers Sam another beer, then holds up the wine and raises her eyebrows at Kate, who shakes her head. 'I'll wait for the sugar hit,' she says.

Ettie fills her own glass, regretting the impulse as soon as she takes a sip. 'Back in a minute,' she says, jumping up and racing down the jetty, where the cool night brings no relief from the heat that's rushing through her body like an electric current. If she's this bad now, how's she going to feel when the next heat wave hits? Temperatures predicted to be in the high thirties. Humidity in the nineties. The kind of weather that turns you into a raging virago or sucks you dry. In her current state of mind, she's not sure she'll survive it. But if she installs an air-conditioner (to save her sanity), will she be helping to wreck the ozone?

Then there's the question of the rat. If she puts down rat bait to remove a pest that could shut down her business, does she risk killing any poor starving bird that takes a bite out of the carcass? To her horror, tears pool in her eyes for the second time in a day. She is worn out by the fact that every thought and deed has far-reaching ramifications and none of them good. Why does every decision have to be so hair-tearingly complicated? Of its own accord and for no reason she can define, her body starts to cool, her panic subsides. A few moments later, almost back on course, she asks herself if most unsustainable decisions come down to immediate survival and if that's when the rot triggers a minuscule knock-on effect that eventually expands to topple the whole shebang. Feeling fully functional and competent now, she makes her way back to the table, back on track. No bridge. No development. Hold back the bridge and resort or watch a way of life come tumbling down to sink forever in the sea. On this, at least, she feels no quivering qualifications.

She slips into her chair at the same time as the chef emerges from his high-tech kitchen, leans across to Sam and whispers: 'We're going to hold the biggest fundraiser The Briny has ever seen. Let's set a date before the night's over.'

The chef trumpets his arrival through pursed lips. 'Tonight, we will have an old-fashioned treat that is no less magnificent for its longevity as a star in restaurants around the world,' he declares, placing a silver serving tray on the table. Six doughnut-sized golden rounds of cake lie in a pool of fragrant syrup. The smell of rum is intoxicating. 'I give you . . . babas au rhum! I have added, of course, my own touches. Lemon and orange zest, a little vanilla in the syrup only to bring out the subtleties of dark Jamaican rum. A symphony of lightness and strength.' He beams. 'At least this is the plan. Now we see if I am right.' He serves from the platter, passing around a glass bowl of cream so thick it falls in folds like a ribbon.

Sam groans with pleasure. 'You are a genius, chef. Never let it be said your talents are wasted on us.' He reaches for his spoon.

Kate kicks him under the table. 'We haven't all been served yet, Sam.'

The chef breaks in: 'You must begin, Sam. It is middle-class to wait.'

Kate blushes. The chef looks frantically to Ettie to get him out of a hole.

'Two, four, six, eight, bog in, don't wait,' she chants. The heat is getting to her again. She wonders if spending so much time working over a hot plate in the café has somehow busted her inner thermostat. 'Where were we?' she asks, smiling brightly.

Kate takes up her story. 'John James specialises in targeting ailing trusts. Quite clever, really. It's a cheap way to acquire first-class properties. Now,' she says, waving a piece of paper covered in small print, 'guess who's the trustee for Garrawi?'

'The bad-tempered colour-blind leprechaun who lives on the eastern side of the Island, right?' Sam says.

'If you mean Eric Lowdon, spot on. He's sole trustee. Turns out he's related to Teddy Mulray, which according to my research, is how he got the job. Spent a few holidays here as a kid, too. So not quite the blow-in everyone thought.'

'Must've been a loner or I'd remember him,' Sam says, struggling to conjure up a childhood image of the current adult version of the man.

'Now, who do you think owns the construction company that's been hired to do the build? I'll give you a hint. It's not connected in any way with the guru.'

The trio looks blank. Kate laughs, pleased with herself: 'Eric Lowdon again. Trading under the name of EL Constructions. Right under our noses if we'd bothered to look hard enough. He's set to make a fortune out of the deal. Oh, and his first cousin is Theo Mulvaney, Minister for Housing and Development.'

'It's bloody outrageous,' Sam says angrily. The foursome goes silent. Appalled by the crushing weight of money and power, struggling not to feel defeated before the battle even begins. The night closes in. Soft and warm. Like velvet. At complete odds with the way they feel.

Marcus says, 'So what is my job on this committee to save the world?'

Sam places a hand on his satisfied stomach and hits on a brainwave. 'You will host the first committee meeting, chef, if you're agreeable. Perhaps one of your light repasts to give us all strength for what is ahead?'

Marcus slaps his thigh emphatically. 'This is my forte, of course. So happily, my friend. Happily.'

Eventually, Kate rises to leave. Sam, unsure since the thumping disaster of his unintentionally light-hearted dismissal of Kate's intense labours, whether he's still invited to a post-prandial – as his dad used to say to his mum with a nod and a wink – assignation at her home, stays seated.

'Your boat or mine?' Kate asks.

'I'll follow,' he says. As he knew he would.

Sam slips into bed beside a drowsy Kate. 'The stuff about the cult knocked us sideways. It was good work, Kate. We're on a learning curve. Most of us still can't understand how all this has happened. I mean there we all are, going along minding our own business, leading halfway decent lives and all of a sudden, someone rips the rug from under us . . .'

'Clichés, Sam. Time to give them a rest.' She rolls deliciously on top of him. Their separate skins joined by the heat of their bodies. In a voice hollow with sleepiness, she says: 'Promise you won't turn rogue soldier and roar off on your own again. No freelancing, OK?'

He grins and runs his hand along her silken back. The power of women. No wonder men go mad. 'Nice to think you care,' he says, dodging the question, knowing he'd never get away with it if she were wide-awake. Just to make sure, he does his best to distract her.

CHAPTER EIGHT

Within a week, the first official gathering of Sam's vagabond committee comprising Marcus, Jenny, Jane, Judy, Glenn the removalist, Ettie, the Misses Skettle, Lindy Jones (who still insists on shouldering the blame for letting Eric Lowdon sneak under her radar to buy properties), John Scott (representing the art community) and Seaweed (a devout rule-bender with a talent for creating top websites) takes place at Marcus's home. Siobhan still hasn't returned Sam's call. A bad sign.

More or less on time (the first in what turns out to be a series of minor but significant miracles), a small flotilla of boats, with Sam in his tiny tinny at the point like an arrowhead, arrives in V-shape formation, setting up a foaming white chop that washes against the chef's sandstone seawall. 'The navy's in port and ready to man the battle stations,' they shout, waving madly. 'What's for dinner, chef?'

Marcus greets them one by one as they disembark with a firm handshake and a slight bow. It is a strangely formal gesture, underlining the grave purpose of the gathering and for a moment the committee is overwhelmed by the seriousness of the task they have set themselves. The fate and future of their small community is in their unskilled and very possibly inadequate hands. The mood goes flat.

Sensing this, Marcus indicates a table and chairs spread out on the deck. When everyone is settled with a drink, he announces: 'We are here to work, of course. This does not need to be said. But if we are not to weary ourselves, and even possibly – Gott Verboten – lose heart, we must also embrace the great Australian tradition of facing even the most dire situations with courage, of course – but, above all, with humour. We have already had our first round of luck, I think. The campaign has been born in the most luscious and bountiful of grape seasons. There is a wine glut, my friends. We will not go thirsty.' Hear, hear. 'Also, we cannot think straight on an empty stomach. This is true. No?' Hear, hear. 'I will attend to our dinner.' Hear, hear! 'So refill your glasses. I will return in moments.' Before he disappears along the gangplank corridor that leads to his state-of-the-art kitchen, he whispers in Sam's ear: 'But where is Kate? Is she ill?'

Sam shrugs. 'She's knows it's on. Left it to her to decide whether to get involved or stick to the sidelines as, er . . . as a consultant,' he adds, hurriedly, not sure whether it's true or not.

Marcus, clearly confused, nods diplomatically. 'Of course. I see.'

Wish I did, thinks Sam, turning back to the throng spilling over the deck and halfway along the jetty. That's when he notices a lone tinny, with a slight figure standing straight-backed, red hair streaming like a Botticelli maiden, at the console. It *putt putts* slowly, almost regally, towards the chef's house. It's not Kate but, in his mind, the appearance of

Siobhan O'Shaughnessy ('We kept the O because we'd rather starve than take the filthy English soup in the famine'), adds up to a poetic moment. He makes a fist with his hand and raises it high in triumph. He's almost starting to feel sorry for the poor bastards they're going to drill into the ground. Metaphorically speaking, of course. He hurries along the jetty to help the most battle-hardened recruit of them all tie up, leap over a few tinnies and arrive safely on terra firma. 'Siobhan,' he breathes, his face lit up like a lantern.

'Just so you know, I'll not tolerate laziness or eejits and there's only one boss. Me . . .' she begins, in a strong Irish lilt that, despite thirty years spent listening to the long flat drawl of down-under, still sounds like music even when she swears. Which she does frequently. But in a singsong way that not even the young Island mums trying to teach their kids some manners find offensive.

Sam holds up his hand. 'Save it until after dinner.' He grins, thinking she'll be as delighted as the rest of them at Marcus's generosity, and continues cheerily: 'The chef's barbecued a heap of king prawns that have been marinating all day. A feast, if he stays true to form – and there's no reason to think tonight he won't.'

Siobhan grimaces, gathers her flaming hair in a fist, lashes it neatly with an emerald-green elastic band wrapped around her wrist like a bangle. 'I knew you'd be faffing around worrying about food and wine like it's a frigging mothers' club meeting. You're going to have to get real, boy. You and all the other freeloaders up there with their snouts in the trough. This is war.'

Jeez, Sam thinks, instinctively taking a step back and

feeling slightly winded. The tiny, pale-faced, fierce-eyed woman, of indeterminate age (the only clue being her public-transport seniors card, although given her low opinion of all governments she could easily be ripping off the system), stares straight back, daring him to contradict her.

'Good to have the gutsy Irish on board,' he finally says, recovering, throwing an arm around her shoulders and quickly removing it when she stumbles under the weight.

Her sharpish features soften, she jabs him playfully in the ribs. 'Wasn't it the English who gave in first, then? Even after a thousand years of bloody tyranny.' She laughs, slips an arm through his and lets him escort her into the maelstrom. 'Jaysus,' she adds, turning towards him, suddenly serious, 'and, you know, this little skirmish could take just as long.'

'Dinner is served!' The chef places a massive earthenware bowl filled with glossy char-grilled prawns in the centre of the table. He fetches a basket of sourdough baguettes, a leafy green salad with a soupçon of lime in the creamy dressing.

Sam rips into the prawns. 'Messy eating,' he says, licking his fingers with a loud, smacking sound. 'The best kind.' It takes enormous personal control to hold back from mentioning that kings used to live like this. He heads for the pontoon with a heavily loaded sandwich. The others, who haven't experienced the chef's hospitality beyond a fireshed dinner now mostly memorable for the fact that it resulted in Ettie and Marcus finding true love, enthusiastically embrace Sam's style and plunge into the bowl without restraint. The chef sits back, smiling happily, his gaze returning to Ettie over and over, as though she's the spreading light of dawn after a black and stormy night.

Siobhan takes a position alongside Sam, dangling her legs in the tepid water. 'A magnificent love affair, eh?' she says, indicating Ettie and Marcus.

'World beating,' agrees Sam, who's noticed that even the most rancorous Island couples have been inspired by the chef's gallantry and Ettie's joyful response to it. All summer the bays have been awash with people relishing the forgotten romance of boat picnics. The bush has been busy with Islanders sheepishly carrying blankets in the direction of the mossy, twilight softness of the waterfall in the deepest crevices of Oyster Bay. A top but no longer secret spot, he thinks with a hint of wistfulness. The Island, too, has been rocking under the sound of popping champagne corks.

'None of me business, of course, but I was thinking Kate might be here to lend a hand.'

Sam chucks his scraps into the water, unable to think of a suitable response. Siobhan lets it go. In the distance, the sky lights up and a few thunderous booms shoot across the water. Another bloody storm, he thinks.

'Watch Jane,' Siobhan says, nudging Sam with her shoulder, pointing a finger. 'She'll be the first to squib if it rains. That colour and haircut cost a fortune.'

It's on the tip of Sam's tongue to ask Siobhan if her astonishing shade of hair also comes courtesy of a bottle.

'Me own's natural, if that's what you're thinking,' she growls, giving him a fierce look.

'Never crossed my mind it wasn't,' he agrees, hastily.

Siobhan walks back to the others and calls the meeting to order.

*

Not much is resolved during the first official gathering of the Save Garrawi committee, which ends early anyway, when the heavens open. Hands over her hair, Jane bolts like someone has set her backside on fire. In her tinny, she opens a brolly, holds it above her head and sets off at a sedate speed to prevent turning it inside out and rendering it useless.

'It's only water,' Ettie yells after her, but she is gone and the mood with her. The rest depart in a ragged, wrung-out pack, Siobhan's words wired into their heads: 'Get people talking,' she said, 'until there's not a soul – not even a babe – from coast to coast who hasn't heard that Garrawi is in danger of being lost forever.' She warns them against using the cult to get attention. 'The leader enjoys a good law suit. It builds his property portfolio. And anyway, soon as you mention a cult, people write you off as a nutter.'

Not sure whether to feel desperate or elated, they go home to think of ways to wake up a nation to what is happening under its nose. What no one dares to ask is whether the nation will even care. At the last moment, unable to contemplate defeat, fists are raised. A battle cry goes up: 'No resort. No bridge. No resort. No bridge.' The chant carries across the water in the heat of the damp night until it echoes back from a band of sympathetic barbecuers on Cutter Island. 'No resort. No bridge.' Bring on the rage. Take up arms. Fight to the end. It's bloody on!

Kate circles Emily's mysterious tin box where it lies on the kitchen table.

Antennae twitching, she scrabbles in the bottom drawer, searching for a screwdriver to pop the lock. Now or never.

Or is it? She hesitates – as she has for days. If the box contains what she thinks it does, lifting the lid means risking everything she believes to be true. Her family tree may not be ideal, but it's all she's got to anchor her, however ephemerally, to her sense of self. 'Your choice, Kate,' she says out loud. Sink the box – unopened – in the middle of the bay and retain the status quo that will mean she can continue to go about her daily darg comfortably and – she might as well admit it – uninspiringly. Or ratchet it open and let loose whatever lies within.

She reaches for the box but withdraws her hand at the last moment, unwilling to touch it. Nighttime paranoia, she thinks. She's letting the dark get to her. There's probably nothing important inside. She cannot imagine Emily saving a lock of baby hair, a tiny shoe, a photograph of a swaddled creature not long out of the womb. *You were a little wolf when you were born, covered in fur. She can't be mine, I told the nurses and I still believe they made a terrible mistake, that you're the progeny of ferals.* It was meant to hurt, but Kate had immediately latched on to the idea. A changeling. Her *real* mother, she dreamed, hoped, prayed in the ridiculously phantasmagorical way of unhappy little kids, was kind and beautiful and compassionate and warm and . . . there was nothing of Emily in Kate's DNA at all. She reaches again for the metal tin. It is cold and smooth except for a couple of shallow dings, a few scratches. No. Not now. Not yet. She isn't ready. She needs more time.

All night, she lies awake, staring at the dark lines of the heavy timber beams holding up the plaster ceiling, listening to the sounds of nocturnal bush life. Wallabies. Owls.

Bandicoots. Thump. Sob. Grunt. A whole new order that emerges at dusk to forage. When she first took possession of her stone cottage on the wrong side (no winter sun) of Oyster Bay, the nighttime rustles, twangs and tunes – so foreign to her inner-city ears, which were used to the caterwauling of sirens – made her anxious. Thump. Sob. Grunt. Reassuring. The box, she thinks over and over. What to do with the box?

Cook's Basin News (CBN)

Newsletter for Offshore Residents of Cook's Basin, Australia

JANUARY

Friday afternoon at the Square

Big Phil and Rexie will be playing their toe-tapping hits to raise money for the Garrawi Park fighting fund. Bring your wallets. Ettie and Kate will provide fish and chips – all proceeds to the fund.

If it's raining? When have offshorers ever let the weather hold them back?

5 pm to 8 pm, the Square. Don't miss it! January 25: a great kick off to the Australia Day celebrations.

NB: Against his better instincts, ferry master Chris Black is offering a late ferry service for post-gig party-goers to return home without incurring undue interest from the Water Police. Fast Freddy will also run a cut-price water taxi service to ensure the evening ends on a high note. (Get it? Heh, heh.)

COMMITTEE TO SAVE GARRAWI ANNOUNCED

The battle begins!

Yesterday, Island resident Siobhan O'Shaughnessy announced that Sam Scully, Marcus Allender, Ettie Brookbank, the Three Js, the Misses Skettle, Lindy Jones, John Scott, Seaweed, Glenn, and her own good self will begin investigating whether due process to buy and develop Garrawi has been followed and to come up with strategies to beat the bastards behind the scheme. Stay tuned. Seaweed's new website (savegarrawi.com), covering possibly the most defining environmental battle of this area, is already on line. This is the beginning of what Siobhan describes as a social-media campaign that will rattle the foundations of the current government. Check out Twitter, hashtag #savegarrawi.

(Editor's Note: This concerns all of us. Do not sit back and think someone else will do the work. We must all carry our share.)

HAZARD REDUCTION BURN

Due to favourable conditions, there will be a late-season Hazard Reduction Burn on Sunday at the peak of the Oyster Bay Trail, continuing down the waterfall trail and around the cliff line. Please ensure roofs and gutters are clear and windows are closed. Be aware of vehicles on the trails.

CHAPTER NINE

On Monday, with the summer humidity not letting up and the stink of a low tide wafting about like ripe garbage, Sam and Jimmy set off to pick up Kate's writing desk. Jimmy – rake thin, frail almost – wears electric-blue clothes that strobe in the sunlight. Barefooted, he dances and prances on the hot gravel like an exotic bird hoping to attract a mate. His spiked carrot hair a handsome cockscomb. Longfellow nips and pounces at his heels. The boy laughs. The pup squeals back, races off, full tilt and fur flying, to incite to flight a flock of seagulls arguing over scraps left over from weekend picnickers. The kid whistles. The dog screeches to a halt, torn between a full-bore chase or boring obedience. After an indecisive second or two he opts to join the hunt for Sam's ute among the bird-shit-splattered rows of rusting vehicles in the shambolic car park designated for offshorers. Smart dog, Sam thinks. Get lost on the wrong side of the moat and it could be forever.

'There it is, Sam,' Jimmy says, excited and pointing out the ute. 'Over there. Under the tree. Aw, Sam, ya windscreen's gunna be a shitty mess. You bring a rag, Sam? You want me to get a bucket of water?'

Up close, the kid frowns. 'Ya taillights are busted, Sam. Both sides. Ya musta hit something big, eh?'

'Eh?' Tiny shards of red plastic crunch under the weight of his boots. Sam steps back. He's either been rear-ended or some funny bugger has deliberately taken a hammer to his lights. He checks the windscreen. No note of apology with a contact name and number. He hadn't expected one but he'd hoped, because he sure as hell didn't want to feel the itchy sensation that this small but effective act of vandalism had anything to do with the campaign to save Garrawi. He counsels himself to stop being paranoid. There's not a car in the park that isn't scarred from vandals, falling branches from the few over-hanging shade trees, used as roosts by incontinent birds, or the erratic reverse parking of a few locals who shall remain nameless. (Although the Misses Skettle could well be among them. On second thought, probably not. They've never reverse parked in their lives. A fact they announce proudly whenever the opportunity arises.) He decides to imagine incompetence instead of conspiracy.

'Hoist that pup in the back seat, Jimmy, and climb in after him. Hold him on your knee good and tight. No questions, mate. Go on. In you get,' he adds, holding up his hand. 'The mutt will be safer in the back. First we'll get the lights fixed. Then we'll pick up the desk.'

They set off sedately, slowing even more for school zones until Jimmy thoughtfully points out the kids are still on holi-days and the law is on temporary hold.

Pretty quickly, the pup starts to whine. Scrabbles at the half-open window. Sniffing land smells. Anxious to explore. Jimmy lifts a furry ear and whispers a litany of soothing sounds into it. With a harrumph of unwilling surrender, Longfellow settles.

'Someone got it in for you, mate?' asks the mechanic.

Sam shrugs. 'Why d'you ask?'

The young bloke, clean as a whistle in a dark blue shirt and matching shorts, points a finger at the damage. 'Too precise to be caused by a bingle.'

Sam bends down, looks closely into the gizzards of the electricals. 'See what you mean. Yeah, clear as a bell.' The battlefield, he thinks, has just been sign-posted.

'I'll patch it temporarily with tape and order in replacement parts. Bring it back in a week. The new bits'll click in like a Lego set.' He walks to a computer and hits the keyboard.

Sam thinks: No wonder he never gets dirty. It's a weird day in history when blue collar turns white collar.

He whistles up Jimmy and the mutt. Ten minutes later, he swings into the driveway of Emily's retirement village, slipping into second gear, which is as slow as he can go without stalling. He drives aimlessly through acres of well-tended gardens and hundreds of identical units, hoping to find someone to ask for directions. There is not a soul out smelling the roses (so much for the positive spin on reaching the age when no one wants to employ you any more) or walking the shady paths.

'Not many joggers, eh?' he jokes.

Jimmy twists and turns, held fast by the seatbelt, checking for himself. 'Nope. Can't see one. Are we lost, Sam?'

Sam pulls up to get some local advice. A pallid-faced old

man keeps the security door locked while he gives directions in a thin and uncertain voice. Five minutes later, feeling hundreds of pairs of eyes following his progress through lace curtains, they arrive at Emily's unit. Sam takes a solemn oath that when he is too old to fend for himself, he will take the *Mary Kay* way out to sea, drill a hole in her voluptuous rear end and raise a frigidly cold stubby in farewell to what he hopes he'll truthfully be able to describe as a life well lived. Man and vessel going down together. Nobly.

Unless I've got a heap of kids by then, he thinks, coming to his senses, and one of them needs the barge to continue in the Scully family tradition of working on the water. In which case, he'll come up with another appropriate end scenario with the same final result. But god save him from this kind of mortal anteroom where the weekly death rate is probably in double figures so you don't dare make friends for fear of losing them before you finally learn their names. The eternally useful (and therefore youthful) Misses Skettle, he reminds himself, have old age nailed. Feeling less depressed by the minute, he tells himself there are always options as long as you keep your mind open.

'Let's get this desk, mate, and then we'll treat ourselves to a nice long lunch at The Briny until the tide comes in. What do you reckon?'

'Sounds good to me. It sure does. You gunna eat your spinach today, Sam?'

'Trust me, it'll be a pleasure and an honour to slide it onto your plate.' He unlocks the door. He expects the room to be dark and dingy, smelling of decay and dust, but big windows frame a lush garden with a pond where a couple of black ducks dunk their heads to scavenge whatever tasty morsels lurk under water. Wrens, finches and noisy lorikeets play about in a bushy grevillea covered in pollen-heavy lemon flowers. The lorikeets are bullies but the wrens are good fighters with smart, attack-from-the-rear tactics. Despite his prejudices, Sam decides if you're the type that prefers to shoot for unchallenging longevity instead of guts and glory, this isn't such a bad end chapter after all. Never leap to conclusions, old son, he thinks. Or as his father would have said: Walk a mile in a man's moccasins before making a judgment. The unit is bare except for a lone writing desk standing up against a wall, the last remaining evidence of Emily's occupancy, her life.

For some reason, he'd expected a roll top or something equally fancy but it is tall and narrow with head-high glassed-in bookshelves, a drop top and cupboards below. A schoolboy's desk from the early 1900s. Shabby now, but with good bones that will see it through another century if it's restored and cared for.

'Grab the bottom end, Jimmy, and slowly as she blows. No, no, don't say a word. Concentrate or Kate will end up with nothing but toothpicks. This is a frail piece of furniture held together mostly by habit. Your next job is to tie it down in the ute so tightly it doesn't shift a fraction. See that glass? It's a bit wavy, isn't it? Means it's old, Jimmy, and age should always be respected.'

'Ya might want to swerve around the bumps on the way home then, Sam. Ya can't be too careful, can ya?'

'Round up that mutt of yours. It's time to get going.'

*

Ettie Brookbank is in a major flap. The rat-traps, temptingly laced with honey and peanut butter, have remained empty and she's found more poo on the floor near the deep fryer. Every time a stranger walks into the café, she mutters a fervid prayer that he's not from the health department. Just thinking about the problem sends her into a spin. Her face flushes, the strange dizziness she's been experiencing lately returns. Anxiety takes hold until her breath comes in quick little gasps. She feels like Chicken Licken waiting for the sky to crash down on her head.

She cannot think of any new strategies to deter the rats given the garbage is only collected twice a week and if a few cunning little rodents have learned to lift the lid on the wheelie bins, there's nothing she can do about it. Well, one rat, if the single, neat little poo that appears daily is anything to go by.

'Hiya, Ettie!' Jimmy bounces in, skittering in all directions at once. 'Me and Sam, we're here for lunch. A treat, says Sam. But I shouldn't get used to them 'cause then it's not a treat any more.'

'Lamb burger? The works?'

The kid nods emphatically, happily. Ettie could just as well have offered him a winning lottery ticket.

'You got enough saved for a car yet, love?' she asks, feeling the beginning of a plan that is so clever, 'brainwave' is a closer description.

'Rome wasn't built in a day, was it?'

'Well, Jimmy, I think I've come up with an idea that just may earn you some extra dollars.'

The kid puts down the jar of biscuits he's been playing with and spins. A whirling dervish, his face alight. 'How much money? Enough to buy a car next week?'

'Not quite, but my mother always said that if you watch the pennies the pounds take care of themselves.'

'How much is a pound?'

'It's a saying, that's all. It means if you're careful, you'll always reach your goal. Or something like that. Anyway. Here's the idea. I'm going to find a couple of very big compost bins and fork out some of my hard-earned cash to buy you a worm farm. Every night I want you to collect the scraps from the bins and take them home. Within a few weeks, you'll be able to sell compost and worm castings all over the Island. What do you think?' She smiles encouragingly.

Jimmy looks doubtful. 'Me mum's not too keen on worms. Says they make your bum itch . . .'

'Um, these are different worms, love. Good worms. They make the soil healthy so we can grow healthy vegetables,' Ettie explains, her face going puce, sweat breaking out all over again.

'I better ask her, but. Me mum's pretty firm about worms.'

'Righto, fair enough. Here, have a piece of lemon tart while you're waiting for the burger. It's got to be eaten today.'

'I'm supposed to have spinach, Sam says.'

'How about neither of us tells him.'

On the back deck, Sam scoffs down one of Ettie's magic harissa-marinated grilled calamari concoctions with shaved fresh fennel (to cut through but enhance the spices) spread artistically on top. She's even peeled the cherry tomatoes, he thinks, slowing down to give the food the close attention it deserves. But the episode with the taillights has left him edgy.

In his experience, thugs rarely downgrade assaults. They ramp them up.

He drags out *The Concise History of the World* to take his mind off his worries and flips forward to the chapter on Australia.

> *Once upon a time – around forty thousand years ago – kangaroos were ten feet tall and native lions roamed the land along with giant ox-like beasts. All of them were quickly killed off and people settled near the coast to live on fish and shellfish.*

Nothing changes, he thinks. We come, we see and we conquer until there's nothing left.

His phone goes off with the buzz and momentum of an angry fly. He picks up. His face goes black. He pushes back from the table, leaving his lunch unfinished. 'Jimmy!' he shouts en route to the barge. He barely checks to see the kid is on board before setting off.

Sam pushes the throttle forward and urges the normally dowager-sedate *Mary Kay* to her maximum speed of six knots. Under the broad hull, the water is smooth and glassy.

The short waterway from the café to his jetty is alive with traffic. The light southerly has lured out every passionate yachtie from one end of Cook's Basin to the other on a day when there's just enough breeze to fill a sail but not enough for a skipper to spill his drink. Paradise at its best. Except, Sam thinks, for a new underbelly that reckons money calls the shots. Well, he tells himself, the cockroaches behind the development might find they're jet propelled towards a new and gargantuan learning curve. He makes a conscious effort to loosen his jaw to stop his teeth from grinding.

By the time he ties up at his jetty, he feels calmer, steadier. Nobody died, he tells himself. Anything that can be fixed with nails and a hammer isn't worth sweating over. From the water and in the sunlight, the windows of his house look like broken toffee. Despite his good intentions, his (almost) calm rationalisation of what he considers important and what actually matters, a shaft of hatred slips inside his head. For a second all he sees is red. Red house. Red trees. Red sea. He feels his jaw lock tight again. 'Stay on board, Jimmy. Don't move till I call you.' He sprints along the jetty.

Eric Lowdon steps out from behind the boatshed. 'You don't want to mess with us, boy,' he hisses, his chubby little body jiggling with spite. 'Next time, you'll find yourself floating face down in the sparkling waters of Cook's Basin.' He's dressed unbelievably eccentrically in clashing checks and tartans, and a ridiculous tasselled green cap, a relic from the past, shades his eyes. His fingers caress the fat end of a driving iron. He looks like he's off to play a round of golf a hundred years ago instead of what Sam would assume is a regular weekend game on a local course.

'Did you do this?'

'Wouldn't dirty my hands . . .'

'Of course not. You've got the balls of a gnat. You're pathetic, mate. I could almost feel sorry for you if you weren't such a dead-set, over-dressed toad,' Sam says, wagging his head, amazed that this small, fat, unfit parody of a human thinks sending in a few freaky goons under cover of darkness to break his windows will scare him off.

Suddenly, Lowdon rears, thumps Sam hard on the chest with the fat end of the golf club. 'Think you're tough, do you? You're no match . . .'

Sam, driven by a flash of red anger, snatches the driving iron easily and turns it back on the little man, landing a blow mid-stomach. Lowdon doubles over, fights for breath. His face purples. Rheumy eyes water, look ready to pop. Sam pushes Lowdon to the ground, where he lies beached. Emitting strange gurgling noises from blowfish lips. Sam towers over him, golf club gripped fiercely. One strike, maximum damage. The temptation is irresistible. He takes a huge back swing.

Lowdon rolls into a foetal position, knees pulled into his chest, hands covering his face. Whimpering.

Sam throws down the club in disgust. 'It would be too easy. You're not worth the effort. But if you or the goons come anywhere near my house again, I'll know. Trust me, I'll know. You might want to ramp up your insurance too, mate. Hate to think what a hammer might do to that poncy glass dining table of yours.'

Sam reaches down to grab Lowdon's shirtfront and hoists him to a point about a foot above the ground. The fabric starts to rip. Sam holds on. 'From now on, I'll be watching you so closely that you won't even be able to take a piss in private. You get my drift?' The fabric gives way. Lowdon drops to the ground.

Winded, apoplectic, but back in a vertical position, Lowdon finds his voice, points a finger in Sam's face. 'Don't make me sic my boys on you again, Scully, because you don't want to see what else they can do,' he wheezes, in short, pained gasps. Frothing, spitting, his bloated face twisted with rage.

'Love to see 'em. Bring them on. Anytime. Don't forget your golf club, mate,' Sam says. 'And here's your cap, let me adjust the angle. Your tassel is all over the place.'

Anticipating a strike, Lowdon jerks backwards, losing his balance. Almost falls. 'Get your affairs in order, boy,' he snarls. 'You're history.'

Sam dusts his hands, shrugs and, without glancing back, takes the steps three at a time. What a low-class greedy little mongrel bully. 'Jimmy!' he calls, remembering the kid confined on the barge. Two long skinny legs lift off the deck, grasshopper fast. He's airborne, arms windmilling. Lands on feet the size of small boats and gallops along the jetty. The shaggy black-and-white mutt is glued to his heels.

CHAPTER TEN

Inside, the house is trashed. Clothing shredded, mattresses slashed, tomato sauce sprayed in long red lines on walls. Crockery is smashed against his fireplace like the aftermath of a Greek wedding. On the floor, broken glass sparkles obscenely in shafts of sunlight. Helluva party, he thinks, and with his spleen already vented, he feels oddly voyeuristic instead of enraged.

Jimmy begins sweeping the floor. 'Sorry for ya loss, Sam,' he says, eyes filling with tears, using his wrist to wipe his nose.

'Nobody died, mate. There's nothing broken that can't be fixed. He made a bloody mess, though, didn't he?'

'Ya got that right,' Jimmy says, leaning on his broom. 'It's a mess all right.'

Sam scoops the small collection of his father's precious books from the floor, replaces them on a shelf. How come no one noticed? Not even a brush turkey got away with bin ransacking without the whole neighbourhood getting involved. The spine is broken but fixable on Bert Facey's *A Fortunate Life*, given to him by the Misses Skettle all those years ago when they were determined to set him straight on how to deal with disaster. 'Bastard,' he says, under his breath. He lies it flat to fix later. 'You ever heard of the US marines, Jimmy?'

'Sure,' the kid says, uncertainly.

'They believe that if you stop and dig in at the height of a battle, you're rooted. By my way of thinking, if we play by the rules of thugs, we'll lose by the rules of thugs. We have to take the initiative. Be one step ahead. Keep them angry and pissed off so they make mistakes. Step forward when they think they've hammered us. That's what the marines do, mate. They step forward no matter what the odds.'

Jimmy, who's been listening intently, his freckly face tilted sideways like one ear hears better than the other, suddenly straightens, clicks his heels and salutes: 'What's next, Sam? We gunna step forward now?'

'Well, not exactly right now but it's nice to know I can count on you, mate.'

Jimmy, getting the hang of it, straightens and stands at attention, his broom out to one side like a rifle. 'We're a team. Isn't that what you said?'

'The best team a bloke could ask for. When the time comes, we're going to step forward together. But only when the time comes. Got that?'

'Sure, Sam. Long as you know I'm here. I'm not a piker. No way.'

'Never thought you were for a minute.' Sam pats the kid on the back. To hide the fact his eyes are blurry, he steps out of the way, into the bedroom. His old plastic clock, worth as much to him as his father's books, is intact. They missed the real valuables, he thinks. Or maybe nothing quite compares to losing both your parents in a single, devastating, unrecoverable hit. He must have learned young how to recover quickly.

Looking on the bright side – as a man has to if he's to hold onto his sanity – at least one of the enemies has been clearly and irrevocably identified. What was that old saying of his dad's? Keep your enemies where you can see them. Yeah, that was it. No, not quite. The best way to destroy your enemy is to make him your friend. Well, he didn't think he'd be able to pull that trick off for any one of a number of very obvious reasons but he could sure as hell keep him in his sights.

Out on the deck, he breathes in the salt and sun, watches a pulsing sea. Three kookaburras, chests fluffed, scruffy from the rain and heat of the past few days, swoop on to the deck railing, looking for a handout. One by one, they start to laugh. Sam catches the larrikin spirit, the age-old instinct of tough people to laugh in the face of adversity. He slaps his thigh with the sheer beauty of inspiration. He turns towards the house, his backside propped against the railing, and shouts out: 'No matter what hideous, low-life tactics they come up with, Jimmy, we're going to laugh in their dead ugly smug faces.'

Jimmy sticks his head outside: 'We stepping forward, Sam?' he asks, clicking his heels to attention again.

'You bet we are.'

News of the vandalising of Sam's house flies around the Island in no time. All afternoon and well into the night, people drop by with spare cushions for the sofa, bed linen, cakes and casseroles, even a bottle of tomato sauce. 'For your sauso rolls, mate. Wouldn't want you to go without the trimmings.'

Kate rings to offer her help.

'Nah, all good,' he tells her.

'I'm here if you need me,' she replies. 'Ettie, too. She sends her love.'

The magnitude of the wanton destruction fires up the community to unprecedented levels. This isn't a case of throwing a dead bird in a water supply to make a point. This isn't about dropping a spoonful of sugar in a boat's fuel tank to ram home a few basic Island rules. This isn't even calling in at dawn, uninvited and unannounced, to deliver some well chosen words to a lawless newcomer ignorant of the value of a fully functioning community. This is major property damage that goes way beyond cleaning out a water tank or replacing a (usually) clapped-out outboard, and it strikes at the heart of everything Cook's Basin holds sacred. A roar goes up for payback.

CHAPTER ELEVEN

The following day, just as the sun dips towards the hills to cast long pink silken streaks across the water, Siobhan O'Shaughnessy knocks on Sam's back door. Without waiting for an answer, she marches in. Red hair fizzing. Wearing outrage like a fashion statement. 'Bastards,' she says, spitting out the word. She stops dead, looks around. 'Well!' She grins. 'No harm done then. The place has had a free and much-needed clean and update. There's always an upside, eh? I'll have a glass of wine, if you're offering. White. We have work to do.'

Sam scrabbles in the fridge. 'Donations didn't run to wine,' he explains, handing Siobhan a beer and settling on a moss-green pillow embroidered with winking sequins that instantly bite him on the bum. But he can't bring himself to toss it aside. 'What's on your mind?'

'Well, boyo, you've just been elected spokesperson in the campaign to Save Garrawi. What an honour, eh?'

Smelling a rat, Sam ditches the carnivorous cushion and faces Siobhan full on. 'Elected? You're kidding, right?'

'Unanimous.' She crosses her fingers and hums a little tune, her eyes fixed on the ceiling. 'All those do-gooders,' she adds, 'they missed the cobwebs.'

During the next two hours, Siobhan O'Shaughnessy grills, grooms, thrills and threatens Sam Scully until his head begins to throb.

'Never lie, never overstate your case. Make sure all your facts are absolutely correct. If you don't know the answer to a question, admit it. Never, ever make up a story. One wrong move and you'll be dismissed as a dangerous crackpot working with a personal agenda and you can kiss goodbye to any media support.'

Seeing him begin to wilt, she drags a kitchen stool into the sitting room and orders him to take up residence on it. 'Concentrate, you eejit. Pinch yourself hard if you're flagging. Don't let the bastards see you flounder. They'll hone in on your weak spots like sharks smelling blood.'

'I'm the wrong man . . .'

'Oh fiddlesticks. Try to remember where god inserted your backbone and let's get on with it.'

She fires a barrage of questions at him, coming from a negative angle. Surely, more people deserve access to this little paradise you've had to yourselves for so long? What about the pressure of population – land has to open up, doesn't it? What's one less park when there are so many? What about the Square, isn't that enough public space for a relatively small community? Aren't you being greedy?

He stalls and stutters, mumbles his way around the issue,

looking embarrassed and ill at ease. The bombardment begins again and goes on relentlessly until she tells him he is ready.

'Your main asset is your passion and belief in the cause,' she says. 'But never get so caught up in emotion you lose your train of thought. You can't afford to relax for a second. If you feel uncertain, fall back on the stock answers we've prepared and rehearsed. They're factual, understandable and quotable even if they lack a colourful turn of phrase.'

'Not sure I can make this work, Siobhan,' he says, still hopeful he might get a reprieve.

'Well, to be honest, you're my last chance. Everyone else turned down the gig. Now listen up while I tell you about a man called Delaney.'

'Who's Delaney? Not a leg breaker, I hope.' He gets them both another beer, sensing the night has a long way to go.

After Siobhan goes home, to clear his head, settle his nerves, Sam walks around the Island. The darkness is almost disorienting but he uses the lights from windows to get his bearings. Phoebe's house. John's studio (probably working late on Garrawi business). Glenn's back porch light left on because he's a man who prefers to pee on his lemon tree when he gets up in the dead of night and he'd rather not step on a snake in the process. The night smells sharp, like iodine. Another bucket load of rain is on the way and the Island's not even close to dried out from the last week's deluges. As if to prove the point, Sam's foot comes down hard in a puddle. His boots, socks, feet are soaking but he feels full of purpose, a man on a mission who knows his value within a close community. Doing good.

'You got a job for me, Sam?'

Sam jumps. 'Jeez, Jimmy, you just about gave me a heart attack. How many times do I have to tell you not to creep up on a bloke? Gawd, I nearly decked you, mate. Reflex action. Nothing personal.'

'Nah, ya wouldna, would ya?' The kid slips in step alongside Sam, swaggering a little, Longfellow at his heels. His banana-yellow shirt is a beacon, his young eyes spy out the puddles. Sam follows his lead religiously.

'What are you doing out and about? Storm's coming. You should be tucked up at home with your mum.' He points at Longfellow hovering at Jimmy's heels. 'The mutt should be in bed too. He's still a pup and needs his beauty sleep.'

'Storm's a long way off. Ya have to count. That's how ya tell. Ya hear the thunder first, then ya count. If ya make it to ten it's all good. If ya barely make it to one, it's time to skedaddle. And me pup's been snoozin' all day. Me mum said to take him out for a poo and a piddle before bed. He's done the piddle but . . .'

Sam breaks in. 'Yeah, well we're on for an afternoon pick-up at Cargo for Kingfish Bay. I told you all this earlier, Jimmy. You've got to focus, mate.'

'Yeah, Sam. I'm there. Good as gold. I mean me other job.'

Sam struggles to catch on. 'You talking about the worm farm, Jimmy?'

'Nah, Sam. The park. What's me job to save the park?' The kid stops suddenly and turns full on towards Sam, his earnest face struck white by a ribbon of light streaming across the track from a nearby house. His feet uncharacteristically anchored to the ground.

'Ah. Gotcha. The thing is, mate, we're taking it one day at a time. I'll tell you when you're needed, promise you.'

Jimmy reaches out a scrawny arm to grab hold of Sam's shoulder. 'I need a real job, don't I? I'm gunna have kids one day and I wanna tell 'em about me part in the battle. We're makin' history here, Sam. Everyone says so.'

'That's what they're saying, eh? S'pose we are, in a way. Never been a fight like this in Cook's Basin before.'

'So what's me job, Sam? I can do anything, ya know. Ya just gotta tell me what.'

Sam tilts his head gravely. 'You're coming through loud and clear and it's a noble offer, cuts through to my heart. Truly. Give me a couple of days, though, because all new action has to be approved by the committee. You square with that?'

'Sure, Sam. A coupla days. No worries. You wanna hear me idea, but?'

'Go for it!' Sam is barely concentrating. He's reached his house and he's impatient to call it a night before rain buckets down.

'How about I rub out the pink marks on the rocks and trees in the park. I gotta tell ya, they look weird. Pink's no good in a park. Stands out like dog's balls.'

It takes a couple of seconds for the information to sink in then Sam half closes his eyes, thinking. 'Run that past me again, mate?'

'The pink paint on the rocks, Sam. Some fella went round with a spray can of paint today and made a mess. Gotta tell ya, it looks bloomin' awful. Even though me mum says . . .'

'Yeah, yeah, a fresh coat of paint is as good as a holiday. Leave it with me, Jimmy. By the way, you've just been elected to the committee. You've got to be on time for the meetings and all, though. You up to it?'

'I can do anything, Sam. How many times I gotta tell ya that? There he goes, good boy Longfella, he's havin' a poo . . .'

'Keep your eyes peeled, Jimmy. Anything odd, you report back. Got it?'

'We steppin' forward, Sam?'

'No, mate, we're rocketing forward.'

War is officially declared, hand-to-hand combat begun. The Island artists slog through stinking hot and humid nights to create logos, choose powerful typefaces and prepare exquisite artwork showing the fragile flora and fauna of Garrawi. 'It's too hot to sleep anyway.' They shrug, as though it's no big deal.

Huge posters decrying the desecration of Garrawi appear one morning out of John's print works, and are plastered from one end of Cook's Basin to the other, as well as all over the city. Collector quality, everyone agrees, barely holding back from ripping them down and racing off to get them framed for their walls at home. Pamphlets (outlining the background and history of the park) are widely distributed. Emotive letters (Jenny, Judy and Jane) begging for support are sent to environmental organisations around the world including a special hand-written note on quality paper, to the Duke of Edinburgh and Queen Elizabeth. Monarchists and republicans unite briefly in a common cause for the common good.

Next, every heritage and conservation authority is contacted (Jenny, Judy and Jane), as well as the Greens, Liberal and Labor Parties, National Parks and Wildlife, even the Surfrider Foundation. 'We want them all on our side,' Jenny explains. 'So if anyone calls us a bunch of NIMBY silvertails living in waterfront properties, we can tell them we're supported by hundreds of groups across the country.'

The list of impressively credentialled supporters grows longer and longer. Even the National Trust comes on board and agrees to declare Garrawi worthy of conservation — a big win when you consider the Trust doesn't have much money and there'll be even less if it upsets potential donors. The letter campaign continues until every single heritage and conservation authority comes onside. The consensus is unanimous. Garrawi belongs to the people and should be preserved forever. Only the local mayor, Evan Robotham, a confirmed believer in the far-reaching power of the current state government, refuses to support the cause. Hiding behind a blah-blah press release citing the council's mandate is to remain neutral, he ducks and weaves like a professional pickpocket in a holiday crowd.

The promised papier-mâché white cockatoo, about four metres long and two and a half metres tall, is fitted with a fully fanned bright yellow crest and takes up residence in the Square. Passers-by are told to pat it for luck. The Misses Skettle, armed with flyers, set up camp day after day, sweetly cajoling signatures against the development even from tourists who don't speak English. At precisely ten-thirty, they break out morning tea from their picnic basket. Lunch is on the dot of one o'clock. Afternoon tea is at three-thirty.

'You can set your clock by them,' says Kate, standing in the doorway of the café, watching them set out plates, napkins, sandwiches and a Thermos. She puzzles out loud over the old ladies' refusal of free refreshment; they don't even accept a cappuccino.

'They lace their coffee with whisky,' Ettie explains. 'They don't think anyone knows but we all do. The smell of booze that steams out of the Thermos when the top comes off is enough to knock you out.'

'Ah.' Kate understands at last. 'I was worried they didn't like our food.'

Every time it rains, they rush around with a blue tarpaulin, anchor the corners with rocks. Papier-mâché, they explain, is particularly vulnerable to moisture.

Soon, the whole community is revved and ready for a full-on stoush. Excitement is tangible. Defeat is unthinkable. Ettie and Kate are planning a massive black-tie fundraiser to be held in the park. Every woman in the area is combing op shops for glamour gear to wear on the night. There's also been a run on white T-shirts printed with a black bow tie.

Deciding he doesn't have time to wait around for another committee meeting which may or may not end in the kind of action he is itching for, and without discussing his plans with a soul, Sam decides to call on Theo Mulvaney, State Minister for Housing and Development and first cousin to Eric Lowdon. He reassures himself that technically, he's not breaking his word to Kate since he never – technically – gave it. On the way, he detours to get his taillights replaced.

At Parliament House, he expects to get the run-around but all it takes to get him through the door is a single phone call from the guardhouse to an office located somewhere deep in the hallowed halls of power and the mention of Lowdon and Garrawi Park in a manner that – he later admits – is obscure and could be construed as supporting the plan. Without a single hold-up, he is magically waved through security (emptying pockets that reveal two shackles, eight screws, one nut – no bolt – and a ratty wallet that spills its guts the moment he withdraws it) and directed to the plush but deeply masculine inner sanctum of the minister. Leather sofas, mahogany table with lion's-claw feet and four serious chairs, a desk the size of a small dance floor. A barrage of clashing smells – furniture polish, flowery air fresheners, a lemon-scented aftershave – make his eyes water. Were he blindfolded, he couldn't say whether he'd stepped into a toffy club or a toffy dunny. He catches a whiff of something more primal. His mind flashes back to Fast Freddy's tabloid and its recent dissection of questionable executive expense-account use within a branch of a top-ranking union. And we're paying their wages, he thinks. Whatever happened to the good old days when politicians understood they worked for the taxpayers? Not the other way around.

'Call me Theo' arrives a few seconds after his citrus aftershave. He approaches with his hand outstretched, a wide, narcissist's smile on a soft-living, unblemished, beautician-cured face. Beneath fiercely plucked, trimmed and (presumably) dyed brows, insincerity floats in his eyes like an oil slick.

If politicians were meant to be charismatic, then this bloke has had a triple by-pass. Sam stares at the hand as though it might bite, unable to decide whether to take it in his own great paw or let it hang. Before he can make up his mind, Mulvaney, with the finely honed survival instincts of a city rat, picks up an off vibe. The hale-fellow-well-met mask dissolves. His smile disappears; his eyes go hard. He puts the desk between them in a couple of long steps, refrains from offering Sam a seat. 'Friend of Eric's, are you?' he asks. His tone is brisk. Frigid. Sam realises he's lost the element of surprise – never a smart tactic. With nothing more to lose, he goes for broke.

'Sam Scully. Wouldn't mean anything to you, of course, although Eric Lowdon knows me well enough. Might be an overstatement to refer to us as friends, though. Big overstatement.' Despite the fact that he believes unflinchingly in the nobility of his mission, he's surprised to find himself more than a little intimidated by his expensive surroundings. He catches another whiff. This time of power. So strong it's almost tangible. He needs a moment to settle his mind into a customarily stable balance. He shifts a crystal paperweight, a few papers, from the edge of the desk and perches there. 'Nice office you've got here. Good views. Plenty of space. Your own loo?' He points towards a door tucked discreetly off to the side of the room. 'Bet it's got a shower. All the luxuries.'

'Look, I'm not sure what you're doing here . . .' Mulvaney is irritated. He checks his watch, makes a whole lot of other signals that he's a busy man. Sam picks up the paperweight, tosses it from hand to hand. Mulvaney snatches it away. 'If you're here to play catchy, I'm all booked up.'

Sam makes what he hopes is an educated guess and decides to go way out on a limb. 'Just wanted to let you know that the residents of Cook's Basin are fully aware that you, personally, signed off on the Garrawi development and the community is pissed off. Ropeable. No consultation. No environmental studies. No impact statements. Just your name on a document, followed by a champagne toast, I imagine. And, hey presto, a fat cheque lands in your personal bank account and that's the end of it.'

'You accusing me of taking bribes, you numbskull? Get out and get a life, sonny. Before I have you kicked out.' Mulvaney moves a few papers around. Looks up. 'Still here? Go on, get out.' He waves his hand dismissively, like he's dealing with an idiot.

One decent punch, Sam thinks, seeing red. Settle the quarrel like men. One almighty whack on that over-cleansed weak little chin. Even better, two. He clenches his fists by his side. Holds back from striking out with an almighty mental struggle. Hang around scum and you turn into scum. Then where do you end up? With an effort, he smiles, hoping it comes off as more Bond than Clouseau. In a normal voice, he says: 'Thought it only polite to let you know that from now on, every time you turn around for the foreseeable future, I'd recommend you duck real fast because there'll be a bullet coming your way.' He pauses, fixes a friendly grin on his face. 'Figure of speech, of course.' He wipes the grin. 'This time, you've taken on the wrong crowd, mate. Big mistake.'

Mulvaney launches himself around the desk, reaches for Sam's shirtfront. 'You threatening me, you dickhead? Do you know who I am?' Instead of alarming Sam, the assault settles his resolve to stay calm under pressure. He unlocks Mulvaney's fingers, one by one. He briefly – very briefly – considers trying to sell the bloke on the idea of a paradise that's attracted dreamers, poets, lefties, commos, young love, old love, kids and dogs. Realises he'd be mining a barren seam. 'By the time we're finished with you and your dodgy land deals, you won't have the kudos to OK a public lavatory. Your name will be mud. Nah. Worse than that. Slime. Scum. Not even your mother will own up to you.' He dusts his hands, continues, almost conversationally, 'Wouldn't want you to be under any illusions.'

Mulvaney lets rip with a deep, gut-busting laugh. The smile returns, dirty with malice. 'Go home and take a long last look at your beloved park, which according to the report on my desk is infested with ticks and used as a garbage dump. The developers are doing you a favour. In three weeks, the bulldozers move in. You're whistling Dixie if you think a few raddled pot-smokers and bozo surf bums are going to stand in the way. Oh, and just so you know, the government of New South Wales bought the park from the Trust a month ago. Lock, stock and barrel. And we've sold it to the highest bidder. It's a deal as clean as a whistle.'

A well-groomed and discreet assistant or secretary, Sam has no idea which, materialises out of nowhere. But Mulvaney's not finished: 'You say one word about me that I find offensive and I'll sue your pants off. By the time I'm finished, I'll have your house, your car. Even your fucking underwear. Now get out.'

Sam is tempted to make a crack about his jocks. Decides Mulvaney isn't worth the effort. The secretary holds the door open, indicates Sam should go ahead of him.

When it's just the two of them in the empty corridor, the dapper little man, polished from the tip of his balding head to his black leather lace-ups, says, quite pleasantly: 'Don't come back. Not if you want to live a long life.' Said with a poker face, like it's a hack line in a lousy sitcom he gets to repeat over and over.

For some reason he'll never understand – his bloody instinct again – Sam offers his hand, feels heartened when it's grasped almost warmly. 'They play for keeps,' the secretary adds, in a manner that's clearly meant to inform, not threaten. He pauses. Then, 'Is the park really full of ticks, a dump?'

'No, mate, it's paradise.'

He lets out a sigh heavy with regret. 'They always are.' He disappears back into what Sam can only think of as an expensive rat hole.

Out on the street, Sam takes a minute to thank the two sweat-soaked security guards at their sauna-hot gatepost for – as he puts it – looking after a man more at ease on the open waterways, a bargeman named Sam Scully who doesn't set foot on land too bloody often. Not if he can help it. 'And by the way,' he asks, 'just so I can get my bearings, where would Mulvaney's office rank in that three-storey stack of windows?'

The guards, stomachs hanging over their belts, shirt buttons stretched to breaking point, swagger a little and laugh. 'Top floor, mate, three from the end. Right next door to the premier and breathing down his neck like a rabid dog.' Heh, heh.

Heading home, Sam silently declares his mission a success. Mulvaney is as rotten as a week-old sardine. Why do they think they can get away with it? Because they always have, he thinks, feeling a layer of innocence peel off him like sunburn. 'But not this time,' he says vehemently. 'No freaking way.' He pounds the sun-bleached dash of his rusty old ute, then apologises to the car as if it can hear him. Up ahead, flashing orange lights warn him there's been an accident on the bridge. He checks his petrol gauge and crosses his fingers.

Once again, Sam lies in his own bed. Lightning strobes through the window. Thunder rumbles. Once, it cracks louder than a gunshot next to his ear and he feels a sudden lurch of dread. Raindrops tap the roof. He counts the beats between light and boom, following Jimmy's instructions. One . . . *bang*! Another house-rattler. The storm feels like it's on top of him. He'd invited Kate to spend the night in his house but she'd turned him down even though she understood he didn't want to leave the premises unoccupied for a while yet. Come to think of it, she'd barely ever set foot in his home. If he were the kind of bloke who tended towards cynicism he'd put it down to a fear of losing control. His house, his rules. He turns over, punches his pillow into a shape to fit between his neck and shoulders. Curls into a ball. Squeezes his eyes shut tight like a small boy. The wind picks up. He hears bark peeling from spotted gums and crashing noisily to the ground. There'll be a mess in the morning, he thinks. Water in the tanks will go even browner. It's fortunate Islanders favour strong colours in their clothing. Which brings him to Kate's sparkling white T-shirts. How does she do it? And why won't she join the committee? When he asks, all he gets is a shrug and a hard look that warns him it's a no-go zone. Eventually, the monkey in his head tires of the Kate loop. Sam falls into a fitful sleep.

At the tail-end of the following day, Sam is nobbled by Jenny, who roars up to him in the Square, beaming with victory, her hair still wet from a quick swim or a shower, he's not sure which. She waves a fist full of cash under his nose. 'Smell this. Sweeter than roses. Signed up every local to the cause except for three. Two weekenders and Artie. Three thousand nine hundred and seventy dollars. The fighting fund is under way. Gotta run,' she says, shoving the money at him, 'or the kids will take off without me and I'll have to swim home.'

Artie, he thinks. Artie refused to join?

He holds the cash out from his body as though it might bite. Where's he going to stash a shitload of money until the committee opens a bank account? He checks out the commuter crowd with their frigidly cold beers, chewing the fat, hawk-eyes on the puddles to avoid soaking their only pair of going-to-town-shoes. Sees a cheeky, wiry terrier ambitiously trying to mount a thuggish, barrel-chested Staffy. A bad move that ends in flashing fangs and an all-out brawl until the terrier rolls over, four paws in the air, pink tongue hanging out of the side of his mouth. Complete surrender. Two mums strip their red-faced toddlers to splash about naked in the cool water. A bunch of kids help load groceries into tinnies. A few dragging their feet. He'd trust every one of them with his life but he wouldn't put a single soul in charge of a ten-cent coin that wasn't his own. The committee needs a treasurer.

'The one committee job that can't be casually passed around is treasurer,' Sam explains to Kate and Ettie. The two women stare at the pile of notes that Sam holds towards them like a gift.

'So who do you think would make a good treasurer?' Kate asks, ignoring the money.

'Well, you would, Kate,' Sam says, wondering why she's even bothered to ask.

Ettie returns to fastidiously wiping the counter. Kate hangs out the closed sign. Sam shuffles from one foot to the other. Afraid he's come down on the twig again just when he hoped he and Kate might be beginning to settle into a mutually acceptable routine that he reckons any relationship needs, no matter how hot and sweaty at the start, to avoid either dying out or exploding. The silence goes on and on. He looks to Ettie for support. Her eyes are focused on a stubborn dirty spot on the counter, which she's rubbing furiously. Kate begins to refill salt and pepper shakers. Sam shifts about nervously. Not sure what to do with the cash. The summer mugginess feels heavy in his lungs.

'I'm still regarded as a blow-in, Sam,' Kate says eventually, spilling a little salt, picking up a few grains, tossing them over her right shoulder.

'Left,' Ettie says. 'The left shoulder. Right is bad luck.'

'Give the job to someone who is more sensitive to the undercurrents of Cook's Basin life.'

Sam shuffles. 'Aw, jeez, Kate . . .'

Ettie breaks in. 'She's right, Sam. Find someone else.'

Beaten, Sam gives in with a loud sigh and shoves the cash in his back pocket. The best laid plans, he tells himself philosophically, often backfire. But at least he has an idea now of why she's stuck to the sidelines. And even though he hates to admit it, she has a point.

Outside in the Square, his mind switches to Artie. He didn't sign on, he thinks again, puzzled. He makes a silent promise to call in on the old bloke.

On dusk, a strong sea breeze threatens to shift the ballooning humidity but it peters out before it does any good. Dankness settles in once more. Dogs are listless. Birds make short-distance flights. Pythons coil sleepily with fat, rodent-shaped lumps in their stomachs. On the beaches, even toddlers sitting like fat little Buddhas in the tepid shallows lose heart and start to whinge. There will be a run on heat-rash ointment in the next couple of days. Everyone is over it. Blasphemy or not. Sam grabs a Briny take-away curry out of his freezer and heads for the *Mary Kay*. Artie is more inclined towards hot and spicy than sauso rolls, which he once told Sam reminded him unhappily of cheap flagon wine parties in the 1970s. He comes alongside Artie's yacht: 'Fenders are out, I'm rafted up. Permission to come on board?' he shouts.

Artie wheezes assent. Half a second later, Sam's solid legs find the top of the cabin steps. He drops, his hands holding on to the top of the opening. Lands lightly.

'Ya wanna know why I refused to hand over me money, don't ya?' Artie says straight off. He sips from a glass of water like it's poison. He's nursing a black eye and a purple bruise on a lump the size of an emu's egg on one side of his forehead.

'It's a free world, mate. You been in the wars?'

'Felt like a sauna down here around midday. Hauled meself up on deck to get a breath of fresh air. Easy as pie. It was the comin' down that created a few, er, issues.'

'Next time, call me.'

'Watched a sea eagle surf the thermals. Goin' round and round in lazy circles until he dropped like a bullet to the water. Barely broke the surface before he launched upwards again with a bloody great fish in his claws.'

'Bad day for the fish, eh?'

'Evolution. How's the war faring?'

'What have you heard?'

'You need an event. A demo of some sort to get wider attention. Jack Mundey, he galvanised a nation. Not sayin' you can pull off a stunt like that. There's a difference between fightin' for a small park and saving the most historic area this young country's got. Which is what he did even though millions of dollars were shoved under his nose to encourage him to go home and put his feet up until every sandstone building in Sydney was reduced to a pile of rubble and there was nothing more to be done about it. Coulda lived like a king. 'Cept he understood livin' with himself was more important.'

'You need a doctor, Artie?'

The old man gives a bitter laugh. 'What for, son?'

Sam heats up the curry in the close quarters of the galley. The boat will stink of spices for days, he thinks ruefully.

Where's a good blow when you need one? 'An event, you reckon?' he says, placing their meals on the table. 'Been holding a card up my sleeve for a while now. Might be time to play it.'

'Wanna fill me in?' Artie says, his eyes sparkling at the thought of mayhem, leaning forward in anticipation.

Back on the *Mary Kay* two hours later, Sam kicks himself for not paying more attention to the old bloke. Refusing to join the Save Garrawi fund was like sending up a smoke signal for company. Artie shouldn't have had to do it. Not in a community like Cook's Basin where they were all supposed to be looking after each other. It's the stinking humidity, he thinks. Even our brains are turning to mush.

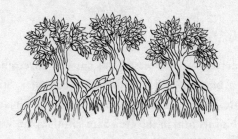

CHAPTER TWELVE

Four days later, Sam treads softly down the steps from his house to the waterfront. He climbs into his tinny and with no more than a couple of pulls, starts the often cantankerous outboard. He *putt putts* across the water. It's almost dawn. He finds his ute and heads out of the car park in the direction of the city. The roads are dead quiet. Only traffic signals keep up their constant routine. Green. Orange. Red. Green. Orange. Red. Go. Caution. Stop. Well, as far as he's concerned, caution's been thrown to the wind and it's all systems go. Clichés or no freaking clichés.

He'd cottoned on to the idea on his way home from his failed mission to convert Mulvaney to the cause. A flashing-orange-lights roadside sign announcing a massive furniture sale had lit up his brain. Couldn't the same device be used to hammer home a few uncomfortable truths if it was stationed in full view of the third window from the southern end of Parliament House? He'd rung a machinery-hire firm, given the manager the full spiel in case he happened to be a card-carrying supporter of the current government, and received a blessing and even better, a cut rate: 'Stick it up them, mate. Third window you say? Top floor? I'll jack up the board till it hits him in the eye.' Sam's initial plan was to run a slogan: *No Bridge, No Resort. Save Garrawi.* But when he found out the machine could be programmed to reproduce the entire contents of *Encyclopedia Brittanica* if that's what you wanted, he shifted the goal posts.

He finds a free, two-hour park half a kilometre from State Parliament. Treads across soft, dewy grass through the Botanic Gardens as the morning light spreads smoothly over treetops. The air is cool, clean. A few birds stir, their rousing tweets cutting through the quiet. He checks his watch. Plenty of time.

Five minutes later, he turns into Macquarie Street. Straight ahead, he spots the flashing screen of his pre-programmed Mobile Electronic Message Display unit. Feeling like he imagines a writer must when he sees his work in print for the first time, he stands still to better admire the show. *Who is stealing Garrawi? Who profits? Why no community consultation? Why no due process? Parks are for people, not profit. No Bridge. No Resort. Save Garrawi now! Who profits? Do you know, Mulvaney?*

A security guard, who's wandered away from his post to take a closer look, saunters up, stands rocking on his heels alongside Sam. 'Anything to do with you, mate?' he asks, tilting his head towards the machine. Heartened by a tone more curious than authoritarian, Sam holds out his hand.

'Sam Scully. You frisked me the other day when I paid a call on the Minister for Housing and Development.'

'Ben Butler. How d'you do?' He scrabbles back in his memory: 'Ah, the bargeman, eh?'

'Good memory. Thought you'd only remember the crackpots.'

Ben Butler, overweight and on the wrong side of middle-age, grins and thumbs the big office at the end of the third floor. 'Just 'cause they're wearing suits doesn't mean they're not crazy. They just hide it better or give it a fancy name. The number of tantrum-throwers hiding behind "bipolar" these days beggars belief.' He gives Sam a serious once-over from head to toe and comes to a decision. 'Would you fancy a cuppa tea, Sam Scully?'

'Good of you to offer, mate. I *am* feeling a little parched. Must be the excitement.'

Ben Butler slaps Sam's back so hard the bargeman coughs out loud. 'Did you know the press cafeteria is right across the road? Give me your phone number, Sam Scully. In case anyone asks for it.'

Back in the Square by midday, after giving the hire firm the go-ahead for a weeklong electronic barrage (that he's funding out of his own pocket) straight through Mulvaney's clear glass windows, Sam keeps to himself. He's tempted to pull the plug on the working day and sink into a celebration frigidly cold like it's Saturday instead of Monday. It's not every day a bloke gets to set a match under the backside of a Minister of State. He's getting the hang of pyromania. Likes – nah, feeds off – the rush of adrenalin that comes from stepping forward instead of standing still like an easy target. Too wound up to consider food, he taps his fingers on the picnic table. Unwilling to let go of the warm feeling of the morning's success.

The phone goes off in his pocket. Sam checks the caller ID but can't place it.

'Sam Scully,' he says.

'Mr Scully? It's Dale Carnegie from the *Telegraph*. I understand you're the genius behind the flashing screen in Macquarie Street?'

'Can't hear you, mate. I'll call you back when I tie up the barge.'

Shit, he thinks, ending the call in a rush. First time he's tested and he tells a lie straight off. He bolts for his tinny, heads for where the *Mary Kay* is tied to her mooring. If he's quick, he may be able to convince himself that – technically – it was only a white lie.

In the tinny, he dials Siobhan. 'I've had a call about Garrawi . . . Who from? . . . The *Telegraph*. Dale . . .'

'Carnegie. Political reporter. How'd he hear about it, I wonder.'

Silence hangs between them like a challenge. Deciding he's no match for Siobhan, Sam breaks first.

'Er, I've been doing a bit of er . . . freelancing.' He is beginning to understand the endless possibilities that open up with the use of a word he'd heard for the first time a few days ago.

'Freelancing, is it?'

'Yeah, it means . . .'

'I know what it means, you eejit.' Siobhan pauses. Sam decides to keep quiet this time. 'You talk to Dale?'

'Caught me on the hop. Said I'd call him back.'

'Thank God. Do not, under any circumstances, call him. If he calls again, let it go to message bank. If you speak to this man, I will personally garrotte you. Clear enough?'

'Crystal,' Sam says, not sure whether he's off the hook or still dangling by his throat.

'Dale's OK, but it's Delaney we'll talk to first. The other eejits can wait their turn.' The phone goes dead. Sam wipes sweat from his brow. His shirt is drenched. He is, he realises wryly, terrified of the woman.

He's due to service three moorings, none of them urgent enough to warrant immediate action. Jimmy's knee deep in worm castings. Becoming quite an entrepreneur. Amazing what having a goal will do for a kid. Although why he's deadset on a ute when a good boat would be much more useful is beyond Sam's comprehension. So . . . nothing seriously urgent. He could – reasonably – skive off for the day. Point the bow of the *Mary Kay* out to sea and rock on the waters near Cat Island, reliving every heady moment, planning the next.

He picks up the scent of roasting garlic. Raises his nose. His stomach flip-flops. His mouth starts to water. He heads for the café.

'A mug of your best brew, love, and something more hefty than a muffin this morning, if you don't mind. Been a long day already.'

Ettie gives him a sideways look. Sam smiles back innocently. Says not a word.

'How about a chorizo and pea omelette, with a few potatoes fried with onions and olives then doused in a little sherry on the side?'

Sam makes a smacking sound with his lips, kisses his fingertips: 'Easy on the olives, if you wouldn't mind.'

Deciding a man has to keep abreast of events if he's trying to influence them in a small way, he forks out $1.20 for a newspaper for the first time in living memory. Ettie almost has to be resuscitated. 'You going to frame it when you've read it?' she asks.

'There's a first for everything,' he replies. He finds a table on the deck in morning shade and settles in. Suddenly remembers he promised to deliver a couple of tons of firewood to a house in Kingfish Bay, so it was just as well he ditched the Cat Island idea. Still, delivering firewood in midsummer went against his grain. As he'd dutifully pointed out, it was like writing an open invitation to a bushfire. The bloke wouldn't listen. What kind of a tight-arse would risk his house burning down just to get timber at half price? Mind you, with the current wet spell, it was an effort to even get a backyard barbecue fired up. People love bargains though, and who could blame them considering the current erratic global economy. If he were the type to worry, he'd be chewing his own nails. Business is down. Everyone's sitting tight and trying not to worry whether they'll still have a job when they wake up in the morning. At least he's his own boss. Anyway, there's no point in sweating what you can't change, as his father used to say.

A shadow falls across the newspaper.

Jenny clutches a small green book to her chest. 'Forgot to give this to you yesterday.' She holds up a slim, dog-eared volume with a lino-cut of banksias, wattles and grevilleas on the cover. *The Battlers for Kelly's Bush.* Sam raises his eyebrows in a query.

'Have a read. It's an eye opener. Just remember that protecting the environment was a new and radical thought when all this happened. Threats and intimidation tactics were rife and it took enormous guts and courage to stand up for what you believed in. Remember Juanita Nielson? Same era.'

'Nothing changes, eh?'

'Really gotta run. Appointment with the skin specialist to remove a few sunspots on my face. Oh, and how about Jane as treasurer? She's still got the first dollar she ever earned.' She's off before Sam can answer which means it's already set in stone. He opens the book as Ettie delivers his breakfast. The mouth-watering smell of chorizo beats the lure of the book. He dives on his food with gusto. Lighting spot fires is hungry work.

'Kelly's Bush?' Sam mutters. He wipes his mouth with a bare arm, his fingers on his shorts. Reaches for the book. His parents' era. The end of the swinging sixties. Wasn't it all about flower power, free love, peace and swarms of dope-smoking students marching in the streets to call an end to the war in Vietnam? He wasn't even born. He's about to skip the details. But nothing changes, does it? He opens at the introduction. Sees Jack Mundey's name. Feels a frisson of déjà vu. Way back in the rip-it-down-to-make-way-for-a-block-of-flimsy-flats days, Sam's father had idolised Mundey. Had a grainy black-and-white picture of him tacked on the boatshed wall near the kitchen table where no one could miss it. 'A man of the people and for the people, son. Why fight for higher wages and better conditions, he pointed out, if there was nowhere left with trees, parks and clean air?'

Sam settles down to concentrate. More useful than heading out to sea and diving into the celebratory six-pack he is fully aware he wouldn't have been able to resist. Gnats hover above the water, playing Russian roulette with fish who strike and win nine times out of ten. The gnats stay put. Literally throwing themselves into the jaws of death. He looks away. Wonders if there's a moment when it's wise to back off and live to fight another day.

Kelly's Bush, eh. He reads it had been used as a playground and picnic spot since the early 1900s with the full approval of the state government. Despite it having been decreed an Open Space, in 1971 the state government and the local council were about to approve a high-density housing estate development on the site.

Out of the blue, thirteen well-groomed middle-class women, mostly housewives and mums who thought lifting a hemline above a knee was about as risqué as it got, decided to fight the development. The men in suits dismissed them as a bunch of twinsets-and-pearls women without a clue. But every time some bureaucrat or politician treated them like idiots, they dug in deeper. Never underestimate the power of a determined woman, Sam thinks. He pulls a pencil out of his pocket, underlines a paragraph:

> *These men invariably behaved as though it should have been a simple matter to persuade these women to their point of view. After all, wasn't money simply everything? . . . Housewives we were, but determined ones with strong principles for which we would fight.*

He reads about the setbacks. He learns that at one point the battle was essentially lost but the women dug in harder. He discovers that a call from Rod Cavalier, a union organiser, set in motion a series of events that literally tipped the power of land developers worldwide on its head. The Builders Labourers' Federation, headed by Jack Mundey, agreed to help out by refusing to work on other sites owned by the developer. The action became known as the world's first Green Ban. Hell of an achievement, Sam reckons, closing the book. If a bunch of gritty housewives could pull off a world-beating victory, the residents of Cutter Island and Cook's Basin should hang their heads in shame if they fail to bludgeon the current proposal to death.

He picks up his mobile. Dials Jimmy. At this stage, he realises, celebrations of petty victories are not just premature: they risk obscuring the main aim. He picks up his plate and takes it inside. Finds Ettie holding open the door of the fridge, her head thrust in as far as it will go.

'Hot, eh?' Sam says.

'Butter was shoved way back,' she snaps.

Behind the counter, her hands deep in a sink full of hot soapy water, Kate rolls her eyes.

Inspired and feeling like he's on an unstoppable roll, Sam decides to call Jack Mundey. He figures if a name keeps popping up it's a sign that unseen forces on the side of good are hard at work. Once, Sam and his dad had watched the evening news on a friend's brand-spanking-new and utterly wondrous full-colour television set, still such a rare commodity in Cook's

Basin, the neighbours took turns to call in. Mundey, his black hair faded to grey, his craggy face filling the screen, was talking about the need to stand up for minorities – feminists, gays, Aboriginals – anyone who was denied a voice on the basis of bigotry.

Sam's dad watched, mesmerised. 'Take a look at one of the few genuine heroes, son. A man who never did deals with one hand behind his back, who never let his ego get in the way of common sense.' He was only a kid but, even then, it seemed to Sam that Mundey had kind eyes, a soft mouth. A noble nose. That he was a man with a soul, a social conscience. A man for all seasons. A man, as Siobhan would say, who never took the soup. Sam badly wants him onside.

He starts at the top of the Mundeys listed in the telephone directory and begins dialling.

'Jack Mundey?'

'Never heard of him.' *Click*.

'Jack Mundey?'

'Wrong number, love, but we're distantly related. No I haven't got his number but I'll tell you about the last family get-together . . .'

Twenty minutes later, his ear thoroughly bashed, he dials again: 'Jack Mundey?'

'No. Great man, though. Do you remember when . . . ?'

Another ear-bashing.

Twenty minutes later: 'Jack Mundey?' The phone goes dead. Rude bastard, thinks Sam, dialling again.

'Jack Mundey?' *Click*. Now he's pissed off. It wouldn't hurt a bloke to say hello. Once more. 'Jack Mundey?'

Almost a whisper: 'Who wants to know?' Bingo.

Sam blurts the cause. Not sure he's making any sense. When he eventually runs out of steam, silence stretches emptily between them. Sam figures he's blown it. Failed to win over this giant of a man. He pulls in his stomach, thrusts out his chest, aware Mundey can't see him but he doesn't care. Taking his courage firmly in both hands, he asks: 'Would you be our patron, mate? Er, Mr Mundey?'

'Why do you want an old ghost like me?' Mundey whispers down the line.

'Why? Well, you're a legend. You saved everything in Sydney that was worth saving. My dad thought you were a hero. So do I. Will you back us? Will you back us?' Sam repeats.

'You going to fight it all the way?' Mundey asks.

'Yeah. Oh yeah. It's on, mate, and we'll die fighting if that's the way it's got to go.'

Again the old man pauses. Jeez, Sam thinks, looking at his phone to make sure the line hasn't dropped out, he's in his eighties. He's got every right to say no. He squeezes his eyes shut, crosses his fingers and invokes the spirit of his father. Waits. Mundey replies: 'I'll help you all I can. Look after you. Tell you who to talk to.'

Sam lets out a breath he's held for so long, black spots dance in his eyes. 'So you'll put your name to it?' he asks.

'Yeah,' says Mundey. Sam's hectic, heartfelt thanks are garbled, idiotic. Mundey laughs, just a dry croak, and ends the call. But it's there. A promise. I just signed up a living legend, Sam thinks, wondering if he's finally starting to seriously get the hang of lighting spot fires. He pulls out a crappy little spiral notebook and pencils in Mundey's name under a new heading: *PATRONS*. Then he turns to the back page and lists his phone number. The campaign has its first official backer; a bloke with the kind of credibility that can't be bought. Who needs celebrities? He's stoked. Bring on the critics, bring on the dissenters, bring on the doubters, he rails inwardly, punching the air with his fist. We're on fire! He feels like kings did, once upon a time. Except this is no fairy-tale. This is a thriller to the bitter end. For the first time, Sam feels a glimmer of hope based on hard reality instead of blind faith.

CHAPTER THIRTEEN

By the time the second meeting of the Save Garrawi committee convenes at seven pm in the cosy front living room of the Misses Skettle, with its views across the water to Cutter Island, there's a buzz in the air and not just because it's the end of the week.

The Three Js take up positions cross-legged on the floor, John Scott perches on a windowsill, Glenn, Lindy, Seaweed, Ettie, Marcus, Jimmy and Siobhan spill into the hallway, balancing yachtie-style on the sloping floorboards. Nobody goes near either of the rosy armchairs where the two old ladies keep watch on stormy days and nights in case some poor wretch's engine fails in dangerous seas and they need rescuing. Small bowls of prunes wrapped in bacon are dotted around with tiny pip saucers and napkins alongside – the dainty embroidered variety used for formal morning and afternoon teas half a century ago. Nobody touches those either.

The Misses Skettle flit around in frothy summer dresses like pink butterflies, filling glasses, patting arms, enquiring after this and that with an old-worldly charm that inhibits anyone normally inclined towards bawdy noisiness at community get-togethers. When drinks are topped up for the second time and the prunes whisked away so they don't get tipped over, the meeting begins. Across the open waterway, the park they are determined to save is a dark and mysterious shadow in the gathering gloom of evening.

With a clap of hands, the meeting is called to order. Siobhan tips John off his windowsill and takes charge. 'Your job was to get people talking about Garrawi,' she says. 'By god, you've done it like bloody pros. And sure and be damned if there's not a tear in my eye when I think of all you've achieved in such a short time.'

'Hear, hear.'

'Laying it on a bit thick, isn't she?' Glenn whispers in Sam's ear.

'She's Irish, mate. It's in the genes.'

'Oh. Orright, then.'

Siobhan goes on to tell them about Sam's impromptu and ultimately fruitless meeting with Mulvaney. She mentions the electronic message board; the coup of recruiting Jack Mundey as a patron; and that the press has already begun sniffing around. 'But it's early days yet. I'm not one for giving orders, as you all know (she grins) but the first person who even says a polite hello to a member of the media without my express permission will be publicly castrated. We are faced with a difficult task. We need the press. Of course we do. But let them get to the bottom of this travesty on their own. Who would believe us if we talked about gurus, human flight, world destruction? As I've said, we'd be written off as nutters and we can't afford to have that happen. Are we all clear on this?'

Hear, hear.

Siobhan crosses her ankles. Her red rope-sole shoes look like they've just come out of the box. She wears faded denim jeans, a red-checked cotton shirt open low enough at the neck to be interesting. There's probably not a bloke in the room who can decide whether he's half in love with her or just plain scared shitless, Sam thinks. He toys with the idea of asking her age when they next share a couple of drinks. Comes to his senses. He'd like to live a suitably long life.

'Right,' she says, dusting off her hands. 'Any ideas for more spot fires?'

'Well, I was thinking a parade of boats,' Sam begins.

There's a collective groan. 'Mate,' says Seaweed, 'in Cook's Basin, there's virtually a parade of boats at peak hour twice a day. Then there's the twilight yacht races, the putt-putt parade, the Three Island race and all the other notable events we're familiar with. No one will even turn a head to watch.'

'I'm talking about a different kind of parade. Using boats to set fire to the sky.'

'Eh?'

Sam explains. 'We rally everything that floats, circle the Island and set off safety flares till the world glows orange. We can use old ones well past their use-by date. We'll call it a donation – might even manage a tax deduction in the form of counting it as a contribution to a cause that has recently been listed as a charitable foundation thanks to the chef –' Hear, hear! Marcus takes a bow '– and replace them with new flares?' Eyes sparkle in agreement. A double whammy with a tuck. Nothing Islanders enjoy more. 'I'll give Waterways a call in the morning to suss out safety rules and regulations. No point in ending up in the clink before the fight hots up.'

Hear, hear.

'Can we set a date?'

Debate surges instantly. They need to take into account the fireshed dinners, kindergarten rallies, Lenny's funeral and wake, twilight racing, Thursday afternoon sailing . . .

Siobhan puts up her hand for silence, checks the events calendar on her mobile phone. 'Listen up . . . according to this schedule, Sunday, February 17, is available. Any questions? Done!'

She reaches for a pad and pencil. 'As we all know, the park's been recently surveyed and trees marked for removal – thank you, Jimmy, for being the first to note the changes. Is Jimmy here?'

'He's taken the dog out to lift his leg. He'll be back in a minute,' advises one of the Misses Skettle.

'OK, I'll come back to the trees. The black-tie fundraiser is set for three weeks from Saturday.' To cut off debate, she adds, 'Don't worry if you can't make it, just be sure to buy a ticket which we'll put down as a donation. But each of you will be given ten double tickets to sell. Payment is in advance. Each payment is to come directly to Jane, our new treasurer.'

'Oh, but . . .' Jane stammers.

Siobhan glares at her: 'If you're not happy, talk to Jenny. She volunteered on your behalf. But meself, I'd be thinking that anything you could do to help . . .'

'Of course,' Jane stammers. Totally cowed.

Siobhan continues: 'Now be warned, all of you. If you sell eight tickets but fail to turn in the remainders, you will be charged. Sure and I know it's not the way we do business in Cook's Basin but we're not talking about a feel-good little get-together here.'

'We're makin' history, Miss O'Shaughnessy. That's what we're doin', aren't we?' Jimmy says, rocketing into the room, the pup tucked under his left arm. 'And I'm not late, Sam, just tendin' to Longfella's business. Me mum says boy dogs lift their legs in strange houses and it's best to be sure . . .'

Siobhan cuts in, not unkindly: 'Good lad and good spotting with those eagle eyes. A fine clean-up job, too.'

Jimmy beams, his face flushes purple. He shifts the dog to his other arm and bounces on the balls of his feet. 'I can do anything, I told ya, didn't I?'

'Right, Jimmy. That's enough now. We've more work to do.' And such is Siobhan's power that even Jimmy goes still and silent on demand.

After the discussion ends and the committee huddles over a plate of smelly cheese and warm bread, John Scott takes Sam aside. 'I had a visit from Eric Lowdon,' he says, in a low voice. 'Pitched up close to midnight. Which is probably smart given the lynch-mob mentality on the Island right now.'

'What did he want?'

John blushes. 'He wants to build an art gallery, Sam. Says the local artists need a showcase and he's prepared to put up the money.'

'Nah, empty promises, mate. He'll get you onside and welch on the deal. Guarantee it.'

'It's not quite that simple. He also made a six-figure offer – half the money upfront – to commission a wide range of local artwork for the walls of the new resort.'

Sam swears under his breath. 'You told the other artists?'

'Not yet. But they have a right to know. It's an artist's dream. Money in the bank and more to come. Like winning the lottery.'

The two men stand silently for a while. Each one scrolling through the ramifications of something too big to be dismissed. Eventually, Sam says: 'What do you reckon? Think they'll go for it? Er, I'm assuming, as you're still on the committee, that you're against the deal.'

'I'm lucky. I make a decent living. I can afford to knock it back but I won't lie – it still hurts to say no. The others? I'm not sure. And you know what? I couldn't really blame them if they rolled over and took the soup, as Siobhan would say.'

'So Lowdon figures he can use his money to divide and conquer, eh? Plunge a knife into the heart of a community and watch it slowly bleed to death? When are you going to mention it?'

'I've asked Lowdon to put the offer in writing. Soon as I get it, I'll organise a barbecue.'

'If you had to guess, mate, which way do you think they'll go?'

'Truthfully? With one less zero attached to the deal, I'd reckon Lowdon would lose. But this is big money. I haven't a clue how they're going to react.'

*

Later, when he's home, Sam considers lobbying the artists against Lowdon's deal and then backs off. If there's no resort, there's no gallery. One step at a time.

He checks his watch. It's still a decent hour. He finds the phone number for the Water Police on a card he keeps secured by a magnet on his fridge door. He writes it in his small spiral notebook: the beginning of his own arsenal of contacts. He likes to think he's a man who learns quickly. He dials. The call's picked up. He hears the smooth and steady roar of a few hundred horse power in the background. He makes his pitch.

'Run that past me again?' says the officer-on-duty, throwing the cruiser into neutral. The noise drops back to a throaty murmur.

'We want to circle Cutter Island in our boats and fire off two hundred distress flares.'

'No, mate, you can't do it. It's illegal.'

'Ah, bugger. It seemed like a cracker of an idea at the time.' For some reason, Sam doesn't hang up.

The officer waits a beat, then speaks: 'Er, is this for Garrawi?'

'Yeah, mate,' Sam replies. 'One and the same.'

There's another pause, a sound like lips smacking. 'Well, you could always call it a flare safety demonstration . . .'

'How do we do that?' Sam asks, unable to keep the excitement out of his voice.

'I'll send you the form. Fill it in and get back to us. No worries.'

Sam disconnects, throws the phone down on the table, spins around four times shouting yippee. Not cool, he thinks, not caring.

An hour later, he puts the finishing touches to his flare safety demonstration plan. In his mind, he sees it as a grand parade of character vessels ranging from svelte little sailing boats to leaky tin dinghies that will probably need to be rescued when the flotilla reaches the unprotected eastern shore of Cutter Island, where a strong wind could whip the seas into a surging frenzy. Which, when he thinks about it, is a perfect result for a flare safety demonstration aimed at saving sinking boats.

Just before he goes to sleep, he calls Jack Mundey. 'There's a top seat on the barge for you, mate. Say the word and we'll spring for a taxi, a hire car, anything to get you here on the day.'

Mundey doesn't even hesitate. 'Do you know the number of the bus from Central?'

'A taxi, mate. Our privilege. It's too far by bus.'

'For an old bloke, you mean.'

'Jeez . . . sorry . . .'

'I'll be there. But I'll find my own way. Save your money for the campaign.'

Next he calls Siobhan. They confirm the date they'd nominated in mid February.

'I'll tell Seaweed to put out the word on the new website,' Siobhan says. 'Check it out, Sam. It's wonderful. You click on the link and straightaway a fierce-looking cockatoo screeches "Stop the vandals!" loudly in your ear.' The notice is also posted in *Cook's Basin News*. The game is heating up.

He's about to call Kate but checks the time. It's just past her curfew and he'd hate to wake her. When you start work at 6 am late nights are a rare luxury. He puts down the phone. He'll talk to her in the morning. He's tired of his lonely bed. That's the truth. He even misses the sparring.

He makes a note to remind himself to ask Seaweed to suss out a simple computer for his personal use. It's time to embrace change, he thinks, with a twinge of regret. And jeez, they can't be that hard to handle. Every Island kid is an expert.

He hits the sack and wakes with a start an hour before dawn, shocked by the feel of a cool breeze on his naked skin. A sou'easterly, he thinks. He gets up to take a piss from the deck, grinning up at a faultless sky. The rank stench of rotting vegetation overlaid with the stink of leaky septics is already fading. He takes a deep breath. The soupiness of high humidity is gone. One or two boats, their red, white and green nav lights moving across the water like large, rare insects in air-force formation, are already about. Sam rubs his arms, feeling almost chilled. He decides to catch another hour in the cot to make the most of the comfortable temperature. Brute summer is on the run for a blessed moment and the fight to save Garrawi is moving up a notch. He needs to stay strong.

Later, with the sun working up enough grunt to burn off the sea mist and the brisk sou'easterly nudging the humidity towards the arid Red Centre where it's more likely to be appreciated, Sam makes his way to The Briny Café. He's looking forward to a mug of Ettie's magnificent brew, a sweet chewy muffin.

He's also kept the news of Lowdon's offer to himself, figuring John will brief Siobhan when the time is right. Anyway, there's no sense in getting worked up until the details are clearly stated in black and white with a cheque – if that's the result – promised by the close of business. It's the kind of issue he could discuss with Kate. She'd tell him straight what would be left of the campaign if the artists defected. He fixes on the idea of a picnic. Good food, a little music, some soft cushions. Winding down on a glorious night is an age-old tradition that ought to be maintained even if you work in a seven days a week business. Kate's got to relax sometime. Relax. The word sounds downright seductive.

Inside the café, a couple of kayakers with damp backsides and dry T-shirts are ordering large flat white coffees. They both look buggered. Sam nods hello. Wonders if they're in training for the Cook's Basin to Port Ready marathon but can't be bothered finding out. Ettie passes them two cardboard containers. Kate takes their money. They leave wet footprints like spoor all over the floor.

'So how's the campaign going?' Kate asks, using tongs to place a muffin in a white paper bag. 'Any fur flying yet?' She passes it across the counter.

'A little. Here and there.'

Ettie hands him his coffee. 'How little and where?' she asks, but six more kayakers roll through the door.

Sam takes Kate aside: 'How about I put together a luscious picnic, tonight? We could head off somewhere quiet . . .'

'OK,' she says. 'But give the sauso rolls a rest, eh?'

Sam reels. Ettie gives him a wink and points at her chest. She'll sort it. He grins. Ettie, as he has always said, is the answer to every man's dreams.

*

By eight am, he's tied up at Cargo Wharf and he and Jimmy are loading the *Mary Kay* with enough heavy chain to service four moorings. The day passes in a blur of dirty work. Chipping cunjies off ropes, lifting marine-life encrusted cement blocks from the seabed. The sun beats down. The kid slaps a hat on his gelled head for the first time Sam can recall. The mutt takes shelter in the wheelhouse, where he flops on his side, panting, his dribbling pink tongue hanging loosely. The kid tips a bucket of salt water on him. The dog raises his head but doesn't stir. Together, Sam and Jimmy hose the muck, swab the deck. The hard physical yakka has the magical effect of making Sam feel cleaner of body and spirit despite the sweat, grit and grease. The kid never complains or shirks.

At the end of the day, they strip naked and jump overboard. The water feels like a cool cloth on their hot bodies. 'Kings never lived this good,' Sam shouts, his spirits high. Jimmy rolls his eyes. Duck dives. For a millisecond his skinny white backside points skywards. The Misses Skettle with their World War II binoculars will be laughing out loud.

At home with an hour to spare before he's due to meet Kate, he grabs a bar of pungent Solvol soap and scours every centimetre of his feet, legs, arms and hands until he reckons he's arguably the most polished bloke in the Southern Hemisphere. When you're on a roll, you're on a roll. Five minutes later, it starts to rain. The best-laid plans . . .

*

The remains of their dinner, a Briny take-away special of lamb rogan josh with condiments supplied out of Kate's fridge (raita, mango chutney, peanuts and tomato and onion sprinkled with paprika and doused in white vinegar that she says is the first feast Ettie ever taught her to prepare), litter the table top. He dabs his mouth with – surprisingly – a paper napkin. Checks his knife and fork are placed at attention on his plate. As far as he can tell, he's been textbook perfect all evening.

'Great dinner,' he says.

Kate smiles, gets up and disappears into her bedroom. Thinking he's meant to follow, he pushes back his chair. Before he can stand, though, she's back. In her hands she holds the grey tin box from her bedside table like it might explode.

'What's that?' he asks, getting a sense that the evening isn't going to unfold in quite the way that he'd hoped.

'Found it at Emily's unit when I cleaned the place after the reading of her will. No key though. Wondered if you would open it for me?'

Sam thinks: So that's where she disappeared to. She hands him the box, finds a screwdriver in a drawer. He pops the lock in about a second.

'Thanks,' she says, coolly.

'Aren't you going to look inside?' He's puzzled. Her responses are off-kilter. He wonders where this is leading.

Kate hesitates. Picks up their plates, stacks them in the sink and then goes to the fridge to get him a fresh beer. She pours a trickle of wine into her own glass. Stares into it. 'If it contains what I think it does, I may be gone from Cook's Basin for a while,' she says.

Sam goes still. 'What are you talking about?' he asks softly.

'My brother. The key to him has to be in this box.'

'Let me get this straight,' he says. 'You haven't got the faintest idea what's inside the box. That right?'

She nods. Her face is pinched. Her eyes cast down and fixed on hands that are balled into fists inside the pockets of her blue jeans. Sam can hear the warm tide slurping against the shore. 'So if it's not a rude question, why haven't you checked it out before?'

'I was afraid,' she whispers.

He chews the inside of his cheek, wondering what strange impulse draws him towards crusades that might rip him to shreds and leave him scarred forever. It's his own bloody history, of course. No one ever gave up on him. His own childhood was idyllic while it lasted. No money, no fancy toys, but there was never a shortage of love. All of it was wiped out in less than a minute, though, when a truck flattened out the new canary-yellow car his parents had saved like maniacs to buy. His mother's last words to him: 'Imagine, I can bulk buy flour and rice because I don't have to carry everything home on the bus. What luxury.'

All he wanted to do was join them wherever you go when your life is snuffed out. The Misses Skettle and Ettie, they saved him. Never let him out of their sight till he came good and realised blame was a pointless exercise. If he thought about it, the whole community had quietly kept tabs. Not in a heavy-handed, eat-your-vegetables way. But gently, as though they realised there was a war going on in his head, a war between grief and a boy's natural instinct to survive. He'd drag himself home from school and find a casserole on the table, a note inviting him over to a barbecue, a message to call, if he had time, to help a neighbour chop his wood. And in those three small gestures, every base was covered: sustenance, human contact and a cash job to help pay the bills.

'You want me to look inside for you?' he asks gently; because he had a dream run, considering, and as far as he can tell, Kate's battled on her own for most of her life. So she's not just smart, she's brave, too.

Kate nods.

'What if there's nothing? What if there's everything?'

'I need to know, Sam. Right now, it's like a sore I keep scratching.'

'He might be a psychopath – or live on the other side of the world. What then?'

'I'll find him. Wherever he is and whatever it takes, I'll find him.'

'I can't help thinking that if this brother of yours has waited this long to be found, hanging around for a few months, a year, until the café is secure and the park is safe won't make any difference.' Where he comes from – and where he'd hoped she was slowly finding the kind of anchors and values she'd been searching for – you hang in even tighter when the shit hits the fan. 'Jeez, Kate, you've got just as much riding on the success of the café as Ettie . . .'

'I can't sleep, Sam. In the café, every time I catch a hint of Emily's smile, the colour of her eyes, the shape of her nose, in a stranger's face, I have to turn away before I make a fool of myself by asking *were you adopted*? Is this the way it's going to be for the rest of my life? Always wondering, never knowing?'

And it occurs to him, his heart hurting with the knowledge, that her cool reserve is a public front and under it, Kate Jackson might be damaged more than most people and it's quite possible that no matter how much love and care she allows him to pour into her, she may never repair.

He lifts the lid of the grey box. It takes two seconds for her to conquer fear. She falls on the box hungrily, scrummaging amongst what looks to him like a load of old scrap paper. Bibs and bobs. Flotsam and jetsam. Rubbish without meaning to anyone except the person who placed it there. Eventually, she extracts an envelope from the bottom, holds it high in triumph. 'This is it. I'm sure it is.' She hurries to break the seal. Her fingers are clumsy with haste. Impatient, she rips the paper at one end and peers inside. Looks back at Sam, her eyes wide, frowning, puzzled. 'Ash,' she says. 'There's nothing here except a pile of ash. It's all a hoax. A shockingly malicious prank devised by my mad mother. And I fell for it.' Her face crumples. She screws the envelope into a tight ball and throws it against a wall, keeping her back to Sam so he can't read her face. He has no idea what to do. Hold her? Leave her alone? Come up with a few soothing but inadequate words? Stay silent?

In the end, he slides the box towards him and takes out each item one at a time, laying them in a straight line. A few blank postcards. From London, mostly. Big Ben, Buckingham Palace. The Tower. A blue foil chocolate wrapper. A folded silver wing from a costume, perhaps. He holds up a parchment-thick card with a coat of arms stamped on the front. 'Looks like a menu,' he says. 'It's from Parliament House in Canberra. Dated 26 March 1962. And here. Another menu.

From the *Oriana*, this time. A cruise ship, wasn't she? Dated a year earlier. Any of this make any sense to you?' he asks, looking at the jigsaw.

'Yeah,' Kate says, sculling her wine. 'My mother was a first-class bitch.' She stands up abruptly. 'Let's go to bed.' Spat out like an order.

He tells himself he should leave; he tells himself turning into anyone's punching bag does a disservice to both parties. He tells himself it would be an act of sensible self-preservation to say something polite and close the front door quietly behind him. He tells himself that if he follows her, he will be drawn deeply into the insanity of Kate and her mother's relationship because his gut feeling – and all men who make a living on the fickle sea know to trust those niggling sensations that are based on nothing but animal instinct – is that this is not the end but the beginning of an odyssey that could well end in tragedy.

'Want me to fill your glass?' he asks.

Cook's Basin News (CBN)

Newsletter for Offshore Residents of Cook's Basin, Australia

FEBRUARY

SAFETY-FLARE DEMONSTRATION

Scrape down your tinnies, trim your sails and prepare for the biggest naval demonstration Cook's Basin has ever seen. In an effort to draw national attention to the proposed rape and pillage of Garrawi Park, everyone and anyone with even vaguely seaworthy vessels should line up to circle Cutter Island for a safety-flare demonstration (approvals granted by the Water Police). Anyone in need of a flare, contact Jane Atherton, treasurer, Save Garrawi Committee.

When: Sunday, February 17

Where: Assemble at Triangle Wharf

Time: 6.45 pm for a 7 pm start

JET SKIS

Cook's Basin will be targeted by police on jet skis this year. Capable of reaching 115 mph, they are apparently being used to increase greater water safety during the peak holiday season. (Editor's note: 115 mph? Safety?) Jet skis were banned (Editor's note: in a rare moment of sanity) on Sydney Harbour in 2001 but can still be used on other waterways. Announcing the new service (Editor's note: ?) today, a government spokesperson said the jet-ski squad would be dedicated to responding to specific needs. "The aim is to provide safer and more secure waterways throughout the state," he said. (Editor's note: Do we want jet skis in Cook's Basin? Have your say on Twitter using the hashtag #jetskisout) (Another Editor's note: I would like to declare a bias against jet skis – if you haven't already picked up on that.)

Black-Tie Fundraiser

A black-tie event to raise money to fund a metropolitan newspaper advertisement campaign against the developers of Garrawi Park will be held next month. So dig out your glad rags (apply lemon juice to dislodge any mould) and prepare for an evening under the stars and the grand old cheese tree. Featuring magnificent food and glorious music, it will be an evening you will never forget. Three course dinner, wine and beer included.

Tickets: $75 each (start saving now!)

When: Saturday, 9 March

Where: Garrawi Park

Time: 6.30 pm

Music: Big Phil and Rexie

CHAPTER FOURTEEN

Sam wakes in the morning to a house that is still and silent. One side of the bed is empty. The place where she lay already cool. He checks the time. Barely six. So she's done a runner to avoid any awkward morning-after socialising. He closes his eyes, remembering. He'd whispered soothing words. Held her fine-boned hands tightly in his great paws. Cupped her pale pixie face and tried to make her see the love in his eyes. In the end, all he could do was to let her talk – spew – until the rage abated and her head cleared enough for the two of them to start sifting through the facts.

If they hadn't been born out of heartbreak, Sam would have relished the halting, tentative revelations. Like someone lifting off dustsheets in a house long locked up, and slowly remembering what had always been there. Which, as it turned out, wasn't much. She knew almost nothing about her mother's life as a young woman. She never met her mother's parents, her grandparents, never heard them discussed. She had no idea where her mother was born, raised or went to school. 'All I know is that I was an unplanned, unwanted late-life baby and my arrival ruined Emily's life.' Over and over, like a bad loop on a CD, Kate came back to that one single fact. 'Well,' he said to her, 'you either let the past dictate the terms or you write your own script.' His words went unheard.

He swings his legs to the floor. Naked, he walks down the hallway to the kitchen. Fills the kettle. While he waits for the water to boil, he studies the enigmatic flotsam from Emily's shabby grey box. The answer is here, he thinks, using a finger to push around one or two pieces. He bends to the task, concentrating hard. Maybe there's a timeline. If he hits on the right order, all will magically be revealed. The kettle clicks off. He sighs with frustration. A heap of mementoes dating back in history. Nonsense to anyone but the owner of them.

He brews a cuppa and carries it into the bathroom, swears when he burns his mouth on the tea. He steps under hot water, turning his back to the spray. Feels a sharp, stinging pain. Yelps. He emerges, wet, to stand in front of the steamy mirror and twists his torso. Red welts crisscross his skin. For a second he feels oddly cheered.

He showers until his skin is lobster red and the pain fades away. Dressed in yesterday's clothes and smarting inwardly from a picture of Sam Scully, a mild-mannered bargeman, trying to pass as a wild crusader in the fight for both Garrawi and Kate, he pulls the bed into order. 'There's no point in being faint-hearted, son; you never know what you're capable of until you put yourself to the test.' The gospel according to his father. Shit, he thinks, slapping his forehead. He closes the door behind him, races down to the pontoon, three steps at a time. He's just remembered an urgent appointment.

Frankie emerges from his boatshed and gives a hoy.

'Not right now, mate. On a mission.' He's due to meet a man called Delaney.

Sam picks Delaney out of the Sunday queue for coffee. A massive man, well past the middle of six feet, with a ruddy complexion that comes from either too much sun or too much booze for too many years, his build runs more towards fat than muscle. His tightly curled fair hair is peppered as grey as his neatly trimmed beard. He wears a baby-pink cotton shirt and drawstring cream linen trousers. A smaller man would have looked foppish. Closer, Sam sees that even if the newspaperman's body is running to seed, his eyes, almost reptilian as he scrutinises the café, the clients, Ettie, miss nothing. Sam can almost hear his brain ticking. Ettie points a finger in Sam's direction. He strides over.

'Scully?'

Sam registers the use of his surname. Journo talk.

'Delaney?'

Sam holds out his huge mitt, which is grabbed by an even heftier one. The two men lock eyes, assessing each other.

(Later, Ettie tells the community it was like looking at a couple of bulls in a ring. 'It felt as though they'd filled every inch of the café,' she explained. 'One wrong move or word, and I got the impression the offender would be shunted onto the back deck and hoisted over the railings. It took a couple of minutes before they each let go of the handshake, the stiffness went out of their shoulders, and their chins stopped pointing towards the ceiling. At that moment, I got started on a couple of mega brekkies because I could sense their backsides were going to be hanging over the edge of our café chairs for most of the day. Thank god it wasn't raining, eh? We'd never have been able to find room for them inside.')

Both men head for a table in the far corner of the deck. 'They got waitresses here or do we order at the counter?'

'You'll have a plate the size of Africa in front of you within about five minutes,' Sam says.

Delaney grins. Drags a small notepad out of his shirt top pocket. He digs deep in a pocket and finds a pencil. 'Just so you know. If I eat, I pay. And if you think a free meal is a peanut kind of bribe I can assure you many people have been persuaded by far less. In fact, it is amazing how little it takes to buy a favour.'

Sam rocks on the legs of his chair. 'Good to hear. Pointless offering you a freebie to our Garrawi fundraiser then. Got seventy-five bucks on you?'

The big man looks startled for a moment. Then he throws back his head and lets loose with a belly laugh loud enough to scare the fingerlings cavorting in the water below. He pulls a ragged leather wallet from his back pocket. Bits and pieces of paper with weird scribblings fall on the table. He fossicks for the cash and slams it under the saltshaker.

'Of course if you'd like to bring someone, that'd be another seventy-five,' Sam says, grinning.

'A wise man knows it's smart to quit while he's ahead, Scully. Now, tell me about Garrawi and why you reckon it ought to be saved. And this better be good because even though I loathe the New Planet Fountain of Youth with a passion I can barely express, there's no point in beating your heads against a brick wall just because a bunch of freedom-loving hippies don't want to lose a prime picnic spot.' He breaks off when Ettie swans up to the table bearing over-laden plates.

'On the house,' Ettie announces, smiling like a lunatic.

'A bill will be fine.'

Ettie's face falls. She goes bright pink. Breaks out in a sweat. Begins to pant.

'Easy on, Ettie,' Sam says, worried she's about to pass out. 'Man's got his principles, that's all. A rare and wonderful thing if you think about it.'

Flustered, Ettie looks around, avoiding Delaney's eyes: 'Oh, yes, of course. Coffee? What kind?'

Back inside the café, Ettie rushes to the office chair and falls in a heap, unable to shake the feeling the world is about to end. She wants to laugh and cry at the same time; her body temperature is ratcheting up towards boiling point. She wonders, not for the first time, if she is going mad.

'Lord, Ettie, you feel like you're burning up. Are you ill?' Kate asks, placing a comforting hand on Ettie's shoulder.

'Look! Over there! That bloody rat is still in residence. See the poo? God, we've set traps, Jimmy's taking the garbage every night. I don't know what else I can do.'

'It's just one tiny pellet of poo and, by the look of it, I think that rat's not long for this world anyway. No need to get so worked up, Ettie.'

Ettie puts her face in her hands, eyes closed: 'I don't know what's wrong with me,' she says softly. 'Maybe I'm terrified because life is just so bloody good I can't help wondering when the axe is going to fall. Know what I mean?'

Kate squats in front of her partner, folds Ettie's hands in hers. She forces her friend to look her in the eyes. 'Your world's gone pear-shaped before, right?'

Ettie nods.

'You've always survived. Right?'

Another mute nod.

'So worrying about what might happen in the future is pointless. And first of all, nothing's going to go pear-shaped. Trust me. Secondly, in the totally unlikely event that it does, you are part of a community that loves you deeply so it will take care of you the way you've taken care of every lost soul for so many years. And thirdly, I think you should have a check-up. I reckon your hormones are all over the place and they need sorting out.'

'Hormones? What have they got to do with anything?' she says dismissively. Her voice is firmer now, the heat draining from her face. 'How about you fix the coffees for those two blokes on the deck while my hormones re-align themselves?'

Kate pushes to her feet. 'Whatever you say . . .'

'And charge that Delaney bloke top dollar. We'll show him what happens to suspicious-minded cynics who turn down the kindness of strangers because they can't believe anyone does anything without expecting something in return. Where's that poor man lived all his life if that's the way he thinks?'

'He's a journalist, Ettie, remember?'

'That's no excuse. You were a journo, too, and you're . . .' Ettie's voice trails off. She looks around, flustered. 'Right, time to peel the carrots.'

Under Ettie's watchful eye, Kate makes two mugs of frothy coffee, each with a double shot, and delivers them to the deck.

'What are they talking about?' Ettie asks, when Kate returns. 'Oh, damn, I've lost count.'

'Couldn't tell you. They went quiet as soon as I got close. Lost count of what?'

'The number of peels off this carrot. Eleven or twelve, I think. Definitely not thirteen. I would've remembered thirteen. Thirteen is unlucky and I would've done one more to make it fourteen. Yep. Eleven. Got to be.' She is distracted, anxious, staring at the peeler like it holds a dark secret.

Kate gives her a queer look. 'There's a magic number for peeling carrots?'

Caught out, Ettie laughs nervously. ''Course not. Time and motion study, that's all.'

'You need a visit to the doctor, Ettie, and the sooner the better.'

Scully and Delaney, as they become known forever after – like two cops out of a TV sitcom – finish their meeting by mid-afternoon. They mutually agree that a member of the community should enrol for flying lessons in one of the umpteen city courses run by the New Planet Fountain of Youth while the newspaperman will cover the flare safety demonstration rally on Sunday evening.

Delaney emphasises the fact that news is an unpredictable and ephemeral creature and the story could very well be blown out of the water by a leadership spill in the nation's capital or a bikie raid on a rival group that ends up a horrific bloodbath. 'Luck of the game, Scully,' he explains. 'I've sweated over noble stories until they were word perfect and still seen them tossed aside without apology for news of a half-baked celebrity on a drug-fuelled spree. It's a national sport to blame the media for dishing up trash but it sells in droves, which ultimately reinforces the practice. I've been in the business a long, long time, and, without wanting to sound like a pessimist, it takes a hero who never loses his moral compass to stand up to the pressure of circulation figures and mostly, the general population gets what it deserves.'

'Jeez, mate,' Sam says, feeling his spirits sinking lower and lower. 'What keeps you going?'

The big man's florid face breaks into a grin. 'Because every so often you win a round against seemingly unbeatable odds and you make a massive difference to the little man, who has no power, no weapons and no way of fighting for what he knows in his gut is right. You live for the golden moments, Scully, and you never, ever let up the pressure on genuine bastards.'

'Good to have you onside,' Scully says sticking out his hand for the second time.

The pleasure goes out of Delaney's demeanour. 'I don't take sides, Scully. I look at the facts and if there's even a whiff of corruption, I dig in. But sides? No. First rule of journalism? Get the facts, remain impartial. Might sound old-fashioned but it works for me.'

'Siobhan said you were a straight-up bloke.'

Delaney leans back in his fragile chair, which creaks alarmingly under his massive bulk, shoving his notebook back in his shirt pocket. 'So how is Siobhan? No one could believe she dumped a stellar career in radio to sit on a deck watching boats chug past in a rundown little coastal retreat. She's much too young to throw it all in.'

Sam feels the hairs on the back of his neck beginning to stick up straight as toothpicks; his eyes take on a distant, glassy quality. He's about to let loose with a harangue about the glories of Cook's Basin but Siobhan's words come crashing into his mind: 'Never piss off the press, Sam. They go away and never return.' He curbs the impulse, sets a friendly smile on his face and offers to take Delaney on a quick tour of the area. 'Sun's out, mate, and so are we. Shouldn't take more than an hour to circumnavigate Cutter Island and snookle into a couple of the Cook's Basin bays for a squizz at some pristine rainforest gullies where waterfalls and lyrebirds make music together. Angels couldn't do better. Trust me.'

Delaney considers his notebook like it holds the answer. 'Works for me,' he says, snapping it shut.

'Give me a minute. I'll ask Ettie to sling together a few supplies and a couple of frigidly colds and we'll be on our way.' He heads for the café, pulling his mobile phone out of his pocket. 'Jimmy!' he shouts loud enough to be heard on the Island without the benefit of technology, 'start up the glorious and voluptuous *Mary Kay* and get your skinny backside over to The Briny Café. We're going on a cruise.' He pauses: 'No, mate, no need to bring Longfellow's dinner. We'll be home before then.' Another pause. 'A cruise can last a year or an hour, Jimmy. There are no rules. Now on your way.' He storms through the back door, a man with a purpose. 'Ettie, a picnic for three humans and our four-pawed friend. Quick as you can, love. I'm going to show Delaney the world of magic and wonderment that we're all fighting for.'

Back on the deck, he gives Delaney a look of pure innocence. 'So the lovely Siobhan retired too soon, you reckon. At what age would that have been, do you think?'

Delaney erupts in laughter: 'If I told you, I'd have to kill you.'

Ettie flings together a basket crammed with some of The Briny's finest food – smoked salmon sandwiches, chicken cold-cuts marinated in lime, chilli and ginger, cherry tomatoes skewered with velvety baby bocconcini and basil and swizzled in olive oil and balsamic vinegar. A tub of tiger prawns. She adds fresh baguettes, a hunk of parmesan, a couple of firm, early season pears, and a slab of her famous double chocolate and hazelnut brownie, slipping in a small container of raspberry sauce and clotted cream as well. She races up to her penthouse and hauls out a few enamel plates, some picnic cutlery and an icebox and finds a chilled bottle of white wine in the fridge. She takes a second to run through the provisions, then adds a bottle of Shiraz. Delaney has the look of a man who's enjoyed a few good reds in his life. In a flash, she strips off her café chef's clobber and changes into a swirling cotton dress that matches the blue of the sky. She slaps a huge straw hat on her head before making her way downstairs.

'Call the chef, will you, Kate? See if he has time to get into his svelte little runabout to pick me up and join the *Mary Kay* on the water. He loves a picnic. You're in charge. I'm going to make sure the journalist is spoiled rotten by the kind of hospitality that Cook's Basin is famous for – whether he likes it or not. Oh, and get on the phone to alert everyone who's around that we're out and about with the journo so no serious rule-breaking in public, OK?'

Kate stands still, in shock. Ettie grins. 'Yep. I'm leaving you on your own. Time to muscle up, love.'

At the last minute, she scoops up a large hunk of banana cake for Jimmy and a small tub of shredded chicken for the pup. Satisfied, she marches onto the deck with her basket just as Jimmy brings the *Mary Kay* alongside with a feather touch equal to Sam's. 'What's a picnic without a bit of female company?' she announces to a bemused Delaney. Without waiting for a reply, she steps on board the pitted timber deck and heads for the captain's cabin. She stows the picnic basket on Sam's comfy banquette, where he's been known to do a lot of deep thinking with his eyes closed on very hot afternoons. 'We need a couple of cushions and a blanket, Sam. They still stored in the hold?'

Sam might be on his own barge, but he nevertheless feels as though he's lost control of the agenda. He nods with a shrug anyway. Sometimes it's smarter to go with the flow.

'Cast off, Jimmy and we're away.'

Jimmy skids up to Sam with a puzzled look: 'We never tied on, Sam. Y'all just jumped on board so quick.'

'Right. All good then,' Sam says, unable to shake the feeling he's lagging behind everyone else. 'Er, Jimmy, this is Paul Delaney . . .'

'Are ya gunna help us save Garrawi?' Jimmy asks, eagerly thrusting out his bony hand in a formal *how do you do*. 'Are ya gunna look after the cheese tree, then?'

Delaney, probably used to people treading warily around him, is visibly taken aback by Jimmy's earnest forthrightness and flounders for a minute or two. Then he recovers and places his huge mitt on the boy's scrawny shoulder. 'How about you tell me all about the cheese tree, Jimmy?'

Jimmy looks towards his captain, ecstatic: 'I'm helpin' the cause, Sam, aren't I?'

'You're a top ambassador, mate.'

Delaney tries to steer Jimmy towards the cabin but the kid points at the bow of the *Mary Kay*. 'Best seat in the house up there. Me and Longfellow, that's our possie. Ya know much about barges, Mr Delaney?'

Delaney smiles. 'Let's talk about the cheese tree first. Then you can tell me all about barges.'

'They're gunna cut it down, Mr Delaney. They're gunna rip off the hands, arms and legs and then cut through the tummy until the tree keels over dead and gone. Me dad proposed to me mum under that tree. 'Course he buggered off after a while but me mum's never forgotten him on his knee and shit-scared she was gunna turn him down . . .'

Delaney reaches for his notebook.

'I can go slower,' Jimmy offers, seeing him making a few scribbles. 'Just tell me if ya can't keep up.'

Hours later, after Paul Delaney has been introduced to the famous cheese tree and when Jimmy and the mutt are home in bed, Ettie, Marcus and Sam sit on the chef's deck in the warmth of the summer night.

'Delaney's travelled to the Planet's headquarters in South America,' Sam tells them. 'He's seen what goes on first hand and he says it terrifies him.'

Ettie, who's had a delicious afternoon break from the café, tips the last of the white wine into her glass, knowing she's going to regret it in the morning but not giving a damn anyway. 'Long way to go for a story, wasn't it?' she asks.

'Nothing to do with work. The cult got its hooks into his niece. He found the girl, starry-eyed, completely brainwashed and running around barefoot and dressed in long white robes with a whole lot of other white-robed chanting and giggling idiots. She didn't want a bar of him or what she called his boring middle-class values. Delaney reckons there are more than two hundred Australians living in the commune, handing over every penny they've got and there's more bad shit going on there than most of us could imagine.'

The chef breaks in: 'This niece, she was a wild child perhaps?'

'Not sure, chef, never asked him. But there'll be no rest for Delaney until he brings her home. The girl's mother is Delaney's sister. Kid's an only child. The sister's divorced. Right now, he's trying to persuade his local federal member to come with him to see for himself what's going on. Delaney reckons it's time the government intervened because he can smell a tragedy of epic proportions – his words, not mine – just waiting to happen. He's also trying to get a US congressman to take a look. Apparently the commune is up to the rafters with young Americans also searching for the meaning of life.'

'Ah, the age-old question,' says the chef, shaking his head. 'What is it all about? At my age, of course, you understand. It is about love.' He reaches for Ettie and encases her hand in both of his.

The trio is silent while the moon plays chords on the water. Somewhere, an owl hoots in time with the shushing sea and the bush whispers soothingly.

Ettie says: 'When Jimmy talked about the cheese tree, I nearly cried. He sees it as a human being, Marcus, a person with arms and legs and a giant torso.'

They talk, then, about the sudden light that switched on in Paul Delaney's bright blue eyes when he first met Jimmy.

'I swear, chef, his nose tilted into the wind like a dog on a fresh scent. It took him two seconds flat to suss out Jimmy's, er, unique way of seeing and interacting with the landscape and the community. He gently eased stories out of the kid that none of us even knew. Said he's got his column for Saturday thanks to Jimmy. Reckons it's a perfect lead into a follow-up story on the flare safety demonstration on Sunday.'

'This man, you trust him to be kind to the boy, yes?' the chef asks. 'Jimmy is not like others . . .'

'This man, chef, may talk like he doesn't have a heart but if you want my sometimes dodgy opinion he's all heart.'

When it is late, Ettie excuses herself. Marcus walks with Sam along the silvery timber planks to the pontoon where his boat is tied. Halfway, Marcus hesitates and reaches out to touch Sam's arm.

'You all right, mate?' Sam asks, alarmed.

'Yes, yes, of course. I am wonderful for a man of my age. But you see, it is Ettie. I am worried. She is so tired and perhaps if I may reveal a fact that many men are uncomfortable to discuss?'

Sam nods, but inside he's squirming. Confessions among men are unfamiliar territory.

'Sometimes,' Marcus says quietly, 'instead of lying close, like two spoons yes? Instead of this, she moves away from me in the bed.'

Relieved, Sam laughs out loud: 'It's been a stinking hot summer, you idiot,' he says. 'Women feel the heat more than men. Trust me, mate, Ettie looks at you as though you've dropped down from the land where Greek gods were born.'

Marcus smiles, but it is thin, uncertain. 'Something is wrong. Yesterday, I am hanging out the washing. I am, after all, a domesticated man. She snatches it from my hands –'

'Helping you out, chef, that's all.'

'Because I am attaching a blue and red peg on the same shirt.'

'Eh?'

'The pegs, which are all doing the same fine job, she wants them to match. This is strange, no?'

Sam gives the chef an understanding pat. 'Women, mate. They have their little routines. I once knew a dame who couldn't sleep unless the pillowslip ends faced out from the centre of the bed. Seriously weird, eh? Knew another girl who would never wear black shoes on Friday. Never did find out what that was about.'

Sam can see that Marcus is unconvinced.

'A month ago, the pegs were not of any interest to her,' he insists.

'It's nothing serious, mate. Promise you.'

'I am afraid, my friend, that it is very serious.'

CHAPTER FIFTEEN

Paul Delaney's column about Jimmy and the fight to save Garrawi is published on Saturday morning. The community reads it and weeps. Young Jimmy MacFarlane's innocent and unclouded vision cuts to the core of what is precious. Islanders are reminded of the many valid and valuable reasons why they choose to live in a water-access only community where sometimes completing the smallest tasks requires five times more effort than it would if they were living on the mainland. But every ounce of sweat and grunt is worth it. Jimmy, whose passion for all wild things including deadly snakes and funnel web spiders shines through, becomes an overnight hero.

The Briny Café has a record day with hungry and thirsty rubberneckers who have come from far and wide to see what all the fuss is about. Sam invites Kate on another picnic to celebrate. 'Weather's going to hold,' he says. 'Opportunity knocks.'

*

Frankie spots Sam heading up the steps to pick up Kate and calls him over. 'This better be good, mate. Women don't like to be kept waiting.'

In the bush, cicadas yammer hysterically, white cockatoos argue their way to bed somewhere high in the National Park. Night comes down like a hot, heavy blanket. Inside the boatshed in Oyster Bay under sickly green-tinged fluorescent lights Sam listens. His face turns black with fury.

'What kind of money did he throw at you?' he demands.

Frankie scratches his head under his cap. 'Free rent for two years.'

'Ah jeez. But what's the point of that? You've got a boatshed that as far as I know you own outright, seeing as how you bought it before god was born. Why mess with something if it ain't broke?'

'Lowdon is talking about a working boatshed attached to a marina. Berths and moorings for forty small boats, twenty moorings for larger yachts and stink boats and a new fibreglass tender boat with a 120-horsepower outboard to transfer boaties from the shore. It's a bloody good deal. All those Islanders without private jetties will have a safe, convenient berth for their tinnies. A blessing for young mums and their babies.'

'S'pose he's going to sling a fistful of cash into your back pocket, too?' Sam is aggressive, accusing.

Frankie's eyes go cold. 'Watch your words, Sam. I'm talking about a legitimate business deal here. Two years to get it up and running and then a market rent. You can't ask for much fairer than that.'

Sam slumps. Wonders what dream world he's been living in. Money talks. Men like Lowdon always get what they want in the end. He gets the sickening feeling that he and the community are living in la-la land if they think they can beat lucrative bribes that are just honest enough to skate across the line. 'So you've said yes, eh?'

Frankie shakes his head. 'Haven't said yes and I haven't said no.'

Sam feels a surge of hope. His eyes catch fire. 'What can we do to convince you to turn it down, mate? What? Give us the right of reply.'

Frankie picks up a screwdriver and walks over to Kate's desk, standing untouched in a back corner with one door hanging open sadly. He begins to pry away the backboard. Sam holds his impatience down with an effort. The backboard loosens. Frankie drops the screwdriver back on the workbench.

'I'm going to look at every angle. Make sure that if I sign up there aren't any nasty surprises waiting. I'll let you know what I decide.' He picks up the screwdriver again. 'You want to call Kate? Ask her to come down. It's time we looked at this desk.'

Sam reaches for his mobile. 'She's on her way,' he tells Frankie. And another picnic bites the dust.

'What do you think?' Kate asks, hands on her hips, circling the desk that Sam and Frankie have pulled away from the wall. It stands mutely, sagging shabbily under the pressure of age.

'The timber is still solid,' Frankie replies, running his hands expertly over the grain. 'One pane of glass has to be replaced. It's very old, maybe eighty to one hundred years. It will take a while to find the right glass.' He opens the desktop, releasing smells of timber, dust, must, olden days. The two men watch Kate almost reel with nostalgia.

'Stamps in this pigeon hole,' she whispers, pointing with her index finger. 'Pencils here, staples, paper clips, envelopes here, here and here. Three bottles of ink in this corner. Indian was black and used for accounts. Swan was blue and used only for letters. My father thought it was bad manners to correspond using a ball-point pen.'

'And the third was red?'

'To be avoided at any cost.'

'He's dead, then, your father?'

'A long time ago.'

Frankie returns to safer ground. 'The hinges are loose but they'll come up good after they're cleaned and polished. The desk is oak, scratched but strong. Should restore like a dream. But this will have to go.' He taps the backboard. 'Masonite. Tough but cheap shit put on some time later.' He grunts. 'Strange,' he says, frowning. He closes one eye, peers into the skinny dark space he's created. 'Look – the original backboard is still here.' He works faster now. His hands are steady, careful. He's more curious than expectant. Tacks release with a small popping sound. 'A mystery, eh?' Frankie murmurs. Sam comes closer. Frankie eases the rubbishy board away from the frame. Lets it fall to the floor. Steps back, one eye shut. Finds a penlight in his pocket. Shines it over the surface in slow sweeping motions. 'Look, here's the reason.' He runs his hand along the timber like it's expensive fabric, squinting through one eye again. 'A secret cavity,' he says. 'You'd never find it if you weren't an expert.'

Afraid Kate's in for another round of crushing disappointment, Sam says: 'Could be anything. Could be nothing.' Under her thin cotton shirt, he swears he can see her heart beating faster.

'See the edges of the cut? There's a tiny fraction of shift in the grain. Shows up because this is a single slab of timber from a great old tree.' Once more, Frankie touches the wood, almost reverently. 'The desk may look simple but there's nothing shoddy about it. Built by a craftsman.'

'I thought people used to hide things behind a brick in the chimney or in old jam jars on the mantelpiece,' Kate says. She looks and sounds bizarrely chirrupy, flirty. She's all over the place, Sam thinks.

'Only in movies. Bad ones.' He circles the desk, wolfish under the green light. Kate bangs the backboard with the palm of her hand. Frankie shakes his head, takes her arm and pulls her gently but firmly away. 'It's always better to think first. Force, which can do more damage than good, is the last resort.' He shoves his cap higher on his head, rubs his forehead like he's trying to get rid of a nagging headache. Steps back for a better overall look and trips on the edge of the Masonite. He picks it up and leans it tidily against the wall.

'No lock, no release, no hinges,' he murmurs. 'So this means we must approach the problem from the inside.' He moves in slow motion.

Kate spins in frustration. Covers it with a thin grin. She says: 'I've cleaned and wiped it from top to bottom, Frankie. There's nothing inside. Truly. I would have seen it.'

The shipwright ignores her and opens the bevelled glass doors. 'They were so precious once,' he says.

Kate looks at him blankly. 'Desks?' she asks.

'Books,' Frankie says. He slips his hand inside the shelving, presses against the timber at the top of the framework. His eyes are closed, his head turned slightly to bring one ear closer to the action, like he's listening for a heartbeat. 'Ah,' he says. There's the sound of a ping. Kate races around the back.

'Don't touch,' warns Frankie, following her at a normal pace. 'Whatever you do, don't touch.' He takes out the penlight for a second time. 'Maybe there's a fortune in jewels? A treasure most of us dream about?' He's teasing. He examines the four sides of the cutting then places a finger in different places, pressing gently.

'Do you need any help?' Sam asks, unable to bear watching the fluctuations of hope and despair on Kate's face, hoping to speed up the process.

'Patience, patience.' He hits the spot. The wood makes a slight cracking sound. Frankie eases the cover off. Stands back. 'Might as well see what we've got,' he says.

Kate looks as though she could throw up all over Frankie's neatly swept cement slab. Sam watches her swallow. She reaches inside. Withdraws a smeary plastic bag.

'A bunch of old paperwork,' Kate says, feigning disinterest.

'So no diamonds, no gold, then,' Frankie says, sounding disappointed.

To make the point, she picks up the pouch and shakes it. 'Nope, nothing but papers. Probably a stack of Emily's old bills. She had a habit of hiding them from my father.' She places the bag on Frankie's workbench, returns to the matter of restoration. Sam moves towards them. 'Don't touch,' she snaps. So not just a bunch of old bills, he thinks, jerking backwards like she's zapped him with an electric prong.

'You reckon you can make this old desk glow again?' she asks.

'It will take time. Each piece must be removed, sanded, oiled and polished. Time costs.' He raises his eyebrows, looks her square in the eye.

'This desk is precious to me, Frankie. Whatever you need to do is OK.'

Sam moves outside the spooky green satellite glow of the boat-shed. Listens to the swallowing sound of tiny waves breaking on shore. A fish jumps. The night is clammy. People keep secrets, he thinks, because they are afraid of triggering havoc. No one keeps a good secret. Not for long, anyway. Sticking your nose where it's really not wanted is a good way of getting it chopped off, as his mother used to say. He feels a familiar surge of dread. He turns at the sound of Kate's footsteps. She slips her arm through his and guides him towards the pontoon. They sit side-by-side, their legs dangling in cool water.

'I could see him there, you know?'

'Your father?'

'Every night before dinner, he'd do the accounts and balance the till from the grocery shop, placing the cash in a bag to take to the bank in the morning. Notes tied with a rubber band. I can't remember how old I was when my father found a secret wad of unpaid accounts stuffed in a jam tin and pushed into the deepest corner of the pantry. Accounts Emily had run up in the city. He was looking for something sweet to put on his toast. It was before they sold the shop, anyway. He was appalled. Humiliated is probably closer to the truth. In country towns, small businesses skate on a thin line between surviving to trade another day or bankruptcy and a family thrown out on the street, so owing money was on a par with paedophilia. Neighbours stopped talking to you, invitations to dinner or tennis dried up, no one even knocked on your door for a donation for the local Scouts group. You didn't buy what you didn't have the money to pay for.'

'They're a bunch of old accounts then, eh?'

Kate avoids the question. 'Emily hid bills, as if that somehow made the debt disappear. She seriously believed it was OK for others to go without, but completely impossible for her. Why would she even contemplate putting someone else's welfare before her own? Law according to Emily.'

'Want me to hang around while you check it out?'

'Thanks. I'm good. No cowardly hanging back this time, promise you.' She smiles, calm now, as though she's passed through the eye of the storm.

He gives her shoulder a brotherly pat. Pushes to his feet, aware she's determined to go it alone on the big stuff again, and he's been given his marching orders.

'Oy!' Frankie's silhouette waves them back to the boatshed. Sam reaches for Kate's hand. Hauls her up.

'Thought you'd like to know straight away. I've found another hidey-hole. Don't get too excited. No jewels. A few old letters, that's all.'

Frankie shows them a second secret cavity behind the first. 'A false back. Genius. You find the first stash, figure that's it, and move on. Just like we did.'

*

Sam makes his way along the jetty to the *Mary Kay*. Every time he feels he's getting closer to her, it triggers a response that catapults him back to square one. That bloody yo-yo syndrome, he thinks, not to mention the freaking twig. He suddenly feels too exhausted to think straight.

CHAPTER SIXTEEN

On Sunday morning Sam wakes with a bad feeling in his gut. His house is already an oven. It would be irresponsible madness if the community went ahead with the flare safety demonstration. Less than a week without rain and already the air crackles with the kind of moisture-less heat that gives a tiny unnoticed spark from a backyard barbecue the power to explode into catastrophic force. They'd all be wiped out in minutes.

He makes a cuppa, wandering around naked. No point in saving a park, he figures, if fire wipes out every house on the Island. He shrugs. He's a practical man who knows how to prioritise. He is also painfully aware of how it feels to push the limits and wear the consequences if events go spectacularly belly-up. He wraps a towel around his waist and takes his tea onto the deck to check the sky. A squillion mares' tails swipe the early-morning blue. He smiles inwardly. If the air keeps moving fast in the upper layers of the atmosphere, there's a chance a storm will blow up and bring a cool change. It could all work out yet.

He sips his tea, wondering if the gods land on your side if your motives are pure and unselfish. Wonders too, if the reverse is true. But pulls up short when he thinks of the New Planet Fountain of Youth. Worth a billion dollars and flourishing without a philanthropic instinct to be found. He tosses the dregs over the side and wanders back into the house, consoling himself with a fact he knows for sure is true even if science with all its tests and calculations sneers in his face: what goes around, comes around. Or as his mum drummed into him *you reap what you sow.* An image of Kate creeps into his mind, her face firm and serious: Steer clear of the clichés, Sam. They're a lazy way of making a point. Well, it is OK for her to think that way: words are – or were – her livelihood. He's just a bargeman who knows good from bad and wants to lead a blameless life. No rocket science involved. Shit, another cliché.

He gives up digging deep and heads for the shower, turns the cold on with a blast and steps under a stinging waterfall that's lukewarm from the early-morning sun hitting his tank full on. Yep, it's hot as the hammers today, he says out loud, taking pleasure this time as yet another cliché rolls off his tongue with ease. He wonders if Frankie has made a decision yet.

The plans are for the community to line up their boats at Triangle ferry wharf at seven pm. Theoretically, there's still enough light to stay safely on course but by the time they're organised it will be dark enough to make a maximum impact with the flares. Sam also wants to do a quick check to list the seriously dodgy vessels that haven't a hope of completing the course without sinking or breaking down. He'll assign people with fully functioning boats and enough horsepower in their motors to tow, as guardians. He mentally maps out the day ahead until he's satisfied that, weather permitting, it should go like a dream.

He makes his way down the steps to his tinny and sets off for a substantial breakfast at The Briny Café. He's going to need his strength. Ettie might even persuade him to eat a little of that spinach she insists on loading onto his plate even though he's told her a thousand times that he's long past his growing years and green stuff is for rabbits. With the exception of peas. Nothing beats a handful of peas alongside four lamb loin chops – their fatty tails crisped to a salted golden crunch – and a serious mound of creamy potato mashed with lashings of butter and not a drop of milk. He feels his taste buds slip into overdrive and saliva fill his mouth. He could wipe out a coffee or two and three helpings of Ettie's spicy baked beans with a fried egg on the top, a hint of greens to lift the look of the plate and about eight slices of toasted sourdough that's solid enough to hold a serious amount of butter without going soggy. By the time he ties up at the end of the deck, he's sorted. He bangs his way into the café, gives Ettie a smooch and a quick swing around the kitchen and places his order with all the fanfare of a prime minister announcing a major, guaranteed vote-winning initiative.

'We're out of spicy beans and I haven't had time to make a new batch,' Ettie says.

Sam is crestfallen. Without expecting any success, he mutters something about a few lamb chops.

'No worries, love,' Ettie agrees. 'How about poached eggs, fried tomatoes and a heap of spuds seared in butter in a hot pan with a little onion, capsicum and chilli thrown in?'

'You're the answer to every man's dream, love. Er, you couldn't whip up a few peas and a little mash, could you?'

'No,' Ettie says firmly. 'This is a take it or leave it, once only, offer.'

'Good as gold,' he says in a hurry, remembering Delaney's sound advice that a wise man knows that it's smart to quit while he's ahead. His mobile phone goes off in his pocket. Sam checks the screen. The loyal Cook's Basin anti-development protesters have woken up and, given the weather, they're edgy and looking for direction. Sam tells them it's all systems go until they meet at Triangle, which is where they will assess the climatic conditions and come to a democratic consensus.

The Islander with a legendary thirst takes umbrage: 'What the hell does that mean? You're getting a bit high fallutin' with your vocabulary, mate.'

'Be there and we'll see what happens,' Sam explains, patiently.

'Orright then. All you had to do was say so.'

Ettie delivers Sam's breakfast with a flourish. 'Have you seen Kate? She hasn't turned up yet.'

Sam's gut somersaults. 'You called her?'

'No answer on the landline or her mobile.' Ettie is puzzled. 'Can't understand it. We made a deal. If she can't make it, she calls. If today is like yesterday, we're going to be under pressure from the word go.'

'Put my brekky in the oven to keep warm. I'll do a quick dash.'

'No, love, I'm sure it's all OK. Eat your food while it's hot. If she's not here in the next few minutes, I'll call Jenny to fill in. It might teach her that rules are rules. And,' she adds with a grin, 'she can dock her own pay.'

Ettie disappears inside the café. Sam drags out his mobile and dials Fast Freddy. 'You pick up an Oyster Bay resident in the early hours, mate?'

'Kate, ya mean? Yeah. She was off to the airport. In a stinking hurry and all revved up like it was life or death. Never seen her so nervy.'

Sam ends the call. Pushes Jenny's number. 'Get over to The Briny asap, love. Ettie needs you.' The phone goes dead in his ear. Five minutes later, he sees Jenny's tinny flying across the water from the Island. Good communities, he thinks, know how to take care of each other and never, ever worry about the details. Kate, he realises, may never get it. For once, he feels sadder for her than for himself.

By lunchtime, blue sky is a fading memory and the sky is bruised and overcast. Heavy rain will mean a washout. Even though the community is hell-bent on saving Garrawi, postponements kill enthusiasm and douse the spark of spontaneity. Sam keeps his fingers crossed, trusting luck to hold off the storm until well after dark. He checks four weather sites. They're all over the place. Anything could happen.

At four pm Delaney arrives at The Briny Café, this time wearing a baby blue shirt with his khaki linen trousers. He looks uncomfortably hot, with large rings of perspiration darkening the fabric under his arms. His trousers give the impression they've been through a mangle. Clive, the photographer, is as ruddy-faced as the reporter. 'Do you reckon Ettie would be able to find a couple of icy cold beers?' Delaney asks, straight off, throwing himself into a chair on the back deck with reckless abandon considering his size and the relative fragility of the furniture. 'Maybe throw in a burger for Clive and a salad of some kind for me? Almost didn't come. The weather. What do you think?'

'Good as gold,' Sam fibs, fingers crossed like he's a five-year-old kid.

Ettie and Jenny appear with a platter of cold-cuts, cheeses and grilled vegetables and a tray of cold beers. 'A few snackettes for the workers,' Ettie says brightly. 'Paid for by the café, if you're worried about ethics, Mr Delaney. An army marches on its stomach. Napoleon, I think.'

'Well, the French understand food better than anyone else . . .' He reaches for a beer with one hand, a snack with the other.

Ettie looks like she's come out of a fierce stoush victorious.

Half an hour later, fed and refreshed, the men step on board the *Mary Kay* for the quick trip across the water to Triangle wharf. The air is still and sharp with electricity. The sky is the colour of an eggplant. Sam begins to worry. He thinks about bringing forward the time of the demonstration to beat the storm. Delaney settles himself comfortably on the bow in a director's chair Sam's loaded on deck. Clive is already snapping, his eye glued to the lens, treading clumsily around chains, cleats and coiled rope. Sam considers warning him about the lack of lifelines, pointing out he should be careful he doesn't topple overboard, but holds back. Clive gives the impression of a man who has learned how to take care of himself the hard way.

'You covered many demonstrations like this?' Sam asks, as much to lure the photographer into the safety of the cabin as anything else.

'Like this?' Clive looks astonished by the question. 'Just how many little water-access backwaters do you think there are around town?'

Backwater? He swallows a retort. 'Yeah. Gotcha. Dumb question. Anything you need, just ask. I'm giving you Jimmy, my first mate, as an aide. He's a good kid. Got a real thirst for knowledge so gear up for a few questions here and there.'

'He the kid Delaney wrote about on Saturday?'

'Yeah.'

'Fine piece. One of Delaney's best. Handled right, Jimmy could be a star. Get him a site on YouTube promoting products. He's got an unforgettable face and a turn of phrase that could sell anything.'

'He is a star, mate, in all the ways that genuinely count.' Sam starts the engine and listens for the diesel thrum to settle into a smooth rhythm before he pushes the throttle forward. The canary-yellow hull (homage to his parents) glides over the water. He steers around yachts on their moorings, feeling a cool afternoon breeze kick in from the north-east. If it freshens quickly, there's a small chance it will hold back the storm looming in the west. Up ahead, he sees Jimmy and Longfellow waving madly from the wharf. Jimmy has outdone himself in a costume of lime green and brilliant orange. His feet, encased in silver shoes, are hippity-hopping with excitement on the weathered timber planks.

'That's Jimmy,' he tells Clive, with a hint of pride in his voice. 'And the black-and-white mutt glued to his ankles is

Longfellow. Hope you like dogs, mate, 'cause the two of them are inseparable.'

But Clive is already out the wheelhouse door, his lens nestled in the palm of his left hand to reduce the rock of the barge, his right index finger on the shutter, lining up a shot of Jimmy and his faithful companion. Sam feels a twinge of unease. It's that bloody invisible enemy, he thinks, the one you never see coming that does all the damage. Jimmy a media star? Open the doors to the bigger world and all of a sudden life gets complicated.

He ties up at Triangle and checks his watch. Plenty of time.

At five pm the old *Seagull* comes alongside the *Mary Kay* to offloads its passengers. They step from ferry to barge to wharf, which violates every safety regulation in the book. The skipper announces he's calling it quits. 'Any bastard who needs a ride can hop the flotilla for a freebie,' he says.

'What about the parade, mate? Aren't you going to be in it?' Sam asks.

Chris looks at him as though he's lost his marbles. Uses his foot to fend off from the *Mary Kay*. 'The *Seagull*'s a tightly woven pack of toothpicks, mate, held together with more faith than finesse. One spark from a belligerent flare and *poof*! Gone in a flash with me on board.'

Clive crosses from the barge to the ferry in a single step: 'Lovely old boat. A real classic. Reckon I could get a shot of you at the helm?'

Chris gives him the same look he's just chucked in Sam's direction. 'No,' he replies flatly.

'Lucky most old fellas aren't like you or I'd be out of business,' Clive mutters. The old ferry master disappears back into the wheelhouse, one shoulder tilted towards the ground, the other hoisted skywards, his legs bowed like two sides of a melon, slightly unsteady as though the sea is pitching hard under his heavy feet. At the last minute, he sticks his head outside and addresses Clive, who hasn't moved: 'If you're stayin' on board, mate, you'll need to buy an overnight ticket.' He revs the engine. Clive leaps aboard the *Mary Kay* before the distance between the vessels becomes more life threatening than athletic.

Sam explains: 'He doesn't want anyone from the Maritime Services Board getting a squiz at any of a hundred safety violations.'

'Ah.' Clive nods.

Sam spends the final hour before mustering time checking hoses and pumps in case of emergency. The weather is stable, the sea breeze carrying a bit of bite and forcing the storm clouds into a holding position. With luck, they'll make it. No bastard's turned up early so getting the parade under way ahead of schedule isn't an option. He starts splicing rope to make a few ties for the crucifix bollards, keeping busy. He's a patient man, lord knows, but he's never been much good at sitting around doing nothing. Time drifts by; the hands on his watch creep slowly towards seven o'clock. The *Mary Kay* rocks under a quickening sea. Not bouncy enough to catapult a few leaky tinnies straight to the ocean bed, though, so his luck is still holding.

He's suddenly conscious of an eerie quietness on board. He puts down the rope and stands up, looking around.

'Jimmy?' he calls out. Puzzled, he wanders the deck, which is ridiculous because he can see quite clearly that he's alone. He looks towards the shore, wondering if the indefatigable Clive has dragged everyone off on a photographic mission to capture the increasingly legendary cheese tree. There's not a soul in sight. Jeez, he thinks, it's almost starting time. Even allowing for the local tendency to arrive late, the protesters are pushing the limits. He pulls his battle plan from his back pocket. According to the list of definite starters, the ferry wharf should be six deep with more than one hundred tinnies. And that's not counting the yachts, stink boats and working barges.

He feels the beginnings of panic followed quickly by despair. Lowdon's got to them, he thinks. Lowdon and the freaking black cockroaches with their shiny black glasses and evil smirks have somehow put the pressure on and everyone's done a runner. Christ, there's not even a tear-away kid to be seen tossing a footy on the bottom track. Irrationally, he thinks of the Pied Piper piping the children of Hamelin away forever and even though he tells himself he's being stupid, he can't shake a black feeling of dread. Where are the kids? He pulls out his phone. Calls Jimmy. The call goes to message bank. He calls Delaney, Ettie, Marcus. Same result. He spins on one foot. It's seven o'clock. Too late to hang around, too late to go off investigating. He'll go it alone. There's no other way.

He unties the *Mary Kay* from the ferry wharf, his eyes wet with disappointment. For a second he can't remember which way the parade was meant to go – clockwise or anti-clockwise. He shakes his head to clear it. Clockwise. Yeah.

He sets off slowly. Keeps trying the mobile phones but no one picks up and nothing adds up. The Island is ghostly quiet, every jetty he passes is deserted and bare of boats. He looks down at the loud hailer on the banquette and feels like a fool. Mostly, he's worried sick.

Five minutes later, the *Mary Kay* rounds the south end of the Island. If he'd been driving a car, he would've slammed his foot on the brake. The sea is a moving landmass of boats. A roar goes up from this massive armada of vessels of all shapes and sizes crammed so tightly on the water people are boat hopping without getting their toenails wet. Everyone laughs, waves and cheers, giving the thumbs up. Skippers sound their horns; the flag-waving is hysterical. Bastards, Sam thinks, so relieved he's borderline furious. Not bloody funny at all. But no Pied Piper, no dastardly threats, no fear of revenge or physical recriminations. The parade is *on*! He'll settle the score with whichever numbskull came up with the idea of scaring the proverbial shit out of him later.

The Three Js, crammed into a tiny tinny weighted down with a large aluminium bucket stuffed with ice and bottles of champagne, cup their hands around their mouths and hoot out loud. He shakes his fist in mock anger and they laugh harder. The curly-headed, mischievous chief of the volunteer fire brigade shouts out an offer to take off her top if Sam thinks that might increase publicity for the cause. He grins but makes a cutthroat signal, not sure whether the sight of Becky McKay's admittedly superb chest would win the right kind of support. Or lose it.

Lindy, who has hung a banner across the bow of her spiffy but honourable timber stink boat to give her real-estate agency a bit of exposure, indicates the huge turn-out with a wave of her hand, and silently applauds. He shakes his head. Nothing to do with me, not really, he thinks. This is community at its best – though he can still feel the bitter taste of failure lingering in the back of his throat. That fear – that his passion to save Garrawi had destroyed Cook's Basin's everyday sense of safeness and replaced it with dread and terror.

He can't help wondering what he would've done if they'd bowed to pressure. Would he have backed off and let the thugs have their way? Or fought on alone? He can't be sure but he makes a guess. If you lie down for bastards and thieves, you end up with nothing. Like he'd said to Kate, over and over, if you don't stand up for what you believe in, you lose it and you never get it back. The balance shifts, your tiny fraction of the earth's surface spins and a new game begins. She always argued that change was inevitable and only fools and reactionaries resisted it, but he'd fought back with force: change for the common good is rarely an issue but change for the profit of a few and the destruction of what is important to many, is untenable. It widens the gap between the haves and the have-nots until it spawns revolution.

He wishes she could experience the force of a good community fighting for what it believes in even though the odds are stacked against it. He does a quick count of the boats. They must have come from all points north and south of Cook's Basin.

Delaney's column about Jimmy has done this, Sam thinks. A kid, who in a different environment would be slapped with a long-winded diagnosis and have a tag hung on his shoulder forever after, a kid who'd be written off as an odd-ball no-hoper without a future, has somehow inspired a wider population to help save a park it will probably never set foot in. Well, Kate told him the media had an awesome power. He's finally seeing it at work.

Marcus breaks out of the crowded boats. With Ettie beside him holding on to her fiery red bandana, he guns his spiffy timber runabout towards Sam. 'It wasn't my idea, Sam,' Ettie shouts when they come alongside. 'I voted against it!'

In the back, Paul Delaney has his arms flung wide over the white upholstery. Squashed next to him, Siobhan O'Shaughnessy looks triumphant. 'We've got ourselves a real campaign, Scully. We're seriously on our way!'

Sam, too emotional to speak, waves his hand loosely in acknowledgment, looking in the direction of Ettie's pointing finger. Ahead, and lining up to lead the parade, Glenn's long flat furniture-removal barge is decked out like an over-dressed float in a mardi gras. The centrepiece is the artists' huge white papier-mâché cockatoo, wearing a bright red sash that reads *Save Garrawi.*

Jimmy and Longfellow prance around the deck of Glenn's barge, each as excited as the other. Clive is not far behind with his camera. And there he is. Jack Mundey. Man of the people and for the people. Once the conscience of a generation. Leaning against the chest of the cockatoo, his legs slightly apart for balance on the water. Glenn is nudging the barge into position with his pissy little tinny, one hand on the tiller, the other thrusting a stubby high in the sky. The atmosphere is electric. Boats manoeuvre into line behind the giant bird. The sea is a churning, frothing cauldron. The noise of engines is like sitting under the fuselage of a jet plane. The sky is black but no rain. Not yet.

'We're going to make it,' Sam shouts out.

Ettie and the chef salute the rough and emotional bargeman with grins that go way beyond their eyes and reach into their hearts and souls, then gun the boat into the queue. Sam steps into the cabin to fire up the *Mary Kay*. He catches a movement out of the corner of his vision and looks behind. 'Ah jeez,' he thinks, this time crying for real.

Artie has slipped his mooring for the first time in years and he's steering his gloriously rundown, shellfish-encrusted and shabby old rusty yacht into the parade with Amelia standing at attention by his side. She's dressed in the same colours as her son and salutes Sam with a laugh as they motor past the *Mary Kay* with an engine that coughs, splutters, occasionally bellows, and barely holds on to the lowest rev.

'Know anything about boats?' he shouts out to Amelia.

'Not a thing,' she shouts back, laughing.

'Right,' says Sam, falling in behind Artie in case he needs rescuing. He loves this place, he thinks, feeling his throat clam up for the third time in minutes. He loves this place with a blind, unswerving passion that will last a lifetime. He slams the helm with an open hand, euphoric. 'It's you and me, Miss Mary Kay. You and me to the finishing line.' Stretched ahead, a glorious procession makes its way around Cutter Island to fight for a cause for the common good. How can they lose?

With the light dropping fast now, Sam releases a flare into the sky. On cue, everyone follows his lead. The smell of sulphur dulls the briny tang of the sea. The Island disappears from sight in an orange fog. It is spectacular, eerily otherworldly, with people dancing on decks and on bows, the high-and-low-pitched thrum and chug of outboards, inboards, diesel engines and putt putts, the background music to a floating party on a serious mission.

For no reason he can pinpoint, he feels his hackles rising. Once again, he looks behind him. Six black-suited goons, legs apart, arms folded, span the bow of a million-dollar stink boat so fancy the deck trimmings are leather. In the faded light, their sunglasses are round black holes in their faces. They look like standing cadavers formally dressed for their own burials.

The pointy-nosed launch – shiny ebony hull, glittering chrome and cat's eyes portholes – speeds alongside. The goons turn to face Sam. Each one raises his arm, makes the shape of a gun with his hand and fires a couple of mock shots. 'You're a dead man,' says one. 'You're a dead man floating.' Then they're away, kicking up a wash that knocks the *Mary Kay* sideways. Eric Lowdon waves from his seat at the stern. His face is smug, his expression cocksure. He holds a glass of champagne in his hands, already celebrating.

'You're a bit premature, you scumbag,' Sam shouts angrily. In the distance, lightning makes a serrated tear in a black sky.

Cook's Basin News (CBN)

Newsletter for Offshore Residents of Cook's Basin, Australia

FEBRUARY

THE BATTLE FOR GARRAWI RAMPS UP!

Massive congratulations are in order for a boat parade with a difference. Anyone who missed it, weep. It was a rock-star event. Young Jimmy MacFarlane's interview with top journalist Paul Delaney was also a triumph. STAY TUNED FOR MORE UP-COMING SPOT FIRES! (Heh, heh).

In the meantime, the editor wishes to catch up on community notices. Life goes on. See below.

Asparagus Fern Out Day at Stony Point.

All are welcome to join in, especially novice bushcarers. Take a ferry or tie up your tinny at Kingfish Bay wharf and follow the signs.

A fabulously delicious and robust morning tea and lunch will be served.

Organisers suggest long pants, long sleeves, gloves, hat and enclosed shoes or boots (not sandals).

Tools and training on tackling asparagus fern provided.

Bring bathers, if you like, as it will be high tide at lunchtime – lovely for a dip at Kingfish Bay beach.

When: Thursday

Time: 9am to about 12.30

LETTER TO THE EDITOR:

I would like to address the issue of the council rubbish skip on the wharf. This skip is for household rubbish only, NOT building waste and broken furniture. Just the other day, a huge pile of cardboard moving boxes (not broken down or flattened) and some old cupboards were dumped next to the skip. The council is not going to magically clean it up!! Also, tradies and builders: please hire your own skips. The one located on Triangle wharf is not for commercial use.

Name supplied

NEW PONTOON

The installation of a new pontoon at Triangle wharf is scheduled to commence next week (Monday). All commuters are advised they will need to trek to alternative Island ferry wharves until work is finalised.

Boat owners who tie up at Triangle will need to make other arrangements for that period. Options include:

- dock your boat in the shallows;
- make a temporary arrangement with a private jetty owner;
- use the ferry for commuting; and
- leave your boat at Commuter Dock until the wharf is back in working order.

Any offers from private jetty owners for that short period would be greatly appreciated (hint, hint).

CHAPTER SEVENTEEN

Earlier than usual on Monday morning, the community flocks into The Briny eager to pick up a copy of Delaney's mass-circulation newspaper. A picture of Jimmy, Longfellow and the giant cockatoo is front-page news. The story is continued on page three, where a collage of shots of the floating protesters takes up half the space. It's massive coverage of the kind that no amount of money can buy. If Delaney would let him, Sam would offer to shout him a slab of the best brew on the market. He pulls out his mobile and calls the big newspaperman.

'Don't get too excited,' Delaney says. 'The bastards will send a counter-attack your way any moment. Watch your backs. They'll be seething.'

Sam mulls whether to mention the fancy boat loaded with goons and decides against it. He'll sound like a whinger. Refuses, anyway, to spoil the moment.

'Glenn's first flying lesson courtesy of the New Planet Fountain of Youth is on this afternoon. He's supposed to take a mattress. It's got me beat why.'

'That's what you sit on when you're airborne, Scully. What else would you think it was for?'

Sam ends the call. He buys a copy of the newspaper and heads off in his tinny to call on Artie who, by all accounts, made it back to his mooring without any major mishap. The old man responds to Sam's knock on the hull with a hacking cough.

'Came by to say thanks, Artie. Helluva spot fire last night, eh?'

'Spot? Nah. I don't think so. It was a full-on blazing hot, voracious bushfire, son. Is that the paper?' Artie stretches to take it from Sam's hands. Holds it up at an angle to catch the light from a porthole, his eyes narrowed for better focus. 'Front page, eh? Not bad, not bad. Little word of advice, though, if you don't mind an old man ramblin' on a bit at this almost civilised hour of the mornin'.'

Sam dips his head.

'Keep Jimmy away from the press. He's easy fodder for every half-baked, snaky-minded current affairs show in town. He'll be chewed up and spat out until his sticky red head is so done in even that poncey gel he uses won't be able to point out which way is up. You gettin' my drift? Water off a duck's back for some folks. But not for a kid like Jimmy.'

'You mention this to Amelia?'

'Yep. But all she can see is that her not-so-little baby boy is gettin' the kudos she reckons he deserves. And as we are both painfully aware, Amelia isn't too nifty when it comes to seein' the long-distance picture. She's a go-for-broke woman. Has a light-bulb moment, chases the dream and then wakes up to find herself hurtlin' into disaster. 'Course by then it's too late. Remember the double registration for the dole that landed her in the clink for a few months? Did it for Jimmy, o' course, and was blind to the downside. Lovely woman, though, not sayin' she isn't. Just doesn't have much of a clue and reckons everyone will see it her way once she explains. Bit like Jimmy, now that I think about it.'

'Her head's been turned, in other words.'

'They'll ruin him, the media. And they won't give a damn. Wouldn't want to see that happen to a kid who's never done a bad turn in his short, innocent and sincerely good-hearted life.'

'Hear you loud and clear, Artie.'

'That Kate would say the same if she was around. Saw her go off with a suitcase yesterday. Any idea when she'll be back? I'll miss me morning confabs with her.'

'Let you know the second I hear.' Morning confabs? He gives the old man a quick salute.

Artie says: 'Was good to feel the fire in me belly again, son. Real good.'

Sam makes it about one hundred metres before swinging his tinny around. Maybe she's left him a note, he thinks.

The house is cool and still. Sam checks for a note under the kettle. On the bed. In the bathroom. On the coffee table. He circles the kitchen table where Emily's treasure trove is laid out in the order of discovery: the mysterious contents of the grey tin, the documents in the plastic bag. A stack of letters. There is no note for him here, either. He considers his options. Takes a seat. Pushes aside the mementoes and pulls the bag towards him. He removes and unfolds the first yellowed document. Neat copperplate writing in faded ink. A deed to a house in the Melbourne suburb of Fitzroy, dated January 27 1938. Not a bill, then. He skips to the names. Phyllis and Robert Conway.

He puts it aside and reaches for the next document, more stained, this time, and worn thin around the edges. It's a death certificate for Phyllis, dated 1963. Cause of death: Suicide. There's another death certificate. Robert Conway, who departed this mortal coil in 1983. Kate would have been eight years old. Next, a birth certificate for Emily Elizabeth Conway. Kate's mother. If he's not mistaken, the old girl was two years older than she admitted. He grins, wryly, impressed. Emily was a law unto herself. There's a wedding certificate for Emily and Gerald.

He looks up at the sound of thunder. Pushes back his chair and goes to the window. The far-off glow of sheet lightning strobes way beyond the escarpment. With a smile, he counts and gets to fifteen before there's another rumble, testing Jimmy's theory. A wind from the west gathers and riffles the casuarinas, setting off a low keening. Leaves start to fall from the spotted gums. A dark shadow makes his way down the steps to Kate's pontoon. Sam knows it is her wildly eccentric and reclusive neighbour on his way to fish off the end. He hopes he doesn't get struck by lightning.

He returns to his seat and pauses for a moment to consider whether he has a right to be in Kate's kitchen, looking through private documents. Too late to think about that now, he tells himself. He reaches for an envelope that's been slit open. And there he is. The long-lost brother: Alexander Conway. Born September 12 1961. Place: Corowa Base Hospital, Victoria. Mother: Emily Conway. Aged nineteen. There is a blank space where the father's name should have been.

So it is true, he thinks, weirdly flat, finally understanding that it's the not knowing that drags a person down, eats away at any idea of who you are and where you come from.

He rocks on the back legs of the chair in a way that sets Kate's teeth on edge. The letters are in date order. He begins with the earliest.

In the Newbury County Court No R 1367 In the Matter of the Adoption Act, 1947

And In the Matter of Baby Conway, an Infant Take Notice that an Adoption order has this day been made in respect of the above-named Infant

On an application under the serial number BQO Dated this 27th day of March 1962.

(Two names are stamped above 'Registrar':)

J F Hampton
G Barr-Jones
3014/27

The address shown is in Newbury, Berkshire, United Kingdom. The opening times for the court are also thoughtfully supplied: ten am to four pm. Mondays to Fridays only.

England. The baby was put up for adoption in England. He reads on.

General Register Office Newbury
Berks PO 27, RG14
Telephone: (0)1635 1356
Your reference: Our reference: RAC 0638202 20 February 1980

Dear Madam,

Thank you for your recent letter containing information as requested. The adoption record of your son has been noted in accordance with your wishes. If he should apply to this Office for access to his birth records under provision of Section 26 of the Children Act 1975, your request will be conveyed to the counsellor conducting the interview which your son will be obliged to attend before particulars of his birth are provided. In order for this office to maintain up-to-date records, it would be appreciated if you would advise us of any change either to your address or your original request. Please quote the above reference number in any correspondence to this Office.

Yours faithfully,
Mrs IL Roberts

General Register Office
Ed Harrison Adoptions
Casework Officer
Date: 22 June 2000

Dear Mrs Jackson,

Thank you for your letter dated 15 May 2000, informing us of your change of address. Our records have been noted accordingly. Should you have any further changes of address etc. please keep this office informed so we can keep our records up to date.

You would not be informed if your adopted son were to die as we do not know this information and would not be informed ourselves. If/when your son applies to access his birth records or applies for entry onto Part 1 of the Adoption Contact Register, your name and address will be forwarded to him.

Yours sincerely,
Ed Harrison

Berkshire County Council
20 January 2002

Dear Madam,

My name is Joe Brampton and I work for the Berkshire County Council Social Services Directorate. One of my jobs is Section 51 Counselling, that is to help people who have been adopted research their birth origin.

I am aware that you have thrice made contact with the adoption registrar to seek information about your adopted son. These enquiries have now been forwarded to me for action.

I am pleased to advise that your birth son has now requested information about his birth and, because of the emotional implications for all involved, we offer to act as intermediary.

My first meeting with your son went well and we are in the process of requesting records from the appropriate adoption agency to enable us to take the next step. He is not yet aware of your contact but was told about the adoption register.

When the records I have requested are received from the agency, we will meet again. May I suggest you write a letter to him via this office to enable me to present this letter at our next meeting.

I realise this letter is out of the blue and perhaps will trigger many emotions and I do hope that you have some support. It goes without saying that we will help all we can.

You will be pleased to learn that his name is still Alexander, the name I believe you gave him at birth. That's as much as I am able to tell you about him at this stage.

I would take this opportunity to wish you a happy New Year and look forward to hearing from you.

Yours sincerely,

Joe Brampton

Family Placement Assistant

Berkshire County Council 10 February, 2002

Dear Mrs Jackson,

Thank you for your telephone call and subsequent letter sent to me for onward transmission to Alexander. I write to advise that our meeting on 28/01/02 went exceptionally well. He was visited in the security of his home. There was a lot of information given in your letter that caused much joy and excitement.

Alexander will be writing to you and will no doubt share with you his life story. You are both sure to be emotional but I sense you'll both handle it well. In the first instance, Alexander will correspond via this address until he feels confident enough to pass on his location. I'm sure you will understand. He has a lot to think about and so do you. I hope you have some support.

I am away on leave for two weeks from today. I would expect that you will receive mail direct from Alexander before I return. I wish you well and feel that your contact is progressing well. From past experience it is advisable to progress at a pace that all concerned can handle and are comfortable with.

Yours sincerely,
Joe Brampton

Berkshire County Council
17 September 2004

Dear Mrs Jackson,

A lot of water has gone under the bridge since I last wrote to you on 10/02/02 about Alexander. Alexander was contacted the moment your letter arrived this week and collected it from my office within the hour. He read it in my presence and was obviously delighted. My understanding now is that he will make contact by letter in the first instance then progress to a phone call at a later time. This being so, and since I am unable to effect a face-to-face meeting locally, the time for me to withdraw has come. I will now place the file back in the archives for safekeeping. I do hope all is well with you. I can imagine the emotions you have gone through and am glad to have been of some service to you. It goes without saying that if there is anything you feel we are able to help with in this regard, please do not hesitate to contact us.

Yours sincerely,

Joe Brampton
Family Placements

Sam leans back in his chair, his head spinning. Emily could have opened the door in 2002. Instead, it took her two years to write a letter to the child she relinquished. Why? She definitely wanted to find him. She first began her enquiries into his whereabouts in 1980. Clearly, it took a long time for Alexander to begin searching from his end. He must have been – he scans the letters, scribbles a few dates – nearly forty years old. Probably with children of his own. Sam mentally puts himself in his shoes. If *his* adoptive parents were good and kind – parents in the true sense – to avoid causing them hurt or grief, he'd delay the search until after their death.

He replaces everything in forensic order. So she's gone to England, he thinks. God knows for how long. He'd better warn Ettie so she can alert Jenny she'll be needed for a while yet. Rain fingers the roof. Then pounds down. Outside, the light is dark purple. The bay froths with white caps. He's going to take a beating in the tinny.

The bow dredges into every second swell before breaking clear. The hull sloshes with rain and seawater. The bilge pump kicks in with a high whine but barely keeps pace. Sam is soaked. The outboard makes death-throe sounds. He is in his element. The boat climbs a wave, teeters, crashes down. Sam drops the revs, hoping the engine doesn't cut out completely. His eyes sting. Hands are slippery. The shore is almost invisible. He wants to shout with the sheer bloody pleasure of it all. Grins when a huge swell hurls him forward. He shifts his weight up a fraction to avoid flipping. A flash of lightning hits. Closer now. He feels a shock run up his arm where he's holding on to the gunnel. The rain keeps coming in solid sheets. Up ahead, he makes out the shallow-water marker and adjusts his course.

Truth is, he thinks, wiping his face with his arm, Kate shies at the first hurdle. Steps to the sidelines and observes. A journalist through to the core. What did she call it? The thrill of the chase. Yeah. Sniffing out secrets and exposing them. Once, he'd asked her if they did any good, these public revelations of private matters. 'Not every private matter, Scully: it's a question of public interest but sometimes it's hard to hold on to your integrity under pressure from the editor for a front-page lead.' She'd absentmindedly called him Scully and he'd asked her why. A journo's habit.

She'd kissed him lightly on the cheek, but he'd felt uncomfortable all the same at the distance the use of a surname instantly put between them. She'd given up the job, she'd said, because once or twice she'd found herself weakening under pressure and she'd known it was only a matter of time until she ended up cynical and disengaged from the people whose lives she pushed, pulled and honed into a series of facts summed up in less than one thousand words.

He rounds Stony Point. Waves towards the Misses Skettle, who'll be watching his clumsy progress through their binoculars. He'd tried to visualise how many pages one thousand words filled and later, still curious, he'd leaned over Fast Freddy's shoulder while he read the Saturday paper at the picnic table in the Square, and counted out loud. He'd made it to five hundred and seventy-three before Freddy lost patience. It was an amazingly small space. A huge last gust knocks the boat, then the squall blows itself out. The wind drops, the sea begins to quiet. He chugs almost sedately to tie up at The Briny's pontoon. If he'd delayed for ten minutes, he would have had a dry run. Timing is everything, as his father used to say.

He waits in the tinny, wiping the moisture from his eyes, tasting salt, removing his shirt to wring it out. The bilge pump slowly clears the hull. No point in coming this far and letting the tinny sink from lack of attention to detail. While he watches the level drop, he decides once and for all to put his relationship with Kate on the back burner. Relationship? Has it ever been anything more than – oh jeez, the black-hearted insouciance of the word – a convenient fling?

It takes a couple of seconds for him to feel a lightness spreading through his body, the heaviness shifting from where he now realises it has laid like a rock pressing on his chest ever since Kate took off for the will-reading and left Ettie in the lurch without a second thought. He has known despair, felt it, tasted it, and once, almost succumbed to it. Love might be an act of courage, as his father told him often enough, but only fools are blind to the truth. There's no way to save a person who can't see she's in trouble. But who is he to judge? He knows very little of the world beyond Cook's Basin. He climbs out of the boat, his clothes sticking to him like a second skin. Helluva ride.

He breathes in the pulse of his chosen territory, feels the strength of his connection to people, community, landscape. In time, the community will forgive and even understand why Kate abandoned Ettie and swanned away from the fight to save Garrawi. But it will never forget. Not that it matters. He has a feeling Kate isn't long for Cook's Basin. She needed a holiday, not a radical change of lifestyle. Hardly a noble end to a relationship. He sighs, wondering if he is as cool as he thinks or if, as after the death of a loved one, grief will smash into him like a ten-tonne truck in three months' time. That's how long it takes, according to the experts who are regularly quoted in Freddy's favourite tabloid, to finally believe a person – or in his case, an affair – is dead and buried.

But shit, a single phone call wouldn't have gone astray, just to let him know she was OK. He'd feel the same way about any member of the community who'd upped stakes on a decidedly iffy mission. Ah bloody hell, he's kidding himself. He wouldn't give a toss about anyone else. Not unless it was Ettie, or Jimmy, or even the chef, now that he thinks it through. Jenny too. The Misses Skettle. A few others he can think of . . .

The list goes on and on. Artie's on it, for sure. Not that the old bloke's going anywhere with his bung legs. Shouldn't write him off, though. He pitched up for the Save Garrawi parade with a hefty slice of his once legendary dash on display. He must have been a rabble-rouser in his day. And a lot more went on behind his dishwater yellow eyes than any of the community gave him credit for. He didn't miss a trick. He's definitely got a thing for Kate, Sam thinks. He watches over her like the old soldier that he is. Sam wonders but wouldn't dare ask what the two of them talk about on those *confabs* Artie misses so much. Ah, move on, he tells himself. Done is done.

He pulls out his mobile. Calls Glenn. 'Mate! You got a rubber mat sorted? You won't be needing it. No, mate. I'll go to the flying thing. You're off the hook. It's my turn to be useful.'

Keeping busy. Keeping busy. Works for him. He stomps towards the café.

Sam hears Ettie whanging and banging inside the café. He pokes his dripping head inside the back door where she's putting away pots and pans. 'Got a minute, love?'

She comes towards him, drying her hands on a tea towel slung over her shoulder. 'You're drenched, Sam . . .'

'Kate's gone. To England, I think. Well, I'm almost certain. You might want to let Jenny know she needs to hang around for a bit.'

Ettie sighs. 'It's the brother, isn't it?'

'Seems to be.'

'What about a shower upstairs and I'll bring up an early lunch?'

'No offence, love, but I'll get going, if you don't mind. Leave you two to sort out logistics for the next . . .' He breaks off. Shrugs. 'Well, who knows how long?' He turns on his heel and makes his way back to the tinny. Another squall is threatening. Not that it matters. He's soaked to the skin.

'How about dinner with the chef and me tonight?' Ettie calls after him.

He gives a backwards wave, suddenly unable to trust himself to speak.

Sam makes his way into the city with a rolled-up exercise mat borrowed from Jenny. 'No time for yoga right now,' she'd told him when she handed it over. The sun is brutal. Steam rises from the bitumen. He copes better with the traffic. Must be getting used to it, he thinks. He wishes he'd brought a CD to shove in the scratchy deck of the ute to treat himself to a little homespun country-music style philosophy to counter the loony claptrap he's about to submit to. Although there are people, he admits, who might find it hard to differentiate between the two.

Unaided human flight. Is there no end to the gullibility of lost and lonely people? He hates to admit it, but he's worried the six goons might be lying in wait like a pack of hyenas ready to pick his bones bare. After he'd showered and changed, he'd returned to the Square and stuck his head inside The Briny. Told the two women to send out a search party if he wasn't home by six o'clock. They'd laughed, thinking he was joking. Which he was . . . in a way.

He swings into a dark street in the inner city where the houses all date back to the Victorian period – though this lot hasn't been discovered by trendy young money-market whiz-kids yet. They're rundown, with peeling paint, loose guttering and forsaken front plots. Bloody depressing, if you ask him, when only two hours away the clean blue sea is there to rest your eyes on for free. He sees a scabby young bloke nodding off in a doorway. Further on, a desperately skinny young woman with dyed black hair and a skirt that advertises her totally naked backside gives him a wiggle and an encouraging look. What the hell is a multi-billion-dollar empire doing hanging out in a street that's a slum? The answer rockets back. Easy prey.

He scans the house numbers, realises he's close to his destination and starts searching for a parking spot, but cars are banked up tighter than cans in a supermarket and most of them look as though they haven't budged in a month. Dead leaves and broken twigs, bird shit and spiderwebs festoon them like gothic flourishes. Could almost be the car park at the Square. It takes him five minutes to shoehorn his ute into a metered parking spot two blocks away. He checks the fee and sighs loudly. Welcome to the exciting city, folks, where every time you take a step you get stung. Shouldn't be legal to charge punters thirty-eight bucks a day to leave a car in a dodgy neighbourhood.

He carries his soon-to-be-flying mat up the dusty, leaf-littered front steps of the Victorian terrace where the New Planet Fountain of Youth teaches and fleeces the gullible. There's not a goon in sight. For the rest of the afternoon, in the midst of forty other acolytes with painfully young faces, he sits (in excruciating discomfort) cross-legged with his eyes closed, chanting: 'I'm light as a feather, I can fly.' He fights hard to control an urge to grab the white-robed leader by his throat to shake some plain, old common sense into him.

CHAPTER EIGHTEEN

After a twenty-four-hour stopover in Dubai, Kate's plane lands at Heathrow airport. Almost itchy with excitement, she completes the formalities of customs and immigration and makes her way to the Underground to hop a train to Kensington. When she comes up from the bowels of the earth, she emerges into the thin daylight of Britain's winter for the first time. She wonders whether it's possible for a native Londoner to eat, sleep, work and play without ever being exposed to daylight. Probably, she thinks, envisaging the Morlocks from HG Wells's *The Time Machine* beavering away underground and sustaining themselves by eating the tanned, healthy, lotus-eating sun dwellers from above. What sun, she thinks?

The weather is bitter. The residual warmth of air-conditioned spaces flows out of her. Cold seeps into her bones. She blinks. Pulls her jacket tighter. People pass in a hurry, huddled inside heavy coats, swaddled in scarves, gloves, knitted caps. Eyes cast down as though the pavements hold some weird fascination. She lets go of her small suitcase and drags a map out of her backpack, vowing to switch to a smartphone as soon as possible. It takes her three minutes to check directions and head in towards the small hotel where she has a room booked.

Half an hour later, she's checked in, showered, changed and back in the busy London streets. It's now three o'clock in the afternoon. She feels pumped with adrenalin. She knows from experience that people find it easy to politely say no when you're calling from the other side of the world. Her brother will find it much harder to ignore her if he knows she's come a long way to meet him. She walks off her jetlag looking for a shop where she can buy a smart phone. She purchases twenty-five pounds' worth of calls and data.

Back in her tiny hotel room, she searches the phone database for Alexander Conway. She hits on twenty-three possible candidates and begins dialling the ones closest to the region mentioned in the letters. It is eight pm. The first seven attempts are duds. A man too deaf to hear her. A young father with screaming kids in the background. Two women who say their husbands are in their early thirties. Two answering machines where she fails to leave messages. Another old habit. Leave a message and if your call is unwanted, all future calls are screened. The seventh attempt is diverted to a mobile. This Alexander is in a bar and he's drunk. He's also twenty-four years old.

She falls back against the pillows in her chintzy English hotel room, where the radiator is so close to the bed the heat is burning her left leg. Crosses her ankles because once, long ago, a healer told her it captured energy in the body. Flimflam superstition of the kind her mother indulged in. The thought pulls her up short. She realises she hasn't thought of Emily, Ettie – and only briefly of Sam – since she boarded the plane. Her old instincts and skills have kicked in. You have to stay focused to get the story. She dials the next on the list.

Her call is picked up: 'Alexander Conway.'

'You don't know me, but –'

'If you're selling anything I'm really not interested.' He is polite. His voice is pleasing.

Kate's heart beats faster. On some primal level, she knows it's him. 'No. Nothing like that. My name is Kate Jackson. I'm from Australia and I think I may be your half-sister.'

She wants to kick herself. She'd meant to reveal a few facts. Give the man time to adjust to what might be coming. She crosses her fingers. The silence goes on and on.

'Is our mother with you?' he asks, after an age.

'No. I'm alone.'

'Kate Jackson, you say?'

'Yes. I'm in London. If you wouldn't mind too much, I'd like to meet you. There's no agenda. More like closure, really. I only found out you existed a few weeks ago.'

An even longer silence.

'So she's dead, then, is that what you mean?'

Kate swallows. 'Yes.' She hears a sigh. Long and deep. She loosens her white-knuckled grip on the phone a little. Waits. She can guess what's going through his mind at a thousand miles an hour. Is she mad? Does he need this kind of complication in his life? Where is this going? Is she after money, does she want to move in, will he ever be able to get rid of her once the door is open?

'I'm a journalist for a financial paper – well, I was. Right now, I'm the partner in a rather wobbly old waterfront café in a place called Cook's Basin on the eastern coast. And I am not, I can assure you, mad or after anything other than meeting you. Just so you know –'

'Ah, so you're a cook?'

She understands he's looking for a link, something that connects them beyond a mother he's never laid eyes on. She's tempted to say yes. It would be so easy. But if she begins with a lie, where will it stop? 'No. I'm a lousy cook. My partner, Ettie Brookbank, is the star; I wash dishes, mop floors and look after the money.'

She strains to hear what sounds like a quick laugh. Finds herself smiling, hopeful.

'If you can navigate your way to Newbury in Berkshire in the morning, there's a café that serves quite a good English breakfast. Not exactly traditional but satisfactory all the same.'

'What time?'

'Catch an express train from Paddington. The café isn't far from the station. Say ten o'clock?'

'Perfect. And thank you. I was afraid you might say bugger off or something.'

'Actually, I'm a little curious myself.'

He tells her the name of the café. They exchange mobile phone numbers.

'See you tomorrow.'

It's only after she disconnects that Kate realises she hasn't a clue whether he's tall or short, dark-haired, blond or grey, fat, thin or just plain ordinary. She likes the sound of his voice, though. Substantial, middle-class British, neither too plummy nor too slangy. He has a measured warmth in his tone so she mentally pictures him in textured trousers – maybe corduroy – a conservative tweed jacket with leather patches on the elbow, lace-up shoes. She stops short of giving him a pipe with vanilla-scented tobacco.

The iron radiator gurgles and hisses and she gets up from the bed to see if there is a thermostat she can turn down. Waking in a lather of sweat isn't going to help her jetlag. Through the window, streetlights throw pools on black streets. No one stirs. In the all-white bathroom, tiles are warm under her bare feet. She stares at her features in the mirror as if seeing them for the first time, wondering if his eyes are blue too.

London looks forlorn under a grey drizzle when Kate sets off. The streets are a moving sea of umbrellas that go up and down in a mad dance to avoid clashing and smashing. Standing on the steps of the hotel, shielding her new phone from the rain with one hand, she calls up street directions on the screen, then hoists a hood over her hair and steps out. She's booked a seat on an earlier express train so she can arrive way ahead of her half-brother. At the last minute, she decided to suss him out before stretching out her hand to shake his. Or should she kiss him on the cheek? She wonders: Is there a protocol for meeting a sibling for the first time?

At Paddington Station, she listens to a mind-boggling selection of ticket options before she buys a return ticket for forty-seven pounds and thirty-six pence from a worn Cockney woman with frizzy bleached hair and a mouth like a thin red slash. 'Same day use only, luv, you got that?' Kate nods, feels the pushing pressure of the man in the queue behind her. She steps aside and he jumps forward, harried and hassled. He gives her a look of disapproval and says, 'Not all of us have all day.'

She ignores him. Glances at the station clock. The trip will take fifty-two minutes. If her brother looks feral, the smartest course of action would be to bolt. But she's come too far to give up at the finishing line. Or perhaps it's the starting barrier? She has no idea.

After twenty minutes whooshing through dimly lit tunnels, brakes squealing, wheels clanging, the train breaks into the low-hanging gloom of a British winter. The rain has stopped but the cityscape is drab and lifeless. Kate stares into bleak backyards where abandoned children's bicycles, rusting barbecues and naked trees line up depressingly. It is all so still, she thinks, except for the neon flash of television sets in nearly every house. She whizzes through more bleak and wintry stations with long corridors of columns and waiting passengers hunched over one electronic device or another. One or two people read newspapers. If ever there was a signal that hard copy was a dying industry . . . People always need to eat, though. The Briny Café will be around long after the last broadsheet folds, the last tabloid, too. For a second she feels a wave of homesickness.

Outside the train station in Newbury, Kate finds herself in a street of quaint redbrick buildings with pretty casement windows. She follows the map on her phone to Northbrook Street where it's market day and the street is awash with stalls selling everything from homemade jams to second-hand clothing. The stallholders are encased in puffer jackets, their hands woolly in rainbow-coloured mitts. They stamp their feet, slap their arms against their chests, and spruik like slick East End showmen. A lone busker strums a guitar and sings a song made famous by Donovan in another era. She struggles to remember the name. Something about wind. Once or twice, the sun makes a half-hearted attempt to break through the low-lying cloud. For a brilliant second, metal bits hanging from noses, lips, eyebrows and ears catch fire and the drizzle sparkles. It is still bitterly cold.

Kate finds the coffee shop easily enough. A bell tinkles when she opens the door then the central heating hits her like a hot slap. She finds an empty corner table with a view of the street and notes the red-checked tablecloth is spotless, the condiments shiny and topped up. She runs her finger along a windowpane, checking for dust. It comes away clean. A waitress bearing a striking resemblance to blonde and bosomy Big Julie, a former employee of The Briny Café, hands her a menu with a smile. Kate orders eggs, bacon, fried tomatoes and toast. 'And a long black with a double shot.'

'English breakfast and a strong coffee. On the way.' The waitress scoops up the menu and walks towards the swinging kitchen doors.

To fill in time, Kate writes a list of questions. How has life treated him? Was he adopted into a loving family? Are his adoptive parents still alive? Light, social chitchat until she strikes out for the mother lode: Why did you decide to seek out your birth mother? Were you ever in touch personally? She glances into the street, checking the passers-by as if a sixth sense might help her to sniff out a matching bloodline. She sees winter-white faces, cold-reddened eyes, a few dogs on leads, people carrying old-fashioned cane shopping baskets as though they are off to buy a pound of blade steak, two lamb's kidneys and a loaf of bread to make a steak and kidney pudding for dinner. As though fast food and supermarkets haven't yet evolved. Kate has the disorienting feeling of having landed in another century.

She checks her watch as her order is placed in front of her. Half an hour to go. She gives the bacon, still so hot the fat is sizzling, a close look, then picks up her knife and fork and hoes in. It's the first meal she's had since she arrived in England and every mouthful is an exquisite explosion of the robust smoky meat, slippery poached eggs, salty fat and sweet tomato. As soon as she finishes, a man who's been nursing his coffee on the other side of the room comes up to her table.

'I heard your accent. Australian?' he asks.

Kate nods, but offers nothing, thinking it's a bad pick-up line.

'Your name wouldn't be Kate, would it?'

She sees a man of medium height dressed in faded jeans and a heavy cream Aran sweater over a pale blue shirt. His hair was once black but is now flecked with grey, his lean face is clean-shaven, his gaze direct. He is crisp and soft, a bundle of contrasting textures that add up to a man who seems comfortable in his skin. He has Emily's nose. Her mouth, too, but without the twist of dissatisfaction that defined her face. His almost feminine hands belong to a man who has never known physical work.

Kate silently pushes back her chair and stands. 'Yes,' she says, looking into eyes that are indeed as blue as her own. 'You must be Alexander?'

'So, do I look a little like her?' he asks, smiling.

Kate shakes her head. 'Sorry. Didn't mean to stare. It's just that you've been a ghost till now. And yes, you do look like her. More than just a little.'

'May I?' He indicates a chair opposite. 'I came early so I could take a good look at you before I decided whether to proceed. You obviously did the same? We were both being so careful we could've missed each other altogether. It would have been shockingly ironic, don't you think?'

Kate nods, scrabbling for something to say, unable to find her voice.

He grins, and holds out his hand. 'So now we know we're neither lunatic nor dangerous, tell me how long you plan to be in London. How long do we have to get to know one another?'

'A few days, that's all. Businesses don't run themselves and, at the risk of sounding pathetic, your English weather is pretty depressing.'

'Well, who knows? I might make it to the other side of the world one day and look you up on your own turf. Look, I don't know about you, but I've had enough of this place. How about we move on to somewhere we can get a sinful pastry or a rich slice of cake and spend some time sorting out a few facts? Then we can decide whether to wave goodbye forever, no harm done and on the mutual understanding we have nothing in common beyond a woman who once made a mistake and paid for it for the rest of her life. Or we can decide we like each other, get along, might even develop a sibling fondness in time and continue with the contact. Deal?'

Kate shrugs wordlessly, won over by Alex's easy charm. 'One thing,' she says, standing up and gathering her belongings. 'What made you decide to look for Emily?'

He laughs: 'You mean did I have an ulterior motive?'

'No, no . . .'

'Relax, Kate. It's quite possible I might have wanted revenge, to upset whatever family she had, to put in a bid for the family fortune – if there happened to be one.'

'Well, there isn't –' She swallows.

He holds up his hands, cutting her off, as though it's irrelevant: 'As it turns out, I have a very rare medical condition. I wanted to find out whether it was hereditary or just one of those things that afflict people for no reason at all.'

'Oh.' Kate blushes. 'Are you worried you might pass it on to your children?'

'Children? No. I don't have any. Never been married. Commitment doesn't seem to be a strong point.'

'Well, that's certainly hereditary.' Kate gives Alex a wry smile. 'Is it too rude to ask what the condition is?'

'I'm afraid it's not very glamorous. Intermittent fibrillation, that's all. Had it all my life. It didn't bother me when I was young. I made a point of eating properly and keeping fit. Which I still do. But as I age, I wonder whether heart attacks have been a family curse . . .'

'Emily was completely indestructible until she had a massive heart attack, which is not the same thing, is it? And she would've survived if she'd gone to the doctor instead of stubbornly refusing to have a check-up.'

'So. That leaves my father's side of the family.'

'Any idea who he is?'

Alex calls for a bill. 'I was hoping you might know.'

He pays for Kate's breakfast over her protests and they leave the restaurant together. Outside on the pavement, he reaches for her backpack. She gives it up without a word.

'Would you care to adjourn to a typical English pub?'

'Actually, I'm not much of a drinker.'

'Neither am I.'

Relieved she's not being invited to a drink-a-thon in a bid to loosen tongues and unearth deep family secrets – a journo's tried and true formula – Kate smiles brightly: 'I've always loved English pubs. What the walls must have heard from one century or another, eh?'

'Would you like sixteenth, seventeenth, eighteenth, nineteenth or twentieth century?'

'Anywhere warm. My toes are already going numb. Does it ever stop raining?'

'This is only damp air. You'll know when it rains. The whole of Britain is sodden and everywhere you go you can smell the ripe odour of wet wool and wet dogs.'

'Ah, I wondered what that smell was . . .' A thunderclap explodes like a cannon, the heavens disgorge a blinding torrent and they dash for an impossibly small pub called Bird and Barrel, nestled at the end of a cul-de-sac. It is crooked, uncannily reminiscent of The Briny.

'You think that's our mother making her presence felt?' Alexander shouts above the storm, pulling her into the doorway.

'I wouldn't put it past her,' Kate shouts back, amazed to find that she's laughing. They stand for a moment and watch a torrent rush down red-tiled roofs to find its way along ancient gutters. 'What century have we been flung back into?' she adds, looking around at a tiny pocket of slouching redbrick houses where a horse and carriage would not have seemed out of place.

'Mostly eighteenth.'

An icy, waterlogged gust whacks them hard up against the pub door; it swings open and they fall inside a warm, dark room with low, beamed ceilings, cherry-red carpet and enough space to hold about fifteen people at the most. They shake off some of the water. The barman holds up a towel with a question in his eyes. Alexander strides over and grabs it. He throws it to Kate, who catches the faint whiff of stale beer embedded in the fabric. She dries off. The barman passes him another.

'They know you well here?' she asks, towelling her hair, curious at the easy familiarity of the barman.

'You could say that.' He pauses then seems to come to a decision. 'Actually, I own it. So we're in the same sort of business, you and I. Weird, don't you think?'

Kate hands him back the towel. 'I've given up being surprised by anything.'

Alexander leads the way up a flight of creaking stairs so skewed they make the Misses Skettles' hallway look like an airport runway. The timber smells of wax and polish. The hall runner, a colourful kelim that she'd feel happy having in her own home, might be faded and worn but it, too, exudes a dedicated and fresh spotlessness. A monumentally different cultural environment, she thinks, and yet the details of their characters are essentially the same. Which makes her wonder about research that insists environment is the driving force in character. Emily used to say it was all in the genes – usually as a prelude to another cruel quip about Kate being swapped at birth.

'My parents owned the pub, passed it on to me. I make a decent living but I would have gone broke long ago if I'd had to buy the place.'

'Are your parents still alive?'

'No. I wouldn't have opened the door to you if they were. I loved them both and they were spectacularly good to me. I wouldn't have hurt them for the world.' He lifts a latch, opens one of three doors leading off a small landing and waves his hand to usher her in.

A wall of glass overlooks a wide canal beaded with old river barges. Despite the foul grey weather, the boats are bright and joyful, painted yellow, red, sky blue – all the colours of the rainbow. She could almost be looking out from Ettie's penthouse.

'I live in a world where the only way home is by boat,' she says.

He slides Kate's damp backpack onto a darkly gleaming round oak corner table. Indicates she should sit on one of a pair of wingback chairs on either side of a small cast-iron fireplace. He lights a match and opens the glass door, sets newspaper and kindling alight. After the cold and wet of the outdoors, the warmth and comfort makes Kate want to curl up and sleep. She yawns loudly: 'Sorry. Jetlag.'

'Now,' he says, 'tell me about our mother.'

'Would you like the short or long version?'

'Start with the short.'

CHAPTER NINETEEN

Three days after Kate's disappearance – or desertion as some of the less understanding locals describe her dawn flit in the midst of the busy late-summer season at the café and the battle to save Garrawi – the scuttlebutt switches from the effect on Ettie to the impact on Sam. No one dares broach the subject except Fast Freddy, who deliberately hangs around the Square longer than usual after coming off his water-taxi shift to catch up with his friend. 'She didn't say much when I picked her up before dawn,' he says. 'Just that she'd never forgive herself if she didn't follow through. Nothing to do with you, Sam, or the way she feels about you. Not that I'd know much about all that,' he adds hastily. 'What goes on between two people is their business. But in all my years of ferrying broken hearts around the waterways, I've learned to read some of the signs. Tears. Anger. Sadness. Disbelief. Occasionally, resignation or relief. She showed none of them. Seemed more like a woman on a quest, if you know what I mean. She gets a look in her eye . . .'

'Yeah,' Sam says. 'Know what you mean. Like an avenging warrior.' Or a cat waiting to pounce, he thinks.

Fast Freddy beams: 'That's it! You got it in one. So you're all right, then. It's just when you called asking if I'd picked her up, it occurred to me she'd obviously forgotten to mention she was taking off and I thought you might be wondering or unsure . . .' He breaks off. Out of puff. Out of ideas. Out of his comfort zone.

'Thanks for the concern, mate, but it's all good. She'll be back when she's ready. Count on it.'

The third meeting of the Save Garrawi committee takes place four days before the black-tie fundraiser. The group convenes at Sam's house. Shoes are kicked off in a mess at the door. Backpacks dumped in the hallway. Bottles of red wine are slammed onto the kitchen counter, beer and white wine stashed in the fridge before they lose their frigidly cold edge. The house smells of buttery pastry with savoury overtones. Mouths water. The mood is upbeat. Sam and his sous chef, Jimmy, produce a medley of sausage rolls from the oven, including his newest experiment, a tasty mixture of pork, veal, ginger, garlic, chilli and shallots.

'Hold off on the tom sauce with these little beauties,' Jimmy advises, his freckly face red from the heat of the oven.

Sam says: 'Try them with the sweet chilli or on their own.'

Even the chef is impressed. 'You are becoming adventurous,' he says, slapping Sam on the back. 'Next we can expect the Sam's Sauso Roll franchise, no?'

'Ya reckon?' Jimmy asks. He swallows one whole, licks

his fingers. Reaches for another. Blows on it and passes it to Longfellow. 'They're bloody delicious, Sam, I'm tellin' ya. Longfella's a pretty good judge.'

Siobhan calls the meeting to order. People plant their backsides uncomfortably on deck rails. Two mouldy canvas chairs are reserved for the Misses Skettle, who have rung to say they are running late. Something to do with setting the custard for the desserts for the fundraiser on Saturday night.

Jane reports that the treasury is in the black. The gala dinner is a sell-out. She will have a more accurate figure after expenses are deducted. Ettie breaks in: 'I've worked out the food costs. Around five hundred dollars . . .'

'I'll need receipts,' Jane says, a tad officiously. Ettie looks bewildered. Marcus rushes to her side. 'I will organise this aspect,' he announces. 'Kate is away. It is too much to run a café and separate the costs, yes?'

'Good idea, chef,' Siobhan says, smoothly. 'Ettie's generosity often means she ends up out of pocket. We can't have that.' Jane retires to a corner of the deck, unsure whether she's had a win, a loss or a rap over the knuckles. Sam's phone rings. He races off. Reports back with the news that the Misses Skettle apologise. They regret they will be unable to attend this evening. The custard has curdled and they must begin again. Everyone feels deeply for them.

Jimmy announces with a swagger that's new to him that there has been no new paintwork in the park. 'But a lotta blokes have been trampin' around lookin' under rocks and takin' pictures. Bloody shifty-lookin' lot if ya want my opinion.'

Siobhan gives the kid a hard look. 'You're an expert now on shifty looks, are you?' Jimmy grins, missing the irony.

'Watch you don't get too big for your boots, sonny. Or you'll come a cropper.'

Sam steers Jimmy back to the kitchen, out of harm's way. 'Another plate of sauso rolls, mate. And don't forget the dog. As you rightly deduced, he's a downright connoisseur of life's little luxuries.'

Jimmy, bamboozled by the rhetoric, catches the bit about feeding the dog and follows through. One bite for the dog. One for him. By the time he returns to the meeting, it's well under way. He sits in a corner with his knees pulled into his chest. Wipes a few flakes of pastry from the mutt's jowls. They both fall asleep.

'We're doing well, so far,' Siobhan says. 'But in another week or two, the safety-flare demonstration will be forgotten and, along with it, our campaign. More ideas, if you please. Keep the spot fires burning.'

She goes on to report that continuing responses to the Three Js' letters asking for support are still flying in from the Greens, individual members of the Liberal and Labor Parties, particularly local members who, she warns, can't be trusted beyond the next election. The Conservation Foundation, the Heritage Council, the Surfrider Foundation – every single official body contacted including unions and mothers' clubs – are asking if they can help out. There's even finally been a positive response from the office of the Duke of Edinburgh, that commends the preservation of the environment.

'This is all well and good but if you think Mulvaney's going to take any notice of a few letters, you're all off in la-la land. He's just going to play dirtier. I've heard, by the way, that sneaky son-of-a-bitch who's swanning around like he's the newly anointed king of Cook's Basin is looking for barges to carry three bulldozers into the park.'

'Ah, bloody hell . . .'

'No takers, so far. But don't get too cosy. As we all know, money talks and it takes very little effort to become fluent in the language of cash.'

John Scott steps forward, his face beetroot red. 'I've been holding back on reporting an offer to the artists from Lowdon.'

Siobhan nods: 'The art gallery and commissions, eh? No secrets on the Island, John. You should know that by now. So have you come to a decision?'

'No deal.'

'Hear, hear!' Loud clapping. Another cheer.

'And if I may ask, what was the deciding factor?'

'There were a few. Lowdon's a deadshit. The money would be spent in a flash. We'd all have to move because the Island would be ruined. And we're planning to set up our own galleries in our boatsheds, which we'll open once a month for organised tours. Phoebe's working on a design for the website as we speak.'

'Hear, hear!'

Siobhan turns towards Sam: 'And Frankie? Has he made up his mind yet?'

Sam sighs. No secrets on the Island all right. 'I'll let you know as soon as I hear.'

Siobhan rubs her hands together like they're cold, paces for a second: 'I've been thinking,' she says. The committee leans forward. 'After the fundraiser there'll be money to burn, eh? We should move on those advertisements in a major metropolitan newspaper. Nothing terrifies powerful men more than the thought that they're up against money. They're scared rigid it will mean spending some of their own.'

Hear, hear.

'If the artists could come up with a design?'

John nods.

Siobhan smiles: 'Haven't I always said? There's no situation that cannot be further inflamed.'

Hear, hear.

Seaweed stands and clears his throat. 'If ya interested . . .' he begins, hitching frayed shorts kept up by a string around his waist. Every head turns in his direction. He squirms. 'I'm not sayin' I've done the right thing . . .'

'Well get to the point, Seaweed, and be sure that we'll tell you,' Siobhan says, with what passes for kindness.

'I came across a few files er, by mistake. Yeah. That's it. By mistake.'

'And?' Siobhan says.

'I was checkin' out me own bank balance, when – by mistake, you understand – I found myself lookin' at an unfamiliar set of figures for an account in the Cook Islands, which as it turned out, appeared to belong to Theo Mulvaney. At least, he seemed to be a director of the company I accidentally came across.'

'You hacked –?' Jenny says, incredulously.

Siobhan snaps, 'Did you not hear how the man made a terrible mistake?' Her voice softens: 'Well now, I'd call that the luck of the Irish. If I still believed in a god in heaven I'd say he was well and truly committed to our cause.'

Jenny grins. The whole committee grins. Siobhan wriggles

her shoulders in happy anticipation. 'And from this terrible mistake, Seaweed,' she wheedles, 'what did you discover?'

'That Mulvaney received a payment of five hundred thousand dollars from the New Planet Fountain of Youth six months ago.'

'Ah,' everyone murmurs.

Sensing there's more, Siobhan makes a beckoning sign with her hand. 'Give, give.'

Seaweed delivers with a flourish: 'He also received twenty-five grand from Eric Lowdon.'

'Ah.' Another collective response.

Siobhan says: 'What a cheapskate the bald little toad is, eh?' She sighs almost dreamily. 'Since the Misses Skettle aren't with us tonight, I'll indulge in a little colourful language, if you don't mind. My friends, we have got him by the proverbial balls.'

'Hear, hear.'

She stands, unlashes and re-lashes her long red hair. 'So we'll keep this to ourselves for the moment, are you all clear? Print out a file, would you, Seaweed, and deliver it to my door when you have a moment. From now on, we've no idea how we came by this information. An anonymous benefactor, we'll say. The file dropped at my back door and none of us the wiser. You'll wipe your hard drive, of course.'

Seaweed digs into a stained knapsack at his feet. Hands Siobhan a file. 'The hard drive's so clean you could eat off it,' he says smugly.

'Good man. It's a question of how we use this amazing insight into a man's uncanny ability to make such massive amounts of money in the flicker of an eyelid. I need to think long and hard.'

When the meeting breaks up, Siobhan takes Sam aside: 'Now tell me, are you able to fly unassisted, then?' she asks. 'Can we expect to see you floating around the Island on a magic mattress in the not too distant future?'

'Ah, mate, trust me, the whole experience beggared belief. I still can't figure out whether it was crazy, misguided or just plain weird. About forty – I dunno, what would you call them?'

'Eejits,' Siobhan suggests drily.

'Well, anyway, they were a bunch of barefoot, beaming innocents – no women – with neat haircuts and dressed in white tracksuits. They sat on thin mattresses on the floor in a dingy old room smelling of a blocked drain that made the toxic-smelling recent septic gasses on the Island seem like a sweet perfume. Although no one seemed to notice. They were too busy bouncing up and down on their backsides with their legs crossed in a position I have just learned is known as lotus. I'll tell you something else for nothing, mate. The lotus position is the nearest thing to torture I've ever experienced.'

'But the flying part? How did they get around that?'

'Ah. The backside raising was stage one. I would be inducted into Stage Two after signing a form agreeing to pay a further three thousand bucks. All for a good cause, you understand. The money, I was told, would go towards creating a philosophy that will lead to world peace.'

Siobhan snorts.

'Not a goon in sight, though. No black suits or sunglasses. Just a bright-eyed leader lifting his backside over and over and chanting loudly.'

Siobhan stands to leave. 'Watch your back, boyo. They'll know you were there. Trust me, they'll know.'

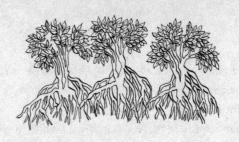

CHAPTER TWENTY

Kate watches a hot orange sun rise slowly above a cushion of white clouds, turning them the colour of one of Jimmy's traffic-stopping orange T-shirts. The quality of light shifts from thin and wintry to richly tropical. Two hours later, she makes it quickly through customs and immigration and through the International terminal to the escalators leading to the rail shuttle service to the city. At Central Station, she waits at the bus stop. The switch from icy to hot weather is almost an assault. Every so often she checks the schedule printed on the sign. The bus is running late.

By the time the double-length blue people carrier with its accordion midriff screeches to a halt in a cloud of thick exhaust, she has stripped to a T-shirt and pulled off her woollen socks. After just ten days in Britain, the tan on her arms has faded to a faint stain. She stands aside while people stumble down steps and onto the footpath to head off in different directions. When the last passenger, a young woman with an iPod plugged into her ears and wearing denim shorts over thick black stockings like she can't decide on the season, topples out, Kate steps on board. She rummages in her bag to find the right currency among her pounds, shillings and pence and takes a seat up front. There are just two other passengers heading out of the city instead of into it. The bus roars off, buildings pass in a blur.

Just over an hour later, she wanders into the Square, where the giant white papier-mâché cockatoo, with its arrogant yellow cockscomb fanned out like a clownish hat, takes up most of the space. It takes her by surprise until she remembers the fight to save Garrawi. There is no sign of Sam or the *Mary Kay* but Fast Freddy is dressed in rainbow colours as usual, supping his usual coffee, breaking apart his usual raspberry muffin and contemplating – as usual – what the astrology column says is in store for him during the day. He sees her and his tired, water-taxi post-nightshift eyes, light up. 'So you're back then,' he says.

Kate throws her gear on the picnic table, stands back to take in the sight of The Briny Café, still leaning, still in need of a new roof, still in business. 'Nobody walks away from their investments, Freddy.'

As the words fall out of her mouth, Kate hears the cold practicality of them. Fast Freddy, one of the few locals who embraced her from the very beginning, flinches.

'But the bottom line, Freddy,' she adds quickly, 'is that it's good to be back.' Fast Freddy nods. Kate kisses his cheek. He blushes so furiously his skin clashes with his sky-blue beanie. He shoots off like a frightened rabbit, upsetting a couple of scrounging seagulls, before leaping nimbly into his water taxi (nimbly for a man on the wrong side of fifty), and gunning the engine home.

After a while, when the sun has tainted her face with a layer of pink over her English pallor, she picks up her gear and heads across the Square to The Briny Café. At the last minute, she hesitates in the doorway. She knows she's broken every Cook's Basin code. She has no idea how Ettie will react to her return. She takes a deep breath and steps inside.

'Kate!' Ettie flies around the counter, leaving three tradies hanging out for their cappuccinos, and throws her arms around her partner. 'You're back. Well, of course, you're back. Any fool can see that. Did you find what you were looking for? My god, you've lost weight. Come inside. Let me fatten you up until you're back to your old self. My goodness, you look wan.' She breaks off. Takes a long, apologetic breath. 'Sorry. I'll slow down. But lord, there's a lot to tell you. So much has happened. What about a coffee, love? And a good brekky. What do you say?'

'It's good to be home and the old Briny looks terrific. Smells good too . . . something new on the menu?' She slips her luggage on her desk under the stairs, turns back to Ettie.

Behind the counter, Jenny casually waves a tea towel.

'Pikelets. We're making huge batches for the tradies to take for their smoko. They've been a hit,' Ettie explains. 'Blokes feel a bit wussy buying a slice of cream cake, but a blueberry pikelet spiced with a little orange or lemon zest has grunt.'

'So how was it?' Jenny asks, coming over after seeing to the tradies' order and without a hint of warmth in her voice. 'Worth high-tailing it out of here at a crucial time?'

'Yeah.' Kate feels the animosity, backs away a little. 'I can't thank you enough for filling in –'

'Didn't do it for you. Did it for Ettie. Had a ball, actually.' She points to the Save Garrawi contribution jar on the counter. 'The café has become the campaign headquarters. Have to empty it every night and there are more notes than coins. Hope you keep it going now you're back.'

'Why wouldn't I?' Kate asks, puzzled.

Ettie, who's been silent, hastily grabs Kate's arm and leads her onto the deck. 'Come and sit down, love and I'll tell you what's been happening. Since you left, our tiny little cause has had so much attention it's on the national map. It's given us such heart we feel we're unstoppable.'

The two women settle into a corner table. Jenny brings out a couple of coffees. 'Might've sounded a bit grumpy back there. Bad manners that I wouldn't let my kids get away with. Sorry.' She turns on her heel and leaves before Kate can respond.

Ettie reaches across the table for Kate's hand: 'So did you find him?'

'Yeah. I did.'

'And was it all you expected?'

'Better. But I don't know, Ettie, I feel edgy. Not sure why. Just feel that something's not quite right.'

'Trust your instincts, love. But remember, you could be over-reacting because you've been dealing with fairly traumatic situations for a while now.'

Kate shakes her head, dismissing the idea of trauma.

Ettie pushes the point: 'Think about it, love. In the last six months, you've quit your job, bought and renovated a house where the only way home is by boat, sunk your life savings in a crumbling café, your mum's died and you've discovered you have a half-brother on the other side of the world. Not exactly low-key stuff, is it? And I'm not even going to mention Sam.'

'Depends on how you look at it. Think of it this way: I escaped a job I'd begun to loathe, I found a glorious cheap piece of waterfront property and restored it to its former glory, learned the mostly joyous thrill of boating in even uncertain conditions, and landed in a bright new career as my own boss in a wonderfully vibrant community of stand-up anarchists. And while my mother may have died, I also gained a brother. And you. So tell me, Ettie, where's the downside?'

Ettie grins: 'Is that what's called spin, love? Now. I've got forty minutes until the morning-tea crowd arrives. Tell me every detail from the beginning.'

'Ettie? You coming in soon?' Jenny yells.

Ettie jumps up. 'Oh god, I lost track of time. I've got to run, but . . . it was all worth it, eh?'

'It's the not knowing that drives you nuts, Ettie.'

'So it's over then? You're back for good?'

'Ettie!' Jenny sounds desperate.

Ettie grins. 'Better get going or she'll fire me. Have a shower upstairs, love, and whack on an apron. We've been so busy lately three pairs of hands will make a huge difference. I'm afraid the paperwork is behind, too.'

Ettie helps with the rush and then begins making hazelnut pastry for a strawberry, mascarpone and toffee tart. Jenny washes up with more force than absolutely necessary. She gives Ettie a hard look: 'You're a good woman. Never known anyone with your ability to forgive and forget.'

'There's an old saying – forgive but don't forget. That's me.'

Jenny nods. 'Hate to see you get burned over and over, that's all.'

'It's so sad, you know. She could have it all if she'd give herself the chance.'

'Maybe she doesn't think she deserves it . . .'

Ettie looks up from her pastry, eyes wide with surprise. 'Yeah. You might just be right.' The discussion ends with the sound of Kate's footsteps on the stairs.

An hour later, Kate takes a break from paperwork. She waits a little longer for the late-morning lull to set in and then suggests she and Ettie go over the figures upstairs on the deck where there's more space.

'The pikelets must have been a massive success,' Kate says. 'Revenue has more than doubled since I went away. Journalists have a saying: *Never take a holiday because before you're even out the door, someone else will be warming your seat.*'

Ettie glances up, not sure how to reassure her. 'Jenny's a wonderful asset but her skills are different from yours. Business is good because the fight to save Garrawi has brought people to the area. It's really got nothing to do with the pikelets. Well, not much.'

'Come on, Ettie. There's no need to be diplomatic. Even with idyllic weather and the Garrawi interest, the increase is historic and, to be ruthlessly honest, disturbing. Jenny's ideas and ability have made an impact. It would be unfair if I didn't offer to step aside.'

Ettie sighs, looks towards the drooping casuarinas in the Square – why do they always have to look so sad and hopeless and yet sing so beautifully when the wind flows through them? 'You are an equal partner in the café, Kate. In the end, the choice is yours. But if you're here, I expect you to work. I'd prefer it if you didn't take a wage for the time you were away. Frankly, you haven't earned it.'

In the distance, the canary-yellow duckbill bow of the *Mary Kay* rounds the northern end of Cutter Island, far enough away to give it the size and fragility of a toy boat. Kate quickly stacks the spreadsheets. 'Fair enough,' she says.

'I'd like to keep Jenny on staff for the time being, too,' Ettie says. 'For as long as business stays booming. Deal?'

Kate hesitates for a fraction of a second. 'Deal.'

CHAPTER TWENTY-ONE

On the *Mary Kay*, Jimmy is sweeping dirt overboard from the mess made by a landscaping pick-up and delivery of twenty tonnes of rich black soil to Charlie Smithers, a city-based bloke with the heart of a genuine country boy. The dirt, stored in massive bags, is destined to be spread over the rocky shale of the shoreline at the nub of Kingfisher Bay. 'First grandkid,' Charlie explained, when Sam gently tried to point out the downside ahead for anyone who tried to twist Mother Nature into an unwilling new shape. 'The missus wants a deep green lawn right down to the beach so the kid doesn't hurt his tootsies when he dashes off for a swim. Never mind some years it forgets to rain. Never mind the salt in every high tide will kill it off. Never mind if by some miracle it takes hold, I'll have to bust my gut mowing it every weekend.'

Sam grunted in sympathy. Charlie, on a roll and with a like-minded audience, continued, sounding sad: 'The kid's a boy. Named after me. If my wife, bless her, has her way, he'll never know a moment's grief. How's he going to learn if he's never tested? That's what I want to know.'

Sam saw anxious eyes and struggled to find something solid for Charlie to grab on to. 'It's a different battlefield out there, mate. Kids are tested every day in new ways that you and I never even dreamed of. Wouldn't worry too much anyway, until he's old enough to toddle. By then the grass will be dead, the rocks sticking up like needlepoints and your missus will be relieved 'cause the little bloke won't be able to make a beeline for the ocean before he can swim without turning the soles of his feet into mincemeat.'

Charlie's face cleared. 'What do I owe you? And add a hundred bucks for the fighting fund. OK?'

'Too bloody right.'

Sam watches Jimmy finish clearing up. Coiling ropes tight as grass mats, stowing hoses and checking the hook on the crane is secured good and fast so no unsuspecting pirate steps on board to do a runner with the *Mary Kay* and, instead, gets his head knocked off. Truthfully, if any outlaw tried to hijack his barge, Sam would prefer to do the decapitating himself.

Charlie's words swirl uncomfortably. In his pocket, he has the name and number of the producer of one of the more decent television current affairs shows who wants to interview Jimmy. They've offered a fee, which Sam thinks is astronomical, given they're asking for just a day of Jimmy's time. He'd have enough to buy the car of his dreams (within reason), a warehouse full of fabric for Amelia's thriving patchwork quilt business, a rhinestone collar for the dog and a new tinny as long as he settled for a second-hand outboard. Sam knows he has to discuss it with the kid and let him make up his own mind but there are ways of presenting cases that can sway a person further one way than the other. Artie's given fair warning about the evils of fame, even if the limelight is only temporary. But Jimmy's eighteen. If ever there was a right time to muscle up for testing time, it's now. He mulls the pros and cons in an internal conversation with Kate as adversary. What would she think? What would she advise? What does she *know* about the downsides? But he finds himself circling his and her arguments without any clear-headed result. He tries Delaney's mobile for the tenth time and the call goes straight to message bank.

'Jimmy!' he yells out.

The kid bounces up from his cross-legged position on the bow, Longfellow by his side, and tears along the deck to the cabin.

'Aye, aye, Sam!'

'How much money you got saved, son?'

'I'm watchin' the pennies, Sam, but the pounds are gettin' slower and slower.'

'What kind of a car are you after anyway?'

'A ute, just like yours. But new. Me mum reckons rust kills a car, Sam, and you got rust all over.'

'Yeah. Right. So how much would it cost? Have you done the sums or are you just dreaming?'

'Single cab. Tray back. Diesel. Eighteen thousand if I go for one of them new China utes. Why you askin', Sam? You got a deal goin' or somethin'? I'd go second-hand as long as the seller was legit. Know what I mean?'

Sam sighs. Has one last go: 'What's this damn ute for, Jimmy? You're an ocean boy, mate, with the feel of swells, not potholes, under your two platforms called feet.'

'I just want it, Sam. I want a car of me own.' His tone is wistful, the yearning so palpable Sam feels he could reel it in with only a fly for bait.

'When we get to The Briny, you and me are going to have a chat. Man to man . . .'

Jimmy hippity-hops, fixes excited eyes on Sam. Sensing big news, Longfellow yips and chases his fluffy tail for two spins before realising it's a loser's game. 'What about? About a ute?'

'One step at a time, Jimmy. Now, fenders over the side. We'll soon be alongside the glorious Briny to tie up. Smell that, mate? That's the sweetly spicy scent of one of Ettie's famous summer prawn curries. She's the answer to –'

'Aw, cool it, Sam. Ya done that line over like a dinner for too many years.'

Sam grins. In the distance, he catches movement in Ettie's penthouse. Gives a wave. Then sees there's no one there. The shadow of a passing cloud, maybe. But the sky is big and empty.

Inside the café, the lunchtime rush is on. Ettie and Jenny dodge and weave, their movements counter-intuitive as they load fillings on to fat slices of sourdough bread, plate the daily special of a coconut-rich red prawn curry, slam the on switches on the espresso machine, and deliver the goods without spilling or dropping a single morsel. From where Sam stands in the doorway, they look like dancers in a frantically modern pas de deux, as his mum, who was a ballet nut, would have said, although he's not sure she ever got the pronunciation spot on.

'Ya better hurry up,' Jimmy says, craning his neck around Sam's blocky body, 'the curry's goin' faster than daytime.'

'Eh?' Sam says. Then he gets it. Jimmy's in a bigger hurry than normal. He wants to settle the food issue immediately so they can find a spare table on the deck and focus on the ute that Sam's dangled in front of his eyes like a lottery win. He wonders if he should have kept his big mouth shut. Too late now, he thinks. 'OK, mate. Order me a curry and whatever you fancy long as it's got green stuff in it somewhere. Water for you, coffee for me. No arguments, mate. You run on rocket fuel without any help from Mr Coffee Bean. No saying where you'd end up after an espresso. Other side of the world most probably.'

'Ya lookin' out for me, Sam?'

'Always.'

Sam picks his way through the crowd to the last empty table. Ever since Delaney's coverage of the fight to save Garrawi, business has been booming. Good and bad, he thinks, remembering Ettie's swollen feet and small groans of exhaustion. He leans back in his seat, gobsmacked as usual by the beauty of Cook's Basin. Wonders idly if he'll ever lose sight of the fluid details that weave the real magic. He stares through water that beats steadily as a heart to where the sun strikes golden sand. Starfish – he stops to count – seven of them splayed out as still as statues.

'Sam!' Ettie shrieks, loud enough to splinter the frail timber walls of the café.

He leaps out of his chair, dashes inside. Ettie has Jimmy by the collar of his T-shirt. Her face is bright red, dripping with sweat. She's a bundle of nerves, anger and anxiety. 'Get him out,' she hisses. 'Right now.'

Jimmy looks distraught. He holds out his hand, palm

turned upwards for Sam to see. 'Poo,' he says. 'Picked it up off the floor, Sam, to tidy up.'

Ettie rolls her eyes, looks about to faint.

Jenny rushes forward to shield her from a cluster of curious customers. 'Er . . .' she says, lost for words.

'Out, out! Right now,' Ettie orders, her voice louder, higher.

'But we've gotta find the skink, Ettie. The skink'll die if we don't. They gotta have fresh water, ya see . . .'

Ettie's eyebrows shoot up as high as they'll go; her vocal cords are twisted so tight her words come out in a long squeak: 'We can talk about the er . . . skink, later, Jimmy. Jenny's got your lunch ready. I'll bring it out.'

Jimmy, feeling he's edging his way back onto more stable ground, holds out his palm again: 'See, ya know it's a skink from the white tip on the end of the poo . . .'

'Enough!' Ettie looks even fainter.

Jenny holds her up, patting her soothingly at the same time. She only lets go to grab a bottle of water out of the fridge. She lies the ice-cold length of it on the back of Ettie's fiery red neck. 'Take a break, Ettie. I'll get Kate to fill in for a while,' she advises.

'Kate?' Sam says. 'She's back?'

Before Ettie can reply, one of the customers, a nerdy-looking bloke with bloodhound eyes and large teeth, says: 'Could I get a look at that scat, kid?'

Jimmy holds his hand out proudly, a smile splitting his face.

'He's right,' says the nerd, sounding surprised. 'It's a skink . . . odd place to find a skink. Thought it might be a rat, but it's not.'

'Kid's a genius, no doubt about it,' Sam mutters, pulling

Jimmy away, figuring he'll deal with one crisis at a time. Jeez, what's he talking about? Kate doesn't fall into the crisis category. But his pulse is thumping hard and fast, he feels short of breath and he's fighting back a heap of contradictory emotions. He wants to rush upstairs and grab her in his arms so tightly neither of them can breathe. He wants to never lay eyes on her again. He wants to settle opposite her over a bowl of steaming hot spaghetti Bolognese but couldn't bear to share a meal that ended in a polite cheerio instead of a sweaty night in tangled sheets.

He'd like to ask her how she'd handle Jimmy's sudden media desirability; the fight for Garrawi; flying mattresses and how anyone could think reciting a secret mantra – to be revealed sometime in the future – for extended periods of time with your eyes closed and your legs crossed, could end in unaided human flight; and then there's the goons and a strategy to neutralise them.

At the same time, he doesn't want to start any conversation because he's terrified he will bend the drift of it into another shape that includes love, marriage and a handful of kids. He tells himself to get a grip. He reminds himself he's already made the decision to walk away, that he's better off out of it. The fact brings him a degree of calm. He wonders how she got along with her brother. Ah jeez, who's he kidding? He's still besotted.

Back at their table, Jimmy refuses to sit: 'The skink, Sam, it's gotta be thirsty. We gotta get Ettie to put out a saucer of water. Or maybe milk. I'll ring me mum and see what she says about the milk. I think they like milk.'

'We'll work it out, mate. Trust me. And that skink's been OK for weeks now so another day without a saucer of water or milk isn't going to hurt . . .'

'Ya sure? Ya sure he won't cark it?'

'Positive,' Sam says firmly.

'Ya didn't cross ya fingers behind ya back, didja?'

Sam shakes his head: 'No, mate, promise you.'

Five minutes later, Ettie is flat out on the sofa. She lies as still as possible, waiting for the sudden onrush of anxiety to dissipate. Kate dumps her paperwork and brings her a cold, damp flannel, which she places over her eyes.

'I would've laughed off all that kerfuffle six months ago,' Ettie murmurs. 'Now, any little tilting of the normal daily axis feels like the earth is splitting open under my feet.' She removes the cloth, stares into Kate's eyes. 'You don't think I'm losing the plot, do you?'

Kate shakes her head, smiling. 'No way.'

'God, I've got a mongrel headache coming on,' she moans. 'Flashing slivers of light in my left eye. Need painkillers fast please or I'll end up with a full-on migraine.'

'Coming up,' Kate says, heading for Ettie's medicine cupboard. She fills a glass with water and carries it to her friend. 'I'll call Marcus and ask him to come and get you.'

Ettie shoots up, almost panicky, groans, drops down: 'No. Please. Don't say a word to him. I'll be fine in half an hour, truly. Off you go. Jenny must be frantic by now.'

'At some stage you're going to have to admit you've hit menopause with a vengeance . . .'

Ettie raises her voice angrily: 'I will not, I refuse point blank to have anything to do with that . . . that business. I have finally found a man I adore and who loves me. I am having the best sex of my life. I am happy, for god's sake. I am also tired, stressed, and probably having a niggling and inconvenient bout of temporary hormone havoc caused by all of the above. Not to mention coping with a disappearing partner . . . Sorry, we've been through all that already.'

'Fine. Whatever you say . . .'

'Now go. Go!' Ettie says, sounding exasperated, covering her eyes once more with the damp cloth and letting out a little whimper of pain. 'Bloody migraines. Never had them in my life until a couple of months ago.'

'I rest my case.' Kate flees before Ettie has time to react.

At the bottom of the stairs, she runs smack bang into Sam 'Hiya, Sam,' she says, as if she's never been away. 'How's it going, Jimmy?' She reaches for two plates ready on the counter. Holds out the curry, her eyebrows raised in a question.

'That's Sam's,' Jimmy says. 'Mine's the other one.'

'Nice to see you home safe and sound,' Sam says, taking his plate. Besotted, yeah. But hurt, too. She could've called. 'Let's find a table on the deck, Jimmy. Tuck in, before our lunch gets cold. Catch you later, Kate. And like I said, great to have you back.'

Kate hesitates. 'Sure.' She turns on her heel.

Jimmy leans towards Sam, his voice a whisper: 'You two havin' a barney, Sam? Or what? Ya can tell me, ya know. I'm ya friend for life. Honest. And me lips are sealed. I don't hold with gossip and neither does me mum.'

Sam smiles. 'So a secret is safe from everyone except your mum, eh?'

'Well, me mum says it doesn't matter what I tell her, she's on my side. So all bet's are off with me mum, right?'

Sam considers explaining the morality, legality and philosophical implications of secrets then gives up the idea. Not many secrets last for more than a nanosecond in Cook's Basin anyway. Spices – cumin, coriander, chilli, and probably a dozen more he can't identify – spiral up from his curry to his nose. The rice is white and fluffy, with a thin slice of lemon buried loosely among the grains. Best of all, the appearance of Kate has distracted Jimmy from the question of the ute. He forks a prawn into his mouth. A symphony of flavours skirts the edges of his tongue. He catches Jimmy pushing his salad aside while he hoes into the lasagne. 'How many times have I got to tell you, Jimmy? Eat your greens.'

'Ya gunna tell me about the ute, Sam? Man to man, like ya said.'

Sam sighs. Puts his fork on the side of his plate. 'Do you have a dream, Jimmy, a real dream that you had long before you wanted a ute or a tinny?'

'O' course,' Jimmy says, his normally childlike expression morphing into his serious version of adulthood.

'Can you tell me?'

'Ya won't laugh, will ya?'

Sam shakes his head.

'I wanna get married and have me own kids, Sam. At least two. Me mum says one kid can end up cranky 'cause they get too spoiled. Spoiled kids are brats, ya know what I mean? She said you and I were the . . . er, expection to the rule, but mostly it was a dead-set certainty. Mind you, me mum was one of thirteen. She reckoned that wasn't much chop, either.'

A germ of an idea begins to take hold in Sam's head.

'You need to save hard if you want to have a family. You up for that?'

'Once I get me ute, Sam, I'm up for anything, aren't I?'

Sam rolls his eyes, cursing his idiot impulse to mention the car. He pulls out his mobile phone and dials the chef. He needs help on this one. He walks away from the table to have a quick conversation that clues in Marcus, who has his own take on the subject, to the upside and downside of fame and makes arrangements for Jimmy and his mother to meet him on the chef's deck at sunset.

Pleased he's sorting through at least one problem, he sits back down and tucks into his curry with renewed gusto and an even deeper appreciation of Ettie's unerringly exquisite talents in the kitchen. He's not the kind of man who often contemplates the follies of happenstance but jeez, there was something wrong with the order of the universe when it saw fit to link Ettie and the chef. Two great cooks in one household was borderline criminal. Not that they weren't a great couple and didn't appreciate each other's culinary skills to the maximum, but good cooks needed to be shared around the greater unskilled population who otherwise relied on meat – mostly lamb chops till the price sky-rocketed – and potatoes for sustenance. Not that he isn't a devout aficionado of the humble lamb-y chop, which in his opinion runs a close second to sausage rolls, it's just that variety, as anyone with half a brain is well aware, is the spice of life.

Realising he's sending his thoughts off in haywire directions to switch his mind off Kate not even bothering to let him know she was home, he decides to focus on the upcoming black-tie fundraiser. Five minutes later, his head awash with dead ends (Does black tie mean tables, chairs, and matching cutlery for chrissake?), he gives up and orders Jimmy aboard the *Mary Kay.* He lumbers into the café to pay the bill. It's a pointless exercise. The joint is jumping with tourists in search of food and drink and no one's got a second to scratch themselves. He slaps enough notes on the counter to cover the damage and heads for the barge with his woolly head down. He's ready to tackle the business of Jimmy's magic windfall that if mishandled – despite everyone's best intentions – could turn into a nightmare and ruin the life of a kid who was born with enough personal, er, glitches to challenge even the toughest hombres. Hombres? Where the hell had he found that word when *bloke* was a more than decent description for a . . . well, bloke?

Amidst the rush, in a tone she hopes is tinged with the right degree of nonchalance and self-deprecating humour to pass off as casual interest only, Kate says: 'Sam seems to be so busy I don't think he even noticed I was gone.'

Jenny, furiously working the grill and plating up six orders at a time, swings around, her face red with effort. 'Oh, he noticed. He's just finally realised that, at best, you're a seriously dodgy bet. At worst, you'll bleed him dry of every one of his generous instincts and then leave him wrung out forever.'

Kate grabs the plates, a flush of her own rising from the base of her neck. 'Wouldn't want you to hold back, Jenny.'

'Not in my nature. Not when a good-hearted man whose natural impulse is to save souls lays his own wellbeing on the line for someone – and Kate, I'm not beating around the bush here, either – who may not be worth the effort. And for your information, I'm not talking about romance, love or even a full-on fling. Go figure the rest for yourself.' Jenny turns back to the grill, tossing a tea towel over a shoulder, and diving on the hamburger buns. 'Bugger,' she says crossly. 'Burned.' She tosses them in the bin and starts again.

Kate bolts, like she's been slapped hard in the face.

The Misses Skettle, who stood aside through the discussion, heads at an angle all the better to catch every word, step forward, smiling serenely. 'Feel better now you've got it off your chest?' one of them asks.

Jenny swings around, spatula raised, her eyes blazing. When she spies the two old ladies, resplendent as usual in shades of pink, she smiles wryly. Violet Skettle, the older of the twins, reaches across the counter and pats Jenny's shoulder. 'You're under pressure, dear. Kids, saving Garrawi, the café.'

'It's just that Kate –'

'We're all built differently. Nothing wrong with that as far as I can see. Makes the world more interesting, doesn't it, Myrtle? Be a terrible thing if we were all the same. And Sam can take care of himself. He learned long ago where rock bottom lies and he's smart enough to quit long before he gets close to it.'

'What can I get you?' Jenny asks with a loud sigh, knowing when she's defeated.

'Nothing, dear. We just called in to give Ettie some sweet-potato cream to rub on the inside of her thighs. It might help to get her hormones back on track – at least until she admits she's going through the change and not simply unravelling as the day progresses.'

They plonk a jar that looks like it's been recycled many times since it first appeared filled with Pond's cold cream, probably in the 1950s, and twitter off back into the Square.

CHAPTER TWENTY-TWO

Sam dashes home to clean off the sweat and dirt of a hard day's work before his meeting with the habitually immaculate chef on his spotless deck overlooking the large flotilla of holidaying yachties moored in the shelter of a tiny bay fringed with a golden crescent of beach. In the bathroom, he catches a quick glimpse of his face in the mirror. He pauses. He is unable to recall the last time he took a long, hard look at himself. Well, he thinks, that's not quite true.

The last time he looked closely he was thirty instead of forty years old and pissed as a lizard. The image that bounced back then – bleary-eyed, slack-mouthed, red-faced and slightly off-balance – shocked him into sobriety. Long ago, he'd come to grips with the idea that he'd never give Tom Cruise a run for his money, but until that defining moment, he'd always thought he could handle the booze with gentlemanly valour, without the boring, self-absorbed sloppiness of most drunks. Since then, if a few of his old demons seemed to be gaining the upper hand and he felt like tying one on till they were beaten back into submission, he took to the water on the *Mary Kay* and got quietly shit-faced in private. Better than revealing the darker side of Sam Scully, known far and wide as a mostly cock-eyed optimist and generally decent bloke, to the impressionable Island kids.

Today, he might be in full control of his faculties but he's shocked to see someone slightly feral gazing back. Hair turned into dreadlocks by the salt air. Face well weathered, as square as the rest of him. A two-day stubble flecked with grey. Grey? Jeez, when did that happen? He pulls a tape measure out of his back pocket. According to one of Fast Freddy's latest dips into the shifting sands of modern health research, the average life span for a bloke is now eighty years. He stretches the tape along the rim of the bathtub and locks it at eighty centimetres. Places his callused thumb on the forty-centimetre mark. So, he thinks with a feeling that's not unlike rising seasickness, if he's average and barring accidents or some hideous life-threatening disease, he's half done with making a footprint on this earth. Christ, what happened to the last ten years? Where did they go? What's he got to show for them? He casts his mind back, sees the seasons scroll in a fast rewind through a mish-mash of fireshed dinners, community meetings where the problems are mostly the same and never change, picnics, a few (quite a few) casual summer romances and days plotted and planned around the rise and fall of the tides.

He turns away from the mirror, feeling slightly shattered. He is not the man he dreamed of becoming. A family man like his ferry-driving father, who slowed his hell-for-leather young son every so often, to point out the small details that truly enriched life. 'See the tiddlers, son? Watch how they play in the shallows where they're safe from sharks that gulp them down. See the octopus? Watch how she shields her babies from predators. We should all have eight arms, eh, and turn red to frighten enemies away? See the tawny frogmouth babies? They're learning to fly. They'll crash and bang for a while but they'll never give up. Remember, life can be tough so it's the way you handle problems that really counts.'

Sam presses a button and the tape measure winds back with a lethal speed before snapping shut. He opens the bathroom cupboard, turning the mirror towards the wall. He reaches for shaving cream and a razor and, from memory, slides the blade along his sun- and salt-blasted cheeks. He's had enough of the sight of his freckly, messy, boofy phisog for one day.

Three hours later, scrubbed and feeling slightly less pessimistic about his future, he leaves the *Mary Kay* tied safely to his jetty and jumps in his tinny to make the trip across open blue water to Kingfish Bay. The engine starts with the first pull of the cord; he opens the throttle slightly and lets the salty tang of a brothy summer sea invade his senses. The sun is a sinking hot orange ball shooting fiery blades that bounce off the water. He closes his eyes against the glare. How, he wonders, do you explain to a boy who knows only how to live in the moment that planning for a secure future is far more important than a ute?

He scrummages through his past until he finds a memory of his father sitting at the kitchen table, his hand on a chipped old money box his mother had picked up at Vinnies. 'You ever heard about saving for a rainy day, son? Well, here's how you do it.' And he put the box in front of Sam and handed him a one-dollar coin. 'In the box, Sam, because the sun can't be relied upon to always shine.' Sam had held the coin in the palm of his hand, burning with a desire to race out and spend it on something. Anything. A few years later, he realised what he'd felt was the raw and heady power of money and he'd understood that if you let it take hold of you, it could twist your head away from what really mattered. That's what the bastards planning a bridge and a resort on Cutter Island had lost sight of. What did Delaney say the New Planet Fountain of Youth was worth? Billions. And yet it still wasn't enough. He could almost feel sorry for the boys with black holes where their eyes should be, for the paltry meanness of their narrow little lives.

Thinking of Delaney, he pulls out his mobile. His call goes to message bank. Christ, he mutters, journos have a bad habit of stepping into your life and taking over, then jumping out as soon as something new catches their imagination. You wouldn't call them stayers, that's for sure. He drags his eyes back from the beauty of the rolling hills, blue in the evening light, and aims the bow of his tinny at the chef's house. That's when he notices the snub-nosed outline of Kate's boat tied to the pontoon and his stomach goes into free fall. He deliberately stalls the engine to give himself time to think, rocks on the water while the last warm breath of a nor'westerly dries his recently shampooed hair. He watches as Kate and the chef emerge from the house carrying trays and sighs before firing up a suddenly reluctant engine once more and wheezing towards his fate.

Kate tried to resist the chef's invitation, citing jetlag and exhaustion, but he was adamant. 'For Jimmy's sake,' he said.

'Be strong for a little while longer. For Jimmy's sake.' He'd pounced on her like a saviour when he found her back in harness at The Briny. 'This is fate, yes? To arrive on this most important day of a meeting about Jimmy's future.'

He told her that he and Sam were worried Amelia would push the kid to take the money and run without any clear-headed plan about what to do with it. Even less of an idea of how national exposure on a top-rating current affairs show might affect Jimmy's unique and essentially fragile view of life. Outside the secure boundaries of the Cook's Basin community, Jimmy would be easy prey for anyone with a sob story or a grand plan. 'This is true. We all know this. But what we don't know, is what is a fair price for a television interview?' the chef asked.

She floundered. Her background was finance, where stories were sought but never bought.

'The top offer is forty-five thousand dollars,' the chef whispered in her ear. 'It would take Jimmy close to a lifetime to save forty-five thousand dollars, now it drops into his lap like a gift from heaven. We must consider this opportunity wisely, no? It could set him up forever.'

In the end, she couldn't refuse.

'Thought you'd've crashed by now,' Sam says, as coolly as he can manage.

'Marcus was very persuasive,' Kate replies. 'Glass of wine? Or beer as usual?'

'A frigidly cold, thanks. Where's Ettie?'

'Helping the chef load another tray with nibbles.'

'She er, OK, after the skink episode?'

'She's fine. Just in denial about aging.'

Sam takes a swig of beer, choosing his words carefully: 'Whatever gets her through . . .'

'If she'd just face up to the fact that she's hit menopause full on, she could get some decent drug therapy. It would solve all her problems. But every time I've tried to open the subject, she bites my head off. Quite frankly, the Misses Skettles' jar of mashed sweet potato won't help.'

Sam raises his beer in a truce. 'Well, the old girls are always well-intentioned and in their funny way, they know a lot –'

'She needs modern science not witchcraft,' Kate says, sighing. 'Menopause isn't a new condition –'

'Hey! Here comes Jimmy with his mum. Back in a moment.' He races down the jetty where he stands waiting for five minutes, wiping the nervous sweat from his brow. Jeez, what does a bargeman know about menopause, for chrissake? Women are a mystery. He finds himself wondering whether he should find a dog to keep Longfellow company. Who's he kidding? Longfellow? Sam Scully, more like it. He helps Amelia disembark. Indicates she should go ahead. Jimmy chucks a stick from the end of the pontoon. Longfellow plunges into the water and, black-and-white fur fanning out like seaweed, swims after it. Man and boy walk up the jetty. For once, Jimmy is silent.

The group assembles around the table like they've pitched up in holiday clothes for a board meeting. Longfellow returns triumphant and drops the stick at Jimmy's feet. Shakes his furry body enthusiastically. Water flies. Ettie rushes to cover the nibbles with her hands but the damage is done. The crackers go soggy. Amelia, who has no idea what's going on, is thin-lipped and nervy. In the past, no meeting called to discuss Jimmy has begun or ended on a high note. She thought those days were over. Since her boy signed on with Sam, she's watched him grow into a functioning young man. Well, almost. He'd never lose the wondrous naiveté that the massive newspaperman had explained with such tact and insight and that seemed to have captured the imagination of a world weary of juvenile super brains and hard-boiled delinquents. And she's glad. She doesn't want a kid like other kids. Jimmy suited her fine. They complemented each other. And he wouldn't hurt a fly.

Sam picks up on Amelia's tension and shoots her an encouraging smile. 'It's all good, Amelia. Just got a few things to nut out with you both because the offers for Jimmy to appear on television are flowing in thick and fast.'

Amelia leaps to her feet. 'A star? Are you saying my boy's about to be a star?'

Sam sighs, trying to backtrack from what he silently admits is a super clumsy starting point. 'Let's just lay out what's been happening, one step at a time, OK? That's what the notebooks are for. To work through Jimmy's future, point by point.'

'Is this about the ute, Sam?' Jimmy asks, his eyes as bright as his mum's.

'Up to a point, mate. Right. So let's get started.' Sam pulls a sheaf of crumpled yellow Post-It notes out of his back pocket and places them in a long line in date and time order.

Amelia leans forward, trying to read the scribble. 'Never thought to bring my glasses,' she mutters.

During the next twenty minutes, Sam outlines the offers. Then he hands over to Kate, who runs through the television shows, the type of audience they attract and whether the fee offered is fair or a try-on. 'Truthfully, if you prefer one presenter to another but you think the show should pay more, you can have a go at upping the ante. I'd advise hiring a manager. I'd also warn you that the whole deal might fall in a heap if you ask for more money than the original offer. Another word of advice? Make up your mind really fast. By the end of the week, there'll be a whole new crisis unfolding or star being born and Jimmy will be old hat. The offers will be withdrawn without qualm or conscience.'

Amelia stands up and circles the group, wringing her hands in an old-fashioned way. Jimmy, who's been uncharacteristically silent the whole time, kicks the table leg. No one reprimands him. Even Longfellow, curled in a sodden ball at the kid's feet, picks up on the tension and quizzically eyes first one person, then another, as if he's waiting for an answer. Or direction.

'If we start by agreeing that it would be madness to turn down a heap of money that could set my son up for the rest of his life, then where do we go from there? Bear in mind that I have his best interests at heart, too. But I have more faith in his good sense and ability to judge right from wrong, sleaze from sincerity than you do. My boy,' she adds, getting up to stand behind him and placing her hands on his thin bony shoulders, 'is nobody's fool.'

Kate plays with her pencil, her eyes fixed on her notebook where she's scrawled a heap of numbered points and underlined key words. 'I'm sure you know your son. But truly, Amelia, you have no idea about the media. All it takes is one cunning producer who takes a dislike to Jimmy for no reason any of us will ever understand, and the kid will be set up to take a huge fall. How do you think he'll feel when he walks through the Square and people point at him and laugh?'

Jimmy's face goes pale, he knits his eyebrows and pulls at the one or two coarse hairs that have sprung up on his chin in the past few weeks. 'A good laugh or a bad laugh?' he asks.

'That's the point, Jimmy. You don't need to know and you shouldn't care. Think you can manage that?' Kate asks.

'We talkin' 'bout Fast Freddy laughin'? Or Jenny? Or Ettie?'

'No, mate, strangers. We're talking about strangers,' Sam says gently.

The kid's face lights up with relief. 'Aw jeez. Is that all? They can laugh all they want, Sam. Nothing to do with me, is it?'

Amelia stands back with a smug look that says the deal is done. Sam fears the worst. Kate offers to find a manager who'll charge somewhere between ten and forty per cent of the fee (Amelia almost reels then says she'll manage her son's media career with a little input from Kate, if Kate doesn't mind), Marcus says he will phone his lawyer who will be on call to make sure the contracts are fair.

Amelia's enthusiasm falters for a second. 'Thank you, chef,' she says. 'Never been crash hot with the fine print.'

'And perhaps,' Marcus suggests, 'it might be permissible to draw up a trust for Jimmy to access at the age of twenty-one, or even twenty-five.'

Amelia looks nonplussed for a second, then nods. 'It's his money, chef. I'm well aware of that fact.'

Ettie, who's been quiet all evening, finally chips in: 'One way of keeping a little control over the interview might be to suggest it is done right here in Cook's Basin where we can all keep an eye on proceedings.'

Kate nods. 'Good idea. All we have to do is make sure it's stipulated in the contract. If we explain Jimmy gets confused and agitated in foreign environments, they'll have to agree.'

'So it's on then?' Sam asks. Every head around the table nods, with the exception of Jimmy, who's focused on the dog. Sam walks away with his phone and makes a call to say yes to the highest bidder. He can't shake the feeling he's participating in a form of child abuse.

'When do I get me ute?' Jimmy whispers, coming up behind Sam and cupping his hand around Sam's ear so no one else can hear.

'Rome –'

'Wasn't built in a day.'

'You understand what the saying really means?'

'Sure, Sam,' he replies uncertainly.

'Patience, mate, that's what it means. Have patience and you'll end up with an empire.'

'I know that, don't I? But we've started buildin', haven't we? We getting' the foundations laid, right?'

'Yeah. I guess so,' Sam says, hoping like hell they're not ripping them apart.

Kate, pleading genuine exhaustion, is the first to leave. Amelia and Jimmy follow. Sam says yes to a second beer. 'You're a smart man, Marcus. How do you think this is going to pan out?'

The chef shrugs. 'No one can even guess. But the boy, he has a good heart, no? It would take a criminal to try to crush that for a little entertainment. And this show, it is the best, I think. The reporters do not look for scalps unless they are political, of course, but that is to be expected, yes?'

'Hope you're right, mate,' Sam says.

For no reason at all, Ettie suddenly stands and excuses herself, putting her hand on Marcus's shoulder, telling him to enjoy the summer night with Sam. After she's out of sight, the chef turns to Sam: 'You see? She is ill, of this I am sure. But she won't talk to me. Me, the man who loves her like no other.'

'It's menopause, mate. According to the Misses Skettle, Jenny and Kate, Ettie's just hit middle-age with a vengeance.'

'Menopause? What does this mean?'

Sam shrugs, grins: 'Beats me. Secret women's business. But it's not life threatening, so you can relax. A word of warning. Whatever you do, don't mention the word in her hearing. She's liable to clout you with a cast-iron frying pan. One of the symptoms, apparently, is a short fuse.'

Sam's phone goes off. He checks the caller number, puzzled. 'Freddy, you all right? Broken down and need a tow? Calm down, mate, I can't understand what you're trying to say. Easy, Freddy. Start at the beginning again.'

Sam listens. His face goes white, he ends the call gently and gives a *stop* hand signal when the anxious chef makes a move towards him. Then walks slowly, almost blindly, to the end of the jetty where he bends from the waist and dry retches over the water in violent, noisy spasms. A couple of minutes later, he straightens, wipes the back of his hand across his mouth and shuffles back along the timber boards, holding onto the painted white rail like an ill old man in need of physical support: 'It's the *Mary Kay*. She's been scuttled.'

CHAPTER TWENTY-THREE

Sam Scully takes a deep breath and dives into tepid black water, pushing through a burst of phosphorescence that sparkles festively, obscenely, in the moonless night. On his jetty, a hundred Islanders in pyjamas, nighties, crumpled boxer shorts, or just a towel wrapped around a waist lean forward in anxious silence. Everyone is aware, without a word being spoken, that the battle has ramped up to a notch they have never before experienced and have no idea how to handle. Sam's busted taillights were bad, the smashed windows and trashed house were shocking. Sinking the *Mary Kay*, a much-loved local icon that has rescued, resurrected and stalwartly provided for any vessel in strife and never failed the community, is one step short of murder.

Islanders gaze into dark water where she lies silent and lifeless, a heartbreaking, ghostly sight as the pale green torchlight washes over her. One or two women swallow sobs. A couple of the blokes wade in deep to rescue whatever floats. Ropes. Fuel containers. The flashy red cushions from the infamous banquette. Sam surfaces, gasping. Duck dives again. Anxious eyes follow his beam of light. She looks so perfectly undamaged and inert, like she's sleeping soundly with just a slight lean where she nestles into the seabed, but the *Mary Kay*, once the beating heart of Cook's Basin, is going nowhere.

After six dives, Sam hauls himself on to the jetty, where he sits dripping wet with his legs over the side: 'Hole in the hull the size of an orange,' he says, to no one in particular. 'Perfectly round – edges neat enough to satisfy a shipwright. Done from the inside by a pro.'

A hissing sound caused by quick intakes of breath passes through a crowd that suddenly parts to let Jimmy, approaching at a flat-out sprint in nothing but a pair of banana print boxers, to line up alongside his captain. The black-and-white mutt, ears flying, is not far behind. He drops down. Flings his painfully young arm around Sam's neck: 'Me money's all yours, Sam. Every penny. Soon as I get it.'

Sam shakes his head. 'We're good. Mate. All good.' But in his heart, he knows the *Mary Kay* will never be the same again. She will take up her old career with a new crane provided by the insurers but she will wear the scars of her time on the seabed forever. So will I, he thinks, feeling a terrible sadness for his own loss of innocence. He gets to his feet, stumbles under the heavy weight of consoling hands on his back, shoulders, even his cheek. Jenny slips an arm around his waist and falls in step beside him.

'So it's over, eh? They've won,' she says, her eyes focused on her feet, tears in her eyes.

Sam stops short, trying to get his head around what she's saying. 'Won? Not bloody likely. The thing is, Jen, I can't stand bullies. Never been able to. But it's my battle now. Mine alone. And I'll die before I'll let them get away with this.'

Jenny lets out a long, sad sigh. 'Well, it looks like if you die, you won't be alone. We're all with you, Sam. Whatever it takes, we're up for it. So you better make bloody sure we win.'

He nods. He feels a warm, wet touch on his hand. He looks down. Longfellow gazes up with button brown eyes full of sorrow. He gives the hand another lick. And it is the dog's mute tenderness during a horror night that brings Sam undone. Without another word, he runs up the steps to his house and locks the door behind him.

At dawn the next day when the first light is nothing but a pale grey loom and it's still too early even for the cockatoos to rant, Sam is wakened by his mobile phone. Eyes closed, he fumbles on his bedside table, feeling for the off button. Then he remembers. The *Mary Kay.* His eyes flash open and he checks the caller number. *Private.* The goons.

'Yeah,' he says sharply.

'Figured a man with a barge, you'd be up and around by now.' Gravelly voice, a hint of humour in the tone. So not the goons. Not unless one of them has had a recent lobotomy reversal and found his laughter gland.

'Who'm I speaking to?'

'I wanna help you. Help you fight for Garrawi.'

'Great. You know any politicians? Celebrities? Journalists?'

'No.'

'Well, thanks, mate, I'll put your name on a list and if I need you to write a letter . . .'

'I'll give you a million dollars.'

Sam sighs. A nutter, he thinks in despair. Jeez, it's too early in the frigging morning to have to deal with nutters.

'I'll give you a million dollars now. Who do I write the cheque to?'

Mad as a cut snake, thinks Sam: 'Look, mate, I can't take your money, but thanks –'

'I'll give you a hundred thousand dollars now.'

'No. I can't take your money.' Trying to humour the bloke.

'I'm gunna pull out my cheque book. I'll write a cheque for fifteen thousand dollars right now. Who do I make it payable to? Sam Scully?'

'Jeez, mate. No. Don't give me any money.'

'How about the campaign? You got a fund? I can transfer the money to the fund right now.'

Pigs might fly, Sam thinks, but he gives him the details and hangs up. Then he heads for the shower. Onwards and upwards, as his dad used to say. No use crying over spilt milk, according to his mum. He comes up with one of his own: Don't let the bastards wear you down. At least he thinks it's an original. Maybe. He nicks himself shaving and sticks a bit of loo paper on the cut to stop the bleeding, then he ignores the early hour and calls the Water Police and the insurance hotline. It's time to resurrect the *Mary Kay*. He can't help wondering how she'd look with a cannon on her foredeck. Jimmy would love it but there's probably a law against installing major artillery in peaceful times. Peaceful? Who's he kidding? He'll get the bastards. He really will. He just needs time to come up with a plan. On an impulse, he dials Delaney's number. The big man picks up.

'Where the bloody hell are you?' Sam shouts in relief.

The big man goes in fast and hard: 'Heard they're out to skin you,' he says like he's talking from the bottom of a canyon. 'I'm out of the country –' The line drops out. When Sam redials, the call goes to message bank. Bloody journalists. You wouldn't want to depend on them for the time of day.

It takes all morning to raise the bedraggled *Mary Kay* from deep water, drain her and plug the fist-sized hole in her hull. Then she's towed to Frankie's boatshed with a support flotilla of banged-up tinnies guided by angry Islanders on full battle alert, itching to fire up their arsenal of leftover flares at any bastard who looks even slightly dodgy. At the boatshed, the dishevelled but still essentially grand *Mary Kay* is gently positioned between the two steel arms of a boat cradle and hauled up the cement slipway into dry dock in small, smooth increments. 'No bumps and bangs for the old girl. She's been through enough,' Frankie says, patting the hull like she's a frail old lady.

The classic 1960s, low-speed, high-torque Gardner diesel marine engine, designed to drive sewing machines in the early 1900s then tanks during World War II, will be pulled apart, wiped down and restored to former solid, workhorse glory. If a war couldn't wipe out the machine, a simple saltwater dunking hasn't a hope.

On the other hand, salt water is a fatal mix with the delicate electronic wiring of the crane's gearbox. There is no choice but to dismantle it and consign it to the tip.

The insurers send in a team to assess the damage and sign off without quibbling over the dollars and cents. Sam's never made a claim in more than twenty years of hauling. 'We'll need a report from the coppers, though,' they tell him. 'Nothing flash. Just a note the barge was sabotaged.' He nods.

Frankie puts all his other work on hold without bothering to call a single client to say they'll have to wait. 'They'll know what's going on.' He shrugs, tilting his black cap over his eyes. 'If they don't like it, they can go elsewhere.' They won't, of course. Sam nods a thank you and the work begins. 'A week,' Frankie estimates. Sam nods again. In any other boatyard it would take a month. 'Get the bastards, eh?' Frankie says. 'Scum's got to be scrubbed off with a wire brush.'

'Still thinking about the marina?'

'What marina?'

Sam gives him a quick salute and climbs into his tinny. It's the middle of the working day but without the *Mary Kay*, he's stymied. He feels like a man who's lost his connection to reality and he hasn't the faintest idea what to do next. He detours to call in on Artie. The old bloke might have one or two ideas. Long as he doesn't suggest shooting the bastard that did in the *Mary Kay*, he thinks, because right now, I won't need a heap of persuading. Which brings him to another thought: What are the odds of getting away with murder? He sure as hell is tempted.

He knocks on Artie's hull and climbs aboard the yacht at the old man's invitation. When he goes below, he finds two glasses filled with rum and Artie looking as businesslike as Sam's ever seen him. No bed hair today. And he's wearing a shirt, for chrissake. Sam didn't know he owned one.

'This calls for new strategies, son,' Artie says, straight to the point. 'I've called a few of me old pals who know a bit about the danger of dark alleys and the power of crowbars.'

'Call off the dogs, Artie. Not that I don't appreciate the sentiment behind the action but that doesn't make it right.'

Artie sculls his tot of rum, coughs as the fire runs down the back of his throat: 'Wouldn't have expected you to say anything else, I s'pose. It'll hurt though. Kinda lookin' forward to seeing a few ugly heads roll. I saw 'em, ya know, when they shipped into the er, flare safety demonstration parade in that ugly black torpedo that passes for a boat. Didn't say nothin' at the time. No point. But I recognised the type. Not a brain the size of a pea between them. The kind of idiot that shoots first. Asks questions later. So you watch out, son. They're after ya and even if they're only aimin' to hurt, they're dumb enough to kill you by mistake.'

Sam uses his finger to slide his glass across the table into Artie's easy reach. 'Long as it's only me,' he says.

'Ya might think about shiftin' the battleground under their noses, if ya get my drift.'

'Not sure I do, mate.'

'Keep tabs on Mulvaney's movements. Send in the hecklers every time he gives a speech. Annoy the shit out of the bastard till it feels like a bad itch that won't go away. It'll get you prime-time coverage. Guarantee it. Round up a few protesters and set a day to march in the streets of Sydney. Placards and kids, a few good-lookin' women in low-cut tops –'

'Jeez, Artie.'

'Orright, orright. But think about getting' yourself a mob, mate, and storm the palace. This is an election year.'

'Ah jeez,' Sam says again, sliding out of his seat in a hurry. 'I forgot. Jimmy's big media debut is being filmed today.'

'Pity,' Artie says, drawing the glass towards him. 'Bloody pity. It'll ruin the boy.' But Sam is long gone.

In the Square and under the shade of the giant white cockatoo, its heat-stressed cockscomb wilted by the weather to a custardy mush, an elderly woman with pale blue hair sits at a fold-up card table (red-check tablecloth circa 1970) with a Thermos, cups, apples, a bag of nuts and a large cake she's cut into small slivers. 'Anyone can join me,' she tells passers-by, who mostly nod and smile and write her off as batty. She says the same to Sam when he rocks up searching for a dog, a kid and a television crew. He can't think how to refuse politely, so he pauses.

'Sam, right? Lost your beautiful barge this morning. Same barge I've been watching out of my window for years.' She points at a cluster of buildings up the hill to show him where she lives. 'Thought you might be having a really bad day so I decided I'd prop here for a while. It's time you lot on the other side of the moat know that onshorers have hearts, too, and we're with you all the way. You're going to win, you know. Right always knocks the stuffing out of might.'

'Thanks for the vote of confidence,' Sam says, bowled over, suddenly less heartsick and more heartened. She hands him a slice of chocolate cake, beckons him closer to whisper in his ear. 'Could claim I made it but I bought it at the café. I'm a lousy cook. Least that's what they tell me at the bowling club where I run the chook raffle every Saturday night.'

Sam laughs, scoffs the cake, suddenly famished. 'You happen to see a kid and a television crew around here?'

She points a red-painted fingernail at the Island. 'Took off about an hour ago. Nice kid. Different. But definitely made of the right stuff.'

'Thanks, love. And . . . well, thanks.'

Sam finds Ettie getting ready to close up. She's packed a pile of leftovers into a basket, which she passes to Sam without comment. Then she comes around to the public side of the counter and wraps her arms around his beefy body in a clinch so tight she cuts off Sam's oxygen supply.

'Easy on,' he says, trying to lighten the moment. 'It's all good, love. The gearbox for the crane was just about buggered anyway and now I'm getting a new one courtesy of the insurance company that I've been supporting single-handed – if their criminal rates are anything to go by – for more than twenty years. And the *Mary Kay*? She's tough. She'll come back all cylinders firing.' He grins, gently disengaging Ettie's arms.

'The horror of it, Sam. The sheer horror of it.' On the verge of blubbing.

'Nah. Stuff like this happens everywhere. We're just not used to it. As my dad used to say, doesn't matter what hand you're dealt, it's how you cope that counts.' He's been rolling out that out a fair bit lately. 'Any idea where Jimmy and the crew have ended up? I clean forgot it was on today.'

'Kate's got it under control. Turns out she knew the cameraman. He told her the producer wants a feel-good story so the twenty fiercely protective mother ducks hovering around the kid and ready to kill on the strength of one wrong word could get back to their daily business without fear. Or words to that effect. Kate, all smiles and charm so the sting didn't hit straight off, sweetly suggested that *he who trusts busts*, and she and Amelia would stick around to see he kept his word. Smart girl.'

'Jimmy OK?'

Ettie laughs. 'You should have seen him, Sam. He outdid himself. All red and orange flames and silver and gold sparkle, like a comet streaking across the sky. Or Elvis on a bad night in Vegas. He was off in all directions. In his own sweet way, without having a clue what he was doing, he ran the whole show. It's going to be fine. Feel it in my heart. Goes to air on Sunday night. Jenny got a bit carried away and wanted to set up a huge screen at the top of the Island. Bring the community together sort of stuff. But it's hot on the heels of the black-tie fundraiser. Not sure how many people will be up for it.'

'It's a top idea, love. Jimmy's moment to shine. It'll hold him up every time some yobbo has a go at him for being exactly who he is because he knows, now. He's a star.'

As if on cue, the kid explodes through the door: 'Forgot to get me scraps for the worms, Ettie. They need their dinner and I almost forgot. Cripes, I nearly wet meself with worry although me mum says they can manage for a few days. But ya never know, do ya?'

'How'd it go today, Jimmy?' Sam asks, ruffling the kid's iron-gelled hair.

'Aw, Sam. OK, I s'pect. But jeez, they work slower than Glenn after a coupla grogs. Ya wouldn't put up with them on the *Mary Kay*, that's for sure. When's she gunna be back in the water, Sam? Tomorrow?'

'Next week, mate, but that doesn't mean a holiday so don't go getting any fancy ideas. We'll both help Frankie. Nine to five, round the clock.'

Jimmy looks puzzled. 'Ya mean seven till four, don't ya?'

Ettie explains: 'It's an expression, love. A saying.'

'On ya, then. See ya.' He's out the door like a rocket with his two green garbage bags of scraps. A second later he bounces back. 'Me ute, Sam. When are we gunna get me ute?'

'One step at a time, mate. Got to teach you to drive, first.'

'Aw, that'll take a minute.'

'Might take longer than that but we'll get started on it soon.' The kid's yips echo through the café, the Square and across the water. Pure joy. Life is good.

Sam's mobile goes off. He takes a call from Jane: 'Someone loves us. Fifteen grand went into the fighting fund today. Any idea where it's come from?'

'Jeez,' breathes Sam, looking at Ettie in wide-eyed astonishment. 'Who says there isn't a god?'

Sam stows his basket of provisions and pulls the starter cord on his wussy little fifteen horsepower outboard until his arm is almost broken. In the end, all he gets is a wheeze. The engine is dead. He sighs, defeated. Tilts it out of the water. The old *Seagull*, her bow slicing through the water like a knife, heads towards the ferry wharf. He tells himself that using public transport is a civic duty anyway and it's time he supported the service. He checks his pockets for his wallet. Dashes back inside the café and borrows five bucks from Ettie. Hopes it's enough. It's been close to two decades since he's stepped on board and he figures there've probably been a couple of price rises since then. He saunters along the jetty. Gives Chris a hand to tie up. Gallantly positions himself to help passengers disembark, figuring it's a perfect time to thank the community for its care and support.

The first man to appear is Eric Lowdon. Sam comes unglued. He lunges. Savage. Lowdon squeals. Retreats with a blind backward step. His foot gets jammed between the pontoon and the rocking ferry. The crunch of breaking bones is so loud homebound commuters hear it from the picnic tables where they're knocking back their beers. Lowdon roars with pain, goes white, almost passes out. Sam curses. Against his better judgment, he hauls him to safety then lets him drop to the pontoon like a sack of potatoes.

Ferry riders step around the beached man in his sombre going-to-town clothes as though he's contaminated. Not one hand is extended to help. He lies there, eyes closed, his breath coming in short sharp gasps. 'You, the kid and the dog. You're all dead,' he pants. Sam steps forward, his boot *accidentally* coming down hard on Lowdon's broken bones. He yowls like a wild dog.

Sam bends to whisper in his ear: 'Touch one hair on that boy's head, even go near the dog, and you'll be in a wheelchair for life. Boats. Water. Danger everywhere. A simple accident. No one will ever know how it happened. Not even you.'

He feels a hand pulling him away.

'How about I give you a lift home?' Kate asks. His blood still boiling hot, he nods. He doesn't trust himself to speak.

She says, 'Sorry doesn't cut it about the *Mary Kay* –'

Sam puts a finger to his lips. Kate goes silent. Together,

they tie his tinny to the stern of her boat and slowly – much too slowly – tow it towards the Island. He knows he should tell her to speed up a little, at least until the towrope goes taut, but he hasn't got the energy. Every so often, he gets up and fends off. It's easier than words.

When they are almost at Sam's wharf, she says: 'The real problem with campaigns that run a long time –'

Sam holds up his hand, again. 'Not right now, if you don't mind. I'm about as buggered as I've ever felt in my life.'

She continues, as though she hasn't heard him: 'People get tired of the story. Reporters figure they've covered it and lose interest. Readers go on to the next big issue. The trick, if you want to win, is to keep the flame burning.'

'More bloody spot fires,' Sam says gloomily, coming alive despite himself.

'Ye-es. But you need new angles. Stuff no one's heard about before.'

'Such as?'

'I'll try to come up with a few ideas.'

So here it is, he thinks, the olive branch. 'Why would you do that?'

'I live here, too, Sam,' she says softly, rounding up at his jetty. Sam recalls the days before she fully grasped the fact that boats didn't come with brake pedals but she comes alongside without chipping the woodwork or scratching the paint on her hull. Expert. His tinny glides in on the wake. For a second he's tempted to slip back into the blind faith he once had in her. But he's older now, about a hundred years older, so he unties his tinny. Holding the towrope, he steps out of her boat and onto his wharf.

'Any help is appreciated, Kate. But run your idea past Siobhan. She's handling the media campaign. And she's got a shitload of info –'

'I think I can manage this on my own,' she says. She roars off without a wave. Once, he would've bemoaned his foot coming down on the twig. Now he wonders if the twig is all about Kate getting her own way. Nothing to do with him at all. Well, not much, he admits wryly.

Suddenly, she circles and zooms back, the wash from the boat splashing up against his jetty like a tiny tsunami. 'You could always pose naked for the local paper,' she shouts, grinning. 'You don't look too bad with your clothes off.'

Sam makes a rude sign. But he's laughing, as she knew he would, and it feels good.

Three days later, the more square-eyed members of the community lean forward in front of their television sets when an advertisement for the latest edition of *Woman Magazine* flashes on screen promoting a story by *Australian journalist Kate Jackson, whose international search for a long-lost brother becomes a heart-breaking analysis of the deep complexities of mother–daughter relationships*. In The Briny Café, where *Woman Magazine* sells an average of one copy a month and the remaining (well-thumbed) five are regularly returned to the publisher, the issue sells out by noon the following day. Sam snaffles Ettie's copy and takes it out on to the back deck with a double-shot flat white and a slice of Ettie's strawberry tart. He lines up the vittles like rations for a long haul and starts to read.

OPENING THE DOOR
by
Kate Jackson

Until my mother died last Christmas, I had no idea I had a half-brother. After I found out, I wasn't even sure I wanted to find him. But how do you close a door once it has been flung wide open? How do you deny a cold hard fact and squeeze it back into a dark place once it has escaped into the light? There was no way, I realised, unless I could cope with being shadowed by a ghost for the rest of my life.

My mother, Emily, who died before I could even ask his name, played Agatha Christie from the grave. She left clues to his identity and whereabouts that would become apparent only if I did my duty as a daughter – a role she was fully aware I would be reluctant to assume. Our relationship – mildly combative at best – was mostly defined by anger and bitterness. I was an unwanted, late-life baby and she never let me forget it. When I look back on my childhood, I see myself scrunched in a quiet corner, knees pulled up against my cheeks like armour, a spectator determined to remain aloof from the struggles of my parents' damaged relationship – the uncontrolled velocity of my mother's disappointments, my father's desire and inability to fulfil her extravagant dreams.

As children do, I shouldered the guilt and responsibility for ruining the carefree, glamorous life she told me she'd aspired to – until I was old enough to know better. Then I exchanged guilt for resentment. Not a helpful choice but much easier than struggling towards détente in the bloodied arena of our relationship. Like most selfish decisions, it did neither of us any good.

My mother was an extraordinarily beautiful woman. On the street, people stared after her, tripping over their feet, falling into gutters. At parties, men flocked to her side. Years later, she told me she'd never understood how she failed to be a star on a far bigger stage. Instead she married a country boy and was restricted to a small country town, standing – when she couldn't avoid it – behind the counter of the family grocery store where – among everyday staples such as bread and sugar – red, green and yellow cocktail onions were sold to housewives determined to put a bit of pizazz into their cheese-and-biscuit morning teas. It was a rare admission. My mother never acknowledged defeat or failure.

She told me the secret that I can only guess defined her life – the child born out of wedlock and relinquished forever – in a bitter deathbed confession that I was sure was intended more as a shotgun blast aimed at my heart than a clearing of the decks – a tidying up – of the loose ends of a life governed by unwise choices. Am I being harsh? Perhaps. Probably. Children have ringside seats in families but rarely influence the daily mechanics. Parents lay down the rules, which makes it easy to blame them for our own shortcomings, every knock and lack of success. How gratifyingly simple it is to dodge personal responsibility by pointing a finger at the past. My tragedy, if I can give it such a dramatic word, is that it took my mother's death for me to grow up and accept that every choice – and its ramifications – is mine alone. I am the designer of my own life. A revelation that must seem paltry to many, but to me, was like finding myself with wings to fly.

How fortunate it was that I fought off a childish desire to inflict hurt on someone who was, anyway, beyond hurting: that I did my duty as a daughter. By cleaning my mother's home, I discovered a small tin box filled with clues to my brother's existence. By restoring my father's dilapidated old writing desk for sentimental reasons instead of weighing expense against practicality, I found precious family documents hidden in a secret compartment. If I'd forgone those ancient family rites and left them in the disengaged hands of strangers, I would have paid a terrible price. My brother would have remained a ghost and I am sure that every time I caught a glimpse of a likeness of Emily in a crowd, I'd wonder: Is it him?

Emily's strategy could have gone either way. I can see her smiling at the thought. A game player to the end. Strange behaviour for a mother, perhaps, but she was always a woman who lived for drama and excitement. How I wish now that I'd made a genuine effort to put aside our frictions and stretched wide my arms, even for a moment, when my father, her husband, died. But I didn't. I continued to lay the blame for every family flaw like a wreath at her feet – and turned my back on her.

The first document I unfolded from the secret cavity of the writing desk, turned out to be a deed, dated January 27, 1938, to a house in the Melbourne suburb of Fitzroy. The owners' names, Phyllis and Robert Conway, meant nothing to me. The next document revealed that in 1962, Phyllis took her own life. Robert Conway, who never remarried, died in 1983. I also found a birth certificate for Emily Elizabeth Conway. My mother. I discovered she was two years older than she ever admitted and she also fibbed about her age on her wedding certificate. I smiled at what I instantly recognised as her vanity, when once I would have sat in judgment and labelled her a liar. I wept, too, as I began to discover the forces that built Emily. How does a child cope with the knowledge that her mother took her own life?

Last, there was a sealed envelope with nothing written on the face to indicate who it was meant for – if anyone. I fetched a knife from the kitchen and slit it open. And there he was, appearing like magic in the form of a birth certificate. Alexander Conway. Born September 12, 1961. Place: Ninga Private Hospital, Victoria. Mother: Emily Conway. Aged nineteen. There is a blank space where the father's name should have been.

Emily had a child born out of wedlock in an era when abortion was illegal and an illegitimate pregnancy, if it became public knowledge, was enough to ruin a young woman's life. Contraception was the sole precinct of married women. Her son was born in a quiet country hospital, run by a strict religious order. It's almost certain she never laid eyes on him. As we now know, in those days illegitimate babies were snatched away from mothers who were mostly children themselves and placed in the eager arms of childless couples chosen for their economic and emotional stability. It was a system that both succeeded (young woman goes off free to get on with her life) and failed (young woman spends a lifetime searching for her lost baby). Another era; a different concept of philanthropy. Either way, Emily's entire existence was based on keeping up acceptable appearances and ignoring the messy facts. You had to be tough to live a lie forever. And somewhere in that knowledge, I find the first grains of respect for a woman who did the best she could with what she had.

To be truthful, when I found my brother on the other side of the world, where it was a white winter instead of a golden summer, there was no flash of recognition, no residual genetic impulse that made him stand out in the traditional village teashop in the heart of rural Britain where we'd agreed to meet. Our physical and intellectual similarities were a gradual discovery, each one a small shock, no stronger than the slight electric charge you feel from touching metal on a hot, dry day. A frisson, if you like, of recognition of small things. Blue eyes. One dimple. Unusually small hands. Uncannily similar gestures – rubbing our noses when we're thinking, raising one eyebrow in a question – and a shared preference for very good tea made properly with loose leaves. Small connections but, in their context, also huge.

The search for my brother was like completing a complex puzzle but then my mother, I am beginning to understand, was a complex woman. As a child, I judged her through a child's eyes. Now I am older and know more about the demons that go hand in hand with a reckless moment, I wish she were alive so I could recant my disapprovals and we might work towards understanding and compassion. Is that also a childish impulse made from the safety of impossibility? I will never know. What I do understand is that I have a sibling; and now we have found each other, we will not lose touch.

Emily, I hope, might have been happy about that.

Sam closes the magazine. The story doesn't entirely ring true to him. It's the tone, he thinks, and the way Kate is shouldering the responsibility for events over which she had no control. Maybe she's generously spinning the facts so her half-brother is spared the knowledge that his birth mother was an egocentric, selfish woman without a soft edge anywhere. Nice move. Bloody nice. If he's making the right assumption.

In a slow sideways shuffle, the community decides to forgive Kate for leaving Ettie in the lurch. She was on a great mission to find a family member, they tell each other, and who could blame her for that? Each and every one of them probably would have done the same. Holding grudges anyway, as they are well aware, takes too much energy when there is such magic in everyday moments. But strangers wander in and out of the café to steal curious, sideways looks at Kate. One or two shyly confess their own strained mother–daughter relationships and vow her story has convinced them to try harder in future. Then a woman with mad eyes and dried spittle in the corners of her mouth marches straight up and accuses Kate of being a judgmental little bitch who should be hung by her ankles from a high beam. Kate flees to Ettie's penthouse to hide. She calls Sam, distraught: 'I feel like I've been stripped naked in public.'

'Well, what did you expect?' he asks. 'You virtually gave strangers a written invitation to walk through your front door without knocking.' He waits for a sharp comeback, her reflex response to criticism. And it's her silence that cuts through his defences.

He says, 'If I promise not to offer to bring a sauso roll, as universally acclaimed and magnificent as they are, would you like me to stop by Oyster Bay for a quick drink tonight?'

'What time?' she asks.

As Sam makes his way up the steps to her home, he reminds himself to keep his emotional distance. Commitment, kids and a soft-shoe shuffle into a contented old age that comes from the joy of knowing you've together raised a couple of decent children who love you almost as much as you love them, seems to terrify her. And given her current form, he'd be a fool if he trusted her to hang around long enough to understand the rich, complex but ultimately rewarding layers of family. He knocks lightly and walks in. He'll hold her hand for a minute or two until she settles, then he'll take an official position so they can both move on.

She's sitting on her sofa. He stands in front of her in what he senses is one of the least noble moments of his life. He takes his time, searching for the right words. She stares up at him with a clear blue gaze softened by the residual hurt and shock of the lunatic woman with the flying spittle and he nearly caves in.

'You and me,' he says.

'Hmm?'

'We'd be better off as friends.' He winces. Wants to snatch back the blunt delivery and begin again, more softly and gently this time.

Kate turns away from him and heads for the kitchen and the fridge. She hands him a beer, pours herself a glass of wine.

'Suits me,' she says, at last.

CHAPTER TWENTY-FOUR

The day of the black-tie fundraiser is pure bedlam. The smell of lamb cooking with garlic, rosemary, oregano and thyme fills the Square like an old-time Sunday roast. Upstairs in Ettie's penthouse, the Misses Skettle are blind-baking tart pastry shells to load up with a (successfully set) brandy-laced custard. 'Brandy lifts the spirit, dear.' A massive bowl of deep red strawberries is macerating in more brandy and a sprinkling of sugar. 'Brandy brings out the flavour of the berries, dear.'

The Three Js, carrying lists, mobile phones and wearing severe expressions to discourage any would-be anarchists tempted to insist they know a better way, are flat-out on Ettie's deck peeling green prawns to be stir-fried in vegetable oil and spicy tamarind chutney broken down with a little water. The prawns, not quite completely defrosted, are painfully cold but no one bothers whinging. There's work to be done.

Eighteen Styrofoam containers are stacked two deep and three high to be filled with provisions and shipped across to Garrawi Park, where the boys from the Regal Tinny Yacht

Club, including the Three Js' handy husbands, are using their sailing skills to rig a marquee of white canvas from the soaring limbs of the now famous cheese tree. A precaution only. The weather is tipped to be hot with a light sea breeze to take the steam out of the humidity. 'Another sign we're on the winning team, dears, if you're the type that has more faith in omens than god.' More wisdom from the Misses Skettle.

Despite the hefty price tag per head, in the end it was decided to make it a BYO event. 'No point in seeing the profits pizzled into the creek, is there?' the elder Miss Skettle argued.

Ettie let out a little squeak. 'You mean piddled, don't you?'

'No dear, pizzled. It has infinitely more and much further-reaching connotations.'

Ettie and the Three Js turned away to hide their laughter. 'Well,' Ettie said, 'I'm OK with that.'

Jenny nodded. 'Me too. Might as well get everyone to bring their own glasses as well. Less washing up.'

Marcus, unable to ditch his businessman past, is nevertheless anxious that guests should feel they are getting value for money. He offers to create a range of hot and cold savouries that will 'tickle taste buds and set a mood of glorious extravaganza. We are, after all, dressed up to our head tops. Is it not so?'

The event is sold out. The fighting fund is looking deadly serious. The community is ramping up to fight tough but clean. The law according to Sam. 'Let's not lower our standards, dears, or we're no better than them.' The word according to the Misses Skettle.

The first newspaper advertisement opposing the development will appear on Monday morning (for maximum follow-up impact after Jimmy's television debut) with front-page exposure at an inside-page rate. Kate, 'Bless her!' (the Misses Skettle again), led the committee through the mind-boggling fog of figures relating to buying media space and hard-bargained her way to a deal that opened everyone's eyes to the elasticity of ad rates in a post-GFC market. Not to mention the fragile grip of newspaper circulations in the wake of internet news and social media.

'If I fall under a bus tomorrow, promise me you will never, ever accept the first quote from an ad man no matter how many beers he buys you or how persistently sparkly his assurance that the inside gutter on page twelve is a top spot. Promise?' Kate eyeballed every face in the room. The committee, feeling like fresh bait in a pool of circling sharks, nodded seriously, each member silently vowing to keep Kate away from all buses in future. She was definitely earning her way back into favour. Even Jenny was starting to show signs of softening.

'It's a hard cruel world out there if you're a babe in the woods,' Myrtle Skettle suddenly announced. She was up there with Sam when it came to clichés.

Siobhan asked Kate if she'd like to write the copy for the ad. Kate declined.

Downstairs in the café, the daily specials have been ditched to make room for the slow-cooked lamb and punters are offered strictly a choice of big breakfasts, burgers, fish and chips or sandwiches. 'No exceptions!' Ettie insists, when regulars feign disappointment, despair even. 'If you're feeling deprived, a generous slice of something sweet and creamy such as my triple chocolate cheesecake might help,' she adds, with the hint of wheedle in her tone. Flirting shamelessly.

The recent spell of sunny weather toned down by a constant fanning from a refreshing nor'easterly and the campaign to save Garrawi has boosted the café's earnings to mega levels and Ettie is flying high. 'A virus was all that ailed me and now I am well again,' she tells herself convincingly. Nothing to do with the surreptitious dabbing of the Misses Skettles' sweet-potato salve on the inside of her upper thighs and a daily dose of evening primrose oil. Nothing at all.

She goes to the front door and puts up a sign announcing the early closure of The Briny Café due to commitments to the community and the fight to save Garrawi from developers. Even tourists resist quibbling and get their orders in before the four pm deadline.

Without the large hauling facilities of the *Mary Kay* at their disposal, the committee calls on Glenn, the removalist, to pitch up at The Briny with his barge for the export of the massive amount of mouth-watering fare to the Island. He arrives, stone cold sober, on the dot of four thirty and begins lifting the lids on the Styrofoam boxes to check out the contents. The Misses Skettle watch from a distance, ready to pounce if he tries to rip a little tender moist flesh from the shoulders of lamb that, they agree among themselves, have been cooked to velvety perfection. They'd been doubters at the start, fearing food poisoning from meat coaxed to doneness over seven hours in an oven temperature of just 80 degrees Celsius (add an hour to rest before carving). 'We're not too old to admit were wrong,' Violet told Ettie. 'But we probably won't be using the method ourselves. At our age, we could be dead by the time dinner is ready!' And they'd gone off, giggling, to hitch a ride home on Glenn's increasingly holey barge where there was nothing to hold on to except each other in the event of a passing rogue wave. Fearless and feisty to the end. In their wise old eyes, there was no other way.

Garrawi Park is a festival of coloured lights, red-checked tablecloths and wings of white canvas stretching to a purple sky. The evening star, the first to claim its heavenly rights, shines down like a silver spotlight on women swishing about in sequined gowns and men (well, some men) in crisp white dinner shirts and black bow ties. Even the normally irrepressible Island kids have been stunned into acceptably benign behaviour by the sight of their parents dressed up like movie stars. It is, everyone agrees, a stellar occasion.

The chef arrives with platters of sashimi created from what he believes is the best fishing expedition of his life. 'The gods are smiling on us, no?' He beams, handing around little tubs of dipping sauces with the pearly white flesh of kingfish and flathead.

Fast Freddy, who has taken the night off so he can step into Sam's traditional role of picking up and safely delivering home the two Misses Skettle, arrives with one proud woman on each arm. Freddy is resplendent in a peacock-green suit and a deep blue shirt teamed with a yellow bowtie. The old ladies are a vision in voluminous folds of pink taffeta, pink silk roses in their hair – which is sprayed pink for the occasion. Jenny insists they raise their skirts so she can check they are wearing matching shoes. 'Of course you are,' she says, laughing. And in an odd way, the Misses Skettles' religious devotion to their beloved hue gives a wondrous sense that despite their community being in the crosshairs of violent and vicious predators, the centre of decency and decorum is somehow holding firm.

There is, however, a moment's shocked silence when a smoothly coiffed Jimmy steps into the party wearing black from head to toe. Then he asks Ettie to help him turn on his flashing bowtie and the relief felt is universal.

When dinner is over, Big Phil and Rexie drag out their guitars. Big Phil's flame embroidered cowboys boots are polished to mirror brightness and his red polka-dot bandana is pulled low on his forehead to soak up the sweat. Rexie wears a Mambo shirt with flying saucers, dogs and satellites. The two men riff the chords until their fingertips bleed. The Island rocks.

'Kings never lived better than this,' Sam says to Ettie, swinging her in a circle to a tune made famous by Lyle Lovett. Or was it Willie Nelson? Right now, he doesn't give a damn. He notices Kate slink off. Squishes a twinge of regret tinged with yearning. Life is complicated enough.

While the Island parties in the name of a good cause, Kate sits at home alone. The contents of Emily's grey tin box are laid out in military order on the kitchen table. She's exhausted from the lingering effects of jetlag, the fundraiser preparations and running a café that's somehow somersaulted from bust to boom against all odds. One way or another, though, she is aware that nothing lasts forever and is suddenly overwhelmed by a terrible sense of the likely reality twenty years into the future. Ettie will be seventy-five years old and long retired from the café. She will be fifty-five – Ettie's age now – and, like Ettie, probably menopausal. The business will be sold and either thriving or struggling under the control of others. The end game is the same for everyone. In the final analysis, there's nothing but a handful of dust to show we were here.

She'd had the same conversation with Sam one day. He failed to follow her meaning, looked at her as though she was talking in tongues. 'I don't want to get all lyrical on you, sweetheart,' he said, 'but look around.' Then he'd laughed because he could see she still didn't get it. 'Well, dust turns into compost. Compost grows plants. You never know, we might both come back as a magnificent cauliflower one day with a double cheese sauce, browned under the grill.' She'd smiled to show she appreciated the effort he was making but to her horror, found herself thinking of him as a spear-carrying, animal-skin-clad Neanderthal with a vocabulary of six grunts at varying pitches.

To her, Sam oozed so much ill-conceived optimism he was a danger to himself and everyone else, jumping in blind without thinking through the consequences. She comes to the conclusion that he and Jimmy aren't so different, really. They think small acts of kindness made a difference in the long run. But beyond the invisible line of the Island safety zone, out where dog-eat-dog is often a daily mantra, they'd be quickly devoured. Or is she being deliberately cruel? She's been the one to sound the death knell on relationships in the past. She's in new territory and she isn't sure it feels too great.

The time on her watch says midnight. She throws a last quick look at Emily's pathetic little trove and moves towards the bedroom. The way they talked about good hearts in Cook's Basin, you'd be forgiven for thinking that's all that counted. Out in the rancorous maw of real life brave hearts were the first to be skewered. She glances over her shoulder. Slowly walks back. She fingers the menu from the cruise ship. The invitation to dinner at Parliament House towards the end of 1962. She is struck by a series of quick connections like sparks going off one after another. She hits her computer. Flails through squillions of cyber channels, searching. Eventually, she calls up the passenger list for the *Oriana* on an early 1962 cruise from Sydney to Southampton. Then she cross-references the names with federal members of parliament for the same year. It takes a while. She almost gives up. But bingo, there he is. She's not a betting woman but she'd lay odds of a hundred to one if Jake the Bookie was mad enough to take her on, that Timothy Terence Martin O'Reilly, a first-class passenger, is the father of her half-brother, Alexander Conway.

There's no photograph to compare eyes, noses, the shape of a chin. She checks his biographical details. Retired. Not dead. Her hands are clammy. She clicks the mouse on the White Pages, and finds him listed in a small country town in Victoria. She flops back. Then books an early-morning flight to Melbourne. She returns to the official biography site. Married in 1955, two children, born in 1956 and 1957. So he was married when he had a fling with Emily. With a name like O'Reilly, he was probably a card-carrying Roman Catholic. Divorce would have meant the end of his career. End of his community standing. Far tidier to ship the baby off to foreign climes and get on with being a fine upstanding member of the establishment: church on Sunday, a sufficiently weighty tithe slipped into the offering plate as it passed under the wrinkled noses of his freshly scrubbed, legitimised children and hallelujah! Absolution of all mortal sins in a jiffy. Poor Emily. Poor, poor stupid Emily. Kate tries to imagine being in the same situation but struggles. Her generation has the luxury, if that's the word, of legalised abortion. No loose ends. Havoc denied. On with the show, situation normal.

She places Emily's mementoes in the box and closes the lid. It will come with her to country Victoria as proof – of a sort – of her right to enquire. She prints out the passenger list. She doesn't bother to pack a bag. If she is forced to overnight somewhere, she'll wear the same clothes.

She undresses and climbs into bed. Her tiredness overcome by nervous excitement, she lies flat on her back, wired and wide-eyed. In the still of the night, she hears the rapid drumroll of her pulsing heart. No more loose ends. Alex will know his father. Closure. She wonders if he smokes or smoked, cigars. Wishes she'd kept the ash and the envelope.

Kate crosses the water in the silvery gloom of pre-dawn, a note for Ettie held in one hand as she steers the boat towards the café pontoon. Saturday night's carnival lights – red, blue, yellow and green – are still blazing on the Island but Garrawi Park is abandoned. The party is over. The residents of Cutter Island will be nursing fierce hangovers well into the afternoon. They'll straggle in to The Briny in search of vats of deep-fried food and caffeine hits strong enough to wake the dead. She feels a twinge of guilt but shrugs it off. As Emily, who'd mastered the art of buck-passing, used to say: 'Guilt is a wasted emotion.' She ties up at the pontoon and unlocks the back door, places her note fair and square on the counter where Ettie won't miss it.

'Hello? Who's there?' Ettie's sleepy voice echoes from upstairs.

'It's Kate. Sorry. Thought you'd be staying with Marcus after the party.'

Ettie comes downstairs, rubbing her eyes, finding a smile: 'You lovely girl. Here to get a super early start, are you? So I can sleep in.'

Kate blushes. 'Not exactly, Ettie. Sorry. God, all I ever do is say sorry. The thing is, I think I've found Alex's father. I'm off to the airport.'

Ettie sits on a step halfway down, dragging her nightie over her knees. 'Another trip to London, is it?'

Kate catches the coolness in her tone, feels a wave of guilt and makes a silent vow this is the last time she'll give in to what has become an obsession. 'No, nothing quite so dramatic this time. Turns out he lives in Victoria. Plan to be there and back in one day. Figured Jenny is still on board and it'll be a slow day anyway after last night's big bash.'

'Do whatever you have to do, Kate,' Ettie says, resigned, using the railing to pull herself to her feet. 'We'll see you when we see you.' She is gone without another word.

Jimmy's television debut is watched by the entire, seriously hung-over but intensely contented Island population; who have plodded up the steepest part of the track lugging rugs and picnics to find a spot on the ground in front of old white sheets strung between two spotted gums. The television, which has been channelled through a video projector and sound system, courtesy of Big Phil and Rexie, is set up on the back of an old trailer with electric leads running fifty metres and through a window into the closest house. Considering the historic financial windfall of the black-tie fundraiser and the recent anonymous donation, nobody bothers to hand around a collection plate. By the time the art auction takes place, the war chest will be overflowing and capable of inflicting massive and completely legal damage (fully aware of how far you can push the libel laws without it being worth anyone taking action, Siobhan has shouldered responsibility for ticking off the copy before it goes to press).

As the sun drops behind hazy blue hills and a few clouds scud across the sky turning fiery red, the volume is raised as high as the most headache-afflicted viewer can tolerate. Jimmy's freckly, smiley, guileless face fills the screen. His hair as iridescent as the clouds above. 'Me mum,' he begins, and the rest of the line is lost in the roar of laughter. Jimmy and his mum. It was ever thus.

The interview runs for twelve minutes. The camera follows his barefoot way as he scrambles along the honeycomb shore, the lollopy, grinning, black-and-white mutt at his heels. He shows them what it's like to dive from the ferry wharf into the boiling water left in the wake of the *Seagull*. Still wet, he sprints to the top of the Island and shows them the glorious view right to the vast pale blueness of the Tasman Sea. He rides the back of a turtle that lobs in like a groupie looking for his five minutes of fame. Tells them about another turtle called Tilly and how fishing line in her gut nearly killed her but he and Sam, the bargeman, saved her. He points out a cormorant popping out of the water like a periscope. 'Watch! There it goes!' The bird dives. Emerges with a large wriggling fish in its beak.

He chucks sticks for Longfellow and tells them about a race for mutts that takes place on Christmas Eve, when the whole community gets together to say Merry Christmas. 'But really, we're checkin' even the loners 'ave got a seat at a table somewhere.' He shows them dewy spider webs glistening like crystal palaces. The perfect, tiny five petals of mauve flowers called Love Flowers, 'Which kinda suits the park given so much of it goes on there. Heh, heh.' He points out the furry foetal curl of tree-fern buds. Directs them to see how such tiny perfect swellings transform into 'the world's biggest umber-alla'. He plants his skinny backside on a mossy boulder and points a finger at the creek. 'Ya never go thirsty on the Island. Creek never lets ya down.' And he scoops pure water into the bowl of his hands and drinks thirstily, raising a wet face with such a radiant grin that the audience spontaneously grins right back.

At one point, he puts a finger to his lips: 'Shhh. See there. Red-bellied black havin' a snooze. Poor bugger's tired out. If ya see a brown, get the hell outta there. They'll go ya if they're feelin' cranky enough.' Is it everyone's imagination, or does the camera jerk a fraction at the news? Towards the end, the reporter lays out the plans for the resort against the flaky breast of the papier-mâché cockatoo in the Square.

'So what do you think of this, Jimmy?'

The kid's eyes almost pop: 'Weren't ya listenin' to anything I said, then?' In a world of spin-doctors and truth-benders, his shiny-eyed view of the physical world feels like a cool hand on a feverish brow. There's not an Islander whose chest isn't puffed with pride. The kid, after all, is one of theirs. Island conceived, born and bred. Love of landscape and community locked in his DNA. Jimmy, Sam thinks, is now officially grown up.

CHAPTER TWENTY-FIVE

A little after two o'clock, when the summer sun beats down relentlessly, burning farmland already crisped from drought, Kate pulls off a dirt track opposite the gateway to number 12 Cavendish Road. An impressive redbrick house shrouded with verandahs and grapevines stands at the end of a straight driveway lined with ancient peppercorn trees. A small herd of black cows, heavily pregnant, graze nearby on tufts of yellow grass. In a good season, it would look utterly bucolic. It makes her think of frocked-up ladies and gentlemen sipping gin and tonics at sunset while a string quartet saws lazily in the background. But puffs of dust kick up under shuffling hoofs. The vine is scorched brown, the lawn more dustbowl brown than garden-party green. A strong wind and Mr O'Reilly might find all his precious topsoil stripped and relocated on the rich black plains of the Western District, two hundred kilometres away, reinforcing Kate's belief that what goes around comes around and she's not referring to the dirt.

She takes a long swig from a bottle of water, restarts the car and rattles over a cattle grid into the shaded driveway. Nothing stirs. Not even a dog barks. She'd envisaged a thousand different scenarios but never considered the fact that Timothy Terence Martin O'Reilly might not be home. She gets out of the car and walks up to the door. Lifts a heavy brass knocker and pounds hard. The sound cuts through the silence like a gun going off. In the distance, a crow laments. Emily would call it a bad omen but, like Kate, she wouldn't back off. Emily never understood the meaning of retreat. In most people, that's a strength. In Emily it led to one exploding episode after another. Kate tries the door handle. To her surprise, it is unlocked.

'Emily's girl, aren't you?' Kate jumps. Spins around. Almost losing her balance. 'Saw you through the window. Same eyes,' he explains, without being asked. He is small-boned and lean, still handsome in the landed-gentry fashion of crisp checked shirts, faded blue jeans and elastic-sided boots. A leathery, white-haired version of Alex? When he holds his head a certain way, perhaps. Kate, caught wrong-footed, could swear his blue eyes are twinkling in the style of old men who realise they can afford to flirt outrageously with young women without fearing they'll offend or be forced to follow through.

'Good memory,' Kate manages, thinly.

'Not that good. She was here. Couple of years ago. Barely recognised her at first, not till the colour of her eyes clicked in. How is she?'

'Dead.'

O'Reilly remains expressionless, takes in the whole picture of Kate, detail by detail, like he's trying to get a handle on whether she's feeling grief or relief. After a while, he beckons her to follow him inside the cool gloom of the house. 'Just me here,' he says. 'And a few cows to remind me that I was once a farmer. I can rustle up a cup of tea and a biscuit. That do you?'

'A politician, I thought. Not a farmer.'

'A politician for a while. Nothing to be proud of. More like a descent into petty nonsense. Bad times and a bad bunch I thought back then, but nothing much has changed. You either play the game or quit. I quit.'

'Before they dragged out the dirt on you?' she asks, deliberately trying to shock. But he responds with a shrug, a slight raising of the corners of his mouth. 'Emily said you were blunt. No, not blunt, judgmental was the word she used. Said you two didn't get along.'

'Doesn't matter much now, does it?'

'More than you think, probably.'

In the kitchen, shadowy with wear and filled with the lingering scent of lemons and soap, he fills an electric kettle and reaches for a commemorative tin of Arnott's Anzac biscuits. He lifts a couple of mugs off hooks and slings in a teabag each, pours hot water. Points to a chair at a scrubbed pine table. 'There's no milk. Got sick of it going off before I could finish it. Dirt? In those days, parliamentary debates never got personal. Unspoken rule or we'd all be hanged by the electorate. You don't find many saints in politics. What got Emily in the end?'

'Heart attack. Quick, clean and efficient. A throwaway line the day before she died revealed the existence of a half-brother.' She comes down heavily on the word, making sure he doesn't miss it.

'Ah,' he says, drawing out the sound. He calmly bites into his biscuit. Chews noisily. Kate waits him out. She wonders if Alex will grow to look just like him, although there's an indefinable remoteness in the son that she can't find in the old man. Against all the odds, he seems kind. 'Ah,' is all he adds, after a good while.

'I found him, if you're interested.'

If she'd expected the old man to be surprised and even a little fearful, she was disappointed. 'Ah,' he says again. 'So, Emily's daughter, tell me about yourself.'

His question catches her off-guard. 'Why me? Don't you want to know what happened to the inconvenient kid you dumped?'

'Alex?'

Kate's head starts to spin. 'But I thought –'

'That I dumped Emily? Dumped the baby?'

'You were married when you had an affair or a one-night fling or whatever it was with Emily. The boy ended up being adopted and raised on the other side of the world, for god's sake. What else can I think?'

'My dear, if I may call you that, how much do you really want to know?'

'All of it!'

'It's not pretty. Not at all pretty.'

'All of it,' Kate says vehemently.

The old man is silent for so long Kate worries he's fallen into a light doze. But his eyes are wide open, his gaze directed through the window to a grove of slumped, drought-stricken paperbarks. Unable to sit still, she pushes back her chair. Wood scraping on wood breaks the afternoon inertia. In the paddock, the cows shuffle towards the shade of the trees, moving through dry grass with a sound like rustling paper. Dead twigs snap underfoot occasionally. The low hum of insects filters into the kitchen.

'I met Emily on a cruise ship,' says O'Reilly, his voice so soft, Kate leans closer to hear. 'To say she was incredibly beautiful is to do her an injustice. She was flawless.' He takes a sip of tea but the cup is empty. Without a word, Kate refills the kettle. 'Everyone on board was in love with her but for some reason, she chose me. Yes, I was married. Yes, I had children. I didn't try to hide the facts. If anything, I tried to use them to make her see the futility of having anything to do with me. But she laughed and said she didn't care. "Live for the moment," she said. "Once we hit London, we'll never see each other again. No harm done, what your wife doesn't know will never hurt her." I was flattered, of course. She could have chosen anyone but she wanted me. That laugh, like the warm rich notes of a cello, mocked and dared simultaneously. Cast a dangerous spell. I should have known better, of course. I can't make any excuses. But imagine how it felt to have a glorious young woman offering you a wild holiday romance, no strings attached? Pure fantasy – at a time when my marriage had fallen into a black hole.'

Kate raises her eyebrows.

'Yes, yes. Does a more threadbare justification for infidelity exist? But for what it's worth, I'll explain. My wife, whose religious devotion prevented her from practising birth control, didn't want any more children. I was still a young man. Not even thirty years old. If I played by the rules of the church, I was looking at celibacy for the rest of my life. One fling, I told myself, and then I'll follow the faith. Lunacy, of course.' The shrill whistle of the kettle interrupts. 'Something's broken. You've got to turn it off manually. I like the sociable sound of a kettle on the boil so I've left it.'

There is a long silence while Kate finds a fresh teabag. She hands the mug to the old man. He sips noiselessly in quick increments, like he's thirsty or dehydrated from the heat of the day. It takes him a long, long time to pick up his story. 'For some reason, though, I held back. When I stepped away from the flirtatious orbit of Emily, I understood quite clearly that if I embarked on an affair, I would be betraying every standard I lived by and once I had failed in the first real test of my adulthood, what would be left of the man I thought I was? Once a Catholic, always a Catholic, I suppose.'

'But nevertheless, you managed to put aside your conscience –'

'Do you have any idea what it's like to lose all reason? Any idea at all? Your whole world narrows down to one person. You spend every waking moment thinking about her, reliving the smallest nuances of a word or a gesture when you're apart, holding them close like a blanket on a freezing night. You read greatness and glory into a condition that's as old as time, telling yourself this is the love of a lifetime, that it would be pure madness to deny yourself. But it's not love, is it? Not when it puts the welfare and happiness of others at risk. Forgive me if I use a dreadful line here, but love endures. Mad passion – which is essentially what I felt for Emily – is unsustainable. The ferocity of it also brings about the death of it. When it finally burns out, it's like waking from a different reality. It's only then that you realise you have been quite insane. Have you ever felt any of this, Kate?'

'No,' she says. 'Never.'

'Lucky you. About three weeks into the cruise, when our final destination was as many weeks away, the ship held its traditional fancy-dress ball. It was a crazy night of devils, gorillas, fairies, gnomes, wolves, milkmaids, Mickey Mouses and Cinderellas – god, every cartoon character you'd every heard of – prancing about without restraint, playing the fool. Anonymous and therefore blame free.

'Emily stepped into a kaleidoscopic ballroom in a cloud of pure white chiffon with two silver sequined wings clipped to her shoulders. The room, raucous and uproarious, fell silent. Here was an exquisite angel appearing in the midst of bacchanalia. In my demented love-struck state, I read it as a sign from well, if not God, then from the very least, heaven. She was allowed – ordained – to be mine if only for a single night. I stepped up to her with my arm held out and we danced all night.'

'I'm curious. What were you dressed as?'

O'Reilly makes a choking noise and grimaces. 'The devil, of course. From this end of my life, it's hard to remember the relentless self-absorption of the young. How every tiny decision – including choosing a fancy-dress costume from the bowels of a cruise ship – had to have some personal significance to back it up.'

Kate says: 'Emily probably read it as a sign, too, that you were ready to fall from grace. When I was a child, family life was ruled by omens as banal as the progress of a neighbour's black cat from one side of the street to the other.' Outside, the flat, colourless post-midday light is softening. Shadows are growing longer. 'It was that night, wasn't it? The beginning of your affair.'

'Yes and no. We went to her cabin, both of us drunk on wine, the promise of sex, the hot tropical night. I felt as though we were disconnected from reality. Ships do that, I think. There you are, floating way out to sea among disinterested strangers, without any responsibility for day-to-day decisions except whether to choose fruit or pastry for dessert. It feels deliciously like anarchy although perhaps hedonism is closer to the truth. So, yes, we went to bed. But it never became an affair. I believe that these days our experience is commonly referred to as a one-night stand.'

'Oh, come on.' Kate is incredulous.

'Would you like a drink? It's my habit to indulge in a whisky at this time of day.' O'Reilly stands, taking a moment to straighten his back, as though it is a painful process. 'After all this time, do you really think I have any reason to lie? I could have sent you on your way, you know. Probably should have instead of indulging an old man's desire for exoneration.' O'Reilly pours his drink. 'I have wine, if you'd like to join me. Or a beer?'

'White wine. Thank you.'

He finds a bottle in the fridge and pours a glass, handing it to Kate, tilting his head to indicate she should follow him. They move along a dim, bare passageway. O'Reilly pushes open a door and waits for her to go ahead.

'My study,' he explains. 'I have some photographs you might like to see. Absurd to keep them, but I could never quite bring myself to throw them away.'

'Emily?' Kate asks.

'Yes. They were taken by the ship's official photographer on the night of the fancy-dress ball.' He sculls his whisky. Slams down the glass. After a while, he gets up and goes to a wall of books. He finds the title he's looking for without hesitation and pulls a thin envelope from between the pages. 'Here she is, in full angel regalia. Quite beautiful, don't you think.'

'Her eyes . . .'

'A coldness, calculation? If that's what you're thinking, you're right. After our one night together, Emily cut off contact with me. She was full of regrets, she said. I had a wife, children. It was all impossible. Naturally, I thought I'd been a disaster in the sex department, if you'll excuse the bluntness. Or worse, offended her badly in some way and that was the real reason she wanted nothing more to do with me. I'd never lied to her about my family so that couldn't be the real reason. We avoided each other for the rest of the voyage. If it's possible to feel heart-broken and relieved at the same time, then that's how I was. I was slowly coming to my senses.

'A year later, when I was back home and fully immersed in my career as a member of parliament, trying to run a sheep and cattle property, scrabbling to hold my marriage intact, I attended an official dinner at Parliament House for a visiting head of state from somewhere I'd never heard of. I rarely went to them but the PM had been adamant. He wanted a show of force on the night.' His voice softens: 'I felt her presence before I saw her. It was like a blast of heat coming from my left. I have no idea how she'd arranged to be there. Didn't think to ask. I was quite mad with any number of emotions.

Hope and fear being the two strongest. I'm not sure what I expected. A polite hello? The brush-off.

'But she walked up to me with a smile, much harder than the one I remembered: "We have a son. What are you going to do about it?" There we were in a public place, I hadn't seen or heard from her for more than a year, and suddenly she announces she has a baby and I am the father. Remember, we're talking the start of the 1960s here. Didn't matter how you looked at it, it was a scandal. But you know what? I didn't give a damn. I still loved her, you see. I quickly decided the church would give my wife a face- and soul-saving annulment. Oh yes, it would have been possible. A large cash donation . . . Anyway, I would quit politics and marry Emily.'

O'Reilly's voice is wearing out now. He is white-faced, exhausted. Kate offers to fetch him another whisky. He smiles assent. She takes her time in the kitchen, letting him rest for a while.

'But something went wrong?' she suggests on her return.

'My dear, that hardly begins to describe it. I drove for six hours and walked straight in the house – this house, by the way – and confessed with much wringing of hands and contrition. I thought Chloe would be outraged, but she left the room without a word. I waited. A couple of hours later, when it was nearly midnight, she returned. "Arrange for us to meet. Tell her to bring the baby."' O'Reilly lets his head fall back, closes his eyes. 'I can't explain the horror her words invoked. What on earth was she thinking? In the end, I told her I would leave the decision to Emily. If she agreed, we'd go ahead with the, er, introductions.'

'And did she agree?'

'Oh yes. Why not? She knew she'd won. We were to meet in the foyer of the Australia Hotel. My wife's choice. She was so bloody civilised about it all. A luncheon in the dining room to follow, Chloe suggested, as if we were all old friends.

'Emily arrived late. The baby, she explained, refused to settle. My wife, sweetly implying a strong bond of motherhood between them, said she understood completely. Then almost in the same breath, Chloe dropped her bombshell. She would happily apply for an annulment of a six-year marriage resulting in two children, she said, on the condition that Emily and I take total responsibility for the offspring of said marriage. It was what some would call a show-stopping moment. I turned to Emily, over the moon. Her face was ashen; she looked ill. I put a hand out to steady her while Chloe marched over to the baby and threw back the blankets. Emily came out of her trance, pushed Chloe away. People were starting to stare at us. "Let me know what you decide," Chloe said, walking away.'

'Emily said no?'

'She handed me the baby. Then she left. I never saw her again. Not until a couple of years ago.'

'But why didn't you keep your son?'

'It's not quite that simple. When I went back to our hotel room, Chloe took the baby from me without a word. She laid him on the bed, checked his nappy then she rang room service and ordered a double whisky for me. After the drink was delivered, she advised me to get a copy of his birth certificate if I didn't want to be lumbered with another man's son for the rest of my life.'

'How could she tell he wasn't yours?'

'She couldn't, of course. It was a wild guess. But I can't exactly explain how I knew instantly it was true. Instinct, perhaps? Or a string of odd episodes that alone could be excused but herded together should have gone off like a siren if I'd been in my right mind. Emily's clothes were more priestess than siren. Near the equator, when the heat was almost intolerable, she stayed away from the pool. The night we spent together, she hurriedly snapped off the lights before even taking off her shoes. So many little signs. But I was blind.'

Evening closes in. O'Reilly switches on a table lamp. Outside, one of the cows moans softly as though the heat has sapped her strength. O'Reilly, who's ignored his whisky until now, quietly drains the glass. 'I have some cheese . . .'

'Did you confront Emily? Did she tell you who fathered the child?'

'Emily disappeared.'

'But I don't understand . . . How did Alex end up in Britain?'

'My wife arranged everything. I was . . . I was unwell. I believe the correct term, in this era, is depression. For two years, I railed against God, as if it were His fault. As if my own hand in events had been divinely guided. In the end, I grew up. I put aside my soul, if there is such a thing, and accepted that I was fortunate in many, many ways. Just not in matters of the heart. I had two beautiful sons, a wife with whom I'd achieved an uneasy truce.'

'Did Emily ever get in touch? Looking for news of her son, maybe?'

'I had no idea what had happened to her until two years ago when she turned up here like a ghost. Said she'd been feeling sentimental about the past and was on a sort of pilgrimage to set old wrongs right. She asked about my wife, my sons. But I'm sure she knew.'

'Knew what?'

He seems to struggle then lets go: 'A Greek Island holiday. A ferry carrying too many passengers in rough weather.'

'But you survived?' Kate catches a hard note of accusation in her voice, the journalist in her rising. Eases off. 'It must have been terrible. Your worst nightmare.'

'Worse, in a way. If I still believed in a god, I'd say he exacted a heavy price for my sins. You see, I wasn't with them. It was hay-cutting season. I couldn't leave the farm.'

They are both silent for a long time.

'Emily asked you for money, didn't she?'

'I gave it to her. A small price to pay for a promise never to return. You see, old people learn to blot out the infamies and pains of their youth. It's the only way to achieve a small measure of peace.'

'I'm not sure how much you gave her, but there's around seventy thousand dollars in her account. I'll make sure it comes back to you.'

He shakes his head. 'Keep it . . .'

'No,' she says, breaking in. 'Blood money never does anyone any good.'

It is almost eight o'clock when Kate begins the drive back to the city, the grey box still on the seat where she'd forgotten it. Against the odds, she'd liked Timothy Terence Martin O'Reilly. Been seduced by his dignity under what she is ashamed to admit was an intense and biased grilling he didn't deserve. She'd made the very basic mistake so common to inexperienced journalists and leaped to conclusions without real evidence. She is appalled by how quickly the rules and ethics of her profession collapsed when the story got personal; she is quite sure a lesser man would have thrown her out. She should have given him the box. Filled with mementoes from that awful voyage, they indicated that, at least on some level, Emily had cared enough to hold onto reminders of him. The folded silver wing. It makes sense now. But the ash? Timothy O'Reilly looked surprised when at the last minute she'd asked him when he'd quit smoking. 'Never had a cigarette in my life,' he said. 'Filthy things.'

She dials the café, planning to leave a message on the machine. Ettie picks up on the first ring.

'I'm on my way home,' Kate says. 'I'll be back on deck in the morning.'

'No need to rush. Business is under control.' The phone goes dead in Kate's ear.

CHAPTER TWENTY-SIX

Early on Monday morning, with the sun refusing to bow to the changing season and already hot enough to sting, Sam borrows Jimmy's tinny and zooms to The Briny to check out the newspaper advertisement in the campaign to save Garrawi. Tying up at the pontoon, he races up the gangplank and explodes through the back door. 'Ladies!' he announces.

Before he can say another word, Ettie hands him a frothy mug of coffee. Jenny thrusts an egg-and-bacon roll at him. The two hard-working women look fit to bust. Success is catching. 'Jimmy was brilliant, wasn't he?' Ettie says.

'Always said the kid's a genius. In my humble opinion, last night he galvanised a nation. If there's anyone between here and the Kimberley who isn't onside they're either asleep or dead. If you're interested in a second opinion, I reckon you ought to batten down the hatches because you're about to have the biggest day in the almost two-hundred-year history of The Briny Café!' He jerks his thumb towards the Square. A crowd is building. 'But for starters, you might want to unlock the door.' He grabs a paper and takes off to avoid the stampede.

'Shit,' says Jenny, rocketing forward. Ettie slams eight cups in the coffee machine, presses the button. It's going to be a long – and very profitable – day.

On the back deck, which he doesn't expect to have to himself for very long, Sam lays the newspaper flat on a table, shocked by the difference between seeing a small piece of artwork printed on A4 paper and a full-colour advertisement at the bottom of page one of a mass-circulation daily newspaper. The impact is massive. '*NOT FOR SALE*', '*OUTRAGE*'. The two words are plastered in red across an idyllic photograph of Garrawi Park.

The ad draws your eye quicker than the headlines (another pointless opinion poll rating the premier and the leader of the opposition – as if anything matters except election day) and dares you to ignore it. He whacks up his feet on a spare chair, crossing his ankles, and reads the ad line by line, letting his food go cold.

Too beautiful to lose! Garrawi Park is a pristine public space and natural wonderland on Cutter Island in Cook's Basin. It is in danger of being stolen from the people of NSW and turned into an exclusive resort for the wealthy. The destruction of this unique and historic site is vandalism. Show you care. Join the Save Garrawi Campaign online by going to our website – www.savegarrawi.com – to register your vote against any future development. Join the fight to stop our beautiful beaches falling into the hands of profiteers. Force the State Government to abide by the wishes of the people. Vote now! Make a difference!

It couldn't be a better end to a top weekend, he thinks, wishing Delaney had been around to share in the triumphs. He flicks through the news. Murder. Cricket. Tennis. Road accidents. War in the Middle East. Remembers the day he found an old newspaper under linoleum he was ripping out of the kitchen. Murder. Cricket etc. He scoffs his congealing roll and sculls his lukewarm coffee. Leaving greasy thumbprints on the newspaper.

Jeez, he's late for work at the boatshed. Not good for a man who tries to lead by example. Star or no star, young Jimmy better be there. Fame is fleeting, according to Kate, and anyone who chases it better have a bread-and-butter job to keep from starving when the lights are turned off. His spirit falters.

Before the year is done, he predicts, Kate will coolly pack up, sell out and move on. A blow-in after all, despite Ettie's faith, his hopes. By then, if business stays strong, Ettie will be in a position to buy out Kate's share. The café will survive, Cook's Basin will prosper. And inevitably, so will Kate. People who have little perspective beyond their own tend to come out on top. Must be a lonely life, he thinks. The tragedy – the big freaking tragedy – is that although Kate thinks she's survived Emily's influence unscathed, she is like a pot that's on a slow simmer until someone suddenly turns up the heat. He can't help wondering whether her latest flight to the wilds of Victoria has answered all her questions. Christ, as long as it hasn't opened up an even bigger black hole.

If she'd asked his opinion, he would've told her to quit while she was ahead, cliché or no freaking cliché. Emily was as mad as a cut snake and the only way to deal with madness is to cut it out of your life. He heads for the café pontoon. Jumps into Jimmy's tinny and roars off to Oyster Bay. A furry black-and-white dog streaks down the boatshed jetty, his tail whipping up a force forty gale, to greet him. He breaks into an ear-splitting grin.

'Where you bin, Sam?' shouts Jimmy, his red hair jammed into one of Frankie's Greek fisherman caps. Sam waves. In the slip, the *Mary Kay* is on her way to full glory. He pats her hull as he passes. 'All good, Frankie?' The shipwright nods, keeps filling small cracks in the timber with putty. 'She was due for an anti-foul anyway,' Sam says. 'Tell me, just how many caps like that have you got?'

'The kid was going to need a number one. More shit in his hair than on the hull till he got the hang of it.'

'Knew you were a soft touch under the bluff. How you doing, Jimmy?' Sam tests the texture of the fill with a fingertip. Massages a little between his thumb and index finger. Satisfied, he flicks it away.

The kid slides back his cap, jiggles, giving the question serious consideration: 'Rome wasn't built in a day, Sam. Ya gotta have patience. But me an' Longfella, we're doin' good.'

Sam pulls the kid's cap over his eyes. 'You're a fast learner, mate.' He looks up at Kate's empty house, pleased to note he's feeling more wistful these days than wounded. Soon, he'll convince himself he's had a lucky escape. Soon. Trouble is, every time he writes her off, she comes up with a thought, a gesture, that rips out his heart. There's gold in her, he thinks, a pure seam of kindness that's based on clear-headed common sense without any fiddle-faddling sentimentality. Made her effort to contribute worth more, if you took the time to think about it.

The phone goes off in his pocket, making a noise like a fly caught in a bottle. No caller ID. The press, he decides. The world, it seems, wants more of Jimmy. He dumps the call. 'Jimmy!'

'Yar, Sam.' His freckled face pokes out below the hull.

'You want to do more interviews?'

'They offerin' to sling me another fistful of dollars?'

'No, mate. You're not an exclusive story any more. You're just fodder.' He sees the lack of comprehension in the kid's eyes and back tracks. 'It's like this. You did a good job last night and now more journalists want to talk to you but because you've already told your story once, no one's willing to pay a fee. The law according to Kate.'

'We got work to do, Sam, don't we? How we gunna do our work if we're buzzin' all over the place?'

'Decide what you want, and we'll manage no matter what. Is it a quiet life or the limelight?'

'What's the limelight, Sam?'

'A star, mate. Do you want to be a star?'

'Aw jeez, Sam. Not unless there's a dollar in it. Just a waste of time, me mum says.'

'She's a wise woman,' Sam says, feeling a tide of relief wash through him; Amelia has clearly had an epiphany or Artie's had a quiet but forceful word in her ear and explained the downside of celebrity. Who was it that said everyone would experience fifteen minutes of fame in a lifetime? The artist, what was his name? Loved Campbell's soup cans. Warhol, that was it. Personally, he was a Heinz tomato soup man. Tip the contents in a saucepan with the same amount of milk and as much sweet sherry as you thought you might need to get you through the night. It was one of his mother's favourite winter stand-by dinners, served with heaps of hot buttered toast. Guaranteed to ward off colds and flu. He didn't remember spending much of his childhood prone on the cot with a runny nose and red eyes so she may have had a point. 'You thought about this long and hard?' he asks, giving the kid one last chance at the big time.

'Bunch o' wankers, if you'll excuse me language.'

'Your mum say that?'

'Nah. That's me own version.'

Sam is floored, as he is so often, by the kid's ability to cut through the crap without ever being seduced by it. He watches Jimmy work for a while longer. Seeing a new focus, less frenzy. A boy starting to figure out what makes him tick. Who he is and where he belongs. According to Fast Freddy, who sees his fair share of the Island's more intellectually endowed kids searching for self-knowledge, Jimmy's come from a long way behind to lead the pack. If everyone's due fifteen minutes of fame, Sam's sure as hell happy that Jimmy's time has come and gone. No harm done, thank god.

The payment should hit the kid's bank account by the end of the day. Jeez, the press weren't a trusting lot, were they? No money up front – nothing till after the story went to air. Even a hint of a sneeze in the direction of an opposition television station, and all bets were off. Meaning no money because the exclusivity clause was broken. Anywhere else, and Sam was sure Jimmy would have blown the contract in happy innocence. But in Cook's Basin, where strangers stood out like bad debts, the community – already on full alert after the sinking of the *Mary Kay* – was ready to steer the kid away from any wandering press people intent on wrecking the deal with what Kate called a 'spoiler'. Which meant, she told him patiently, taking a couple of hiyas and giddays and fleshing them out with dodgy stuff based on quotes from 'sources close to Jimmy'. He'd argued the point, insisting no bloke, no matter how great a bastard, would motz a deal that was going to set up a kid with one or two unique personality issues for life. Kate had given him one of those looks that made his toes curl, like he was two cards short of a full deck. 'You think they care about Jimmy? They'd trample over their grannies to get a story,' she said. He wanted to know if she'd been like that when she was a fully operational journo. 'I worked in financial news. It's a different scene.'

He finds a scraper on Frankie's bench and goes to work alongside Jimmy. The kid gives him a comrade-in-arms grin that almost blows up his heart. If he was going to make a habit of picking up waifs and strays he'd be a fool to think he'd manage a one hundred per cent strike rate. Kate was a gamble from day one. You win some, you lose some. 'Ya missed a bit, Sam. Ya gotta concentrate, ya know.'

'Where's your whip?'

'Daydreaming again, were ya? Doesn't get ya anywhere, ya know?'

'Who said that?' Sam, a great believer in the power of day-dreaming to restore the spirit, is curious.

'That TV bloke. Said we were daydreamin' about savin' the park.'

'Bloody knuckle-head. What would he know?'

'We gunna save it, Sam?'

'The great lesson to be learned from this campaign is that no matter what gets thrown at you, never give up or give in. They can change the rules, break your windows or sink your barge, but you keep fighting. You getting my drift, kid?'

'Never take no for an answer, right?'

'Right.'

'So what are we gunna do next, Sam?'

'I'm working on it, mate. Trust me. It's going to be big.' Jeez, how often has he said that and how often is he going to have to say it?

A short time after café closing hour, Kate walks past the boatshed on her way home. He waves.

She comes over. 'As a friend,' she says with a wry grin, 'would you be able to call in tonight?'

'Sure,' he says. 'Give me half an hour.'

'I'll make dinner.'

'I don't need bribing, Kate.'

'Didn't think for a moment that you did.'

Under a canopy of stars made brighter by a moonless night, Kate tells Sam about her trip to Victoria to meet the man she thought was her brother's father. Sam listens, stupefied by her lack of tact and sensitivity.

For the first time since he spotted her back in the days when old Bertie was behind the counter of The Briny Café serving shocker coffee and life-threatening egg-and-bacon rolls, the golden flame of infatuation flickers for what he honestly believes is truly the last time, before dying out.

Thank Christ the old bloke was waiting with a confession he'd obviously been desperate to unloose for decades. Probably did him more good than harm to get it off his chest. He wonders if Kate will stay in touch. Realises he couldn't even hazard a guess, which doesn't say a lot about his genuine understanding of a woman he was supposed to be in love with. Maybe falling for her simply came down to timing. Forty years old, a string of light summer romances in his past that required neither effort nor commitment, he was ready for more. He'd always thought there was something sad about aging men chasing young women. Never dreamed he'd be on the brink of becoming one.

Kate appeared like a prize. He should have known it was never going to be easy. He resists an impulse to indulge in a round of self-pity. Sacrilege when you live in a strong community that never lets you down. Jeez, what's the point of her sad and pointless crusades to get to truths that should have no real bearing on the way she lives her life? 'The sins of the fathers,' he says, out loud without meaning to.

'That's the point, isn't it? Who is Alex's father if it isn't Timothy Terence Martin O'Reilly?' she replies.

Sam closes his eyes. 'Does your brother care?'

'Of course,' she replies, looking surprised he'd even asked. 'I told him I'd keep looking. And I will, even if it takes a lifetime.' She looks at him defiantly. 'Can you imagine how hard it must be to have no knowledge of who you are? Where you really come from?'

'I've never met the bloke but from what you've told me, he sounds pretty grounded. Reckon he knows who he is, and maybe, just maybe, even though everyone's intentions are pure gold, digging into stuff that Emily went to a lot of trouble to hide, might rock him right off his foundations. It's risky, Kate. If he wants to search, maybe he should go it alone.'

Kate pulls a spag bol sauce out of the freezer, and holds it up in a question. Sam gives in and nods. 'I just can't let it go,' she says, shoving the container in the microwave, putting a pot of water on the stove to boil. 'It's obsessive, I know. Maybe I want to prove once and for all that Emily was a monster in her own right and not one that I created out of . . . well, whatever the many and varied reasons behind some kids turning their parents into fiends.' She throws a small handful of salt into the water. The microwave pings. She tips the softened sauce into a saucepan: 'Ettie says it's OK for defrosting, but warming pre-cooked food in the microwave is like nuking it,' she explains. 'Slow and easy gives a better result.'

'She'll make a chef of you yet.'

'No. I'll always be a read-the-instructions type of woman. I don't have the instinctive flair she has.' She stirs the sauce. Throws the spaghetti into bubbling water. Steam rises and hits the ceiling where it hangs like tears. Kate opens the top of a window. Sam watches vapour twist and curl outwards into the open air.

He asks: 'You sure there aren't any more clues in the grey box?'

Without a word, she leaves the kitchen. When she returns, she lays out all the information she has. Only half engaged, wishing he had the sense to follow his own advice and leave the subject alone, Sam searches for links, a pattern, a joining of action and result. Keeps coming back to the word suicide. It bounces loudly off the inside walls of his skull. A single tone that resonates more and more strongly. 'Why would Emily's mother kill herself?' he asks after a while, more out of curiosity than a belief it holds a vital clue. 'What makes someone decide that death is preferable to life?'

Kate shrugs. 'Where do you start? Grief. Pain. Hopelessness. Or all three. But if there'd been a hint of mental illness, I'm quite sure Emily would have used it as a weapon: You're as mad as your grandmother . . .'

'I've always thought something awful must have happened to Emily when she was very young,' he says. 'O'Reilly's story backs me up, too. No mother, not even Emily, could hand over a baby without a backward glance unless there was something so hideous about the conception she couldn't bear to look at the child.' The sins of the fathers, he thinks again. Ah jeez. The sins of the fathers.

Sam knows he should change the subject. Knows he should stop his thoughts rocketing in the kind of directions that could lead to endless pain and anguish. He knows all this but still he says: 'Has Alex ever considered a DNA test?'

Kate scoffs at the idea. 'What's the point?'

'Maybe,' he says, skirting around the hideous idea that's latched onto his brain and refuses to budge, 'to verify that Alex is really, truly your half-brother and not a kid Emily snatched.' Dumb, he thinks, really dumb. No one snatches a kid and gets away with it. He tells himself to back-pedal fast. Get out of the hole he's digging deeper and deeper. Before he can swallow his words and in a final roll of the dice, he impulsively and foolishly opens what he knows in his gut is the real Pandora's horror box. 'You might want to get Emily's DNA and O'Reilly's at the same time.'

'What? Dig up her grave?'

'I dunno,' he mumbles. 'O'Reilly could be lying. Alex might be a fraud. Or maybe just closure.'

'Crazy idea,' she says. Sam breathes a sigh of relief. He may be a firm believer in steering clear of fibs, but seeking out the secrets of the past when they could do more harm than good is a no-win bet.

Thoughtfully, Kate adds: 'Maybe not so crazy. I'll talk to Alex and Timothy. See if they approve. I've still got Emily's hats. They should do. All I need is hair, don't I? Exhuming a body is going a bit too far.' She grins, to show it's a joke. Sam wants to cut out his tongue.

Jeez, he thinks, sculling his beer. Fighting an urge to jump into the water and start swimming. No good will come from all this. Ah jeez. He feels like he might suffocate if he stays a minute longer.

'Feel a bit fluey,' he croaks, struggling to his feet, ignoring Kate's surprise. And it's the flat-out truth. He feels sick to his gut. 'Might have to skip dinner, love. Sorry. Suddenly feel crook as a dog.'

'You'd be better off with someone around to look after you,' she says.

'Thanks, but when I'm this bad, all I want to do is crawl in a corner and curl up like an old dog. Sorry, love. Just hit me all of a sudden.'

Kate sees him to the dock, holding onto his arm. 'Call me,' she says, 'if you need anything.'

'Of all the shocker clichés,' he says when he's on the water and safely out of earshot. 'A freaking tragedy, that's what it is. I'm as sure of it as I am that the sun comes up every morning. The sins of the fathers. Dear god.' He has never in his life ever wanted more to be wrong.

Sam wakes in what feels like the dead of night. He switches on his bedside light and checks the clock. One am. His mobile phone pulsates. You'd call it the death-throes if you saw a person in a similar condition. *Bzzzzz*. Too late to be anything but a crank call. While he's still deciding whether or not to answer, the call rings out. He rolls over in bed, pulling the sheet up to his chin, hoping he'll be able to go back to sleep. He makes a deliberate attempt to switch his mind from Kate to Garrawi and the urgent need for a new thrust in the campaign. Aside from the art auction, future plans are a blank page.

Ring. Ring. Enough to drive a bloke to distraction. Ah jeez, get it over with, he thinks, reaching for the phone to put it out of its misery.

'Sam Scully.'

'I know who you are. I called you, didn't I? You need any more money? I got a million here that's yours. Say the word and it's in the account.'

Sam sits up. Fully awake now. 'You got a name, mate?'

'Yeah. Max. Short for Max.' He chuckles, like he's making the joke for the first time.

'If you don't mind me asking – and please don't think for a moment that I'm not grateful, mate, when there's no way I could even begin to measure my gratitude and the gratitude of the community – why are you doing this?'

'Sailed past the park every weekend when I was young. Magic, it was. Places like that? They're breathing spaces. Stop people going mad when the pressure gets too much. Know what I mean?'

'Yeah. But, mate, tell me, how can we thank you?'

'I'm not looking for recognition, if that's what you think. Doesn't mean diddly-squat to a man as old – and rich – as me.'

'There's got to be something –'

'Gimme a plaque after I'm buried.' The old man's laugh turns into a coughing spasm. Sam waits it out. Max continues: 'Just wanted to say the ad was good. Real good. Here's my number. When you need more money, call. Any time. Old people can sleep when they're dead.'

CHAPTER TWENTY-SEVEN

The following week, as the summer holidays are almost a forgotten era and the working year is well under way, the *Mary Kay* is ready to return to partial duty. Her resurrection, completed a day ahead of schedule, has the barge looking as fit as a woman who's just spent two weeks at a health farm drinking water, eating vegetables and running marathons. Delivery of the new gearbox for the crane is two weeks away so she'll be taking on light duties only.

Frankie presses a button to launch the cradle down the slipway. Sam and Jimmy, as twitchy as expectant fathers, follow the progress of the freshly painted canary-yellow hull with a mixture of anxiety and pride. Longfellow yips and nips, like he's rounding up a flock of sheep, until the stern rams into the water, sinks alarmingly but steadies quickly.

Half an hour later, ropes stowed, fuel checked, they are on their way. Sam spins the wheel and points the barge towards Cat Island to give the engine a long, flat-out run to smooth any kinks before committing to paid work. Under his feet, the thrum is deep and steady, the engine purring its heart out. He figures he'll wait till he reaches the confused waters swirling around Cat Island sanctuary before giving Frankie a progress report – more out of respect than necessity. Frankie won't let go of his grip on a boat until he's one hundred per cent certain – short of an unforeseen natural disaster such as a tsunami or a hurricane – it's not going to kill anybody. He's a good man. Pity he's never had any luck with women.

Sam grimaces inwardly. He's not travelling too smoothly in the romance stakes himself, right now. For the first time in a while, he hankers for the weedy taste of a rollie, the smell of a thin spiral of smoke curling from his mouth, snaking past his nose . . . Jeez, then landing in your hair so you smell like a bushfire or a barbecue at the end of the day. When a man hits forty, he has to make a few hard decisions if he wants to give himself a good shot at making eighty. Christ, there he goes again, thinking about his own mortality, time running out. He wonders briefly if he's currently engaged in a condition he's heard is called a mid-life crisis. It's mind over matter, he tells himself. Long as he believes he's a man in his prime he'll be OK.

But he's buggered if he can think of what to do next in the fight for Garrawi. He dials Siobhan. Gets The Briny by mistake. He hears Kate call an order, his ear as tuned to her tone as a mother to her baby's cry. The strange chemistry of humans is an utter mystery and he bets he could read *The Concise History of the World* from cover to cover and never discover the reason why, against all reason, one person chooses another.

*

In the pre-dawn light two days later, Sam and Jimmy set off from the car park on one of Siobhan's stealth missions – although stealth is the wrong word. They tow, strapped on a trailer built for ten-metre yachts, the giant cockatoo (cockscomb repaired for its big day out) majestically through the suburbs. Sam takes the opportunity to run Jimmy through the gearshifts. Baulks when, less than five minutes later, the kid offers to take over the driving. 'Rome wasn't –'

'Aw jeez, Sam, ya'r wearin' that thinner than ya top line for Ettie.'

'Well, mate, she *is* the answer to every man's dreams.'

Sam dodges the tunnel (in favour of keeping the cockscomb intact), makes it across the Harbour Bridge without mishap and proceeds, in what he likes to think is a stately manner, through the backstreets of the northern CBD then along Macquarie Street, where once again he makes use of the four-hour parking zone across the road from Mulvaney's office.

'That you, Sam?' asks Ben Butler, sticking his grey head out the door of his guardhouse. 'Would you like a cuppa? Kettle's just boiled.'

'Lovely. And this is Jimmy.'

'Oh, we all know Jimmy.'

Sam nobbles Theo Mulvaney, Minister for Housing and Development, a little before midday as he tries to scoot, head down, past the giant cockatoo: 'Have you seriously sold Garrawi? Are you really going to let a shonky cult take over one of the most beautiful parks in New South Wales and turn it into a Club Med? Are you?'

A television news reporter, who has just finished interviewing the opposition spokesperson for land and environment on the current lack of any credible research into the ongoing side effects of coal-seam gas mining, sees an opportunity for another news story. He and the cameraman shoot across and start rolling. Without any prompting, Jimmy stretches a long skinny leg in front of Mulvaney – like a brolga testing the sand of a riverbank. His going-to-town outfit of cerise and peacock blue is a photographer's dream. 'Why are ya trashin' the park, Mr Mulvaney? Why do ya wanna kill the cheese tree?' he asks politely, seriously and patently anxious to understand how foreign forces can be allowed to threaten the foundations of an age-old community and its sacred icons.

Mulvaney loses his temper and roughly pushes the kid aside. Jimmy stumbles, recovers. Draws himself to his full scrawny height, shakes his head at the politician: 'Me mum says it's rude to push people and right now, I'm findin' it hard not ta give ya a good talkin' to about manners. But ya need to brush up on 'em, ya know? Or you'll never get anywhere in life, so me mum says.' The reporter can't keep a straight face. The cameraman gets a full frame shot of Jimmy's disappointment. Sam stands back with his arms folded across his chest, and a look that spells *gotcha*.

The story makes the six-o'clock bulletin. Prime time. Sam's phone runs hot after it goes to air. Everyone's chuffed. The kid's a natural and turning into a Grade A arsonist. Who would have guessed it, eh?

Sam's mobile goes off for the umpteenth time. He checks the caller ID. The number comes up but he doesn't recognise it. He takes the call. 'Mr Scully? I understand you represent Jimmy MacFarlane.'

'In a manner of speaking,' Sam says.

'I'm a reporter with *Woman Magazine*. We'd like to talk to him and his mother about the relevance of good manners in a techno world.'

Sam sighs. 'I don't want to sound mercenary but I've been instructed to turn down any requests unless there's a fee. The kid's got an eye on building a decent superannuation fund for his old age.'

The reporter dodges the question and talks about the beneficial influence a story like this could have on parents all over Australia.

'You reckon a single kid can change the manners of a generation, eh?'

'Well . . .'

'I don't want to sound cynical, but playing the ego card is a cheap way to try to nudge him over the line for free. Unless you're willing to pay a fee for his time, there's no deal.' Jeez, Sam thinks, he just might be getting the hang of the dark side of the media business.

'I'd have to check with the editor,' the reporter says, the cosiness gone from her voice.

'What's your gut feeling?' Sam asks.

'Well, Jimmy's not a celebrity . . .'

'Can't agree with you there,' he says, and he – politely – declines the offer.

Just on dusk, Sam gets three calls in a row. All he hears on the end of the line is heavy breathing. It leaves him feeling chilled to the bone.

Before he can decide what to do, Siobhan calls. 'Nice work at Parliament House but Mulvaney's going to feel like a rat in a corner,' she warns. 'Jimmy made a fool of him. We've got to seriously watch ourselves now. We're starting to look and sound like winners and he's got a lot of money at stake. Think of it, Sam. If the man was handed half a million before the project started, what's it worth to him when it's finished?'

'I've a bottle of your favourite Riesling in the fridge if you feel like dropping around for a drink,' Sam says.

'What's on your mind then?'

'I'm worried they'll target Jimmy.'

'Polish a glass and I'll be there before it's halfway filled.'

They sit on Sam's mouldy canvas chairs on the deck with the slatted timber table between them. Sam slips his beer into a thermal glove to keep it cold. Siobhan takes a small, considered sip of her wine. She tilts her head in approval. 'A lovely, light drop. Those heavy-wooded chardonnays, they'd put hair on a young girl's chest.'

On the water, with the light falling fast, a couple of kids paddle surfboards from a standing position. No lights, Sam worries. He watches until they make it safely to soggy mudflats on a low tide where sand hills rise and fall like tiny islands. The sky is deep pink behind blue hills, the air ripe with damp earth and the tang of brine and wet sand. Nearly every commuter tinny is high and dry. Frankie will enjoy a small boom replacing props over the next few days. One man's luck is another man's misfortune, as his father used to say. The two paddlers lift their boards and hoof it to shore. 'The kid,' Sam says, 'how are we going to protect the kid?'

*

Sam and Siobhan talk late into the night. Alerting the whole community, they agree, could start a panic. Alerting only Amelia would be sure to start a panic. 'How quickly crumble the foundations,' Siobhan says. 'It's a sad day when we can't feel safe in our environment.'

In the end Siobhan resolves there's nothing to do short of sending Jimmy and his mother on an extended holiday.

'Jimmy won't leave while the park is in danger of being razed to the ground,' Sam says. 'So we're back to square one.'

'I'd ask our local member of parliament to warn Mulvaney to call off the dogs but our relationship is a tad testy.'

Sam raises his eyebrows.

'I felt compelled to correct her press releases, which, as it turned out, were written by her husband. He told me I was creating marital disharmony by interfering. Eejit. I was only trying to make them grammatical. Bad grammar is offensive, don't you think? Like someone singing off-key.'

Sam grins: 'Guess contacting her is not an option, then.'

Siobhan sighs with mock innocence. 'Sometimes I wonder if I should employ a little more diplomacy . . .'

'Nah. Life's too short to mess around.' They both grin.

'We're in need of another spot of arson to keep the media ball rolling. Got any ideas?' she asks.

'How about a hot air balloon over Macquarie Street?'

Siobhan's eyes light up. 'Would the balloon be able to hoist the cockatoo, do you think?'

'Might be a bit heavy.'

'Ah well, it would be a shame for it to smash through the roof of Parliament House by mistake. A lot of effort went into creating that monster bird. I'm quite fond of it by now, you know.'

The next day, in an interview in the *Daily Telegraph*, Mulvaney unwisely refers to Garrawi Park as the local garbage dump. He hurl insults at the locals, calling them 'uneducated, drug-taking ferals who need assistance to flush a toilet'. He goes on to mention the 'handicapped' child being callously exploited by members of the community who are too cowardly to step up to the front line.

The Islanders go into uproar. Siobhan, who is incensed Mulvaney isn't even savvy enough to use the more politically correct term of 'disabled' – which certainly doesn't apply to Jimmy – sends out a message: 'He's insulting Jimmy to destroy the kid's credibility. Don't react. Don't say a word. The bastard is looking to fatten his personal bank account.'

Sam takes Jimmy aside and shows him the story. 'Remember how I said people might call you names? This is how it happens.'

Jimmy glances at the picture of Mulvaney. 'Jeez, Sam, I told ya the bloke had no manners.' And the slur rolls off Jimmy like water off a duck's back. 'I'm off if ya don't need me. The heat's stressin' me worms somethin' terrible. I gotta hose 'em down every hour or they'll cark it.'

'You seen anyone dodgy hanging around your house lately, Jimmy?'

'Nah. Only Kerry. But he comes and goes.'

'Kerry?'

'Me big goanna. Think he might be eyein' me worms. I'm keepin' an eye on 'im, though. Me worms are like family so I'd come down hard on Kerry if he 'ad a go at 'em.'

'Right,' Sam says. 'Anyway, if you see anything weird, call me, OK? Anything at all, I want to know, Jimmy. It's important, mate. So don't go it alone if you reckon something's not quite up to scratch. Deal?'

'Yeah sure, Sam. Anythin' weird, eh?'

Sam suddenly realises the many possible connotations for *weird*. 'Er, I'm not talking Island weird. Just weird, weird, OK?'

'Orright.'

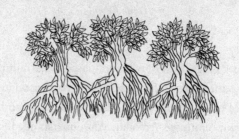

CHAPTER TWENTY-EIGHT

The fundraising art auction takes place on the third Saturday evening in March in the heart of Sydney's posh eastern suburbs. The works adorn the stark white walls of a cavernous echoing gallery owned by Michael Barnes, a very rotund, very volatile, completely passionate curator with big bushy hair; he's affectionately known as the Wombat. The weather is freakish. Stinking hot – forty degrees even with the sun well and truly set. The moon is huge. The kind of night in ancient times that men went mad and women hid. As if to prove the point, a hundred noisy rabble-rousers are gathered with placards denouncing Cutter Islanders as silvertailed toffs trying to prevent others from enjoying their god-given delights.

'Who sent you?' Sam asks the heavily sweating bloke who appears to be in charge.

'Mulvaney,' he responds without hesitating. 'You wouldn't have a cold drink anywhere, would you, mate?'

Sam goes off. The protesters begin chanting: 'Down with NIMBY bastards.' He returns with a large bottle of water.

The leader glugs most of it before passing it around. Figuring he owes Sam a favour, he says: 'Just so you know, mate, we've been told to smash the place. You might want to keep your head down. Nothing personal, you understand. Just earning a dollar here.'

Sam rushes to inform the Wombat, or Barnesie, as he prefers to call him. Wearing a sleek black suit, red-framed sunglasses and vermillion-painted lips that are bleeding into the perspiration running down his face, he's installed in a kissing booth at the entrance. 'Gimme a kiss, lovelies,' he says, mock smooching. 'Five dollars a kiss.' Siobhan, who's dressed in the same glad rags she wore to the black-tie fundraiser and who looks as glamorous as Maureen O'Hara in her Hollywood heyday, gets it instantly. 'He's sending up John James,' she says. 'Sending up the cult.' She parts with her money and leans over. Instead of kissing him, she half-whispers in his ear. 'I will love you forever for this.'

The fake guru gives her a fake blessing and showers her with fake money. The Eastern Suburbs matrons, thrilled to find themselves in the midst of exciting bedlam instead of boring chitchat, line up like over-heated, fluffed-up chooks.

'Those blokes outside. They're going to bust the place, Barnesie. What do you want to do?'

'Ooooh,' he twitters, rubbing his hands in delight. 'I smell a front page. In the art world, all publicity is good publicity. It ramps up prices faster than a freshly dead painter.'

In the midst of what is fast turning into a riot, Jack Mundey steps off a bus and even the protesters go quiet, parting like the Red Sea to let the great man make his way into the gallery, where he's due to make a speech. Soon as he's through the doors, Barnesie bolts inside, shoots the lock and gets on with the show under the happy influence of a noisy air-conditioner running flat out. The rent-a-crowd of hooligans, their moment of reverence for Mundey – whose fame is more apocryphal than real to them – is quickly forgotten. They try to smash their way in. Barnesie calls the media, then waits ten minutes before calling the cops.

Mundey is unruffled and Barnesie leads him to the podium like a precious jewel. Mundey gets straight to the point: 'Parks are for people,' he says. 'To turn public spaces over to private estates for the very rich is unconscionable. We must not allow this to occur. Will neither of our major political parties act to save this beautiful piece of coastline?'

The room erupts in cheers. The art auction raises a whopping fifty-seven grand from the sale of thirty paintings by the Island artists and seventeen works donated by friends of the curator ('I didn't even have to threaten to drop them from my list'). 'At this rate,' Sam jokes, 'we'll be able to buy the park ourselves.'

Siobhan gives him a thoughtful, almost cunning look through narrowed eyes. 'Out of the mouths of babes,' she says.

Later in the week, Barnesie, who's found his inner thespian and is hell-bent on making the most of his newfound role, repeats his performance on the pavement outside Mulvaney's office, tossing fake banknotes into the air with gleeful abandon. 'No resort. No bridge. Save Garrawi, bless you, bless you,' he chants until his voice gives out. One or two passers-by pounce on the money, thinking it is real, before striding off in disgust. Ben Butler calls Sam to give a full and frank account of the reaction of the Minister for Housing and Development to the energetic art dealer. 'He went totally ballistic. Ape-shit,' he reports, 'Completely nuts.'

The following day, the goons descend on the Square. They hang around for hours. Pointing fingers, like guns, at passing Islanders: 'Boom,' they say. 'Boom, boom. Boom. Love your dog? Boom. Love your cat? Boom.'

The Islanders swallow their rage and instead, laugh in the vacant faces. 'Love your *outfits*, boys – off to a funeral, are you?' 'Bit old for cowboy games, aren't you?' 'Could you help carry the shopping, loves? There's more in the boot. No, love, I'll take the light bags. How about you carry the three slabs of beer and two cases of wine?' And on it goes until the Misses Skettle, who are collecting signatures in the shade of the giant cockatoo, which has been returned to its customary perch, finally have enough. Arms linked, brows furrowed, they march in their kitten-heel shoes to the pair of dark glasses they've decided is the leader. Pounding one arthritic old finger each against a gym-toned chest, they utter in perfect unison: 'Bugger off. And take your simpletons with you.'

For the second time in her recent life, Ettie Brookbank, who's been keeping an eye on the women all day, nearly has to be resuscitated. Five minutes later, to everyone's amazement including the Misses Skettle, the goons depart in a cloud of stinking, burning rubber. 'Losers!' shout the Misses Skettle, raising clenched fists high. Ettie reaches for the Thermos and swigs straight from the mouth. 'We knew they'd run,' the Misses Skettle explain. 'Bullies can't handle old ladies. We remind them of their mothers.'

Siobhan O'Shaughnessy literally pops a shirt button when Ettie gives an account of the stoush between two sparrow-like genteel old ladies and six towering muscle-bound goons. 'Oh bejaysus, I wish I'd been there,' she says, wiping tears of laughter. 'They took off like startled crows, you say?' And she bends double, laughing until her stomach hurts.

Then suddenly, everything goes quiet. Lowdon, who's been holed up in his house with a broken foot, disappears. Mulvaney's almost constant presence in the daily press ends. There's not a goon to be seen. Sam tries to call Delaney for a chat. He's no longer surprised when the call goes straight to message bank.

March drifts into April. The heats finally starts to lose its ferocity although the sea is still so warm the fish are sluggish and pathetically easy to hook. Anglers feel like they're cheating and go after bigger game fish to keep the thrill of the challenge intact. Nights are blessedly cooler. A single cotton blanket appears on beds to ward off the chill that creeps in an hour before the kookaburras sound the morning reveille.

The chef cooks like a maniac: fish, fish and more fish. Sushi, sashimi, whole, baked, curried, stewed, grilled and dishes of lemon-cured ceviche. Ettie swears she's on the verge of transforming into a mermaid. The chef smiles with delight: 'You will always be my siren,' he declares gallantly.

Yes, but for how long? Ettie thinks, understanding the time for denial is over. Theirs is not a relationship built on love, children, grandchildren, the richness of family and history, the iron grip of decades of support through good and bad times. She is menopausal. No amount of the Misses Skettles' sweet-potato cream, evening primrose oil or even hormone replacement therapy can hold back aging forever. Her libido, already erratic, will drop. (Never mind the stories octogenarians tell documentary makers about their rampant sex life – fantasy or lies if her own experience is typical and she has no reason to think it isn't.) Her ability to function sexually will diminish. Their relationship will be forced to embrace a new reality. Or end. Squaring her shoulders, she asks for a snifter of cognac that she tells Marcus she would like to sip while she dangles her feet in the bath-warm water at the end of the jetty. Will he join her?

He returns, hands her a brandy balloon and drops to her side with a small grunt. With a pang, she takes in his smooth, tanned legs, where not a single vein has bled into a small blue badge to mark the years. The difference between the way men and women age is a cruel joke, she thinks. Surely, in a fairer world, their diminishing capacities – or does she mean capabilities – would be shared more evenly.

Before she has time to lose her courage, she spells out the future – her future and therefore their future – if they have one after she finishes – in terms that are blunt and even a little exaggerated. She wants him to be under no illusions. It is like taking a knife to her heart and slicing it in thin slivers before tossing it in a smoking-hot frying pan and burning it to a cinder.

The chef listens closely, seriously. He doesn't squirm or fidget. Nor does he try to dismiss Ettie's worries and fears as a momentary bout of female hysteria. He understands precisely the cost to her of these intimate revelations. Who, man or woman, can easily bear to admit they have reached a stage where there is no cure and no going back?

When she is done, he reaches across the short distance between them for her hand. Has he not learned already that to sit too close causes her body heat to soar, brings on discomfort and distress?

'This is about sex, no? Not love?'

She nods.

He is earnest, grappling with words so that when he speaks, they cannot do harm or lead to misunderstanding. 'Sex is a hunger that is never satisfied.' He feels her stiffen. Knows he's already floundering. Rushes to explain. 'Love, Ettie, love sustains us. Not sex. Never sex. It is a side effect, yes, if this is the word. Disappointing, often, unless it is part of love. Do you agree with this?'

She nods.

'If I may explain?'

She nods again.

'When we are together, the world shines. When we are apart, it is like the lights have been turned off. For me, this is love. This doesn't die. Sex, well, of course if you ask, I will never say no. But this is not –'

'Let's go to bed,' she interrupts, breathing in like oxygen every massive nuance in a few simple lines that she knows will be burned in her mind forever. 'While I've still got a couple of hormones left.'

Ettie hosts the fifth Save Garrawi meeting on the back deck of The Briny Café on a spectacular evening stroked by a cool southerly. Members of the committee cannot decide whether to feel jumpy or confident. They all agree, though, that this sudden quietness on the battlefront is eerie.

At a loss about what to do next, they tuck into one of Ettie's new recipes: slow-cooked neck of lamb eased off the bone and swizzled in a sauce based on tomatoes, garlic, anchovies, chilli, capers and olives. Put the same sauce on spaghetti and it would be called puttanesca.

'More chilli,' Sam advises.

'Less chilli,' Siobhan contradicts, entering the food debate for the first time anyone can remember.

'Perfection,' Marcus adjudicates. But no one takes any notice of him because Ettie could dish up raw rats' tails and he would find nothing to complain about.

Siobhan is unusually vague when they look to her for new directions. They worry she might be wearing out, that the pressure is getting to her, but they are experienced enough now in the sleight-of-hand ways of developers and politicians to know that quiet times can be just as dangerous as open warfare. So they wait, worrying they are not as alert or inspired as they once were. That they have lost the knack of stepping forward. But how do you lead a charge when the enemy has gone to ground?

Towards the end of the meeting, Sam tells them about Artie's suggestion for a rally and a march in the streets of

Sydney. Siobhan suddenly seems to wake up and speaks out: 'What day does parliament reconvene? Do we know?'

Seaweed pulls out his phone and Googles the question. 'Second sitting is in a week.'

'Right, well how about we organise a small rally for the Sunday following this one? Seaweed, put out a notice on the website. We're holding a protest march and everyone who fancies a day out for a good cause is invited.'

Reinvigorated by the thought of action, members shrug off their sloth. 'What'll we call it?' Seaweed asks.

They toss around ideas for the next hour. 'RAPE,' Siobhan finally decides. 'Rally Against Plundering the Environment.' Hear, hear. 'We'll need posters, newsletters, placards, banners and loud-hailers.'

'Leave it to the artists!' Hear, hear.

'How about a band? Music is a huge drawcard,' Jenny suggests. 'Big Phil and Rexie might enjoy the opportunity to take their music to a wider audience!' Hear, hear.

'What about a place to set up rally headquarters?'

'How about here at The Briny?' Ettie offers. Hear, hear!

'It's a lot of work for a small rally,' Siobhan muses. For a second, the room goes flat and silent. Enthusiasm falters. She brightens: 'Sure and what would be the point of that? Have you got the list there, Jane, of all the organisations that wrote and said they were with us? Good lass. Let's extend an invitation to every community group in New South Wales with a cause and make it a feckin' blaster of a rally, eh? And Jack Mundey: he'd feel at home at just such a rally, don't you think?'

HEAR, HEAR!

Sam says: 'We need to nail Mulvaney, let everyone know he's on the take and bent as a fork.'

'Whoever says it out loud will end up in court, that's for sure. It's not worth losing your house, now, and even the shirt off your back, is it?'

Glenn jumps forward from the deck rail. 'I don't own a thing except a dodgy Kombi van circa 1973 and a dodgier barge, circa unknown. He's welcome to both along with my collection of stained and holey commemorative Christmas dog race T-shirts. Gimme me a loud-hailer and a script and I'll go the bloke like a bull terrier!'

Hear, hear!

'Only if it will do some real damage, eh?' Sam says. 'We don't want Glenn to sacrifice all his worldly possessions for nothing. And, mate, holes or no holes, those T-shirts are priceless.'

'There's an election in the wind, sonny, and we're standing on a pile of shite the premier needs to flush down the toilet as quickly as he can. It'll hurt. Oh, for sure it will hurt.'

The community, no longer novices, swings into action with efficiency born of experience. Glenn decides to have a practice run at slagging Mulvaney by spearheading an early raid on Parliament House. Sam joins him in the skirmish. They swing into Macquarie Street in Glenn's rattly Kombi, tickled up by the artists so it's a moving billboard of slogans supporting Garrawi. The Misses Skettle, who insist on coming along at the last minute, tumble out of the back of the van. (A luxurious trip, they later reported. The two bunk beds were so comfy they dozed through the entire tedium of the traffic – highly recommended.) The two women, dressed in a shade that's nearer lipstick red than petal pink for a more dramatic effect, promptly set up a card table and a couple of folding chairs on the pavement and, keeping their Thermos handy, they begin collecting signatures. No one gets past them.

During his morning-tea break, Ben Butler hurries over: 'Just heard there's a meeting between the premier and the secretary of the Australian Council of Trade Unions at the Trades Hall in Goulburn Street in half an hour. Get over there and rattle their cages,' he advises. 'Every television, radio and newspaper news crew will be covering it. Rear entrance. He never goes near the front door.' And he scurries off, giving them a V for Victory.

Sam takes the two old ladies aside and suggests they stay safely put on the pavement with their clipboards while he and Glenn do their best to stir up strife. The Misses Skettle pout. Sam caves in, telling himself it's wiser to keep them in sight anyway. Who knows what they might get up to if they're let loose in the city for the first time in thirty years, 'Barring dentist's appointments.'

They all pile into the Kombi and roar off. By the time the premier's official car pulls up, they're ready and waiting. Sam goes into action, circling the vehicle: 'Have you really let Mulvaney flog Garrawi to a dodgy cult? Are you seriously going to approve a resort on a small island that can barely sustain its current population let alone an influx of tourists? Are you going to let a dodgy cult get its hands on a pristine Australian wilderness so close to a major city?'

Glenn, script in hand, takes over: 'How much does it take to buy the Minister for Housing and Development? Half a million? That's what we've heard is the going price.'

The premier's minders step forward and quickly shove him aside. The Misses Skettle take a turn, smiling sweetly. 'No resort, no bridge. Save Garrawi,' they chant. The bruisers are flummoxed. The news cameras are rolling. Pushing old ladies out of the way loses votes. The premier smiles professionally and accepts a flyer. The union bloke on the door blocks the Misses Skettle entrance into the Trades Hall, suggesting they have a cup of tea in the cafeteria.

'Don't take any notice of him, Myrtle,' Violet says loudly. 'They never put a smart man on the door.' They regally swish past him. Outraged but powerless, the doorman, who is a top-ranking union official, slams shut and locks the entrance. Sam and Glenn pick up their loud-hailers and go searching for an open window. Standing on Sam's shoulders, Glenn shouts through the opening: 'Your minister, Theo Mulvaney, is going to let a discredited cult leader desecrate Garrawi. How much did the cult pay him? Half a million?'

A minute later, two police officers round the corner. 'Show's over, boys,' they say, taking possession of the loud-hailers. 'Time to go home.'

Glenn looks them straight in the eye and lies like a pro: 'They've got our fragile –' (Ha!) '– old aunties in there. Can't leave without them, mate.' One cop stays with Sam and Glenn; the other retrieves the Misses Skettle from the inner sanctum, where he finds them sharing a cuppa with the premier. 'We had his ear at least while the cameras were rolling. What a day, eh? Haven't had this much excitement since the war.'

Early on Sunday morning, adults, kids and assorted dogs of Cook's Basin and Cutter Island gather in the Square with placards, posters and banners as well as rugs, picnic baskets and ice boxes. It's going to be a long day and all it takes is a little planning and preparation to ensure maximum comfort because who knows what they'll find in Hyde Park where the rally will begin its slow march to Parliament House? Phoebe, the graphic design artist, even brings a small fold-up camp dunny seat (hole in the top, discreet cover for when it's not in use) in case she gets caught short and needs to dash behind a tree. Her knees, she explains, aren't what they used to be. Anyone is welcome to borrow it, she adds with her usual generosity of spirit.

They load their goods and chattels into the bowels of buses and board one by one, automatically splitting kids and dogs known to have mutual personality issues. The air is both subdued and festive. Everyone hopes for a mega turnout. Dreads a flop.

'We've worked day and night to rally the nation,' Siobhan says. 'We've done our best and can do no more.' In her hands she holds a dossier with bullet point questions and concerns on a single page from every environmental group involved. She just hopes they don't think they've made their points and fail to attend.

Sam and Jimmy, with the massive white cockatoo once more perched on the boat trailer behind Sam's ute, lead a parade of buses from the sandy track of the Square to the bitumen beyond. They are waved off with damp tea towels by Kate and Ettie. Jenny, who's been given the day off, will represent The Briny Café. Ettie is gutted but business is business. Everyone understands.

At ten am the people come over the hill like Indians. Down they come and down they come and down they come. Each group carries its own banner and raises its voice to chant its disillusionment with a government that seems to have forgotten it is there to represent the people. 'Why won't you listen to the people?' 'Why won't you hear our cries?' 'Stop destroying our coastline.' 'Stop trashing our bushland.' 'Stop coal seam gas drilling from polluting our precious waterways.' 'Save our farmland and let our farmers feed the nation.' And ultimately: 'Garrawi belongs to the people. Preserve it for the people forever.' On and on, down they come.

Siobhan, who can't shake a sad feeling of déjà vu when she sees Jack Mundey standing on a truck bed parked outside Parliament House for the occasion, stands alongside Sam, Jimmy and the cockatoo. She shakes her head. 'Every generation finds itself on the edge of a new battlefront. Do we never learn?' She sighs, hands Sam a loud-hailer and a script. 'Up you go, next to Mundey,' she orders. 'And don't fluff a word.'

Sam checks the script. Gives her a wry grin. 'I'll do my best.' He leaps aboard and takes a place next to Mundey. Behind him, Big Phil and Rexie are ready to hit a few riffs and get the crowd launched on an iconic protest song from the 1950s that never seemed more appropriate: 'We shall overcome'.

Sam shouts: 'We are the people. We have spoken. We are the people. We have spoken.' The cry goes up for a long, long time. Then quietly drifts into song as a ten-thousand-strong choir sways to the steady tap of Big Phil's flaming cowboy boot and Rexie's stirring voice.

Later, on Sam's deck, when the moon is high and he and Siobhan are reliving the more historic moments of a monumentally historic day, Siobhan says: 'Did I see a tear roll down your cheek when the singing started?'

Sam shrugs. 'Nah. It was sweat, mate. That's all.'

Siobhan reaches across and slaps his thigh: 'So you think I can't tell the difference between sweat and tears, then? And me an Irish woman whose race has known nothing but tragedy for a thousand years.'

'Yeah, well, to be honest, I was flat out holding back the sobs. Never felt so emotional in my life.'

'Me too, me too.'

Before the community has time to congratulate itself on the success of their rally, it wakes to newspaper headlines and stories that send shockwaves through the nation and cut through the heart of every Islander.

In a mass suicide pact, four hundred and thirteen members of the New Planet Fountain of Youth cult, including leader John James, died after eating food laced with cyanide. At this stage, it is not known whether there are any survivors.

Australian journalist, Paul Delaney, in Qualupe, a small town in Central America, to investigate claims of corrupt land deals with the potential to bring down the NSW State Government, was shot dead as he was boarding a twin-engine plane for his return flight. James McInerney, shadow minister for human rights, who accompanied Delaney to witness the increasing number of allegedly brainwashed young Australians who had joined the charismatic leader, is fighting for his life in a local hospital. Police investigating the shootings drove to the cult's headquarters and described the scene as carnage. Men, women and children lay dead on the ground. John James's remains were found inside his marble palace, surrounded by those of his top henchmen. It is not known why James, who is worth billions of dollars, and his followers decided to end their lives.

The dreadful news flies around the community in minutes. Sam grabs a bottle of Riesling and a six-pack and knocks on Siobhan's door. She greets him with swollen eyes and tear-streaked cheeks. 'Have you got a spare bucket?' he asks.

The idiocy of the question takes her off-guard. 'Are you mad, Sam Scully?'

'There's no loo on the *Mary Kay* and you and I are heading out to sea for a while. No arguments, please. If you stay here you'll have people calling in all day, laden down with sad faces and casseroles. Far better to rock on the roomy deck of a lovely barge that once hosted the ample frame of a great man, eh?'

Ten minutes later, the *Mary Kay* has her bow pointed towards a deserted sandy cove not far from where the beautiful Cook's Basin waterways get unruly with merging inland rivers, bays and a vast blue sea. Sam snookles into a sheltered corner and throws down the anchor. With the engine switched off and the barge almost still, Siobhan tells him how she came to know Paul Delaney.

'With a name like Delaney, he was one of us. We mad Irish, I mean. Even though he was fourth generation Australian, there's a gene – the one that can't abide injustice – that never dies. I first met him when he burst into the newsroom where I worked. I'd arrived in Australia fresh from Ireland with a yearning for the warm sun and a life free from the claptrap of our priest-besotted families. He was like a blue-eyed god with his curly blond hair and his great belly laugh.

'We other reporters learned quickly that here was a man who wasn't afraid to rattle the status quo until it fell off its iron hinges. We admired him. But he scared us a little, too. He gnawed, nagged and raged if he had to, even if it cost him his job. Which it did more than once.'

Sam passes her a plastic beaker of white wine. Knocks the top off a frigidly cold. He wishes he'd thought to raid the picnic counter of The Briny Café for a few nibbles.

'When he was in his early twenties with a wild hunger to see the world, he took himself off to the United States of America. I was already there and, foolish girl that I was, I thought he'd followed because he missed me.'

'You were lovers?' Sam asks, amazed and curious at the same time.

'Not in a way that mattered, as it turned out.'

'He broke your heart, eh?'

'We journos, we're different,' she says, taking her time to find the right words. 'Part of the job is to charm strangers until they're half in love with you. We reinvent ourselves for every assignment, wheedling, smarming and charming until we have everything we need. Then we walk away without a backwards glance. Chasing the next big scoop.'

Sam opens his mouth, about to break in. She stops him with a signal. 'It's the adrenalin that sucks us in, the rush to deliver on deadline. It's like living in a war zone. You never feel more alive. Comradeship becomes indistinguishable from love. A strange bond.'

Sam nods, wondering if he's just been given an insight into Kate. Their closenesss then the sudden distance she puts between them. Her terrier ferocity when she's chasing a lead. Her blindness to the consequences when she loses sight of the difference between a personal quest and a professional assignment.

Siobhan continues with her history of Delaney. 'He landed a job as one of a dozen or so editors on a mass-circulation tabloid with a wicked reputation for gossip and scandal. 'There was a cult, Delaney said in his first news meeting, in Central America, where suicide drills were practised once a week . . .'

Sam looks at her puzzled: 'The same cult? John James? God, even the names are similar.'

'Another name, another place but a copycat all the same,' she says. 'For four weeks straight, Delaney tried to raise interest in the story, upping the ante with more and more horrific facts, not least that children were being lowered into wells and left there for days as punishment for slight misdemeanours. The fifth week, the whole world knew about almost one thousand people dying in a mass suicide pact in a small village that became known as Jonestown. Delaney never got over it. He felt he'd failed every victim.'

'Ah jeez, so that's why . . .'

'There's a thousand stories just the same as Garrawi: wherever you look in this great country that seems hell-bent on trashing its national treasures. It was the cult that lured him in, as I knew it would, because to my endless shame, I was one of those ambitious, toadying young editors on that dreadful rag who failed to support him in his crusade all those years ago. He forgave me, though I've never forgiven myself. The tragedy, eh, of Delaney's niece joining a cult no different from the one he tried so hard to expose so long ago. Sure and she must be dead, too. Delaney's sister, she'll be gutted forever.'

The two of them sit in silence long after the wine is drunk, the six-pack – with just two bottles emptied – put away. After a while, Siobhan stretches out on the deck on the shady side of the wheelhouse, her head resting on a coil of rope. She quietly sleeps.

Sam keeps watch from the bow where he leans against a huge crucifix bollard until it cuts into his skin and he can no longer stand the pain. Then he too lies flat on the deck, gazing at an empty blue sky, wondering how people can bear to do such awful things to each other.

A week after Delaney's death, April is three-quarters done and the Square is full of kids in school uniforms going back and forth, their packs as heavy as their faces. The rainclouds and humidity have long moved offshore to vent their spleen over the empty ocean. Balmy autumn days are sharp with clean light. Nobody wants to go to work. It's the best time of the year. The sea, bluer than the sky and so sparkly it hurts naked eyes, calls like a siren. But the harsh economic realities of paying the mortgage and putting food on the table are inescapable. People count down the days to the weekend, with a longing that's strong enough to call an ache.

There's been no sign of the goons since the Misses Skettle told them to bugger off and the cult went spectacularly belly-up with the death of the leader and his closest followers. No one dares to suggest out loud that the threat is over.

Sam turns on the morning news; the cult mass suicide no longer rates a mention. The focus is on the upcoming state election where the incumbent government is tipped to be facing a nail-biting battle. He's about to switch off in disgust when Theo Mulvaney's face fills the screen. He watches as Mulvaney walks over to the worn patch of grass under the spreading arms of an ancient fig tree where most political television grabs take place and, citing the pressures of family life, announces his resignation. The reporter adds that the Minister for Housing and Development has been under party pressure to quit since it was revealed he had strong links with John James, 'who orchestrated a mass suicide in his cult headquarters in Central America last week for reasons still unknown'.

Mulvaney refuses to answer any questions and ducks unceremoniously out of the grounds onto Macquarie Street, cheerfully waved through the gate by Ben Butler. Sam leans closer to the screen. In the background, he swears Ben's middle finger is somehow raised in a rude sign. Two minutes later, Sam's mobile goes off: 'You fought hard but clean,' Ben Butler says. 'Congratulations.'

'See you've had a bit of finger surgery,' Sam says.

Ben laughs loudly: 'Repetitive strain injury, mate. There's a lot of it going around.'

The premier makes clear the reasons for Mulvaney's exit on the evening news.

'Theo Mulvaney's part in questionable land and development deals, including Garrawi Park, Cutter Island, off the east coast of Australia, cannot be condoned or even tolerated by a government that prides itself on full and frank accountability in all areas.' The man keeps a straight face.

Sam is rendered speechless. He turns to Siobhan, who is tucked onto his mismatched sofa with a glass of wine, and rolls his eyes. 'My dad always said that rot starts at the top. Not one person on Cutter Island will believe him for a second.'

'Sure and Mulvaney's the designated fall guy for the lot of them,' she says.

The premier goes on to mention illegitimate funds discovered in the offshore bank account of a company of which Mulvaney was director. Siobhan leans forward, shocked: 'Tattling on colleagues on the same side in politics is a rare and dangerous act. He must be desperate to make sure Mulvaney's career is dead once and for all. Men like Mulvaney, unless you hammer them into the ground, they pop up in a new guise and start their criminal games again.'

'Bastards, all of them.'

'No, no. It's as well to remember that not all politicians are crooks. There are good men and women doing fine jobs. We just rarely hear about them.'

'Maybe,' Sam says grudgingly, because it has to be true or they're all doomed.

Cook's Basin News (CBN)

Newsletter for Offshore Residents of Cook's Basin, Australia

APRIL

Vale Paul Delaney

An informal ceremony honouring a great and good man who gave his life to fight corruption and injustice will be held in Garrawi Park. A plaque, made possible by overwhelmingly generous donations from the Cutter Island Community, will be erected on the foreshore at noon.

When: Sunday, May 11

Time: Midday

Where: Garrawi Park

CHAPTER TWENTY-NINE

About a month after the rally, the community holds a ceremony to erect (or, technically, to screw onto a large sandstone boulder) a plaque honouring Delaney for his role in the battle to save Garrawi. While every local was expected to pitch in without reward, congratulation or even thanks or acknowledgment, Delaney, though an outsider, deserved eternal recognition for never shirking the hard yards in a cause that really wasn't his own.

The event takes place late on a Sunday when the bay sparkles like jewels and birds are too busy finding soft furnishings for their spring nests to make much of a racket. Islanders stand around and wonder at the compassionate insight of a brawny big man who used words so skilfully to tell the story of a different young boy with such heart and understanding, when it's the nature of the press to tear down heroes. 'Not Delaney,' they agree. 'He wasn't that kind of man.'

The plaque is set next to the one honouring Teddy Mulray for his gift of the land in 1946 to the people of Cutter Island, of which the ownership is still in doubt despite the moral victories of a tiny community with the might of right on their side.

Bill Firth, wearing his hat as President of the Cook's Basin Community Residents' Association, delivers a few quick but well-chosen words about Delaney's influence on the battle to save Garrawi. He finishes with a line that sends a chill through everyone there: 'The park is still vulnerable. We cannot relax. The battle is far from over. To lose at this stage would insult the memory of Paul Delaney. Keep the faith and keep up the vigilance.'

There are a few moments' silence while his words are digested then Jenny fires up the barbecue under the beady eye of a greedy goanna. When he comes too close, his summer skin dulled by heat and wear and tear and ready to be shed, she grabs a big stick. Yelling Geronimo like it's the Indians' last charge, she roars after him. Everyone laughs. Though not Siobhan, who is inconsolable.

Jimmy, spiffily dressed in his most exotic shorts and T-shirt as a tribute to the man who made him a star for long enough to build Rome in short order, wraps an arm around her shoulders: 'He's not really dead, Miss O'Shaughnessy. Not while the park's still here.'

Hurting, and never a woman to soften the facts, she says: 'Oh yes he is, sonny. He's dead all right.'

The kid doesn't miss a beat: 'Not to me, Miss O'Shaughnessy. An' he never will be to me or me kids when I 'ave 'em.'

'You're a good boy, Jimmy, but move along now so I can weep alone.'

*

Life settles down to an easy Island pace. In the wider world, Mulvaney is currently under investigation for corruption but no charges have yet been laid. Eric Lowden is rumoured to be taking an extended holiday overseas. The goons are already a fading memory although when the Island kids play war games, the baddies inevitably wear dark clothes and mirror sunglasses. Despite Bill Firth's warnings, even the Save Garrawi committee loses its edge and when Jane suggests a meeting, Siobhan just shrugs. 'What for? It's a stalemate until after the election.'

'Maybe,' Jane replies. 'But we're still in charge of a lot of money that doesn't belong to us. We need to decide what to do with it.'

The sixth and – as it turns out – final meeting of the Save Garrawi committee once again takes place on the back deck of The Briny Café. The nights are cool and closing in earlier. The Misses Skettle are wrapped in hand-crocheted afghan shawls. Ettie, Jenny and Jane wear cardigans. The men – apart from Glenn and Sam whose sole concession to winter is to wear socks with their shorts – are back in long trousers. Lindy has sent her apologies. She has a parents' and teachers' meeting.

Ettie and Kate dish up early-autumn fare – cheese and onion tarts made with sour-cream pastry and imported Gruyere. 'Imported,' Marcus explains apologetically, 'because even though the cheese of this great country is extraordinary, I have yet to find a local Gruyere with the long sharp bite of the Swiss variety. Perhaps our grass is to blame, no? Or perhaps, as with our wine, it is the soil and climate that make a difference? Certainly not our cheese makers, who are sublime.'

To follow, they serve baked apples stuffed with rum-soaked sultanas and roasted walnuts, presented in shallow terracotta bowls with a large spoonful of double cream. 'Winter is coming,' Ettie says. 'We'll need a little extra padding to keep out the cold.'

When the plates are cleared, Jane stands and clears her throat. 'If everyone is ready, I'd like to give the Treasurer's report.'

Hear, hear. (Muted.)

'Expenses for the rally came to four thousand three hundred and twenty-seven dollars, which includes a small fine of seventy-five dollars for sticking up a poster in the bus shelter. The most expensive items were paper, timber and fabric. All other materials and the execution of props were donated.'

She looks up, aware Glenn is starting to fidget. She gives him a hard look. 'Until two days ago, the net balance was forty-nine thousand, three hundred and eighty-three dollars and eleven cents.'

Siobhan hones in like an Exocet missile: 'And what's changed since two days ago?'

Jane goes pink, runs her tongue along her lips. 'Unless there's been a terrible bank error, someone has deposited a million dollars in our account.'

'Did you call the bank, then, to see whether it was true or false?' Siobhan demands.

Jane shakes her head nervously. 'I had no idea what to do.'

Sam smiles. 'Max,' he says. 'The money will have come from Max.'

He pulls his phone out of his pocket and retreats to a quiet corner. Dials. 'Can I put you on speaker phone, Max? I'm sitting on the deck of The Briny Café with my fellow committee members and we're wondering what you want us to do with the money.'

Sam gets permission. Hits the button. Max's laboured breathing comes across in stereo sound. 'What do you think I want you to do with a million bucks?' he wheezes.

'Haven't a clue, mate.'

'Buy the bloody park, of course. And you'd better get this sorted out before I die or I'll come back to haunt you.' He coughs. The phone goes dead. Max has run out of puff.

Later, when Ettie, Sam, Siobhan and the chef recall the moment, they all agree it felt as though even the pulsing sea under the deck froze hard and solid for a good minute.

'Have we not just learned, then, that money can solve as many problems as it creates?' Siobhan says. 'But I'm wondering – is buying the park the answer? Who buys it? Another Trust and when the money is all used up and we're dead and gone, some other dirty little toe rag like Eric Lowdon can come along with his gutter morality and snap! The community is back where it started. I'm thinking . . .

'Another newspaper ad but a full-on campaign this time, one that runs for as long as the money lasts. We'll slam the government's record on environmental issues and focus on the corrupt mishandling of Garrawi Park. If we get the wording right, it should send every member of the current ruling party running straight to the toilet. And haven't we already been given the green light by the premier to expose Mulvaney's greedy brown-paper-bag deal with a now totally discredited and extremely dead cult leader?' She rubs her hands gleefully. 'Oh this is going to be fun. To be on the safe side, though, would you mind, Glenn, putting your Kombi and barge on the line again?'

Glenn bows with an ear-splitting grin. 'It would be a pleasure.'

The aim is to launch the campaign on Saturday, the biggest circulation day, and ramp up the pressure until the election with a series of shocking facts about the lack of due process in the Garrawi development plan. Kate Jackson is called in to broker a deal for a month-long run of bottom-front-page ads at a cut, bulk rate. The committee stands around during a mid-morning lull in the café and listens while Kate haggles like a Turkish rug dealer. Holds its collective breath when she threatens to take the ads to another newspaper. Gasps audibly when she casually mulls the benefits of television over print. 'With more than a million dollars to spend, perhaps we should think bigger,' she hints. The deal is done half a minute later. 'Clever girl,' Ettie says, beaming like a proud mother. Even Jenny slaps Kate's back in congratulation.

The first bullet in the campaign is fired the following Saturday – six weeks before the election date – with a forty-centimetre-deep, single-colour ad that runs along the bottom of page one of the *Herald*. In blood-red type, it says: '*If this Government busted an iron-clad Trust to sell off Garrawi Park against the wishes of the people, what's to stop it selling off the whole State?'*

On Monday morning, another ad hits the newsstands. *'If this government is prepared to do business with a mad and fraudulent foreign cult leader, what's to stop it doing deals with terrorists, gun runners and drug dealers?'*

Tuesday hits even harder: *'If a former member of this government actively engaged in graft and corruption, shouldn't he face legal action and the full force of the law like anyone else?'*

Late on Tuesday afternoon, the mayor of Cook's Basin, Evan Robotham, calls the Save Garrawi committee in a flap and requests an urgent meeting. 'Not tomorrow. Now!' he insists.

Siobhan, her nose twitching with the scent of something major, rounds up Sam, Ettie, Jenny, the Misses Skettle, Glenn, Jane, John, Marcus, Lindy and gives up on Seaweed after four attempts to reach his mobile. Sam calls Jimmy.

'I'm makin' a worm-juice delivery, Sam. Can ya wait a minute?'

'Now or never, mate. This is history and history doesn't wait for anyone.'

'I'm wearin' me work clothes . . .'

'Just get here . . .'

While Kate keeps the café open, the committee hits their tinnies, illegally roar through the go slow zone with their eyes peeled, slam into the commuter dock, and trot towards the car park, where even the immaculate chef agrees to squash into Glenn's, er, retro Kombi, in which the pong of Jimmy's wet mutt is barely noticeable.

The mayor is waiting for them as they pull into the council car park and points at a space reserved in the name of

Garrawi. 'Sure, they're treating us like royalty,' Siobhan says, falling out of the van, straightening slowly so the kink in her back doesn't go into full spasm. 'I'm getting a warm feeling in the pit of me stomach.'

Ettie rips off her apron. Jenny checks for stains on her shirt. The Misses Skettle reach into their handbags and withdraw scent bottles. They give everyone a squirt except for Marcus and Sam. They rode up front. They follow Evan into the building. 'No dogs,' he shouts. The entire committee instantly turns on its heels. 'Jesus,' Evan whines. 'Don't blame me. It's the rule.'

The meeting that seals the fate of Garrawi is held on the front steps of the council chambers in full view of passers-by who stop and stare as the mayor addresses a motley collection of men and women as though his life depends on it. A few move in to listen.

'The premier,' Evan announces, 'has called me to say he will approve a plan I put forward a week ago to transfer the title of Garrawi into the hands of the National Parks and Wildlife. It will remain under its control and as a heritage-listed site, free from all future development.'

'Eh?'

He beams. 'I'd call this a win, wouldn't you?'

'I'd call it sleight of hand and panic,' Siobhan says in a muttered aside to Sam. 'There'll be a proviso, just wait and see.' She turns a smiley face towards the mayor. 'Well, that's wonderful news. We had no idea the council was so concerned about the fate of Garrawi. None at all. What a dark horse you've been all along, eh? So we're free and clear, then. Nothing else to add?'

'Er, there's just one proviso . . .'

'Well and why is that not a surprise? It's the advertisements, I suppose. If we cancel the remainder, the park is ours.'

Evan nods.

'And if we don't?' Siobhan asks. Nearly a dozen pairs of eyes turn towards her in shock.

The mayor swallows. Looks like he's about to wet his pants. His face goes red. He puts a hand in his pocket and nervously withdraws his mobile phone. 'Er, I'd have to check . . .'

'Ah, no need. I was kidding,' Siobhan says. 'A little joke to amuse myself. No harm intended.' She turns towards the committee. 'Shall we call it a deal, then?'

Hear, hear.

On Wednesday morning, a hastily prepared new ad appears at the bottom of the front page of the *Herald*. *GARRAWI SAVED: THE PEOPLE WIN*. Nothing else. The rest of the campaign is cancelled. Most of Max's money is comfortingly intact.

Sam rings the good-hearted benefactor, whose hefty donations effectively levelled the playing field for Save Garrawi, to give him the news. 'And, mate, tell us where to send your change.'

Max doesn't hesitate. 'Hang on to it,' he wheezes. 'It'll keep any future bastards honest.'

A week later, Lindy Jones reports that Eric Lowdon is selling his Cutter Island properties at a knock-down price. Like worms turning, the mayor and his fellow councillors, religious fence-sitters up to the last moment, step forward to claim credit for saving Garrawi in a barrage of hastily written press releases. Even the Misses Skettle can't hide their disgust.

'Pariahs. Not one of them could find their way here with a hand-written map,' they fume.

The committee, cold hard realists now, with Max's blessing, put aside the remains of the fighting fund in a high-interest account for the day someone else with the morals of a bandicoot tries to steal the park from under their noses. 'Max has a great understanding of human nature,' they say with sadness and resignation. Siobhan asks Sam whether Max might want to reveal his identity to the public as the man who truly turned the tide in the fight for Garrawi. Max declines. He got his money's worth, he says, by tracking the course of the battle from his sitting room, where he's anchored by chronic emphysema.

The great, cracked, mashed and almost collapsed sulphur-crested cockatoo is ceremoniously withdrawn from the Square and returned to the Island kindergarten playground. For as long as she remains in charge, says Trudy Wentwhistle, every child who attends will be told of the brave and noble warriors from far and wide who fought so hard to keep their park so they could play, propose and possibly (probably) procreate under the spreading arms of the cheese tree.

'We made history, didn' we, Sam?' Jimmy asks.

'Yeah, mate.' Sam feels oddly flat. Sensing his mood, Longfellow, who's made the transition from pup to a gloriously full-grown dog with a full deck of impeccable manners that every Island mum hopes to instil in her kids, gives him a quizzical, head-sideways look. He rubs the mutt's velvet ears, sighs loudly. Wonders if chugging the open waterways with a kid and a dog is going to feel a little dull after the past few months of adrenalin-fuelled hand-to-hand combat. In a moment of madness, he considers whether he might swap his barge business for a life in politics. Discards the idea almost immediately. Even on a top day, he wouldn't be able to keep up with the skulduggery. The thought settles his mind, brings peace. He'll focus on keeping his home turf clean and safe. 'Jimmy!' he shouts.

'Standin' right next to ya, Sam.'

'Time for a driving lesson. If you're going to chauffeur me around in my old age, I want to feel confident you're as good as the legendary Jack Brabham.'

'Who's Jack Brabham, Sam?'

The image of a tape measure strung along the edge of a bathtub flashes through his mind. Halfway through my allotted time, providing all goes well, he thinks. But he's content with the knowledge that in a small but critical way he has helped to make a difference. 'You got any shoes with you? You can't learn to drive unless you're wearing shoes, mate. Rule number one.'

'Longfella! Fetch me shoes!' orders the kid, pointing in the direction of home.

The dog takes off. Pink tongue flapping. Fur flying. On a mission. Five minutes later, triumphant, he's back on Sam's dock. He drops a single boat shoe. Looks up for approval. 'Now, go git the other one!' Jimmy orders. Longfellow flies off.

'You're doing a fine job bringing up that dog, Jimmy. First class.'

'Aw. If ya say so.' He blushes red from his toes to his top. The dog returns. Spits out the shoe. It falls in the water.

'Still got a way to go, though, eh?'

'He's a good dog, Sam. We all make mistakes, me mum says.'

The Briny Café declares a record-breaking season. While the two owners expected business to drop off once the publicity about Garrawi faded away, the crowds keep coming. Some are rubber-neckers but there's also a surprising number of supporters and everyday mums and dads who are fighting their own backyard environmental battles. 'Can you give us a blueprint?' they ask, over and over, until one day Sam and Siobhan spend a whole day trying to distil an erratic but passionate campaign into coherent advice.

1) Form an efficient committee
2) Keep minutes of every meeting
3) Be open and completely scrupulous about funds
4) Have a designated media spokesperson and never lie
5) Think outside the square
6) Never give up
7) Always be on the front foot
8) Never pause or let up the pressure even when it goes quiet
9) Never believe what you are told
10) Big business lies. Check the background of every 'official' statement
11) Use the internet to get and spread information
12) Knowledge is a mighty weapon
13) Do not be afraid of bullies
14) Never fight on their terms

15) Be creative, do ridiculous stunts to get attention
16) Line up your patrons
17) Suck up to the media and never lie (repeated for emphasis)
18) Never take a backward step
19) Light spot fires all over the place (metaphorically)
20) With patience and persistence you will prevail

'Twenty steps to victory,' Siobhan says. 'Set out like a women's magazine suggesting twenty ways to drop a dress size. But it's never that simple, is it? We got lucky, sonny.'

'Nah,' Sam says, daring to disagree with her for the first time. 'As my dad used to say, luck is where ability and opportunity meet. He also used to say that the harder you work, the luckier you get.'

'A nice man, then, was he?'

'Yeah.'

'Not much of a realist, though. If you don't mind me saying so. A good man died so we could get lucky. And another man gave us a fortune for no other reason than he'd always loved the park. Truth – stranger than fiction, eh?'

In June, with a new government in power that no one really believes will be able – or even willing – to clean out the stench of corruption in high places, café business shows no sign of slowing. Kate and Ettie sit down in the mostly vacant penthouse with the figures for nearly a year of trading. Ettie, who'd rather eat glass than add up, surreptitiously moves the paperwork to one side.

'The quotes are in for a new roof and it's more than affordable. The builder will replace it section by section so we won't have to close the café for even a day.'

'Who's doing the work?'

'Reagan. From the Island.'

'Ah, good girl. Keeping the money in the community where it does the most good.'

'Best price, Ettie, business is business. And he's near enough to chase up if he does anything dodgy.'

Ettie sighs. Then looks alarmed. 'Kate? Are you all right?'

Kate is on her feet, heading for the bathroom, a hand over her mouth. Ettie hears retching. A flush.

'Sorry. Must have eaten something . . .' she says when she returns.

'Not café food, Kate, don't tell me that.'

'No, of course not.' Kate sits again, pale but functioning. 'I might as well admit that since Jenny joined us, business has boomed. I know outside events have helped hugely, but Jenny's ability in the kitchen means we've doubled our capacity in a way that would never have happened with only my input. I'd like to suggest hiring her as a permanent, part-time – sous chef.'

'But Kate –'

'Hear me out. All three of us work the morning and lunchtime shifts. Jenny quits at two o'clock, in time for her kids, and I work through to closing time, giving you an afternoon break before the school rush. Frankly, most of my work now is routine maintenance, ordering and keeping track of the money. Not physical enough to wear me out.'

'I'm not that smart, Kate, but this has the ring of a long-term plan to give up The Briny.'

'No, Ettie. If I wanted out, I'd tell you. And frankly, there's not enough money yet to buy me out. You'd have to find another partner.'

'I see,' Ettie says. 'God, Kate. Are you sick again? How long's this been going on? Time to see a doctor, love.' The bathroom door slams. Ettie fetches a glass of water. When Kate emerges, even paler and gripping her stomach, she sends her home.

Feeling like she's abandoned a sick woman, Ettie calls Sam and asks him to check on her in the morning. 'Long as you're not trying to play match-maker. We're friends, Ettie, nothing more,' he says.

'That's what friends do, Sam, they look after each other.'

In the morning, when the sun is still no more than a flat orange line on the horizon, Sam follows through on his promise to Ettie. As he guides the *Mary Kay* past Artie's yacht, he hears a kettle whistling and smiles inwardly at the thought that the old man with his buggered legs and razor-sharp mind will live to see another day.

Nearer Kate's house, he feels a shiver. Even in summer, the estuary end of Oyster Bay is a gloomy spot, he thinks. At this time of the year, it broods darkly in shadows until almost noon. He ties up at Kate's pontoon, telling himself a quick *hello* and *how are you* and he'll be out of there in a flash. He and Jimmy have a full day's work ahead and Ettie's a born worrier. Kate's probably only got a mild bug.

She opens the door to his knock in her pyjamas. Reaches on tiptoes to kiss his cheek. The warm, musty bed smell of her almost brings him undone. Without a word, she leads the way inside, leaving him no choice but to follow. In the kitchen, she begins the ritual of preparing a couple of mugs of fragrant tea – her favourite, Darjeeling – without asking if he'd like one. Unless he's prepared to be flat-out rude, he's stymied.

'Feeling a bit crook, love?' he begins.

'Timothy O'Reilly sent me his DNA profile,' she says, pouring boiling water into the warmed pot. 'He's out of the picture.' She fits the lid back on, slips on a plain knitted green tea cosy.

'So the old bloke was fairdinkum, eh? You always thought he was.'

'Alex emailed me a copy of his DNA results, too.' She lines up two very fine white bone china mugs. Pours milk into his. Leaves hers empty. She spins the pot, first one way and then the other. Never looking up. 'I sent them off with Emily's for analysis.' She pours the brew. Very quietly, she adds: 'Just got the results.'

'Ah.'

She finally looks at him. 'You guessed, didn't you?'

'Are you going to tell Alex?'

'Not unless he asks.'

'He will.'

'Yeah.' In the early grey light drifting through the kitchen window, Kate looks haggard. He has no idea how to help her. She hands him his tea then disappears into the bedroom. Returns with the box of horrors, as he thinks of it, and puts it carefully on the table. Like it's a ticking bomb. 'I can't bring myself to throw this stuff away. And yet keeping it feels like picking at a scab.'

'Get rid of it, Kate. Ditch it. Burn it. Bury it. Long as it's here, Emily rules. You're better than that.'

'Am I?'

Trying for lightness, he grins. 'Well, you showed a lot of early promise but fell by the wayside a couple of times. There's nothing holding you back now, love. You are who you are. No secrets. No ghosts. No reason to look back. Time to step forward.' Jeez, he thinks, I sound like a football coach.

'I can't help wondering how it happened. I keep trying to see Emily as a victim, but the image doesn't work. Maybe if she was a kid when the abuse began . . .'

'You'll never know.'

'Trouble is, she always had to be top dog. Maybe she was the instigator –'

'Jesus Christ, Kate,' he says in frustration, 'what does it matter whether a father abused his daughter or Emily seduced her father? Let it go. Or you'll end up as bitter and twisted as your mother.'

'I'm pregnant, Sam.' Her voice is small. Defeated. Trapped.

He closes his eyes, drops his head into his hands and waits for the kicker line he knows is coming. But he's wrong; the silence goes on and on. 'When is it due?' he asks, finally.

'October. I lost track. All the travel. Work. The Briny boom. It's too late to do anything about it.'

'Wouldn't want you to, love. I've always dreamed of having a kid –'

'This is not about you, Sam,' she says, breaking in. 'I don't want this baby. Any baby.'

'Ah jeez, Kate,' he says, wincing. 'A little baby. They're miracles of engineering and evolution, you know.'

She grimaces: 'Evolution! Take a good look at my family history, Sam. A dreadful legacy for a kid. What if it turns out to be a monster like Emily?' She is on the verge of tears. Sam reaches for her hand. She snatches it away.

'There's not a pregnant woman in the world that doesn't fear and hope for her child in equal parts. This little Cook's Basin baby will be fine. Trust me,' he says.

Kate pushes her chair back from the kitchen table, walks to the window and stares out. The light, warmer now, catches her face. 'You have no idea what it feels like knowing there's no way out.'

'It's a baby, Kate. People have them every day. Give yourself time.'

'I don't want it, Sam. I don't want anything to do with it. It's a mistake. A hideous mistake. Oh god, I'm just like Emily. Oh god.' She bunches her fists, pushes them against her cheeks, forcing back tears.

He steps towards her and takes her hands in his: 'Not like Emily, love. Never like that.' He leads her back to the table, takes a seat and guides her onto his knee like a child in need of comfort. 'I've always been good with babies, did I ever tell you that? For some reason, they love me. It's my size, I think. Makes them feel safe. A baby, eh? Girl or a boy, do you know yet? Doesn't matter, of course.'

'Will you be there for the birth?' she asks in a tone that's as close to desperate need as he's ever heard from her.

'I'll be with you all the way and on any terms you set out.'

'I'm scared, Sam. Terrified that being a mother will make me mean and jealous and cruel and competitive like Emily. That I'll end up bending a pure new life into something bruised and broken because that's how I've been programmed.'

'Nah. You're smarter than that. Truth is, you're a realist. That doesn't make you a bad person. Me? I'm an optimist, a dreamer. We're not a bad combination if you think about it.' He rubs her back, unaware he's doing it. She leans into his chest. Looser now. Like the glue holding her tight is melting. Her eyes close. Black lashes fan on her pale skin. He sees the small hard roundness of her stomach under her pyjamas and feels a surge of pure joy. 'You'll be a great mother, Kate,' he whispers. 'You'd be a great wife, too.'

She twists towards him, eyes wet, a tentative smile lifting the corners of her mouth: 'Is that a proposal, Sam Scully?'

'Yeah. I'm not saying we'd have a smooth run –'

She puts a finger over his lips: 'What about you? A great father? A wonderful husband?'

'I'll give it my best shot, love.'

'Then so will I.'

Back on the *Mary Kay*, Sam calls Ettie and tells her Kate's fine and she'll be in later to explain what's going on.

'She's pregnant, isn't she?' Ettie says.

Sam sighs. 'Jeez, Ettie, she was going to surprise you with the news.'

Ettie's voice softens. 'You and Kate, you'll be magnificent parents. And that little baby's going to be loved, cherished and fought over by the whole community. A café baby, how wonderful . . .'

'Barge baby, love. Boy or a girl, it'll be a barge baby.'

'We'll see what Kate says. Early days yet. I might paint the penthouse pink. Or blue. Depends.'

'I was thinking the wheelhouse of the *Mary Kay* might be due for a facelift. A pale, gender-neutral lemon to blend in with the hull might go well.'

'Marcus and me, we'll be honorary grandparents, of course. Pretty dresses for a girl. Boat shoes for a boy. Do they make baby boat shoes?'

Sam laughs. A kid of his own. Not quite the way he thought it would happen, but in four months, he'll have a tiny Scully to hold in his arms. To point out the stars, the moon, the sea and the infinite secrets of the natural world.

Ettie adds: 'By the way, Jimmy's here and waiting for you. Says you're running late for a couple of pick-ups.'

'Tell him they're cancelled, will you? And then give him a slap-up brekky with plenty of spinach. And ask him to give his mum a call. We're going to need a baby-size patchwork quilt the same colour as the *Mary Kay* by October. Jeez. I'd better get a list going. Oh, and inform him that I've put his name down as number-one babysitter. It'll be good practice for when he has his own kids. After that, tell him . . . tell him I've gone fishing and I'll see him and that lollopy mutt of his first thing tomorrow. And Ettie?'

'Yes, love?'

'You'd better start thinking about top nosh for a mega wedding. You might start with a few sauso rolls, eh?'

Cook's Basin News (CBN)

Newsletter for Offshore Residents of Cook's Basin, Australia

APRIL

GARRAWAY PARK STAYS IN THE HANDS OF THE PEOPLE

VICTORY DECLARED

In a massive turnaround, the state government has reversed its decision to allow developers to build a bridge connecting Cutter Island to the mainland. It also quashed plans for a luxury resort that would forever have altered our Island life.

The Save Garrawi Committee, captained by Siobhan O'Shaughnessy with the inspired assistance of Sam Scully as first mate, supported strongly by local residents, fought a long, hard and magnificent campaign to ensure our children and grandchildren will enjoy the beauty and magic of this newly listed heritage site. The park is now in the hands of National Parks and Wildlife.

To ensure this travesty of people's rights can never happen again, Siobhan O'Shaughnessy would like inform the community that all remaining campaign funds have been set aside in an interest-bearing account to be called on in the future if necessary. (We live in uncertain times!)

As part of our Island history initiative, anyone who would like to write about their roles in saving Garrawi may submit stories to CBN for publication. Photographs are also welcome.

We showed the bastards!

WIN! A prize (to be advised) for the best story or photograph from any of the battlefronts of the Save Garrawi campaign. We're also looking for three judges. Any volunteers (thick skin's a prerequisite)?

BLUE PRINT FOR AN ENVIRONMENTAL CAMPAIGN

Due to daily requests throughout the land from people who feel their voices are being ignored, Siobhan O'Shaughnessy and Sam Scully have put together a guide to fighting for your rights. It is available at the front counter free of charge. (Or for a donation to keep the fighting fund growing – who knows what the future holds?) The editor, however, feels that it is worth repeating here the three golden rules:

Laugh in the faces of bullies.

Laugh in the faces of crooked politicians.

Laugh in the (many) faces of adversity. It's the Island – the Aussie – way!

Oh, and one more: Never believe a bloody thing they tell you.

Recipes From The Briny Café

Ettie's roasted potato, zucchini, pumpkin and capsicum oven-baked frittata

Serves 6–8

2 red capsicum
4 zucchini
4 cups butternut pumpkin
4 large potatoes
12 fresh eggs
2 cups pouring cream
½ cup grated cheddar
½ cup grated parmesan
½ cup flat-leaf parsley, chopped

Preheat oven to 180°C. Chop all vegetables into bite-size chunks and tip into a bowl. Sprinkle with olive oil and sea salt, then toss with your hands. Line a shallow roasting tray with non-stick baking paper, spread over the vegetables and pop into the oven until soft and golden, about 35–45 minutes depending on your 'bite' size.

Beat together the eggs and cream. Stir in the cheeses and parsley. Pour over vegetables and cook until centre is just wobbly. Time varies according to depth of mixture.

Ettie's Brown Sugar Shortbread

450 g plain flour
½ cup rice flour

Pinch salt
500 g unsalted butter
1 cup brown sugar
2 tsp vanilla extract

Put all ingredients into a food processor and whizz together until it forms a dough. Remove.

Press dough gently into a large tray lined with baking powder and mark mixture into bars with the back of a knife. Chill for half an hour, then poke the top randomly with a fork.

Place tray in an oven at 160°C and bake for one hour. If it's not quite crisp enough after it's cooled, whack it back in the oven for a while longer. The recipe yields a huge amount; the mixture can be halved.

Marcus's Quick-and-Easy Coq au Vin

Serves 6–8

12 chicken thighs on the bone
20 small brown onions or, even better, shallots
20 button mushrooms
½ kg good-quality smoked streaky
bacon, cut into wide strips
1 cup red wine
½ cup brandy
1 bunch baby carrots, washed and trimmed
Chicken stock
Splash of olive oil

Brown thighs in oil in a deep, heavy-based frying pan. Remove and set aside in a bowl. Brown peeled shallots. Add to bowl. Brown button mushrooms. Add to bowl. Fry bacon until golden. Replace all ingredients in fry pan.

Tip in brandy and carefully set alight. After flames dissipate, add red wine and enough chicken stock to keep ingredients moist – don't flood them. You want the juices to reduce.

Simmer until chicken is cooked through and the juices have reduced to a rich consistency. Serve with garlic mashed potato and beans or a green side salad. (Note: You can use whole thigh fillets but reduce the cooking time.)

Marcus's Prawns in Tamarind Chutney

(Wonderful finger food)

2 tbsp tamarind chutney (Goan Cuisine brand is good)
¼ cup water
Uncooked peeled prawns – fresh or frozen

Place chutney in a bowl and add water to break it down. Toss in prawns and leave for a few minutes. Stir-fry in a very hot wok or frying pan until just cooked through.

Ettie's Delicious Puttanesca Sauce

Serves 6–8, generous sauce serves

2 cloves garlic
½ tsp chilli flakes
8 anchovies
Olive oil
800 g tin chopped tomatoes
Handful pitted black olives
1 tbsp baby capers

Heat olive oil until just warm and add garlic, chilli and anchovies. Stir for a couple of minutes or until the anchovies have dissolved. Turn up the heat and add tomatoes. Simmer for about half an hour.

Just before serving, add olives and capers. Serve like a gutsy gravy alongside slow-roasted shoulder or neck of lamb.

Acknowledgments

This is a work of fiction but it owes much to the courageous and single-minded environmental warriors all over the country who fight so hard to preserve our bush, beaches and, now that coal seam gas is looming, our drinking water and backyards. And of course, to the legendary Jack Mundey, one of the greatest soldiers of all, who kindly allowed me to take some real moments from his life and insert them into make-believe. I should also add that the inspiring story of Kelly's Bush is based on fact. How often I smiled when I read and re-read a slim green volume that explained how thirteen twinsets-and-pearls housewives, sneered at by businessmen and politicians, sweetly and politely managed to redefine the environmental battlefront worldwide. We are all deeply in their debt; they have shown that anything is possible if you refuse to back down or accept what you're told is a *done deal.*

The story of Bruce Robertson is also fact. Bruce Robertson, a softly-spoken cattle farmer from sleepy Burrell Creek on the mid-north coast of NSW, proved – with the help of the Manning Alliance – that escalating electricity bills were primarily the result of over-investment in electricity networks and that the power industry was essentially misleading the State Government by predicting rising energy consumption. In fact, energy use was falling. In a desperate, bullying bid to gag him, Robertson suddenly found that and he and his young family were being sued by six state electricity giants. The public outcry was thunderous. As it turned out, corporations are prevented by law from suing individuals for defamation anyway. The lawsuit was withdrawn within twenty-four hours and plans to build a massive power grid in the Manning Valley were shelved.

The other tilt towards truth is the story of Delaney, which is, in effect, the story of Paul Dougherty, my first husband, who died of a brain tumour in 1993. The tabloid he worked for was the *National Enquirer*, when it was under the tyrannical rule of the late Gene Pope. I used as reference a story by one of those young editors, Shelley Ross, who went on to become a much-awarded executive producer for *Good Morning America*. It was titled 'How the *National Enquirer* Blew a Chance for a Pulitzer Prize – 30 Years Ago'. I have no idea why it suddenly seemed so important to tell this story, but, like Sam, I have learned to trust my instincts. Perhaps it will resonate for all the right reasons with a reader somewhere. Or perhaps it was simply to reinforce that truth is truly stranger than fiction.

Beyond the fictional storyline and the fictional characters of fictional Cook's Basin, the underlying purpose of *Gone Fishing* is to provide a blueprint for anyone who wakes up one morning to find his/her immediate world under threat in ways that seem undemocratic and destructive. I hope it helps or, at the very least, suggests a way to start any action.

Many thanks to author Amanda Hampson (*The Olive Sisters*, *Two for the Road*) for her invaluable advice and input, Toby Jay (who runs the real-life *Mary Kay*, the *Laurel Mae*, with his partner, Dave Shirley), and the Western Foreshores community of Pittwater for their generosity of spirit and many day-to-day kindnesses. Thanks also to Nikki Christer, Beverley Cousins, Kate O'Donnell for her clever edit, and the team at Random House. As always, thanks to Caroline Adams for her sensitive and intelligent reading of the manuscript.

Most of all, thanks to my husband, Bob, for his quiet, unconditional love and support.

The Briny Café

Brimming with warmth and wit, Susan Duncan's first novel is a delicious tale of friendship and love, and the search for a place to call home . . .

Ettie Brookbank is the heart and soul of Cook's Basin, a sleepy offshore community comprising a cluster of dazzling blue bays. But for all the idyllic surroundings, Ettie can't help wondering where her dreams have disappeared to. Until fate offers her a lifeline – in the shape of a lopsided little café on the water's edge. When Bertie, its cantankerous septuagenarian owner, offers her 'the Briny' for a knockdown price, it's an opportunity too good to miss. But it's a mammoth task – and she'll need a partner. Enter Kate Jackson, the enigmatic new resident of the haunted house on Oyster Bay. Kate is also clearly at a crossroads – running from a life in the city that has left her lonely and lost. Could a ramshackle café and its endearingly eccentric customers deliver the new start both women so desperately crave?

Available now

Salvation Creek

The unputdownable true story of tragedy, courage and love, that grips like a bestselling novel.

At 44 Susan Duncan appeared to have it all. Editor of two top-selling women's magazines, a happy marriage, a jetsetting lifestyle covering stories from New York to Greenland, the world was her oyster. But when her beloved husband and brother die within three days of each other, her glittering life shatters. In shock, she zips on her work face, climbs back into her high heels and soldiers on – until one morning eighteen months later, when she simply can't get out of bed. Heartbreaking, funny and searingly honest, *Salvation Creek* is the story of a woman who found the courage not only to begin again but to beat the odds in her own battle for survival and find a new life – and love – in a tiny waterside idyll cut off from the outside world. Combining all the sweeping, rollercoaster style of a bestselling novel with the very best – and most inspiring – human interest story, *Salvation Creek* is a tour-de-force that will stay with the reader long after she has turned the last page.

Available now

The House at Salvation Creek

The wonderful second memoir from Susan Duncan, which picks up where *Salvation Creek* ended.

Continuing the story of Susan Duncan's bestselling and much-loved memoir, *Salvation Creek*, *The House* picks up after Bob and Susan marry and, two years later, move from her Tin Shed into his 'pale yellow house on the high, rough hill', Tarrangaua, built for the iconic Australian poet, Dorothea Mackellar. Set against the backdrop of the small, close-knit Pittwater community with its colourful characters and quirky history, *The House* is about what happens when you open the door to life, adventure, and love. But it's also about mothers and daughters, as Susan confronts her mother's new frailty and her own role in what has always been a difficult relationship. Where *Salvation Creek* was about mortality – living life in the face of death – *The House* is about stepping outside your comfort zone and embracing challenges, at any age. In turn funny and moving, Susan Duncan's beautifully written sequel reminds us to honour what matters in life, and to disregard what really doesn't.

Available now